THE SHŌ
AN

THE SHŌWA ANTHOLOGY

Modern Japanese Short Stories

1929–1984

Edited by
Van C. Gessel
Tomone Matsumoto

KODANSHA INTERNATIONAL
Tokyo • New York • London

The editors wish to thank the following authors for graciously allowing the translation and publication of their stories: Ibuse Masuji, Ishikawa Jun, Abe Kōbō, Yasuoka Shōtarō, Kojima Nobuo, Yoshiyuki Junnosuke, Shōno Junzō, Shimao Toshio, Kurahashi Yumiko, Inoue Yasushi, Minakami Tsutomu, Endō Shūsaku, Abe Akira, Shibaki Yoshiko, Ōba Minako, Kōno Taeko, Kanai Mieko, Kaikō Takeshi, Ōe Kenzaburō, Tsushima Yūko, and Nakagami Kenji.

In addition, the estates of the following have granted permission for the use of the included works: Hori Tatsuo, Dazai Osamu, Kawabata Yasunari, and Mishima Yukio ("Eggs" © 1953).

Concerning works previously published elsewhere, the editors gratefully acknowledge the following:

International Creative Management, for permission to use a slightly revised version of the translation of Abe Kōbō's "The Magic Chalk," which appeared in *Asia Magazine*, translated by Alison Kibrick. © 1982

Peter Owen, Ltd., for permission to reprint "The Day Before" by Endō Shūsaku, from *Stained Glass Elegies*, translated by Van C. Gessel. © 1984

Columbia University Press, for permission to reprint a slightly revised version of "Bad Company" by Yasuoka Shōtarō, from *A View by the Sea*, translated by Karen Wigen Lewis. © 1984

Japan P.E.N. Club, for permission to reprint "The Silent Traders" by Tsushima Yūko, from *Japanese Literature Today* (no. 9, March 1984), translated by Geraldine Harcourt. © 1984

Publication of this anthology was assisted by a grant from the Japan Foundation.

Distributed in the United States by Kodansha America, Inc., 114 Fifth Avenue, New York New York 10011, and in the United Kingdom and continental Europe by Kodansha Europe, Ltd., 95 Aldwych, London WC2B 4JF. Published by Kodansha International, Ltd., 17-14 Otowa 1-chome, Bunkyo-ku, Tokyo 112, and Kodansha America, Inc.

Printed in Japan.

First edition, 1985
First paperback edition, 1989
First mass paperback edition, 1992
95 5 4 3

LCC 88-46052
ISBN 4-7700-1708-1

CONTENTS

INTRODUCTION

Van C. Gessel

The reticent marine biologist who until recently occupied the Japanese throne retained his position for over sixty years. It is sobering to ponder the scope of the changes he saw take place in the lives of his subjects. When he gave his reign the name of Shōwa, "enlightenment and peace," in December 1926, he could have had little inkling how painfully ironic that title would prove to be. It was a period that saw much ignorance pass for enlightenment and a peace that was often sanguinary. From his perch "amid the clouds," Emperor Hirohito witnessed a fourteen-year war that engulfed the entire world, fire bombings that ravaged the landscape of Japan, the visitation of two atomic bombs, the first foreign occupation in the long history of his independent, isolationist country, and a contemporary reputation that remains murky in some parts of the world, due both to Japan's past misdeeds and her present technological virtuosity.

The literature of the Shōwa era is as varied and accurate a portrait of the Japanese nation's meandering, tortuous progress through the past six decades as we can hope to find. The present collection was conceived with the intent of bringing together stories by the finest authors who have produced short fiction during this period, primarily those who have not been adequately represented in English translation. As the anthology took shape, it became evident that the stories were remarkably varied in the experiences they describe as well as in the techniques they employ. This suggested that stories by several familiar writers should also be included, particularly works that display sides of their creators not generally recognized overseas.

It would be foolhardy to suggest that the present collection is in any way a "panorama" of Japanese life in the Shōwa era; Japanese artists are seldom at home in the painting of vast landscape murals. They prefer instead the creation of genre-style vignettes rich in detail and in brief flashes of inspiration. But when these small scenes are placed one beside another and the entire scroll is rolled out before the viewer's eyes, the subtle and complex portrait of human life presented there is truly impressive.

Some critics argue that the modern period has finally severed Japan's literary ties with its traditional roots; that the Shōwa author has once and for all become as artistically deracinated as all his international contemporaries. I for one don't believe that for a moment. It may be possible to cite authors such as Abe Kōbō as evidence of such a phenomenon, but the substance of this anthology strongly suggests that much continuity remains, both in form and in content. The stubborn persistence of that uniquely Japanese literary form known as the "I-novel" (*watakushi-shōsetsu*) is one testimony to the tenacity of literary tradition. These egocentric quasi-novels emerged as a distinct form early in the twentieth century, but they in fact have subterranean links with the literature of the tenth century in Japan. The I-novel has been criticized for being overly precious, too narrowly concerned with the private agonies of its authors, and too little aware of the feelings of surrounding individuals and ideas. While all of these criticisms are justified, Japanese writers have been reluctant to jettison the form altogether, finding it a congenial and fluid means to examine and define themselves and their surroundings. But in the Shōwa period, particularly in the postwar years, authors have been willing to stretch the confines of the I-novel to determine whether it can be employed for a more objective study of human relationships, and for such purposes as satire and religious contemplation. In this attempt, they have poured a new distillation of wine into the old bottles left by their literary predecessors; the present anthology provides several examples of the form for readers to relish, including "Bad Company," "Stars," "The Day Before," and "With Maya."

A further argument for continuity may be found by comparing the anthology's first story, "Kuchisuke's Valley," written in 1929, with such later works as "Mulberry Child" (1963) or "The Immortal" (1984). While even the traditionally pastoral setting of "Kuchisuke's Valley" is shaken by the suggestion that modern technological progress may eventually obliterate every trace of the past, the two more recent stories forcefully reaffirm the presence of an unsevered conduit that allows the contemporary Japanese author to remain in communication with his classical predecessors.

Amid the continuity there is also change; the stories presented here range from the discursive ("Moon Gems" and "Under the Shadow of Mt. Bandai") to the experimental ("Mating," "One Arm," "The Monastery"); some, like "Les Joues en Feu," approach sheer poetry. "The Magic Chalk" is perhaps best described as "scientific surrealism," while "The Pale Fox" is more along the lines of fantasy. Shōwa literature has seen a wealth of trends swell and fade, and has ridden the tides of proletarian fiction, wartime propaganda, Occupation censorship and a myriad of modernist influences. One of the healthiest and most welcome aspects of the postwar scene has been the appearance of many truly talented women writers—six of them are represented in these pages.

In short, there may well be something that will appeal to every literary taste in this compilation of twentieth-century stories. The works in this collection clearly demonstrate that literature in Japan over the past six decades has been a living, changing entity, responding to and commenting upon the many vicissitudes of the society. And since twenty-one of the authors represented here continue to be active on the Japanese literary scene as this collection goes to press, it seems safe to say that the interplay between continuity and diversity will remain strong hereafter. Mirroring the fortunes of the Japanese nation over the past sixty years, the Japanese short story has survived wars and defeats and high-tech and evolved into a durable and universal form of literary expression during the age of Shōwa.

KUCHISUKE'S VALLEY

Ibuse Masuji

Translated by John Whittier Treat

*Ibuse Masuji's long career in literature spans most of the twentieth century and many of its genres and themes. After making a precocious debut in the 1920s with such stories as "Koi" (Carp, 1926; tr. 1971), Ibuse went on to build a diversified yet solid reputation with novellas (*Kawa *[The River, 1932]), modern poetry (*Yaku yoke shishū *[Talisman Poems, 1937]), historical tales (*Sazanami gunki *[A Chronicle of Ripples, 1938]), wartime diaries (*Nankō taigai ki *[Sailing South, 1943]), accounts of shipwrecked sailors (*Hyōmin Usaburō *[Castaway Usaburō, 1956]), and most notably his novel of the Hiroshima atomic bombing,* Kuroi ame *(Black Rain, 1966; tr. 1969). Ibuse's latest work,* Ogikubo fudoki *(An Ogikubo History, 1982), is a memoir surveying the more than fifty years in which he has observed, and participated in, the world of Tokyo writers and their public.*

Born in 1898 in a small village near the eastern extreme of Hiroshima Prefecture, Ibuse grew up in comfortable surroundings with an older brother and sister, parents and maternal grandparents. He left for Tokyo in 1917 to pursue studies in literature at Waseda University, but dropped out in 1922 to devote himself full-time to his own writing. His first efforts at fiction reflected not so much the literary trends of the time as his tentative and plaintive search as a young man new to the city seeking both a voice as a writer and an identity as a person. With style, humor, and sensitivity, the Ibuse Masuji of the 1920s explored with words the uneasy relations between town and country, friend and stranger, self and other. By 1929, the year he published "Kuchisuke's Valley" in the magazine Sōsaku gekkan,

Ibuse had begun to understand much of what he sought to say and how to say it; consequently this story is perhaps the best of his early career. Its assured use of language and secure point of view combine to create a distinct and independent narrator and a finely, believably drawn central character, both of whom resurface regularly as the disinterested first-person observers and willful old men that populate Ibuse's later work. Kuchisuke's old-fashioned ways and his young friend's perspective on them, together with the story's wit, shy eroticism, and even its intimations of violence, make "Kuchisuke's Valley" a veritable catalog of what has earned Ibuse his place as one of Japan's most acclaimed modern authors.

* * *

Seventy-seven-year-old Taniki Kuchisuke is especially fond of me. Each year when fall arrives and one's breath turns white in the air, he sends me a gift of rare pine mushrooms even if I am far from home on a trip. He lines an old noodle box with moss, fills it with the dried morsels, and addresses its cover with the salutation "Happy Autumn."

Kuchisuke is the caretaker of the mountain where these mushrooms grow. Although we sold this mountain to another family back in my grandfather's time, Kuchisuke stubbornly continues to do things as he did in the old days.

Before I forget to mention it, I would like to explain how Kuchisuke and I came to be friends.

My older brother, myself, and a younger sister were each in turn reared in the same baby carriage. It was a present to my family from Kuchisuke when he returned from working in Hawaii. It was also Kuchisuke who, as part of his job, would watch over us whenever we were in the carriage.

On its hood was embroidered a four-line poem in a foreign language. It translated to mean "Sleep, sleep, little child, sleep. The evening sun has begun to set yonder." Since I never felt in the least inclined to nap in the carriage, I did not care much for this alien verse.

Kuchisuke would load me in the buggy and spend all day strolling back and forth through the grove of trees in the garden. He consequently wore a path around the pond under the sweet osmanthus trees that even rain failed to efface. Besides a sty in his eye that slowed him down to a snail's pace, Kuchisuke had the annoying habit of frequently stopping altogether to retie his sash. Not wishing the progress of my buggy ever to be interrupted, I remonstrated with him each time this happened.

"Kuchisuke! Hurry up and get going!"

"I'm adjusting my sash just now. Don't speak to me like that."

"Don't talk so big. Who cares about your sash?"

No doubt because I was trying to rush him, Kuchisuke kept redoing his sash even though he ordinarily wore it loosely anyway.

Beneath the sheets in the carriage was a cushion printed with a pattern of black bats. I was convinced that these bats were escaping from the cushion to fly up into the sky after dark.

"Kuchisuke! The bats are taking off again! Hurry up and catch them!"

"If you'll just be quiet, they'll come back in the morning. Don't worry."

"Really? They'll come back?"

"Yes. All right, let's go around one more time."

"When I close my eyes it feels as if we're moving backward. Shall I let you in with me to try it?"

"Of course not. I'll get in alone later."

As he pushed the carriage Kuchisuke would sometimes attempt to teach me foreign words.

"Things like the osmanthus and pines are called 'tree.'"

I always forgot this word "tree" very quickly, and each time Kuchisuke would scold me for it.

"A child who can't remember anything is 'aizuru.'"

"Aizuru" is how he pronounced the English word "idle."

Eventually I passed the carriage down to my little sister. I was in the first grade at the time, and it was decided that I should continue to see Kuchisuke at his home on Sundays to be tutored in English. His house stood alone in the valley. Apparently he had not learned any farming in Hawaii, and for lack of any other skill he served here as caretaker of the mountain. Still, as a teacher he was extremely strict with me. He always wore the formal *hakama* skirt that my grandfather had given him, even though it was so long that it dragged on the floor whenever he rose from his side of the desk. He sat quite stiffly and read to me from the third volume of an English primer. He never, not even once, allowed me a glimpse of the text. Instead I kept my hands folded on the lap of my formal kimono and struggled to memorize the sentences as he recited them.

"'The night was very dark. The general, leading his desperate men, boarded the boat. The willow branches on the shore brushed against the general's shoulders and wet them with dew. The sound of the oars was very faint. The general surveyed the dark river and began quietly humming to himself. He hardly looked like a man who was going off to battle.'"

When Kuchisuke was done with the recitation, I repeated it.

"The night was very dark. The general boarded the boat. . ."

"The general, leading his desperate. . ."

"The general, leading his desperate. . . ?"

"Leading his desperate men, right?"

"Leading his desperate men. . ."

In this way Kuchisuke eventually corrected all my mistakes.

When each lesson was over and it was time for me to walk home, Kuchisuke always repeated the same warning. "When you cross the bridge, don't stop to look down into the river."

He was warning me about a section of the valley stream where its clear waters collected to form a swirling whirlpool. Overhead huge silk trees reached out with their branches and liberally scattered their peach-colored blossoms in the current below. Floating round and round in the whirlpool, these colorful flowers drew circles, as if with red crayon, only to vanish beneath the surface.

These memories of mine are now more than twenty years old. Today I live in Tokyo where I am trying to become a writer. I have yet to respond candidly to Kuchisuke's inquiries about my choice of career, since I am sure literature would please him the least.

Every time I visit my family in the country, he comes over and immediately interrogates me about my work. I avoid a direct reply and have allowed him to form the false impression that I am a dentist, or at other times, an engineer. On his way home he stops in at the neighbors' and boasts that I am a Tokyo dentist, or engineer, as if it were all his own doing.

I do not mean to ridicule Kuchisuke's great interest in me. After all, I am the only student that he ever had. Twenty years ago, when he finally finished reading all of the English primer to me, he looked up and said, "If you don't succeed in life, it will be harder on me than you. Should you fail, I will be the one who feels badly."

I did not know what to say. Deciding that it was time to leave, I stepped outside only to notice that snow, blanketing both the valley and the mountain peaks, had fallen while I was indoors.

I knew only too well that were I to correct Kuchisuke's latest supposition and tell him that I was not a lawyer in Tokyo, his reaction would be one of disappointment and dismay.

". . . I will be the one who feels badly." It wouldn't surprise me if he placed his hand over his heart and expired from grief on the spot. I had no choice but to continue the charade that I was a young attorney.

I have neglected to say anything about a girl called Taeto. There was not much, in fact, I knew about her until later, when we met. But you can learn something of her past from a letter she sent me, and from which I must quote:

> I hope you are in good health. My grandfather Kuchisuke is doing fine. Since the year before last, construction has continued every day here. Soon the dam will be completed. It is an immense wall that will seal off the valley from one mountain to the other, creating a lake more than five miles around. We will have to vacate our home to make room for it. This is a project authorized by the national government, and we cannot refuse to move out, yet Grandfather still refuses to cooperate no matter what. When the lake is ready and it fills with water, our home will lie submerged in the deepest part. Grandfather tells me that you are a lawyer, and I thought that if I asked you to intercede then perhaps he could be persuaded to leave. Please write Grandfather and talk some sense into him. The other day our local Diet member came by and told Grandfather to clear out and stop being a nuisance. It is a question of his prestige in the upcoming election, he said. Grandfather retorted that the representative had planned this lake in order to buy the voters with it in the first place. The last time we had an election, this same politi-

cian dispatched surveyors with red and white striped poles to take measurements, proclaiming in his speeches that he was having a railroad built, but so far we have seen no signs of it. Even now, Grandfather bothers people by complaining about this. I worry that people will look down on us if he is speaking out for no particular reason.

I must tell you something about myself. My name is Taeto, and I came to my grandfather's place from Hawaii two years ago. My grandparents were both Japanese, but my mother married an American. Some years ago Father left Mother and me without warning and returned to the mainland. I may look like an American, but in fact I am Japanese. My mother brought me here in December of the year before last. At the time, the valley and its trees were barren in the winter and I suffered from the cold and loneliness. Mother, who passed as a Japanese, managed to save a little money and soon found herself a new husband. Only two months later, however, she died. Perhaps the change in climate was too much for her. But she raised me as a Japanese, and I came here with her willingly. Japan is a better place than Hawaii. Japan is the land of my ancestors. I act and feel like a Japanese, and am very content now to live in this valley.

This letter gave me pause for thought. So, Kuchisuke has the unexpected responsibility for a foreign, and loquacious, granddaughter. I imagined him driven by all her chatter into the woods, and sitting there with arms folded, doing nothing. Why had he never mentioned a word about either Taeto or the lake to me? I had to go to him immediately, I had to act in defense of his rights. And if the situation warranted, I would go all the way to the provincial government with his case.

I departed for Kuchisuke's valley.

Walking through a deep valley on a moonlit night can be a very pleasant thing. The road had been widened for construction and was etched with deep ruts made by the trucks. The thick branches of the pine trees cast their speckled shadows onto the illuminated road. I stopped several times to gaze at the distorted reflection of the moon in the waters of a deep pool and to knock the flowers off a vine with my walking stick. However, my pleasant stroll was unexpectedly short, abruptly ended by a stone wall as big as that around a castle. It had been erected to bridge the gap between the two mountains forming the valley. This was the dam.

I calculated the distance from the base of the dam to where I was standing, estimated the angle of my line of vision to its top, and thus determined its height to be more than three hundred feet. The lake this wall would create would certainly leave Kuchisuke's home deep underwater. I walked along its base looking for an opening where I might pass through. I did find a sluice gate, but the river was rushing out of it and plunging in a waterfall with a terrible roar. Beneath was a deep pool. This was obviously the gate that would be closed as soon as construction was complete. Still, there had to be another opening for drainage purposes. I searched for it. Finally, not in the stone wall itself but in a hill of rock I discovered a large tunnel. Using my matches for light, I entered. A cool breeze swept through the tunnel, which was about as high and wide as a railway underpass. Water dripped from the ceiling, carved out in an arch through the thickest section of the hill. Bats dwelled in the crevices.

As I emerged from the tunnel I could see the windows of Kuchisuke's house. His lanterns were lit, and illuminated an apricot tree in silhouette. Wishing to avoid a dramatic reunion, I called out to him still some distance away.

"Kuchisuke! Are you still up?"

The next morning I was woken by the sounds of a cow mooing and a sickle being sharpened. I opened my eyes and saw a small crucifix hanging on the wall to one side of my pillow. I shut my eyes again.

Kuchisuke began to chop firewood outside my window. He opened the screen a crack and asked, "With all this racket out here, you haven't been able to catch a wink, have you?"

I replied that it wasn't loud, and that it wouldn't bother me even if it were.

The sound of logs splitting stopped, and then branches were being violently shaken. It was like leaves rustling in the wind. Soon I heard great numbers of apricots tumbling to the ground. I got out of bed and shouted, "Kuchisuke! All the unripe fruit will fall, too!"

"I don't care. I'm going to try and drop a few more."

He began shaking the branches again. When I looked out the window I saw that he had climbed the apricot tree and, striding a limb, was shifting his own weight to and fro. He rocked the tree so much that it looked as if it were in pain. The ground below showed signs of having been swept clean with a broom, but all the fruit and leaves that came hailing down now covered the area with a layer of fresh litter. The scent wafting from split apricots added a tart accent to the morning air.

I sat by the window and smoked a cigarette. All the construction in that part of the valley which would become the bottom of the lake was finished, the land reduced to a gentle slope of red clay.

Kuchisuke continued rocking the branches energetically in quest of one apricot that remained at the top of the tree. The morning sun shone through the leaves to bathe his face in a rich green light, and drops of dew from the branches clung to his skin. I told him to stop handling the apricot tree so roughly, but he only shook it more violently and said, "You're telling me I should leave, right? So I've got to get out, do I? Well, I've taken the advice you gave me last night. I've given up the idea of fighting it further."

He climbed higher into the tree and shook a smaller branch. "But I still want to hear you talk in front of everyone and defend my right to stay. I doubt I'll ever have another chance to see you give one of your fancy speeches."

I told him that if he had indeed decided to relocate, then there was no longer any need for me to speak on his behalf. Kuchisuke had told me that the construction people would build him a small house, and even try to have him appointed as the caretaker of the dam's sluice gate. He could expect to receive a monthly salary for his services. I had come from Tokyo to change his mind for naught.

When the sun's rays reached the mountaintops, Taeto came home leading a big black cow. She wore canvas shoes and a loose, green, high-collared jacket. She was an attractive foreign girl. Her cow carried four bundles of long green grass, two slung on each side. The beast was six times Taeto's size, but it obeyed her signal and went into its pen after she had unloaded its burden. The cue had been three quick clicks of her tongue. As I put trousers on over the long underwear that doubled as my pajamas, I studied her from behind with interest.

When I arrived the night before she had already gone to bed and I did not meet her. Wearing a thin cotton nightgown, she quickly turned her face away and pretended to be asleep when I came in. This allowed me to stare openly at her sleeping figure while I spoke in a low voice with Kuchisuke. Her short hair owed little to the efforts of a beauty parlor, but revealed instead the simple layered lines of a scissor cut. Her nightgown exposed the roundness of her young shoulders, and in the light of a lamp set on a high footstool I could even see the fullness of her breasts. A paperback book she had cast aside lay near her blue checkered pillow. On the wall was the crucifix which would be beside my own bed when I opened my eyes the next morning. Perhaps it was Kuchisuke, with the unsolicited idea of decorating my room, who moved it sometime during the night.

Taeto was picking up the fruit on the ground. Unable to grasp more than four at a time with one hand, she lifted the front of her blouse to make an apron and placed them in it. Then, laden with apricots, she came up to me and announced in perfect Japanese that last year she had eaten the apricots without washing them first. I did not want her to leave, and so I took one of the apricots from her apron and bit into it, slowly, one mouthful at a time. Kuchisuke had already left for the mountain with the cow.

Taeto stood silently beside me. If I were the romantic type, I would have been more interested in her rolled-up blouse, but I am not. I feigned a total preoccupation with eating the apricot. Yet, in a voice no less intense than that of a seducer, I said to her, "You have one, too. The ripe ones are delicious. A bit sour, but delicious."

Attempting to whet her appetite I deliberately bit into one of the greener apricots and, sucking in my cheeks, let the juices drool from my mouth as if it were indeed that tart. She was unable to resist the temptation.

"Thank you," she said as she took the smallest, greenest fruit and bit into it rather bashfully.

"Good?" I asked. She replied that it was.

It was then that we both noticed a group of six or seven men gathered at the top of the highest mountain. They were shouting something in the direction of an immense boulder that towered over the red clay of the summit like a black cancer.

"I bet they're going to break up that rock."

My guess was correct. Another man appeared out of the boulder's shadow and ran as fast as he could to his associates.

Just as he reported that the charges were lit, a series of explosions went off. The blasts were unbelievably loud and seemed to physically dislocate the entire atmosphere of the valley by several inches. My cheeks were struck by the forceful change in air pressure. I was further surprised to see the boulder split into two equal halves, which soon lost their balance and came tumbling down into the valley. The one in the rear rolled to the front as both increased their velocity.

"Look, the one that's behind now seems to be moving ahead again," exclaimed Taeto. The pursuing fragment crashed into the other with an ominous boom as it launched a wild leap-frogging bound and rolled at full speed into first place. The bypassed boulder now pursued a separate course. Both mowed down the dense mountain forest with cracking and thumping sounds. The two rocks reached the red clay of the valley bottom at the same moment, one teetering onto its side after a waltz-like spin, the other plunging halfway into the dirt.

The roll of the rocks had cut two swaths through the woods. Clouds of dust rose in their wake and a total hush spread over the valley.

"I hear the sound of water," said Taeto.

Later I realized she was listening to the rush of the river.

I know. We see a lot of it. It seems that those girls in the big city dance halls, the ones who are always ahead of fashion, find a look like Taeto's interesting. They apparently think it sophisticated to sport a jacket both one size too big and a bit too worn. But none of the green, high-collared jackets you might see at the dance halls would ever be as grimy or ill-fitting as Taeto's.

Taeto, squinting in the bright sun, was cutting and gathering indigo plants. The plants grew behind the house in the terraced rows alongside the millet and cotton. From the ends of the millet stems peeked budding flowers, and the cotton bloomed with deep yellow petals. Most bore no seed yet, but those that did displayed pure white cotton tufts atop their brown outer coverings. Occasionally Taeto would pause in her labors to wipe the sweat from her cheeks with her sleeve and open her blouse to let the breeze cool her chest. I opened my window a crack and watched how she worked in the fields.

Apparently she did not realize that I was observing her. She began to sing her own little song. It made me smile. The words were in a foreign language, but easy to translate. It went something like this: "I am hungry, I am sweating. My back is all wet, and even the soles of my feet are soaked."

She continued with her little song, repeating the lyrics over and over. Finally the sheer repetition made reading impossible, and I went outdoors to help Kuchisuke heat the bath water.

The tub was located under the eaves by the back door. It was surrounded by thick shrubs and a cherry tree that provided a canopy of branches overhead. The wooden tub was preposterously big.

Kuchisuke and I got in together. We fell into small talk as we sat up to our necks in the hot water.

"When you don't have your glasses on you're even more 'ugly' than usual. Hurry up and put them back on. Wait, let me have them first."

Kuchisuke reached for my eyeglasses from the shelf and tried them on. I took them off him and put them on myself. Now I could see the valley clearly. It looked just like those landscape murals done on the walls of Tokyo bathhouses.

"Somehow you've gotten skinny. You're really 'ugly' these days."

"It must be poverty."

"Come on. You mean women, don't you?"

"If I'm so 'ugly,' my problem can hardly be women."

"Anything's possible."

Kuchisuke lifted the upper half of his body out of the water and slapped his wrinkled chest with the palm of his hands. Then he stepped completely out of the tub.

I got out as well and walked through the thicket of shrubs. As I let the breeze dry my naked body, the afternoon sun shone through the leaves of the trees in the garden and playfully painted my skin shades of green.

Taeto finished her harvesting and now took her turn in the bath. Amid the sounds of water spilling and splashing there was suddenly a shrill scream from a terror-stricken voice. What could have happened? Taeto, without a stitch on, came flying from the bath toward me.

"Caterpillars!"

She pointed to the rim of the tub where one fat caterpillar was crawling in a desperate rush to find somewhere to hide. I brushed it off with a bamboo broom and went back to the far side of the shrubs to watch the green light again filter through the trees onto my body. Taeto, however, let out yet another high-pitched scream and came running to me.

"What *are* all these caterpillars? The branches of the cherry tree are crawling with them!"

The limbs of the tree that extended over the tub were indeed infested with hundreds of big black caterpillars. They wriggled all over each other to form a single massive clump.

Taeto slipped on her pants and went to get Kuchisuke. He took one look at the caterpillars and said with a sneer, "In four or five days we'll be out of here. That's not enough time for them to turn into butterflies."

That evening rain began to fall and the wind rose. Both grew worse as the night wore on.

Taeto knelt toward the wall where her crucifix hung and recited her bedtime prayers. She seemed to be in total earnest as she made her supplications in some foreign language. She got into bed afterward, but turned to Kuchisuke and complained that the wind was keeping her awake. The entire valley seemed to be groaning under the fury of the storm; one might have thought the very earth was howling. Kuchisuke and I played game after game of checkers.

"If you can't sleep, try eating these," suggested Kuchisuke as he handed Taeto some of the apricots. She opened her eyes wide and took two in each hand.

"Close your eyes. Then maybe you'll fall asleep."

She replied that she did feel sleepy, and shut her eyes only to open them a moment later.

It was very easy to beat Kuchisuke at checkers. "Don't be such a show-off," he would say each time he lost. "One more game." This is how we countered the nighttime cacophony of wind and rain.

Taeto, deciding that she must have been negligent in her prayers, slipped out from the covers to say them over again. She wore only her thin cotton nightgown. After making the sign of the cross with an arm bare beneath its short sleeve, she began to mumble once more in a foreign tongue. As Kuchisuke agonized over his next move, I took the opportunity to steal a glance at Taeto in prayer. Her naked legs trembled on the straw mat where she knelt. On her feet were short handwoven stockings the length of traditional Japanese ankle socks.

When these second prayers were done she took four apricots and returned to bed. As soon as she fell asleep and the apricots rolled from her loosened grasp, the wind and rain came to a stop.

Kuchisuke and I concluded our game and retired. All three of us slept in beds side by side. I fell straight asleep even though Kuchisuke continued to speak to me. When I woke a little while later, he was still talking aloud.

"Consider which is tastier, thrushes or shrikes. Shrikes are better, I'd say. But pheasant is better still. What I mean is, a pheasant has some meat on its bones. After pheasants come shrikes, then thrushes, in that order I suppose. Oh well, this rainy valley is about to become a rainy lake. They say it's going to be more than five miles around, but if a mallard or a heron were to fly high enough overhead, it might go right by and never realize there was a lake directly below. They say you'll be able to fish for carp in it. Twenty years from now the carp'll be two feet long. If I live till then, I'll go looking for them. What a sight it would be to see two-foot-long carp leaping up out of the lake in the evenings just before it rains. The water, as it follows the curves of the mountains, will make nine little inlets. I'm saying that if this big rainy valley is going to become a big rainy lake with nine little rainy ravines, well, then, that's what's going to happen. Don't blame me, but as a rule any one lake with eight or more little valleys to it is bound to contain a monster. I don't know, maybe the monster will look like a nine-foot-long carp, and if it does, it will come in all sorts of colors."

I pretended to snore. Kuchisuke gave up trying to talk to me any further and lay down, only to make snoring sounds even louder than my own. As soon as he noticed that I had ceased my performance, however, he stopped too and picked up where he had left off.

"I think that once the lake is full I'll buy hundreds of baby carp and release them in the water. I'm fonder of mountain birds, like pheasants, but human beings can't raise them. It was about ten years ago when I came across a pheasant's nest in the mountains with eggs in it, and made a chicken try to hatch them. Only one of the eggs made it. I put a big chicken coop over the hen sitting on the eggs, and when the mother pheasant came home it cried all night outside the gate before it gave up and went away. Oh, it was pitiful. I brought home the one chick that hatched and tried to feed it, but it died only ten days later. Baby pheasants don't know how to eat without getting excited. It would eat a little bit, then run all around, eat a little more, and run around some more. They don't eat right like chickens. It must have been famished. All that running around probably helped kill it, too. No, now I remember. It died from a bite on its head. I suspect that its mother followed it here and pecked it to death. Could there ever be anything worse than a mother like that? To peck your own child to death, even if it has been stolen out from under you, that's really something. I've seen it lots of times. The mother bird flies right into your house looking for its young. And it doesn't stop there. The cock pheasant then tricks the hen that's been taking care of the chick, and has its dirty way with it. I've even thought of letting the hen's eggs hatch, but I stop myself when I think I might be responsible for creating some kind of half-breed. It would be my fault, all my fault."

Kuchisuke stopped his rambling and heaved a deep, sad sigh. Perhaps the thought of Taeto made him grieve. A little later he spoke again.

"It's all my fault."

Suddenly he was trembling with tears. Anyone listening to an old man sobbing late at night would be moved, and a few tears rolled from my own eyes. I couldn't imagine how I might help him in his sorrow, however, and so I simply began to snore again. Kuchisuke soon ceased his crying and fell asleep with some very noisy snores of his own.

We finished moving. The three of us carried all the small things ourselves and had the cow transport the bedding and the tub on its back.

We went back and forth again and again across open fields of red clay in a caravan of man and beast.

The new house consisted of a six-mat room, a four-and-a-half-mat room, and one large area with only a dirt floor. The design and the materials were no different from where Kuchisuke had lived until now. An apricot tree was planted outside the window of the six-mat room, and a cow stall and latrine had been erected on the east side of the house. The only difference was that everything was new. The six-mat room served as a combination dining room, bedroom, family room and parlor; the four-and-a-half-mat room could be a storage area for the bedding and trunks as well as a hiding place for scolded children to run to and cry.

Once we finished moving we began to clean. We found loquats and apricots strewn on the floor and cigarette butts snuffed out on scraps of tin. Someone had written graffiti on the walls with charcoal, under which others had added their own comments. The workmen had probably done it.

Even after we had cleaned everywhere Kuchisuke found reason to criticize his new house. "I don't feel at home here," he said. "It may be all right now, but there's no cross-ventilation for when it's hot and humid. And this is the sort of worthless house that'll be freezing in winter."

He spat out the window several times and continued his diatribe.

"I feel as if I'm in someone else's home. I never dreamed this would happen to me. My other place was so much better! I'm going to spend one more night there."

After he finished dinner that evening, Kuchisuke did indeed grab his bedding and walk off into the darkening valley. Taeto tied the cow to a stake and plucked the ticks that had burrowed into the animal's brow and sides. She did not reproach Kuchisuke for leaving. Instead, she concentrated on her work, crushing all the mites that she found on the beast under the heel of her shoe. The ticks died smeared in the dirt and their own blood.

I had just finished repapering the sliding screen and was gluing a maple leaf onto its handle when I thought to myself that Kuchisuke, for all of his seventy-seven years, still had his childish moments. Sooner or later he was bound to return.

But I was wrong. Night fell, Taeto was done twisting more than half the rope that she was working on, and still Kuchisuke did not reappear. I went out to bring him home. A fog had completely filled the valley and looked like gray smoke under the glow of the moon.

Kuchisuke was not in bed. He had opened a window halfway and sat by it deep in thought, his elbows on the sill and his chin resting on his arms. The sound of my approaching footsteps broke his concentration.

"It's bad for your health to doze off in a place like that."

"I don't feel like sleeping. I'm just worried and upset about things."

"It's late. Let's go home."

"I like this house so much more. It should be up to me what roof I want to live under."

"Stop being such a 'bad boy.' Let's go."

"I'm going to wage a new fight against this. Don't you worry about me."

There was nothing I could do to dissuade him. I started home but then stopped to glance back. Assuming I was gone, Kuchisuke had put his chin back on his arms and resumed his thoughts. That is how I left him.

Taeto was still busy at work. She was braiding dozens of thin, six-foot-long strands of rope. Seated on a straw mat that she had spread over the earthen floor, she anchored the strands between her knees as she twisted. When she had as much as she could hold in her outstretched arms, she reached behind with one hand and pulled the twisted part through her legs. As she did this over and over, rain began to fall again.

The next morning Kuchisuke came home through the rain with his bedding.

The sound of trees being felled could now be heard in the valley. At first, the echo of two axes suggested that there were only two lumbermen, but gradually their number multiplied. It was obvious they were planning, rain or no rain, to clear in short order all the trees from the land that would soon be underwater. There seemed to be dozens of lumbermen at work, and that evening the sound of the rain was joined by a hail of falling axes.

Kuchisuke stood in one corner of the house and listened to the clamor with close attention. He remarked that the highest-pitched sounds came from three axes chopping away at one huge, dead oak tree. Then there was one sound that reverberated more solidly than the others: this was undoubtedly from the single tree that stood off by itself. It had the measured tone of a cello at the heart of a symphony. Kuchisuke recognized this muted sound as that of cherry wood being chopped.

The downpour did not let up, but Kuchisuke, bored with nothing to do, led the cow out. He wore a raincoat of woven straw similar to the sort that he placed over the back of the animal. I remained under the thatched eaves of the cow stall to avoid the rain as I watched the water rush out of the dam's sluice gate. The river had swollen tremendously and shot out through the gate with full force like a solid column of water. Within this column could be seen a great many logs. The lumbermen were apparently trimming the trees they had felled and floating the trunks downstream through the valley that still resounded with the crack of their axes. Logs flowed out of the sluice gate with no respite.

The water fell in a great cascade that created a pool at its bottom and raised clouds of mist. The plummeting waters generated a driving wind that blew the spray high into the sky. The logs in the pool were standing on end or revolving in perfect circles; one of them slipped in between two others to form a slender raft of three which raced headlong down the river. Another log surprised its companions by throwing itself atop them only to slide back, out of control, into the deep waters.

The rain lasted a full four days. The following morning the skies cleared and the valley shone a brilliant green.

The lumbermen had finished the job by the fourth day, and the sound of their axes did not echo under the blue skies of the fifth. They had carried out their mission in a very short period of time. The mountainsides had been cleared up to the exact height of the dam without a single tree left behind. The denuded area depicted a lake utterly drained of its water; this was how we would last see the valley, and I stood on the grass atop the dam astonished at the transformation.

"Now this is something. It's sure going to be big," Kuchisuke commented.

"From here I can see only five little valleys."

The timberline cut by the lumbermen made five nooks carved into the curve of the mountainsides. Kuchisuke disagreed with my count, however, and pointed out that there were four more small valleys under the shadow of the peak that jutted out to our left.

"So a monster lives here, heh?" I said to Kuchisuke.

"Sooner or later one will, yes."

The steep deforested hillsides were ashen in contrast to the red clay of the gentle incline that would become the bottom of the lake. Through the center flowed the river. At this point the land possessed almost none of the charm associated with a lake. It seemed more like someone's eye wide open in anger. At the waterless bottom of this menacing lake Kuchisuke's house still stood intact. Together we walked down from the dam and toured the area that would be deepest underwater. Kuchisuke stopped on a particular patch of ground and sighed as he stared at it. "Maybe this is where the monster will rise up," he murmured.

Two officials were present. Both had their suit coats off and were directing the workmen. They ordered the gates of the sluice closed. As the iron handles turned, three cogwheels of various sizes spun to lower doors as big as stage curtains to seal off the opening.

The waters flowing through the valley had lost none of their volume. Within moments the river was drowning in its own flood.

Kuchisuke and I, together with Taeto, went down below a grove of trees to watch. A turbid pond began to take shape in the red clay slopes at the bottom of the valley. Its surface was smooth and calm, apparently indifferent to the speed with which it was growing, but the scene at the very edge of the water was one of waves rolling to shore at high tide.

Kuchisuke's old home was increasingly isolated below the terraced fields. The cow stall and the trees around it had been cleared away, but for some reason the workmen had stopped before putting their destructive hands on the house itself. That made it all the worse for Kuchisuke now. The encroaching waters were beginning to trespass on his empty house.

Kuchisuke suddenly became as upset as if he were in the house himself.

"No, it's a tidal wave! It's all over!"

I grabbed his arms flailing in desperation and warned that people would sneer at his angry shouting. He broke loose from my hold and cursed out loud what everyone had done, claiming that people had it in for him and planned all along to sink his house at the bottom of a lake.

The water pressed its unsparing attack and poured into the home through its battered door. Walls were uprooted and eaves inundated; soon the entire structure was trapped in a whirlpool and disappeared beneath the surface.

"Sunk," said Taeto with a nervous sigh. A number of wooden beams forced their way to the surface above where the house had stood. They shot up two-thirds out of the water before they began to sink once more, falling onto their sides only to become pieces of driftwood that floated helter-skelter to shore.

The water began to seep into the fields. There, millet not yet ready for harvest was taken in the effortless sweep of a single wave and reduced to clumps of seedlings in the current. Similarly, the cotton plants with their deep yellow flowers and tufts of pure white vanished with the terraces beneath the deluge. The water started to create two bays. According to Kuchisuke it would be several days before it flooded all the nine inlets. Yet one could see that it was one single lake that was filling the valley. Its surface, dark as mud, reflected the surrounding mountains and blue sky in an effort to mollify the changes it had wrought.

When the sounds of the river flowing downstream died away for good, Kuchisuke tugged at his ears and complained of a ringing in them. The two officials went home with the workers in tow. Kuchisuke and I left for the top of the dam. A small sign there announced that a dedication ceremony for the lake would be held on the first of the month.

We sat down beside the sign and gazed at the lake in common silence. A small bird skimmed the surface of the water and flew about in confusion: the lake was a sudden apparition which had invaded its home. Spying its own reflection in the water, the bird let out a shrill cry and beat its wings excitedly. It soared high into the air, drew its wings in, and swooped down close to the surface again. Taeto had been watching the water too and commented that the creature would soon tire. What sort of bird was it anyway? I replied that it looked like a warbler to me.

It grew dark, yet the bird did not stop its wild flight. As the surface of the water turned the color of tarnished silver, the bird's path seemed to etch a black line across it. Perhaps it was the sound of its own flapping wings that kept it in such a state of agitation.

Kuchisuke spoke. "Just how cruel can this lake be."

Taeto picked up some pebbles and called out to the bird as she took aim and threw them. One stone grazed the top of its head. Surprised, the bird beat its wings desperately as it flew in a parabola and disappeared amid the mountain trees.

Kuchisuke rested his chin upon his knees and began to sigh as though something had just occurred to him. Each sigh was a deep breath followed by a forceful exhalation from the shoulders, as if it were meant to dispel the troubled thoughts from his system once and for all. The tail end of each breath that he inhaled and let out quivered slightly with the emotions inside him. Gradually, the old man's sighs turned into sobs.

I felt tired and did not want to get up just yet.

Taeto patiently waited for us to rise. There was a look in her auburn eyes that told me she would never, ever, leave Kuchisuke behind on the dam.

MATING

Kajii Motojirō

Translated by Robert Ulmer

Kajii Motojirō was born in Osaka in 1901 to a merchant family. Although he originally planned a career as an engineer, Kajii became interested in literature during his studies at the Third Higher School in Kyoto. In 1924 he entered the English literature department of Tokyo University but withdrew two years later due to illness. After spending a year and a half in the hot spring resort of Yugashima (the setting for the second part of "Mating"), Kajii returned to Osaka and lived there with his mother until his death from tuberculosis in 1932. Due to his untimely death, and perhaps to the temper of the times—the proletarian literature movement on the one hand and increasing militarism and government control on the other—Kajii's works were denied serious consideration during his lifetime. After World War II, and especially in the late 1950s, many more writers in Japan came to regard Kajii's writings as an important link between the prewar and postwar periods of Japanese literature.

Kajii's first, and possibly best-known story, "Remon" (Lemon, 1925), describes the ennui of its young hero and how the purchase of a single lemon from a fruit stand rejuvenates and purifies him. Almost all Kajii's stories are brief, prose-poetry pieces, and feature a hero who is a solitary figure or, as Kajii describes him in "Mating," "a lone traveler in the universe."

As in several of Kajii's stories, "Kōbi (Mating, 1931) presents an affirmation of the poet as outsider. His description of the cats and frogs suggests an awareness of the transience of life, the elements of death within life which create a balance that the hero of the story draws from to establish a stability within himself. There is also a total involvement in nature, which does not consume the writer's being but instead enlightens and enriches that inner, private world.

* * *

As I look up at the starry sky, bats are flying silently about. Though I cannot make out their shape, when they momentarily block the glimmer of the stars I can sense the presence of some kind of eerie creature.

People are fast asleep. I am standing on the rotting clothes-drying platform of a house. From here I can look out over the back alley. Like countless ships moored in a port, the houses in this neighborhood are built close together, and many other platforms are rotting like this one. I once saw a reproduction of the German artist Pechstein's *Christ Lamenting in the City*. It depicted Christ kneeling in prayer in the back streets of an enormous factory area. Associating with this image, I feel that where I'm standing now is somehow like Gethsemane. I do not feel like Christ, however. When the dead of night comes, my sickly body begins to burn and I am wide awake. But it is only to escape that monster, fantasy, that I come out here and let the poisonous night dew attack my body.

In every house people are fast asleep. From time to time I hear the sound of a weak cough breaking the silence. Because I have heard it in the afternoon, I know it as the cough of the fishmonger who lives in this back alley. His illness is making it difficult for him to carry on his business. The man who rents the second floor flat from him told him to see a doctor, but he would not listen to this advice. Insisting that it isn't that kind of cough, he tries to conceal the truth. The man who lives upstairs, however, goes around the neighborhood telling everybody about the fellow's illness. In a town like this, where only the rare lodger can pay the rent regularly every month, people can't afford a doctor's bills. Tuberculosis is a war of endurance. All of a sudden the hearse arrives. The memory of the deceased is still fresh in everyone's mind, but it is of him working as usual. It seems he was just in bed for a matter of days, and then died. Truly, in this life everyone brings despair, everyone brings death upon himself.

The fishmonger is coughing. Poor fellow. I listen to his cough, wondering if mine too sounds like that.

For a short while now, the alley has been astir with the activity of white animals. As night deepens they emerge, not just in this alley but in other back streets too. Cats. I've thought about why it is that in this neighborhood cats stroll about as if they owned the streets. First, it's because there are hardly any dogs around here. Keeping dogs is somewhat of a luxury. Instead, merchants keep cats so that their goods won't be destroyed by rats. Without dogs there are many cats, and they prowl the streets at will. Still, it is curious to see so many cats monopolizing the late night streets. Leisurely, they walk like ladies on the boulevard. They move casually from corner to corner like a surveying crew.

From a dark corner of the drying platform next door comes a rustling sound. A parakeet. When it was popular in the neighborhood to have birds as pets, some people even got hurt trying to retrieve these birds. Then, when people began to ask themselves, "Who started this crazy idea?" swarms of these scruffy abandoned birds came flocking with the sparrows in search of scraps to eat. But they no longer come. A few sooty parakeets next door are all that remain. During the day no one pays them any attention. But when night falls they become living things that give out this sound.

Then, to my surprise, two white cats that have been chasing each other in the alley stop near me and begin to grapple and moan. But it is not fighting in earnest. They are grappling on their sides. I have seen cats copulating but it was not like this. I've also seen kittens playing, but it wasn't like this either. I don't know what they are doing, but it is captivating and I watch them closely. From far away comes the tapping of the night watchman's stick. Except for that, there is no sound from the neighborhood; all is silent. Though they are absorbed in their grappling, the cats are quiet.

They embrace each other. They bite each other gently. They thrust their forepaws against each other. As I watch, gradually I become fascinated by their actions. Looking at the nasty way they nip at each other and seeing them thrust their forepaws out, I'm reminded of the sweet way they put their paws on people's chests and the thick warm fur of their bellies which is soft to the touch. Now one of them is pawing at this fur with its hind legs. I have never seen cats appear so lovely, so mysterious, so enthralling. After a while, still embracing tightly, they cease their movement. As I watch I feel a choking sensation. Just then the sound of the night watchman's stick echoes in the alley.

Whenever this man comes I duck into the house, not wanting to be seen prowling around clothes-drying platforms late at night. Of course, if I move close to one side of the platform it's hard to see me. But the shutters are open, and if he did happen to see me and call out, it would be most embarrassing. So when the watchman approaches I usually hurry into the house. But tonight, wanting to see for myself what will happen to the cats, I decide to stay where I am on the platform. The watchman draws slowly nearer. The cats remain embracing each other as before, not seeming to make any effort at all to move. The sight of these two white cats entwined gives me the illusion of watching a man and a woman absurdly doing as they please. I derive an immense enjoyment from this scene.

The watchman has gradually drawn nearer. He runs a funeral parlor during the day, and has an aura of unspeakable gloom about him. As he comes closer I wonder how he will react when he sees the cats. Now only a few yards away he seems to notice them for the first time and stops. He is watching them. I watch him looking at the cats, and somehow have the feeling that I am there with him, observing this midnight scene. But the cats have not moved at all. Have they not noticed him? Perhaps. Yet they do not care, for they are finishing their business. This is one aspect of these brazen animals. If they sense that you won't harm them, they have no fear and remain perfectly calm when you try to drive them off. But in fact they watch you keenly, and as soon as it appears that someone means them harm, they instantly take flight.

Seeing they have still not moved, the watchman comes a few steps closer. Then, without breaking their embrace, the cats turn their heads around. From my point of view the watchman is now the more interesting. Suddenly, he strikes his nightstick sharply on the ground. The cats dart off into the alley, two streaks of light. Watching them run off, the man regains his usual bored expression and, rapping his stick, walks off. He has not noticed me.

I once went to observe some singing frogs.

To see them, one first has to venture resolutely to the edge of the shallows where they sing. Since they will hide no matter how cautiously one approaches, it is just as well to move quickly. One then hides by the shallows and remains perfectly still. Imagine you are a rock. Nothing moves but your eyes. If you are not careful it is difficult to distinguish the frogs from the stones in the shallows and you won't see anything. After a while, from the water and the shadows of the rocks, the frogs slowly show their heads. As I looked on they seemed to emerge from almost everywhere. All at once, as if by previous arrangement, they timidly appeared.

I remained still as a rock. Letting their fear pass, they all climbed out to where they were before. In front of me they took up their interrupted courtship song again.

I was overcome at intervals by an odd feeling, watching from this proximity. Akutagawa Ryūnosuke wrote a novel about men going to the land of the mythical *kappa*, but in fact the land of the frogs is much more accessible. Through observing just one frog I suddenly entered their world. This frog sat by the small current that ran between the rocks in the stream and, with something uncanny in its look, stared at the rushing water. Its appearance was exactly like the human figures in classical literati paintings: something between a fisherman and a *kappa*. As I thought about this, the small current suddenly widened and became an inlet. And, in that instant, I had a sense of being a lone traveler in the universe.

That is all there is to the story. And yet, it may be said that I observed the frogs in the most natural of conditions. Once before, though, I had the following experience.

I went to the shallows and caught a frog, planning to study it carefully. I placed it in a bucket from the bathhouse and filled the pail with water. I put in some stones from the stream and, using a piece of glass as a cover, carried it back to my room. The frog, however, would not act naturally at all. I caught some flies and put them in the pail, but the frog just ignored them. Bored with this, I went for a bath. I had forgotten about the frog and was returning to my room, when all of a sudden the sound of a splash came from the bucket. Thinking to myself, "At last," I hurried over and looked. But just as before, the frog remained hidden and would not come out. Next I went for a walk. When I returned I again heard the sound of a splash. Looking in, it was just like the time before. That night, placing the bucket at my side, I sat down to do some reading. I forgot all about the frog, but when I moved it jumped with a splash. It had been observing *me* in my natural condition. The next day, because all I had finally learned from the frog was that it jumped from fear, I uncovered the bucket. It leaped toward the sound of the rapids outside my window, to cleanse itself of the dust in my room. I never tried this experiment again. In order to observe them naturally, I had to go to the shallows.

The day I went the frogs were singing loudly. Their voices could be heard clearly from the main road of the village. From this road I walked through the cedar grove to the shallows where I always went. In the thicket opposite the stream, a flycatcher was chirping prettily. The flycatcher was a bird that, like the frogs in this valley, always gave me a pleasant feeling. The villagers said there was only one of these birds in the whole valley, where the woods were thickest. If another flycatcher went there, the two fought and one would be chased away. Whenever I listened to its song I was reminded of the villagers' story and felt it must be true, for this was the song of one that rejoiced in hearing its own voice. The bird's voice carried far, echoing in the valley as the sunlight changed. Idling my time away in the valley, I would hum this ditty to myself:

> If you go to the bridge of Nishibira
> You'll hear the Nishibira flycatcher;
> And if you go to Seko Falls
> You'll hear the Seko flycatcher.

One of these birds was near the shallows. Just as I expected, the frogs were wailing. Quickly I walked over to the edge of the shallows. At that, their music ceased. Following the plan I had formed, I crouched and waited. In a while they began to sing as before. Their many voices resounded in the shallows, reverberating like a wind coming from afar. From among the small ripples of the current nearby it grew louder, and moved en masse to reach a tide. This diffusion of sound moved delicately, steadily swelling and rolling phantomlike before me.

Scientists say that the first living things with a "voice" were amphibious creatures that appeared during the Carboniferous Period. Thinking of their voices now as the first living sound to chorus forth on the face of the earth gave me a sense of the sublime. It was the kind of music that touches the listener's heart, makes it throb, and finally moves him to tears.

In front of me was a male frog. Obviously drifting with the waves of the chorus, his throat trembled intermittently. I looked around, thinking that his mate must be nearby. A foot or two away in the stream, in the shadow of a rock, another frog was sitting with quiet reserve in the background. I thought it must be the mate. Whenever the male croaked, I noticed that the female answered "geh! geh!" in a contented voice. As this went on, the male's voice grew clearer. My heart responded to his earnest cries. Then he suddenly broke from the rhythm of the chorus. The intervals between his cries grew shorter and shorter. The female continued to reply. And yet, perhaps because her voice did not carry, she sounded a bit nonchalant in comparison to that other passionate call.

But now something had to happen. Impatiently, I waited for the moment. As I expected, the male frog abruptly stopped his ardent croaking, smoothly slipped off the rock, and began to cross the water. Nothing has ever moved me so much as the tenderness of that moment. Swimming across the water toward the female, he was like a child who has found its mother, crying appealingly as it runs to her. As he swam he cried out, "geeyo! geeyo! geeyo! geeyo!" Could any other courtship be so tender and devoted? I watched, feeling an awkward envy.

He arrived happily at the feet of his mate, and there they copulated in the fresh limpid stream. Yet the sight of their desperate mating came nowhere near the tenderness of his crossing the water. Feeling I had seen something in the world that was beautiful, for a while I submerged myself in the cadence of the frogs' voices vibrating in the shallows.

LES JOUES EN FEU

Hori Tatsuo

Translated by Jack Rucinski

The fragile, poetic writings of Hori Tatsuo (1904–53) are unique in the annals of Shōwa literature. In an age fraught with war, extremes of experimentation, and despair, Hori wrote poems and stories for that minority of the human race for whom wild roses and dreams are the vital concerns of life. He stood for artistic conscientiousness and propriety, and his finely wrought prose remains a model of a chaste, poetic style.

As a sensitive, lonely young man, Hori enjoyed the association and tutelage of such important literary figures as Murō Saisei, an important avant-garde poet, and Akutagawa Ryūnosuke. It was Murō who first took Hori to the locale with which his name will always be associated, the fashionable summer resort town of Karuizawa. At Tokyo University, Hori read French literature voraciously: Stendhal, Anatole France, Gide, and Mérimée. His own poetry was highly influenced by Cocteau and Rilke, while in prose his models ranged from Proust to the Heian court ladies who penned personal diaries.

In the 1930s, when other writers turned either to the new revolutionary literature of the proletarian movement or to the opposing forces of pure aestheticism, Hori was left to the pursuit of the introspective, the refined, and the delicate in literature. His first prominent story, "Seikazoku" (The Holy Family, 1930), derived from his personal reactions to Akutagawa's suicide three years earlier, but it is noteworthy for its attempt to achieve objectivity and consciously battle the tendency toward autobiography that was overwhelming the literature of the period. Hori carried this attempt even further in Utsukushii mura *(Beautiful Village, 1933; tr. 1967), set in Karuizawa, and* Kaze tachinu *(The Wind Rises, 1936–37; tr. 1958), an attempt to objectify the days Hori spent caring for his fiancée as she slowly succumbed to tuberculosis, a disease that constantly plagued and finally killed Hori also.*

In the late thirties, drawn to the portraits of docile women resigned to their fates that he found in Heian court diaries, Hori began writing works in the classical mode, adapting Kagero no nikki *(The Gossamer Years, 1937) and the eleventh-century* Sarashina nikki. *His final works were poetic evocations of the beauty of the Japanese natural landscape in the environs of Nara and Kyoto.*

"Moyuru hoho" (Les Joues en Feu, *1932) was intended, like Mori Ōgai's famous* Vita Sexualis, *to be a frank account of sexual attitudes and experiences. Hori's title is taken from an expression much used by Cocteau and Radiguet; the image of "flaming cheeks" aptly captures the mood of the story, a shy and hesitant awakening to sexuality. To reveal the universality of the emotions of young love, Hori draws upon his own experience, but avoids pure autobiography again by the use of other sources. Various scenes and characters are borrowed from Cocteau's* Le Grand Ecart *and Proust's* A la recherche du temps perdu. *As in Proust, women in Hori's literature are the personification of the ideal, almost more divine than mortal. Saigusa here is a near forerunner of the pure heroines of* Beautiful Village *and* The Wind Rises. *Kawabata Yasunari noted the absence of carnality in Hori's treatment of sex, and remarked of "Les Joues en Feu," "What a wonder it is that the author should have such purity of perception, like the innocence of a naked child!"*

* * *

I turned seventeen. I had just gone from middle to preparatory school. My parents were afraid that life under their roof might be bad for my nerves and had me board at the school. This change of environment could not but have had a great impact upon me. Because of it, the shedding of my childhood was to be curiously hastened.

The dormitory was divided up for all the world like a honeycomb into many small studies, each one kept in a perpetual state of turmoil by the ten or so boys occupying it. These "studies" were furnished with nothing more than a few huge, scarred tables, each heaped high with school caps, dictionaries, tablets, ink bottles, and packs of cigarettes and such, all languishing for want of an owner. Among all this might be found a boy doing his German, or another precariously straddling the old chair with the broken leg, idly puffing away at a cigarette. Of all the boys I was the smallest. To be one of them, I tortured myself trying to smoke and timidly took a razor to my still beardless cheeks.

The bedroom on the second floor had a strange smell of soiled linen that made me queasy. The smell even found its way into my dreams while I slept and imbued them with sensations unknown as yet to my waking hours. But gradually I grew accustomed even to that.

And so my innocence was tottering. It needed only the final blow.

One afternoon recess, I was wandering alone in the deserted flower garden to the south of the botany laboratory. I halted all of a sudden. A honeybee, dusty with pollen, flew up from a great riot of pure white flowers I did not know, blooming in a corner of the garden. I thought I would watch and see to which flower the honeybee carried the pollen clustered on his legs, but he appeared indecisive and not about to settle on any of them. At that moment, I sensed that every one of the flowers was coquettishly arching her styles in a stratagem to entice the bee to herself. He finally chose one and alighted upon her. He fastened his dusty legs around the tiny tips of her styles and presently flew up again. As I watched, I suddenly felt that cruelty only children are capable of and yanked at the fertilized flower. I scrutinized her styles flecked with the pollen of the male, crushed her in my palm, and wandered on again through the garden blossoming in flaming reds and purples. Just then someone called my name through the glass doors of the botany laboratory. It was Uozumi, an upperclassman.

"Come and have a look. I'll let you see the microscope."

Uozumi was on the discus-throwing team and seemed about twice my size. When he was on the field, he bore a slight resemblance to *The Discus Thrower*, one of the Greek statues on the German picture postcards that we circulated among ourselves. Consequently, the lowerclassmen idolized him in spite of his perpetual look of disdain for everyone. I wanted him to like me. I went into the laboratory.

Uozumi was the only one there. His hairy hands were fumbling with a specimen. Every now and then he peered at it through the microscope. Then he let me have a look. I had to hunch over, shrimplike, in order to make anything out.

"Can you see?"

"Yes."

Awkward as my position was, I still was able to keep a secret watch on him out of my other eye. I had already noticed a peculiar transformation in his face. Whether it was due to the bright light of the laboratory or to his having removed his mask for once, the flesh of his cheeks was oddly slack and his eyes were deeply bloodshot. A faint smile, like a girl's, kept flickering on his lips. For some reason, I thought of the honeybee and the strange white flowers of the garden. His warm breath grazed my cheek.

I abruptly raised my head from the microscope and, with a look at my wristwatch, stammered, "Well, I . . . I've got to get to class."

"Oh?"

His mask was already deftly back in place. He stood looking down at my face drained of color, with his customary expression of disdain.

In May, Saigusa, who was in the same class as myself though a year older, was transferred to our study. He was known for being a pet of the upperclassmen. He was a slender boy and made me envious of his fragile beauty, for his skin was translucent, blue-veined, and fair, while his cheeks still retained the tint of roses. In the lecture hall, I went so far as to steal occasional glances from behind my textbook at the back of his slender neck.

At night he would go up to the second-floor bedroom before anyone else. This was about nine o'clock even though there was a regulation that lights could not be turned on in the bedrooms until ten. After he went up, my mind would evoke a phantasmagoria of his faces, all asleep in darkness.

I had acquired the habit of not going to bed until midnight, but one evening I had a sore throat and I seemed to be running a slight fever. Soon after Saigusa went up, I took a candle and climbed the stairs. I opened the bedroom door without a forethought. It was pitch-black inside, but suddenly a strange shadow in the form of a large bird was thrown on the ceiling by the light of my candle. It flapped about eerily, as if in a fierce struggle. My heart skipped a beat. Then it was gone. My only thought was that the phantom on the ceiling was created by a caprice of the flickering light of the candle, for when the flame stopped its wavering, except for Saigusa in his bedding against the wall, I saw nothing more than a dark, sullen form in a hooded cape, sitting beside him.

"Who's there?" the huge boy in the cape asked, looking around.

When I realized it had to be Uozumi, I became flustered and put out the candle. Ever since that time in the botany laboratory, I was sure he hated me. I didn't say a thing and crawled under my shabby quilt next to Saigusa's. Saigusa too was silent all this time.

I lay there choking for several minutes. The man I took to be Uozumi eventually got up. Without a word he stomped through the dark and left the room. When his footsteps grew fainter, I told Saigusa in a suffering tone that I had a sore throat.

"You must have a fever, too."

"Maybe just a little."

"Here, let me see." He stretched over and laid a cold hand on my throbbing forehead. I held my breath. Then he grasped my wrist. If he intended taking my pulse, it was a strange way of doing it. But all that worried me was that he might find the beat had suddenly quickened.

All the next day I stayed buried under the covers and even wished my sore throat might never get better so that I could go up to bed early every night. Several days later, my throat started hurting again in the evening. Deliberately coughing, I went up to the bedroom soon after Saigusa, but his bed was empty. Wherever he had gone, he was a long time coming back. A whole hour went by as I suffered in solitude. It seemed to me my throat had taken a turn for the worse and might well be the end of me.

He finally reappeared. I had left a candle burning beside my pillow. Its light traced a weird, writhing form on the ceiling as he undressed, and the memory of the phantom of the other night came back to me.

I asked him where he had been. He hadn't felt sleepy, he said, and had gone for a walk alone around the playing fields. Something in his tone made me think he was lying, but I didn't question him any further.

"Going to leave the candle burning?" he asked.

"As you like."

"I'll put it out then." To blow out the flame, he drew his face close to mine. I kept my eyes raised to his cheeks where the shadows of his long lashes fell and flickered in the candlelight. Compared to mine, flaming as they were, his cheeks seemed celestially cool.

At some point, my relationship with Saigusa passed beyond ordinary friendship. If he grew closer to me, Uozumi, on the other hand, became all the more overbearing to everyone in the dormitory, and from time to time was to be found alone on the field, practicing discus throwing like a demon. He disappeared altogether while we were in the midst of preparations for the half-year examinations. The entire dormitory knew he had gone, but not one of us said a word about it.

Summer vacation came. Saigusa and I planned an excursion of a week or so to the seacoast. We felt somewhat heavy-hearted, like children sneaking off from their parents, as we set out one leaden gray morning.

By leaving the railway at a seaside station and then walking a mile on a road that followed the shore, we came to a small fishing village cradled in the jagged hills. Our inn had a woebegone look about it, and the smell of seaweed came drifting in with the night. A maid brought in a lantern. Saigusa took off his shirt to go to bed, and in the dim lantern light his bare back showed a peculiar ridge on his spine. An unaccountable urge to touch it came over me.

"What's this?" I asked, putting my finger to the spot.

"That?" He reddened a little. "That's a scar from tuberculosis of the spine."

"Let me feel it, will you?"

I stroked the curious ridge on his spine as I might a piece of ivory, not allowing him to dress. His eyes were closed and he shuddered slightly.

The weather had not cleared by the next day, but nonetheless we set out once more over the pebbles of the road that led us through the little villages along the sea. Around noon, we were coming upon yet another village when the sky grew ominous and rain threatened to fall at any moment. Furthermore, both of us were tired of walking and somewhat cross with each other, so we decided that when we got to the village we would ask when the bus passed through.

On our way was a small wooden bridge where five or six village girls, each with a fish basket on her arm, had stopped to talk. When they saw us coming they fell silent and watched us with curiosity. I discovered among them a girl with particularly beautiful eyes and kept looking just at her. The girl, evidently the oldest, gave no sign of annoyance at my stare. In order to make the best possible impression on her in the shortest possible time, I attempted that swagger boys affect in these situations. I wanted to say something, anything at all, but my wits completely failed me, and I was just about to pass by without a word when Saigusa suddenly slackened his pace and, to my surprise, went boldly up to her. He was asking her about the coach—quite a shrewd maneuver. Now this tactic of his was likely, I thought, to give her a better impression of him than of myself. Not to be outdone, I went up to her and, while they were talking, took a look in her basket.

She was answering him without the least trace of shyness. Her voice was unexpectedly rasping and failing in its duty to the beauty of her eyes; yet, the very harshness of it added mysteriously to her charm.

I decided to speak up. I pointed at the basket and faintheartedly asked what the little fish inside were called. There must have been something odd about the way I asked, for she seemed to find it unduly funny. The other girls followed her lead and burst out laughing. The blood rushed to my cheeks and, with a glance at Saigusa, I caught the flash of a malicious smile. A sudden hostility toward him came over me.

We headed for the end of the village where the bus was to stop, neither of us saying a word. We had a long wait and it had already begun raining. Once aboard, we were left largely to ourselves and hardly spoke; I was depressing him as much as he was me. We finally arrived in a misty rain at a town by the sea, where we might find lodgings for the night. The inn was just as gloomy as that of the night before. There was the same faint smell of seaweed and the same light from the flame of a lantern, conjuring up hazy ghosts of ourselves as we were twenty-four hours ago. The restraint between us eventually melted. We blamed our low spirits on having had such bad weather for traveling. My proposal was that the next day we go directly by bus to a town where we could get a train and return to Tokyo for the time being. He agreed, evidently not knowing what else to do. In our exhaustion both of us soon fell sound asleep.

Some time close to dawn, I happened to wake. Saigusa was sleeping with his back to me. I noticed the small ridge on his spine under his bedclothes and gently stroked it as I had done the previous night. When I did so, I found myself thinking of the beautiful eyes of the girl on the bridge. That strange voice of hers still echoed in my ears. I heard Saigusa lightly grind his teeth as I drifted back to sleep.

The next day as well brought rain, or rather a dense mist. We no longer had a choice; the trip had to be given up. In the bus rattling on through the rain, and later in the crush of the third-class carriage of the train, both of us did all we could—and it is this that marks a full stop to love—to spare the other pain. Something made me feel that hereafter we were never to meet again. A number of times he seized my hand. If I did not give it to him, neither did I withdraw it from him. All the same, when fragments of a strange rasping voice came drifting to me from time to time, I was deaf to all else. We were all the sadder when we said good-bye.

The most convenient way for me to get home was to get off the train at a station along the way and change to a branch line. While I made my way through the crowd on the platform, I kept looking back at him in the railway carriage. To see me better, he pressed his face to the window beaded with rain but succeeded only in clouding the glass with his white breath, and hid me all the more from sight.

August came and I went with my father to a lakeshore in Shinshū. I hadn't seen any more of Saigusa but he sometimes wrote what might be called love letters to me at the lake. In time I gradually stopped answering. Echoes of strange voices had effected a change in my love. From one of his last letters, I learned he was ill. I gathered he was suffering again from his spinal tuberculosis. Regardless, I wrote no more.

The autumn half began. On my return from the lake, I once again moved into the dormitory. Everything was different now. Saigusa had gone somewhere by the sea for a change of climate; Uozumi took no more notice of my existence now than he did of the air around him.

With winter, there came a morning all encrusted in a thin shell of ice, when I discovered Saigusa had died. The announcement was on the school bulletin board. I read it through vacantly, as if it concerned someone I had never known.

Several years went by. Every now and then I would recall all that had happened in the dormitory and could not help feeling that I had ruthlessly stripped away the beautiful skin of childhood and left it to lie like an opalescent snakeskin entangled among the brambles. In the course of those years, how many were the strange voices I heard! There was not one among them that did not lead me to grief; and I was all too fond of grieving over them, until one day I was finally dealt a wound to the heart from which there was no recovering.

In the uplands near the lake I had once visited with my father was a sanatorium, and here I was sent after a serious hemorrhage of the lungs. The doctor's diagnosis of tuberculosis has no particular importance to this story save to demonstrate that the petals of the rose must fall and that I, too, had now lost the bloom from my cheeks for all time.

There was, besides myself, only a single patient in what was known as the White Birch Ward of the sanatorium. He was a boy of fifteen or sixteen and had been treated for tuberculosis of the spine but was simply convalescing then, and for several hours a day he would conscientiously sunbathe on the veranda. When he learned I was confined to bed, he took to paying me calls occasionally. On one of his visits, it struck me that his lean face, although darkened by the sun until the only trace of red was in the lips, bore the stamp of the dead Saigusa. From that time on, I did my best not to look directly at him.

One morning was so fine I had a sudden desire to get up from bed and ventured cautiously over to the window. There, on the opposite veranda, was the boy, totally naked, sunning himself. He was leaning slightly forward, intent on a part of his body. He could not have known he was being watched. My heart was pounding. I am nearsighted, and squinted for a better look. When I made out on his dark back what seemed to be that distinctive ridge of Saigusa's, a sudden dizziness came over me. I managed my way back to the bed and collapsed.

The boy left the sanatorium several days later, without the slightest notion of the great shock he had given me.

MAGIC LANTERN

Dazai Osamu

Translated by Tomone Matsumoto

Dazai Osamu (1909–48) was born in Aomori Prefecture, the tenth of eleven children of a grand landowner. Raised by his aunt and servants, Dazai, precocious and sensitive, never had the feeling that he belonged to his own family. He excelled in composition, and his interest in literature led him to organize a literary group at Hirosaki Higher School. With his sponsorship this group published periodicals to which he contributed short stories. Dazai entered Tokyo University in the French Department in 1930. He was involved as a student with the then ebbing Marxist movement, but withdrew from it after two years.

After he made his literary debut in 1933, he published short stories such as "Romanesuku" (Romanesque, 1934; tr. 1965) and "Dōke no hana" (Flowers of Buffoonery, 1935). He was nominated for the Akutagawa Prize in 1935, but was never able to obtain it. Despite his literary success his personal life was chaotic: he was disowned by his family because of a continuing relationship with a geisha; one of the women who participated with him in his four suicide attempts died by drowning; an operation left him addicted to drugs, and he had to be committed to an asylum for treatment.

Dazai's marriage in 1939 to Ishihara Michiko, a secondary school teacher, changed his personal life as well as his writings. The structure and style of his work became much clearer, more natural and simple. This happy period lasted until the end of the Second World War.

His third and final literary peak came in the post-1945 era, but lasted only a year and a half. He produced Shayō *(The Setting Sun, 1947; tr.*

1956), Ningen shikkaku (No Longer Human, 1948; tr. 1958), and "Viyon no tsuma" (Villon's Wife, 1947; tr. 1956), the works regarded as his masterpieces. His fifth suicide attempt was successful: he drowned himself with a lover in 1948. As one of the most controversial writers in modern Japan, Dazai's popularity has increased after his death, and a gathering on the anniversary of his suicide has become a yearly event.

* * *

The more I talk about it, the more suspicious people become. Everyone I meet is wary of me. Even when I go to see them for the simple pleasure of their company, they greet me with the strangest of looks, as if wondering why I've come. I find it unbearable.

I no longer want to go anywhere. Today I went to a public bathhouse near my home, but I waited till early evening so that no one would see me. Back in the middle of summer, my cotton kimono still shone white at dusk, and I was worried how conspicuous I must be. But it has turned noticeably cooler since yesterday. It won't be long before we're using our fall wardrobe, and I'll be changing to an unlined kimono with a black background. I can't stand the thought of having to spend another whole year with things the way they are—to have people staring at me in that white cotton kimono again next summer. . . No, it's unthinkable! By next summer I must attain a social position that will allow me to go out in public dressed even in that eye-catching kimono with the morning-glory pattern. And I want to wear a little makeup as I walk among the crowds at the festivals in the temples and shrines. My heart throbs with emotion when I think how wonderful that would be.

Yes, I committed a theft. I won't deny it. I'm certainly not proud of what I did, but, well . . . let me tell you how it all began. Not that I care what people think. Their opinions don't matter to me. Still, if you can believe my story . . . well, so much the better.

I'm the daughter of a poor Japanese clog-maker—his only daughter. As I sat in the kitchen last night cutting up a spring onion, I heard one of the neighborhood kids out back call, half in tears, "Hey, Sis!" I stopped cutting for a moment and sat motionless. I realized that my life might not have turned out quite so miserably if I'd had a younger brother or sister who needed me from time to time, who called out to me like this child. Hot tears welled up in my eyes, already smarting from the onions, and when I tried to wipe them away with the back of my hand, the stinging worsened. The tears streamed down endlessly, and I felt helpless.

It was last spring, when the cherry trees were past their prime and pink and blue-fringed flag irises were beginning to appear at the flower stands, that the gossip started down at the hairdresser's: That spoiled girl has finally started chasing men.

I was still happy then. Mr. Mizuno would come to see me each day at dusk. Before nightfall I would change my kimono, put on some makeup, and wait for him, stepping in and out of the house to see if he'd arrived. I was told, later, that the people in the neighborhood were well aware of all this, and would secretly point at me and whisper among themselves, "Look! Sakiko from the clog shop is in heat," and laugh at me. I think both my parents were vaguely aware of what was going on, but they couldn't bring themselves to speak to me about it.

I'm twenty-four years old this year but still unmarried. The reason I haven't yet married is, of course—other than being poor—very largely Mother. When she was still the mistress of an important landowner from the neighborhood, she had an affair with my father. She ran off with him, forgetting everything she owed her former patron, and soon gave birth to me. The problem was, however, that I didn't look like either the landowner or my father. Mother became more and more isolated, and for a time she was a social outcast. Being the daughter of such a woman, I naturally had little chance of marriage. But, with my looks, my fate would have been the same even if I'd been born to a wealthy aristocrat.

I don't bear a grudge against my father, though, or against my mother. I am most decidedly my father's child. I firmly believe that, no matter what anyone else may say. Both my parents look after me well, and I take good care of them. They are vulnerable people. Even toward me, their own child, they behave with a certain restraint. I believe that we should be kind to weak and timid people. I thought I was prepared to endure any pain and loneliness for my parents. Until I met Mr. Mizuno, I never neglected my obligations to them.

Though it's embarrassing, I should explain that he is five years younger than I am, and that he's a student at a commercial school. But you must understand that I had no alternative. I met him in spring, in the waiting room of an eye specialist, when I was having trouble with my left eye. I'm the sort of woman who falls in love at first sight. He had a white bandage on his left eye, just like mine. He was leafing through a small dictionary, frowning and looking uncomfortable. I felt sorry for him. I too was depressed because of my bandaged eye. The young pasania leaves I could see from the windows of the room looked like blue flames flickering in the heat-laden air. Everything in the outside world seemed to fade from reality, and his face had an unearthly, even uncanny, beauty about it. I'm convinced that all this resulted from the sorcery of the eye bandage.

Mr. Mizuno is an orphan. He has no blood relations to look after him with loving care. His parents were fairly well-to-do, but his mother passed away when he was a baby, and he was only twelve when his father died. After that the family business, a pharmaceutical supply store, declined. His two older brothers and an older sister were taken separately into the care of distant relations. At present, as the last child of the family, he is supported by the head clerk of his father's store, and goes to commercial school. I was afraid he must have had a rather restricted, lonely life, for he once confessed that his most enjoyable moments were when he went out walking with me. I also suspected that he lacked many personal belongings. He told me that he had promised to go swimming with a friend, but he didn't look happy at the prospect. In fact, he looked quite downhearted. That night I stole a man's swimsuit.

Quickly and quietly I entered Daimaru's, the largest store in my neighborhood. Pretending to look at this and that among the simple cotton dresses for women, I stealthily removed a black swimsuit from the counter, tucked it under my arm, and left the store. I hadn't walked more than five yards when someone called out, "You there!" I was so frightened I was ready to scream, and I ran like a madwoman. I heard a shrill cry of "Thief! Thief!" behind me, felt a blow on my back, and stumbled. When I turned around, I was struck across the face.

I was taken to a small police station. Quite a crowd of familiar faces from the neighborhood assembled in front of it. I noticed that my hair was in disarray and that my knees were showing beneath my summer kimono. I must have looked awful.

A policeman made me sit down in a cramped tatami room in the inner part of the office, where he interrogated me. He was a vulgar fellow, about twenty-seven or twenty-eight years old, with a fair complexion, a narrow face, and gold-rimmed glasses. He asked me my name, address, and age and wrote them down in his notebook one by one. Then suddenly he began to grin and asked, "How many times does this make it?"

I shuddered to think what he had in mind. I simply couldn't think of anything to say. Yet if I didn't reply, he would undoubtedly put me in jail and bring serious charges against me. I realized that somehow I had to talk myself out of the situation. Desperately I searched for explanations, but felt as if I were lost in a thick fog. I had never had such a terrifying experience before. When I finally managed to say something, it seemed clumsy and abrupt even to myself. But once I'd started, I raved on as if possessed:

"You mustn't put me in prison. I'm not bad. I'm twenty-four years old. I've been devoted to my parents all my life. I've looked after both of them with all the love in the world. Is there anything wrong about that? I've never done a thing that would make people point and whisper about me.

"Mr. Mizuno is a good man. He'll soon make a name for himself. I'm sure of that. I don't want him to be humiliated. He had promised someone he'd go swimming, and I wanted to send him there dressed like everyone else. What's so wrong with that? I'm a fool. A fool! But I'll make a fine man out of him, and present him for your inspection. He comes from a good family. He's different from other people. I don't care what happens to me as long as he goes out into the world and does well. Then I'll be happy. I have to help him.

"Don't put me in jail. I haven't done one thing wrong until now. I've looked after my poor parents as best I could. No! You can't throw me in jail. You can't! For twenty-four years I've tried my hardest, and just this once I made one stupid little mistake with one straying hand. You can't ruin these twenty-four years—my whole life, for that. It's wrong.

Why should you think I'm a thief simply because once in my life my right hand moved twelve inches without thinking? It's too much. It's just too much! One slip—a matter of a few seconds.

"I'm still young. I have a lifetime ahead of me. I can see it stretching in front of me—exactly the same sort of life I've been leading till now. Just the same. I haven't changed at all. I'm the same Sakiko I was yesterday. What trouble did I cause Daimaru's with this stupid swimsuit? There are crooks around who extort one or two thousand yen from people—no, worse than that, an entire fortune—and yet they're admired for it, aren't they? Who are the prisons for? Only the poor go to jail. I feel sorry for thieves. Thieves are just harmless little people, too weak and honest to go out and cheat other people so they can live in comfort. So they get backed into a corner, steal something worth two or three yen, and end up in jail for five to ten years. My God! It's grotesque. Crazy! I mean it: really crazy!"

I think I must have been insane then. The policeman had turned pale, and was looking at me speechless. Suddenly, I felt I really rather liked him. Through my hysterical tears, I made an effort to smile at him. He must have thought I was a lunatic. He escorted me to the central police station with great care, as if he were handling a bomb. I was kept in custody that night in the detention ward. The following morning my father came to pick me up, and I was released. All he asked me on the way home—and very timidly at that—was whether I had been beaten while I was there. He said nothing else the rest of the way.

I blushed to my ears when I saw the newspaper that evening. I was in the headlines: "ELOQUENT SPEECH MADE BY YOUNG DEGENERATE LEFT-WING WOMAN." That wasn't the end of my disgrace. Neighbors loitered near the house. I didn't know what it meant at first, but I soon realized that they were trying to get a glimpse of me and see how I was doing. It made me tremble. Gradually I began to understand how serious my small offense really was. I would have taken poison without hesitation had any been available; I would have gone and calmly hanged myself had there been a bamboo grove nearby. We closed the shop for a few days.

Before long I received a letter from Mr. Mizuno. It read as follows:

I believe in you, Sakiko, more than anybody in the world. But you lack a proper upbringing. You are an honest woman, but in some respects you are not quite upright. I tried to correct that part of you, but I failed. Individuals must be educated. I went swimming with a friend of mine the other day, and on the beach we talked for a long time about ambition. We were sure that we would eventually be successful.

Please behave yourself from now on and try, even in some small way, to atone for your crime by apologizing to society. We condemn the sin but not the sinner.

Mizuno Saburō

P.S. Be sure to burn this letter and its envelope after you read it.

That was the entire content of his letter. I suppose I had forgotten that his family had once been wealthy.

Days passed. I felt I was sitting on a bed of needles. It is now approaching early fall. Father said that he was depressed because the light in our six-mat room was dim this evening, and he changed the bulb to one of fifty watts. Beneath the new light the three of us had dinner. Mother kept saying that it was far too bright. She shaded her forehead with the hand that held her chopsticks, and was very cheerful. I served Father saké, too.

Mentally, I tried to convince myself that, after all, this was the sort of thing we find happiness in—putting in a brighter light bulb. In fact, I didn't feel miserable at all. On the contrary, I thought that, in the light of this humble lamp, my family was like a magic lantern, and I felt like saying, "Well, take a look at us, if you please. We make quite an attractive family, my parents and I." A quiet joy welled up in my heart, and I wanted to let it be known, even if only to the insects chirping in the garden.

MOON GEMS

Ishikawa Jun

Translated by William J. Tyler

". . . The breezes that stir the pages of the novel are very different from the gusts of the mundane world." (Fugen.)

A native of Tokyo born in 1899, trained in French literature and accomplished as a translator of André Gide, Ishikawa Jun made his literary debut with the publication of the "récits" Kajin *(The Beauty, 1935) and* Fugen *(The Bodhisattva, 1936), works that represent his satirization and rejection of the Japanese "I-novel" and, simultaneously, his desire to create a "roman" on the order that Gide envisioned in* Les Faux-monnayeurs. *Ishikawa's career can be viewed as his struggle to introduce the concepts of European modernism into Japanese prose fiction, to search for their literary and philosophical correspondences in the indigenous tradition, and to create what subsequently he called the* jikken shōsetsu, *or experimental novel. This was a task attempted unsuccessfully by other members of his generation, most notably Yokomitsu Riichi (1898–1947), and not fully achieved by Ishikawa himself until the 1950s when he began producing his most experimental works,* Taka *(Hawks, 1953),* Shion monogatari *(Asters, 1956; tr. 1961),* Aratama *(Wild Spirits, 1963) and* Shifuku sennen *(The Millennium, 1965). These novels are highly fantastic—*Taka *speaks of a mysterious language called futurese; in* Shifuku sennen *crypto-Christians exploit the chaos attendant on the arrival of Commodore Perry's black ships to bring the Apocalypse to Japan.*

While one may be tempted to treat such works as purely fictional constructions, Ishikawa's novels also incorporate elements of literary parody nd satiric allegory. This is apparent from the all-important seriocomic tone f the writing, which is heavily influenced by Edo period literature, especially he mystification style (tōkaiburi) of the literati, or bunjin, of the Temmei ra (1781–88). Unable to escape Japan during the war years, Ishikawa aunched upon a course of inner emigration that he refers to as his "study abroad in Edo" (Edo ryūgaku). In the "mad verse" of Temmei kyōka poetry, and the covert criticism of society that the kyōka coteries practiced through the medium of pure play (asobi) and parody of the classics (mitate), he found in Japanese tradition the incipience of a style and movement analogous to European modernism and the inspiration for a form appropriate to the modernist Japanese novel.

The present work, "Meigetsushu" (Moon Gems, 1946), represents the genesis of Ishikawa's postwar experimental fiction. It looks back to the parodying techniques of Kajin and Fugen (the watashi-shōsetsu in contradistinction to the watakushi-shōsetsu), yet moves toward greater fictionalization and more fantastic treatment of the material. It is also a paean to Ishikawa's literary mentors, namely, the bunjin tradition that flourished in the Temmei era. This tradition was transmitted to twentieth-century Japanese letters chiefly by Nagai Kafū (1879-1959), who appears in the story as Mr. Gūka, "the Lotus," a play on Kafū's sobriquet of "Lotus Breeze." Gūka's "Liaison House" (Renkeikan) is also a play on the name of Kafū's Azabu residence, Henkikan or "Eccentricity House," which was destroyed in the bombing raid of March 1945. Like Ishikawa's short story, "Marusu no uta" (I Hear the War God Singing, 1938) which was banned by the military authorities, "Moon Gems" is a poignant allegory describing the tension between aspiration and despair in the life of a writer who would defy his times but lacks the means to effect active and meaningful resistance.

Ishikawa's most recent novel is Kyōfūki (Record of a Mad Wind, 1980). Although too difficult a stylist to be a popular writer, Ishikawa has been the recipient of the Akutagawa Prize (1937) and other distinguished literary awards. Because of his singular erudition in Chinese, Japanese and Western literature, he is often referred to as "the last of the literati." Of late his experimental fiction has frequently been compared in the Japanese press with that of Nabokov and Borges.

* * *

New Year's Day, 1945. I rose early and went into the city to a certain Hachiman Shrine. I went to greet the new year and to receive a lucky arrow as a souvenir. As I stood in the crowd before the shrine and was bathed in the light of the rising sun spreading across the cold, windy sky, I composed a crude *kyōka* verse.

> Though their gabled peaks
> Are enshrouded in the mists
> Of the New Year,
> As ever I entrust
> The sum of my hopes to the gods.

I returned to my lodgings at the edge of the city and stuck the arrow in the strip of molding that ran along the upper half of the room. Together with the three branches of holiday green that earlier I had arranged in a cheap vase, it became my sole concession to the new year in an otherwise drab bachelor apartment. Nursing my government ration of saké, I yielded once again to the temptation to compose another dubious *kyōka* poem—in honor of the saké, said to dispel all care with the sweep of its "jeweled broom," and the *senryō*, the holiday green which, bearing its felicitous red berries in the dead of winter, is worth a "thousand *ryō*."

> Sweet elixir of the jeweled broom
> And holiday green bedecked in red,
> T'is a *senryō* spring,
> And its light pours forth, glittering
> Like a thousand thin pieces of hammered gold.

No doubt the great *kyōka* poets would chuckle at my feeble imitations of their famous Temmei style. My visit to the shrine, and the receipt of a lucky arrow, had been a matter of whimsy; and I had felt no need to celebrate simply because today was the beginning of a new year. Yet I was possessed of a secret longing and wished to secure for it a propitious resolve. The desire? I am under no obligation to keep it secret: I longed to learn to ride a bicycle, and the sooner the better. It was in December that I conceived the idea of taking bike lessons, and I was determined to proceed with my plan.

By nature I am disposed to the quick and convenient although there is nothing about my person even vaguely suggestive of agility. My hands move only to let a ball tossed gently my way fall to the ground. Let a trolley stop across the street and my legs will not carry me the few yards to board it in time. Given this state of affairs, I must admit that I had little hope of initiating any movement that might prove equal to the harsh realities of our times. My profession too is devised to eliminate the need for nimble hands and feet, and so it has been my destiny to let them content themselves with inactivity.

Indeed, were one to seek the mathematical equivalent of this thing I call myself, it would be an exercise in the calculation of the square root of minus one. I think of myself as not inhabiting the face of the earth but rather a space one foot under, living in shame yet loath to abandon it. I know that I must rise, cast off this ignominy, and crawl out upon the ground, there to climb to the height of a single foot and make my mad dash through the reality that impinges on us all.

Were this longing ever to assume some concrete form, nothing would suit my needs better than the self-propelled mechanism of a bicycle. I could at least manage the cost of a used one; it would require no gasoline, and it ought to be relatively easy to operate since bikes are also ridden by women and children. What is more, the fulfillment of my wish lay readily at hand. I had only to obtain the bike and, with a contemptuous look over my shoulder at the crowded commuter trains, be off to negotiate the city. Moreover—the benefits are too many to enumerate—by and by my small coup might attract a particle of attention and lead to the desired movement. . . My heart leaped at the thought, but I had yet to master the rudiments of the vehicle.

Some time ago a friend gave me a letter of introduction to a certain corporation. He felt that I had a role to play in what he called "the essential business of the day." His intentions were well meant, and I rejoiced at this stroke of luck. Thinking that at last I had found a way out of the snake hole in which I lived, I set out one day late last year to call upon a gentleman who held an important post in the company.

It would be more correct to say that what I met was not the man but his boots. As he lounged in his chair with one leg extended casually over the other, the room was so overwhelmed by his pair of spit-polished, ox-blood red leather boots—so tight-fitting as not to show a single crease, so spanking new as to still reek of a live steer—that the man's face, poor fellow, seemed disproportionately small and insignificant, as though it had been relegated to the back of the room.

Admittedly, there was good cause for my being impressed by a pair of boots. For what I coveted second only to a bicycle was a fine pair of boots. Need I recite the litany of their praises? When the air raid siren goes off in the night, how much simpler it would to ease one's feet into a pair of boots rather than fumbling in the dark with puttees and getting them on inside out. Or, rather than cringing in the shadows and tiptoeing along a thief-infested street in an ordinary pair of shoes, imagine how boldly one could strut about in boots! Besides, boots are essential footgear for bicycles. They look stylish, and one pedals better. There need be no fear of brushing against objects along the way and scraping an ankle.

It may sound extravagant of me to speak of boots, however, when I have yet to attempt the bicycle. I shall content myself with a pair of plain, even slightly faded, black leather boots . . . although that too is a dream I only halfheartedly believe will materialize. But now that the man's boots appeared on the scene to make sport of the unprepossessing pair that I had only dreamed of owning, I ceased to recall what errand had brought me to his office in the first place. There was nothing for it but to submit to the beautiful shine of his boots, however intimidating that might be.

The résumé examined by the face at the far end of the boots was virtually blank. There was but one line to record, and that to distinguish me from the ranks of the unemployed and uncouth. It was a candid statement of my abilities that read, presumptuous as it may sound, "writer by trade." It did not appear to help the man much. The operation of the firm was divided, he said, between those who handled goods and those who moved papers, and his manner suggested that he would find a way to work me into the latter.

"No," I replied, "I'd appreciate being put in merchandising. That's why I've come." I was quite sincere. I wanted nothing to do with paperwork and its blurring profusion of figures and letters.

"Training in the business end of our firm," he said patiently, "begins with recruits of seventeen and eighteen years of age."

"But couldn't you let me do their work?"

No sooner had I asked my question than there flashed before my eyes the sight of young boys dashing about the city proudly conducting company business on their bicycles! Had I known how to ride a bicycle I might have pressed my case, but I felt a twinge of embarrassment, and it seemed to have crept into my voice. My request sounded weak.

It was then that "Boots" cut me to the quick.

"Can you ride a bicycle?"

His tone was pleasant enough, but he emitted a crude chortle as though he pitied me. He was every inch a man dressed in boots, and possessed a sharp, discerning eye. I was too devastated to speak. I blushed and backed from the room.

Thus the search for a job undertaken so lightheartedly came to an abrupt end after a three-minute interview. I had spoiled the goodwill of a friend, wasted three minutes of this man's busy day; and, in seeking the favor of both and pleasing neither, I had put myself to a great deal of trouble. I felt obliged to remonstrate with myself since this wretched state of affairs was due solely to my inability to ride a bicycle. As long as the bicycle eluded me, I was destined to similar failure should I in a nervous moment decide to crawl out of my hole and seek refuge in the "essential business of the day." The repetition of this failure would only deepen my shame and entomb me forever one foot underground. How unhygienic that would be!

As for lessons of any sort, the younger the age at which one starts the better. And how much more so for operations requiring physical dexterity. To be quite honest, I have reached an age that can hardly be called young . . . and a state in which, having inevitably started down the path that links physical time and the human life-span, I am helpless to reverse matters. Yet inasmuch as I am able to tie my obi and walk on two feet, it is imperative that I mount a bicycle without further delay.

Today, namely, New Year's Day, is the occasion of my first lesson.

To the rear of my lodgings is a small vacant lot. There one used bike and an instructor await me. The one who is to instruct me is a little girl who lives in the neighborhood.

"*Ojisan*, where are you? Aren't you ready yet?"

I can hear her voice outside the window. She has called me two or three times now.

I hurry to finish my saké and, pulling on my tired puttees and worn-out tennis shoes, I rise.

In a moment like this, who has time for comic verse?

Those familiar with the layout of the older, densely built-up sections of downtown Tokyo will recall how, if one followed the covers of the drainage ditches along a back alley, at the point where the alley narrowed and appeared to dead-end, one might discover a large vacant lot. These lots were often quite extensive in size, like those used by dyers for stretching kimono cloth. Today they can be found only in a few neighborhoods on the edge of the city. The back lot of which I speak, while not a dyer's lot, is one of the few remaining.

It did not appear to belong to anyone, and it saw little human traffic except in the hot summer months when a Sumo ring was improvised and the children of the neighborhood came for wrestling practice in the evenings. Thus it was a lively spot until the coming of autumn. At this time of year, however, the ring had been plowed under, and small fox-holes had been dug as bomb shelters alongside the vegetable patch planted by the neighborhood patriotic association. There was adequate space to practice riding a bicycle, and the plowing had the salutary effect of softening the earth along the edges so that one was unlikely to injure oneself in a fall.

My lodgings were at the back of the east end, and a small cliff overshadowed the lot to the south. To the north was the alley that led to the street where the trolleys ran; to the west, the back doors of the seven or eight houses engaged in the businesses that fronted on the main street. The bicycle shop was one of them.

The shop had long ceased operation, and its proprietor, now a civilian conscriptee, commuted each morning to an armaments plant located on the Chūō Line. All that remained in his shop was two used bikes. The fact that I was allowed to borrow one was due to the largess of this man who, despite his nearly fifty years, looked healthier and heavier—one wonders why—than the rest of us. Although the bike would have been better described as dilapidated rather than used, its age and rickety condition made it all the more serviceable for my purposes as a beginner. The owner and I agreed that, once I had mastered it, he would let the bike go—"at a special discount"—in monthly installments of ten yen. One could not have asked for a better bargain. Moreover, he had a daughter, aged sixteen; it was she who volunteered to take me as her pupil.

A spiteful person seeking to find fault with this child, innocent by nature and soft of limb, might have detected that her right leg appeared a fraction shorter than her left. She was not handicapped, although certain boors in the neighborhood complained about her being too lame to be inducted into the civilian girls' work corps.

Admittedly she dragged her right leg when she attempted to run, but the limp was scarcely noticeable and did not seem to trouble her in the least. Once she mounted the bicycle, her forte, she would throw her hands in the air and, like a cherry petal fluttering upon the breeze, go round and round, cutting smaller and smaller circles on the ground. She had the poise of an equestrienne. Those who have watched her ride would agree that the bicycle was her true set of legs.

A description of the events of that first lesson on New Year's Day brings no honor to my name. The girl's instruction was thorough and without fault. But since I was new to the task, I spent much of the time sprawling on the ground rather than mounted on the seat. The vehicle disdained me as a beginner and, no matter how often I rose undaunted by a spill—or how much I attempted, first, to mollify it or, growing impatient, to conquer it by force—it dumped me on the ground like so much unwanted furniture. I was at a loss to deal with its stubborn frame which would not yield to my entreaties. I perspired. My clothes became muddied. My hands were scraped and cut. At times I collapsed struggling to catch my breath. And, as if that were only the beginning of my torture, from every quarter of the neighborhood came children, forming a circle around me and greeting my every fall with noisy shouts of glee.

There were so many that one wondered where they had been hiding. A Frenchman I once knew would throw his arms into the air and shout, "Des gosses, des gosses," when exclaiming about the hordes of children that descended on him wherever he traveled in Japan.

Likewise, on this day a considerable number gathered, even though many children had already been evacuated to the countryside. Their presence was unwelcome, but the final blow came when the little girl on whom I relied also joined their ranks and, joyfully clapping her hands, made fun of me. She grabbed the bike and, letting her foot glide over the crossbar, began to ride. In her hands the recalcitrant machine seemed to breathe new life and went round and round as it was directed. I lifted my weary body from the ground and brushed the dirt from my clothes.

"Enough for today. Enough, enough. . ."

I persevered with the lessons, however. I went to practice in the back lot whenever the weather permitted. But my clumsiness persisted and I made no progress. The bicycle continued to make sport of me, but at least I mastered the art of falling without injury and suffered less.

As for the children, they soon stopped coming. The weather was cold, and their interest waned. Occasionally, one of their parents passed through the lot, but the adults were always in a hurry and they gave no heed to my lessons. The little girl patiently taught me the fundamentals of the art but, since she was under no obligation to stay continually by my side, I spent many hours struggling with the bicycle by myself.

Confronted alone, the bicycle assumed a sinister, almost lethal, air, and as I spat the dirt from my mouth, I knew that I was engaged in a life-and-death struggle. I had ceased to understand the purpose of spending an hour of each bright morning with it, or why I had originally imposed this task on myself. What I did know was that this hour had encroached upon the time I once spent sleeping, spread large upon my bed, and that it was propelling me in the direction of violent, almost murderous action. I would forget all else until I fell to the ground exhausted.

Ludicrous as my behavior may have seemed to an outsider, the back lot was a quiet place removed from the clamor of the world and I felt little embarrassment in practicing there. Although the lot served as a shortcut to the top of the cliff to the south, the north wind whipped across it and no one darkened the path where withered bamboo grass clung to the frozen and exposed earth. No one, that is, except an old man who appeared from time to time on the path atop the cliff.

Though I say old, there was nothing remotely old-fashioned about him. He walked tall, his back erect, a soft black felt hat making his silky white hair seem youthful. He wore a great black coat over what appeared to be the fine black tweeds that had been available before the war. On his feet were a pair of low clogs looking very worn. At times he carried an umbrella; at others, a Kodak leather bag, as he strode briskly through the dry grass. For the moment, I need only identify this elderly gentleman as Mr. Gūka, "the Lotus."

Gūka is a poet of great renown. His residence is located five or six neighborhoods away, at the end of a quiet lane. He calls it "Liaison House." Even the most common of men, who may know nothing of what Gūka has accomplished in poetry in the last decades, have heard the rumors about the Parnassian existence of the owner of this mansion—of how, loath to waste even a word of vituperation upon the sleazy claims of our society, he sealed his gates and refused categorically the traffic of the mundane. I too rank among the common lot who have heard them. Lacking any true profession, I have maintained appearances by proclaiming myself a "writer by trade," but all that I have authored is of questionable value, totally and completely; and since I am congenitally given to laziness and am no more than an impoverished dilettante, too indolent to rouse myself for a trip to a library to peruse Gūka's works, I have been content with knowing him secondhand. As the world would have it, the Lotus lives alone and is said to be engaged in the composition of a work to be kept from the eyes of men. He handles his own daily chores and, on the occasions when some philistine wanders beyond the gate, trespassing upon his yard, it is Gūka who goes to the door and sends him away with the words, "The Lotus is not at home."

If indeed this is his wont, I would not presume to peek through the trellis or tread the perilous space before his door, even though I live nearby; nor have I the curiosity. Whenever he has come my way on the street, I have expressed my respect inwardly. I have never addressed him nor been so frivolous as to doff my cap. We have never met, and on his constitutionals he has passed unaware of my lessons in the vacant lot at the bottom of the cliff, just as I have continued them with blithe unconcern for his opinions.

One matter troubles me, however. It relates not to Gūka's poetry but his clogs. I have heard that in better days he paid meticulous attention to the details of his dress and insisted that clogs be worn only with kimono. No chronology of an artist's life would gloss over the point at which he switched to wearing clogs with Western attire, but my random guess is that this innovation is of recent origin and that it is indicative of a sudden increase in Gūka's spiritual energies. As his clothes faded, and the clogs became chewed and worn, he began to move forward—in the area of literature at least—at a pace equal to the speed of light. At first the combination of a suit and clogs belonged to the realm of eccentric dress, and no doubt the world has had its laugh at his expense, but today fashion runs far behind, breathless in an effort to catch up with the tracks of Gūka's clogs. One can never be too vigilant, given the speed with which poets advance.

But as for myself, his junior, I run still further behind a world that lags behind him. I have only begun to take bicycle lessons and distantly approach the mastery already achieved by a child of sixteen. I feel profoundly ashamed of myself.

And yet, despite there being virtually no correlation between my existence and Gūka's, one could perhaps claim that the relationship between his clogs and my bicycle is not entirely tenuous. The course that he has run in a decade, I must compress into a few hours.

There is a Chinese maxim to the effect that cold and impoverishment make a man brilliant and agile. As for being cold and poor I have no peers; but, as for brilliance and agility, I have no confidence whatsoever. . . Were there a saying that cold impoverishment makes a man weary and ignorant, how appropriate it would be for me!

As I stood beneath the cliff and gazed at Gūka, was it merely false pride, the inability to admit defeat, that prompted me to say, "Damn you, Gūka"? From time to time I raised my eyes and studied the master of Liaison House. Was it an illusion? Did he stop and look down at me? Perhaps there is a link between us after all.

Yet, while his clogs fly across the face of the earth like the eight swift stallions of Emperor Mu Wang of the Chou, my bicycle has not described an arc even a yard wide. To close the gap between us, I needed to extemporize and, in my limited way, I conceived a plan of action. It was extremely simple: deep breathing exercises in the morning.

On the days when I awoke early, I would go outside at dawn and aerate my lungs. The little girl was asleep, and Gūka had yet to appear. I alone possessed the back lot. The city lay darkly frozen in the cold light of morning sunrise. As though to warm the very core of my body in their eastern light, the clouds swelled in the sky and gradually turned a bright, flaming red. Catching the wind as it whipped at me, I threw out my chest and took a deep breath.

There arose out of the dawning sky three stripes of blue, white and red which resembled neither wind nor light and which intertwined as they raced across the sky and, as though thrown with deliberate aim, poured into my mouth. No sooner had their cold seared my tongue and entered my lungs than my body became cool, and the impatience and irritation within me seemed to issue from the soles of my feet. This is what is known in the Chinese art of wizardry as *tai-su nei ching*, the Inner View of the Great Principle. What had I gained? My body became lighter, a most convenient state for a cyclist. For me, still unschooled in this Taoist art, the experience lasted only a few moments. But in that instant I had my sextant, so to speak, and by setting it I was able not only to learn how Gūka had made his dash through terrestrial time but to measure the agility with which the little girl rode.

Chance yielded yet another discovery. I happened upon the practice of riding my bicycle late at night.

These were the hours when the world lay asleep, though men seldom rested lightly upon their pillows. When the sirens wailed I too would kick back the covers and jump, winding on my puttees in the dark (no doubt inside out), and with fireman's ax in hand rush outside to crack the ice in the rainwater barrels. If the raid ended without mishap, instead of crawling back into bed I went to the lot and practiced riding my bike. I seemed to do it somehow better then, and would deceive myself into thinking that in fifteen minutes I had compensated for an hour of useless effort during the day.

One needed moonlight to practice at night, and for the first time I discovered how bright the moon can be. There is a famous *kyōka* verse in which the poet suggests that a man "dare not ask" (*mōshikane*) of life more than a full rice bowl and a moonlit night—only to add, in a facetious play on words, that "perhaps money" (*mōshi kane*) might also be desirable. Leaving the matter of money aside, there was not a soul living at the time who did not offer thanks for a bowl of rice and a moonlit night. Houses were blacked out early in the evening, the darkness so thick that one stumbled to find a foxhole.

One night, after rising from a brief sleep, I stepped outside to find that the moon had risen and the back lot was flooded with light. The old bicycle seemed rejuvenated. Even the spots where the black paint had chipped away shone with the look of the original lacquer and, while the chrome fixtures seemed icy enough to freeze and snag off a finger, I was reassured by the glitter and sparkle playing about the handlebars. I reached for them and pulled myself onto the saddle.

As I rode, the wheels streamed round and round like sprays of water circulating in a fountain. They spun and gained momentum until before long I began to wonder where the bike would carry me. Iridescent stones! Moon gems! How rare they are! The jewels I held in the small grip of my hands were shards of pure moonlight that fell upon the handlebars. How wonderful it would be to master this bicycle . . . at least half as well as the little girl . . . faster . . . one fraction of a second faster . . . it's been misery struggling with you, bicycle . . . let me ride smoothly, gracefully, naturally . . . we're no longer here . . . but long, long ago . . . once upon a time . . . even a poet from the West was warning . . . "Nothing is more likely to propel us headlong down the path to barbarism than a singleminded application to the concept of spiritual purity. . ."

"*Ojisan*, hold on. Hold on tight."

To my surprise my instructor had come into the lot and was calling me from behind. She urged me on. I felt so confident. Going round and round . . . round and round . . . unless one hand lost its balance . . . no, no . . . and I was dumped on the ground with a thud.

We had a great deal of snow this year; seldom was a winter as cold. Moreover, there were numerous fires; the heavens were often enveloped in flame. In spite of my determination, it was not possible to continue my lessons each night. January and February came and went and, by the beginning of March, I had grown accustomed to the bike. Physical object though it was, it came to treat me with more consideration. I reached the point where I could ride with no hands. As long as I maintained my balance, I managed to stay aboard for nearly an hour.

Moreover, the bike was in the process of becoming my own. I had spoken with the bicycle man and, in line with our earlier agreement, it would be mine for monthly installments of ten yen. I made my first payment on the first of March. According to him, I also needed to pay an additional ten yen each month for maintenance, which indicates how antiquated the bicycle was. It was the only conveyance I possessed, and I did not dare suggest that it was unworthy of the additional cost.

One night that first week of March, the wind blew hard as the hour grew late and, at the height of the gale, the air raid sirens began to whir. The neighbors jumped from their beds. We cultivated a sixth sense about such matters, and this did not seem a typical drill. A crowd had gathered by the time I reached the lot, and everyone was hard at work preparing for an attack. Belongings were carried into the air raid shelter and piled in a heap. The radio crackled in the driving wind. A fire hose stretched across the ground and a hand pump had been readied.

The horizon turned bright red above the city and, as we watched, the fire spread, narrowing the distance between us and the flames. We could see it dancing madly out of control as it was flailed by the wind. Nor were the flames confined to the city by now. Pockets of fire broke out to the right and left of us. The sky was filled with an ominous light, making the faces of those gathered at the shelter, and even the colors of our clothes, quite distinct. Sparks twirled about our heads.

I walked back to the rear door of my lodgings where I usually parked my bicycle, and stood ready to defend the building. The fire buckets were filled with water. I had no family heirlooms to remove from my room. Besides, I assured myself that the nearby flames would not spread within our reach. Preventive measures would work and the fire be confined to a small area. Still, it was too soon to relax one's guard.

Suddenly I realized that the little girl was standing next to me. She had stolen up from behind and, leaning on the seat, let the bike press against me. She said nothing as she looked deep into the sky. Although she seemed unafraid, what vague foreboding caused her shoulders to tremble slightly? It was then that I fully understood for the first time that her right leg was not normal. She was no longer the little girl who rode the bicycle with the greatest of ease but a pitiful young lady who would go through life handicapped by a bad limp.

I forgot my usual ineptitude and resolved then and there that should a crisis ever arise I was prepared to sacrifice to the flames the only real possession I had in this world, namely, the collection of rare and used books that I kept in my apartment. To save this child, I would put her on my bicycle and ride to the ends of the earth.

Fortunately there was no need to carry out this resolve. The fires in the vicinity were extinguished by daybreak, and our quarter had not reported a single casualty. That the color in the sky above the city gradually paled and died out was not due solely to the breaking of the dawn. The flames were dying out. I heaved a sigh of relief at the thought that the fire fighters had been victorious.

"We've won, *ojisan*, we've won. I promise to give you another lesson," shouted the little girl as she ran toward her house. Her step was smooth and self-assured; she had reverted to being the little acrobat of the bicycle.

"What's this?" I thought. "Doesn't she realize how worried I was about her?" I raised my hand in the air as though to bless her as she ran.

"Yes, we've won. I'll ask you again soon."

I returned to my room and collapsed on the floor. I had not meant to fall asleep, but it was nearly noon when I awoke. The neighborhood seemed changed. The sky had cleared but the air made one feel irritated and nervous. The relief I had felt at daybreak disappeared, and an indescribable anxiety swept over me. I could not bear to sit still and, going out, I grabbed the bike. Of its own accord it headed in the direction of the city and the shrine I had visited on New Year's Day.

This was my first excursion. Never would I have believed it would occur on a day like this and, lost in thought, I sped along untroubled by the mechanics of the bike's operation, pedaling madly in my old tennis shoes.

I had yet to obtain a pair of boots. Perhaps it was for the best. All my dreams would have been fulfilled, and I would no longer have known what to do with myself.

Presently I found myself in the vicinity of the shrine. I cannot remember in detail what I saw either there or along the way. Nor would I have wished to. The shrine had been obliterated. There will never be a *kyōka* verse appropriate to it again.

Hurriedly, I retraced the route I had traveled. As I entered the lodging house I realized that my clothes were covered with a thick layer of gray dust. I grabbed a brush, and, standing in the doorway, began to beat the dust from my shoulders. I choked on the odor that filled the air.

A scene floated before my eyes. It was not the scene I had witnessed along the road to the city. It was from a passage I had read long ago in a book . . . a description of the cremation grounds at Toribeno in Kyoto. Larks danced in the sky and the spring sun shone brightly, but columns of smoke drifted slowly from the pyres in the fields and an acrid smell hovered over the grasses and mingled with the shimmering heat. That was the smell that permeated my clothing. I stopped and, letting the brush drop listlessly to my side, fell into a wooden silence. My sadness knew no bounds.

I became anxious about the welfare of Mr. Gūka and his mansion. On my way into the city I had passed along the street that ran behind his house and, relieved to see everything in order, I had not troubled myself about his welfare. But hadn't flames shot up the previous night from the area in which he lived? The property may have appeared safe from the rear, but wasn't it possible that the front had been hit? I turned and started out again, this time on foot. I climbed the path running from the back lot to the summit of the cliff and took a shortcut through the adjoining neighborhoods. My feet hurried along only to come to a grinding halt. The quarter visible from the top of the cliff, the quarter where Gūka's mansion was located, had been leveled.

I walked amidst the ruins. Before the now nonexistent house, at what appeared to be the remainder of a gatepost, I stood on its small threshold stone.

Night was beginning to fall, and the dull light of the sun gave the whole area the look of a ravine bottom. Here and there victims of the air raid had fire hooks and were turning over the smoldering ash in an effort to salvage what they could. There was no sign of Gūka.

An elderly woman was sifting through the rubble that lay behind

Gūka's mansion. From time to time she looked up, as though aware of someone standing absentmindedly in the distance. Eventually she approached and, as though inviting an explanation, she studied my face in silence.

"This was Mr. Gūka's residence, wasn't it?" I said.

"Yes. As you can see, it burned down."

"What happened to him?. . ."

"He's safe. He escaped in time."

"I see. And his possessions?"

No sooner had I asked my question than I was embarrassed by its irrelevance. Her reply was firm, as though to emphasize her point.

"No, Mr. Gūka was not the type to bother with his belongings. This section was the last to burn but, even if there had been time, he wasn't the type to bother. He carried out a manuscript wrapped in a cloth bundle, and that was all. He walked to that small rise across the way and watched the house burn. He stood there until it burned to the ground. Until about dawn. He watched it to the end."

I knew nothing about the old woman but I found her direct and articulate manner refreshing. At the same time it reinforced my feeling that my question had been quite frivolous. There was nothing more to say.

"Toward morning a party came for him. I'm a neighbor and have known him for years. You know that he lived alone and was a quiet, retiring sort. When finally he got ready to leave, there was a little bread in the house, and since I know he is partial to bread, and I even had a little butter, I gave it to him. He was delighted. I expect he will return tomorrow."

I was no longer concentrating on what the old woman said. Instead there arose before my eyes the vision of a man stripped of everything but his manuscript, standing on the rise, blown by intemperate winds, bathed in a shower of sparks and quietly watching his house collapse in flames. I sought to capture in my mind this vision of a great poet, old but undaunted.

If a man draws a bow, let him draw it boldly. The bow that Gūka has drawn in the belles-lettres of our day is no ordinary one.

I thanked the old woman as I turned to leave.

That evening I went to the vacant lot and, wiping my bike clean of the dust that had collected on it earlier in the day, I gave it a polishing. Although the hour was early, the neighborhood was quieter than usual. The houses had turned off their lights and closed out the world. It appeared that the little girl would not be joining me tonight. The heat of the flames that had ravaged the city still hung in the air, but the moon rose in the sky, bathing the back lot in a cool, white light.

The mad winds had ceased to blow. The days were getting warmer. Had life been otherwise, we would have counted the days until the cherries blossomed. Polishing the bike bolstered my spirits, and I composed in my mind a *kyōka* which I entitled "Love Song for a Bicycle."

Although the bike ought not to have responded to polishing, at length it began to acquire a small shine. Perhaps it was the brightness of the moon. Instead of parking the bike under the eaves once I had finished my work, I straddled the seat and began to glide about the lot. In a single breath I rounded it six times, cutting a sweeping arc across the earth.

My movements were light and supple, as after doing deep breathing exercises in the morning. I had finally got the hang of it.

To tell the truth, my infatuation with the bicycle had begun to wane even as the machine was about to become my own.

If someone were to express a genuine desire for an old, used bike, I would be ready to make a present of it.

THE MAGIC CHALK

Abe Kōbō

Translated by Alison Kibrick

Abe Kōbō (1924–) was born in Tokyo, but he spent virtually all his youth on the outskirts of the great Manchurian deserts, an experience that in one critic's view has shaped his shifting conception of reality. Mishima Yukio once described Abe's fiction as being particularly low in the "humidity" content of most Japanese literature, and it is indeed as an author totally detached from his environment that contemporary Japanese readers understand his writings. Abe's defenders in Japan and the West consider him their only "international" author, by which they mean a writer free of essentially all the features that distinguish him as peculiarly Japanese. It has been suggested, in fact, that the Japanese language itself is an unsuitable medium for Abe—that he might be more at home writing in katakana, *the phonetic syllabary designed for a hybrid vocabulary that is neither completely foreign nor completely integrated into native Japanese discourse.*

Abe first attracted attention in Japan as the creator of avant-garde stories that were part Kafka, part scientific rationalism, part absurdism and part science fiction. Stories such as "Mahō no chōku" (translated here) and "Akai mayu" (Red Cocoon, 1950; *tr.* 1966) *are based on logically absurd premises described with the most detailed and convincing logic, a mixture of Abe's training in medical school and an unrestrained literary imagination. While many of Abe's techniques and motifs can be traced to common roots in both Japanese and Western writing, the seriousness with which he ap-*

proaches the nonsense of his narratives has proved intriguing to readers throughout the world.

Abe's most important novel, Suna no onna *(The Woman in the Dunes, tr. 1964), appeared in 1962. Since its publication, he has struggled in a number of directions to expand or alter the vision he proposed in that renowned work. He has, in addition, turned to active participation in the theater, forming his own acting studio and producing his own scripts, often adaptations of his early stories. His best-known play is* Tomodachi *(Friends, 1967; tr. 1969), which received the Tanizaki Prize for literature. Most recently, Abe published a new novel after a seven-year silence in the genre:* Hakobune Sakura-maru *(The Ark Sakura-maru, 1984).*

* * *

Next door to the toilet of an apartment building on the edge of the city, in a room soggy with roof leaks and cooking vapors, lived a poor artist named Argon.

The small room, nine feet square, appeared to be larger than it was because it contained nothing but a single chair set against the wall. His desk, shelves, paint box, even his easel had been sold for bread. Now only the chair and Argon were left. But how long would these two remain?

Dinnertime drew near. "How sensitive my nose has become!" Argon thought. He was able to distinguish the colors and proximity of the complex aromas entering his room. Frying pork at the butcher's along the streetcar line: yellow ocher. A southerly wind drifting by the front of the fruit stand: emerald green. Wafting from the bakery: stimulating chrome yellow. And the fish the housewife below was broiling, probably mackerel: sad cerulean blue.

The fact is, Argon hadn't eaten anything all day. With a pale face, a wrinkled brow, an Adam's apple that rose and fell, a hunched back, a sunken abdomen, and trembling knees, Argon thrust both hands into his pockets and yawned three times in succession.

His fingers found a stick in his pocket.

"Hey, what's this? Red chalk. Don't remember it being there."

Playing with the chalk between his fingers, he produced another large yawn.

"Aah, I need something to eat."

Without realizing it, Argon began scribbling on the wall with the chalk. First, an apple. One that looked big enough to be a meal in itself. He drew a paring knife beside it so that he could eat it right away. Next, swallowing hard as baking smells curled through the hallway and window to permeate his room, he drew bread. Jam-filled bread the size of a baseball glove. Butter-filled rolls. A loaf as large as a person's head. He envisioned glossy browned spots on the bread. Delicious-looking cracks, dough bursting through the surface, the intoxicating aroma of yeast. Beside the bread, then, a stick of butter as large as a brick. He thought of drawing some coffee. Freshly brewed, steaming coffee. In a large, juglike cup. On a saucer, three matchbox-size sugar cubes.

"Damn it!" He ground his teeth and buried his face in his hands. "I've got to eat!"

Gradually his consciousness sank into darkness. Beyond the windowpane was a bread and pastry jungle, a mountain of canned goods, a sea of milk, a beach of sugar, a beef and cheese orchard—he scampered about until, fatigued, he fell asleep.

A heavy thud on the floor and the sound of smashing crockery woke him up. The sun had already set. Pitch black. Bewildered, he glanced toward the noise and gasped. A broken cup. The spilled liquid, still steaming, was definitely coffee, and near it were the apple, bread, butter, sugar, spoon, knife, and (luckily unbroken) the saucer. The pictures he had chalked on the wall had vanished.

"How could it. . . ?"

Suddenly every vein in his body was wide awake and pounding. Argon stealthily crept closer.

"No, no, it can't be. But look, it's real. Nothing fake about the smothering aroma of this coffee. And here, the bread is smooth to the touch. Be bold, taste it. Argon, don't you believe it's real even now? Yes, it's real. I believe it. But frightening. To believe it is frightening. And yet, it's real. It's edible!"

The apple tasted like an apple (a "snow" apple). The bread tasted like bread (American flour). The butter tasted like butter (same contents as the label on the wrapper—not margarine). The sugar tasted like sugar (sweet). Ah, they all tasted like the real thing. The knife gleamed, reflecting his face.

By the time he came to his senses, Argon had somehow finished eating and heaved a sigh of relief. But when he recalled why he had sighed like this, he immediately became confused again. He took the chalk in his fingers and stared at it intently. No matter how much he scrutinized it, he couldn't understand what he didn't understand. He decided to make sure by trying it once more. If he succeeded a second time, then he would have to concede that it had actually happened. He thought he would try to draw something different, but in his haste just drew another familiar-looking apple. As soon as he finished drawing, it fell easily from the wall. So this is real after all. A repeatable fact.

Joy suddenly turned his body rigid. The tips of his nerves broke through his skin and stretched out toward the universe, rustling like fallen leaves. Then, abruptly, the tension eased, and, sitting down on the floor, he burst out laughing like a panting goldfish.

"The laws of the universe have changed. My fate has changed, misfortune has taken its leave. Ah, the age of fulfillment, a world of desires realized. . . God, I'm sleepy. Well, then, I'll draw a bed. This chalk has become as precious as life itself, but a bed is something you always need after eating your fill, and it never really wears out, so no need to be miserly about it. Ah, for the first time in my life I'll sleep like a lamb."

One eye soon fell asleep, but the other lay awake. After today's contentment he was uneasy about what tomorrow might bring. However, the other eye, too, finally closed in sleep. With eyes working out of sync he dreamed mottled dreams throughout the night.

Well, this worrisome tomorrow dawned in the following manner.

He dreamed that he was being chased by a ferocious beast and fell off a bridge. He had fallen off the bed. . . No. When he awoke, there was no bed anywhere. As usual, there was nothing but that one chair. Then what had happened last night? Argon timidly looked around at the wall, tilting his head.

There, in red chalk, were drawings of a cup (it was broken!), a spoon, a knife, apple peel, and a butter wrapper. Below these was a bed—a picture of the bed off which he was supposed to have fallen.

Among all of last night's drawings, only those he could not eat had once again become pictures and returned to the wall. Suddenly he felt pain in his hip and shoulder. Pain in precisely the place he should feel it if he had indeed fallen out of bed. He gingerly touched the sketch of the bed where the sheets had been rumpled by sleep and felt a slight warmth, clearly distinguishable from the coldness of the rest of the drawing.

He brushed his finger along the blade of the knife picture. It was certainly nothing more than chalk; there was no resistance, and it disappeared leaving only a smear. As a test he decided to draw a new apple. It neither turned into a real apple and fell nor even peeled off like a piece of unglued paper, but rather vanished beneath his chafed palm into the surface of the wall.

His happiness had been merely a single night's dream. It was all over, back to what it was before anything had happened. Or was it really? No, his misery had returned fivefold. His hunger pangs attacked him fivefold. It seemed that all he had eaten had been restored in his stomach to the original substances of wall and chalk powder.

When he had gulped from his cupped hands a pint or so of water from the communal sink, he set out toward the lonely city, still enveloped in the mist of early dawn. Leaning over an open drain that ran from the kitchen of a restaurant about a hundred yards ahead, he thrust his hands into the viscous, tarlike sewage and pulled something out. It was a basket made of wire netting. He washed it in a small brook nearby. What was left in it seemed edible, and he was particularly heartened that half of it looked like rice. An old man in his apartment building had told him recently that by placing the basket in the drain one could obtain enough food for a meal a day. Just about a month ago the man had found the means to afford bean curd lees, so he had ceded the restaurant drain to the artist.

Recalling last night's feast, this was indeed muddy, unsavory fare. But it wasn't magic. What actually helped fill his stomach was precious and so could not be rejected. Even if its nastiness made him aware of every swallow, he must eat it. Shit. This was the real thing.

Just before noon he entered the city and dropped in on a friend who was employed at a bank. The friend smiled wryly and asked, "My turn today?"

Stiff and expressionless, Argon nodded. As always, he received half of his friend's lunch, bowed deeply and left.

For the rest of the day, Argon thought.

He held the chalk lightly in his hand, leaned back in the chair, and as he sat absorbed in his daydreams about magic, anticipation began to crystallize around that urgent longing. Finally, evening once again drew near. His hope that at sunset the magic might take effect had changed into near confidence.

Somewhere a noisy radio announced that it was five o'clock. He stood up and on the wall drew bread and butter, a can of sardines, and coffee, not forgetting to add a table underneath so as to prevent anything from falling and breaking as had occurred the previous night. Then he waited.

Before long darkness began to crawl quietly up the wall from the corners of the room. In order to verify the course of the magic, he turned on the light. He had already confirmed last night that electric light did it no harm.

The sun had set. The drawings on the wall began to fade, as if his vision had blurred. It seemed as if a mist was caught between the wall and his eyes. The pictures grew increasingly faint, and the mist grew dense. And soon, just as he had anticipated, the mist had settled into solid shapes—success! The contents of the pictures suddenly appeared as real objects.

The steamy coffee was tempting, the bread freshly baked and still warm.

"Oh! Forgot a can opener."

He held his left hand underneath to catch it before it fell, and, as he drew, the outlines took on material form. His drawing had literally come to life.

All of a sudden, he stumbled over something. Last night's bed "existed" again. Moreover, the knife handle (he had erased the blade with his finger), the butter wrapper, and the broken cup lay fallen on the floor.

After filling his empty stomach, Argon lay down on the bed.

"Well, what shall it be next? It's clear now that the magic doesn't work in daylight. Tomorrow I'll have to suffer all over again. There must be a simple way out of this. Ah, yes! a brilliant plan—I'll cover up the window and shut myself in darkness."

He would need some money to carry out the project. To keep out the sun required some objects that would not lose their substance when exposed to sunlight. But drawing money is a bit difficult. He racked his brains, then drew a purse full of money. . . The idea was a success, for when he opened up the purse he found more than enough bills stuffed inside.

This money, like the counterfeit coins that badgers made from tree leaves in the fairy tale, would disappear in the light of day, but it would leave no trace behind, and that was a great relief. He was cautious nonetheless and deliberately proceeded toward a distant town. Two heavy blankets, five sheets of black woolen cloth, a piece of felt, a box of nails, and four pieces of squared lumber. In addition, one volume of a cookbook collection that caught his eye in a secondhand bookstore along the way. With the remaining money he bought a cup of coffee, not in the least superior to the coffee he had drawn on the wall. He was (why?) proud of himself. Lastly, he bought a newspaper.

He nailed the door shut, then attached two layers of cloth and a blanket. With the rest of the material, he covered the window, and he blocked the edges with the wood. A feeling of security, and at the same time a sense of being attacked by eternity, weighed upon him. Argon's mind grew distant, and, lying down on the bed, he soon fell asleep.

Sleep neither diminished nor neutralized his happiness in the slightest. When he awoke, the steel springs throughout his body were coiled and ready to leap, full of life. A new day, a new time . . . tomorrow wrapped in a mist of glittering gold dust, and the day after tomorrow, and more and more overflowing armfuls of tomorrows were waiting expectantly. Argon smiled, overcome with joy. Now, at this very moment, everything, without any hindrance whatsoever, was waiting eagerly among myriad possibilities to be created by his own hand. It was a brilliant moment. But what, in the depths of his heart, was this faintly aching sorrow? It might have been the sorrow that God had felt just before Creation. Beside the muscles of his smile, smaller muscles twitched slightly.

Argon drew a large wall clock. With a trembling hand he set the clock precisely at twelve, determining at that moment the start of a new destiny.

He thought the room was a bit stuffy, so he drew a window on the wall facing the hallway. Hm, what's wrong? The window didn't materialize. Perplexed for a moment, he then realized that the window could not acquire any substance because it did not have an outside; it was not equipped with all the conditions necessary to make it a window.

"Well, then, shall I draw an outside? What kind of view would be nice? Shall it be the Alps or the Bay of Naples? A quiet pastoral scene wouldn't be bad. Then again, a primeval Siberian forest might be interesting." All the beautiful landscapes he had seen on postcards and in travel guides flickered before him. But he had to choose one from among them all, and he couldn't make up his mind. "Well, let's attend to pleasure first," he decided. He drew some whiskey and cheese and, as he nibbled, slowly thought about it.

The more he thought, the less he understood.

"This isn't going to be easy. It could involve work on a larger scale than anything I—or anyone—has ever tried to design. In fact, now that I think about it, it wouldn't do simply to draw a few streams and orchards, mountains and seas, and other things pleasing to the eye. Suppose I drew a mountain; it would no longer be just a mountain. What would be beyond it? A city? A sea? A desert? What kind of people would be living there? What kind of animals? Unconsciously I would be deciding those things. No, making this window a window is serious business. It involves the creation of a world. Defining a world with just a few lines. Would it be right to leave that to chance? No, the scene outside can't be casually drawn. I must produce the kind of picture that no human hand has yet achieved."

Argon sank into deep contemplation.

The first week passed in discontent as he pondered a design for a world of infinitude. Canvases once again lined his room, and the smell of turpentine hung in the air. Dozens of rough sketches accumulated in a pile. The more he thought, however, the more extensive the problem became, until finally he felt it was all too much for him. He thought he might boldly leave it up to chance, but in that case his efforts to create a new world would come to nothing. And if he merely captured accurately the inevitability of partial reality, the contradictions inherent in that reality would pull him back into the past, perhaps trapping him again in starvation. Besides, the chalk had a limited life-span. He had to capture the world.

The second week flew by in inebriation and gluttony.

The third week passed in a despair resembling insanity. Once again his canvases lay covered with dust, and the smell of oils had faded.

In the fourth week Argon finally made up his mind, a result of nearly total desperation. He just couldn't wait any longer. In order to evade the responsibility of creating with his own hand an outside for the window, he decided to take a great risk that would leave everything to chance.

"I'll draw a door on the wall. The outside will be decided by whatever is beyond the door. Even if it ends in failure, even if it turns out to be the same apartment scene as before, it'll be far better than being tormented by this responsibility. I don't care what happens, better to escape."

Argon put on a jacket for the first time in a long while. It was a ceremony in honor of the establishment of the world, so one couldn't say he was being extravagant. With a stiff hand he lowered the chalk of destiny. A picture of the door. He was breathing hard. No wonder. Wasn't the sight beyond the door the greatest mystery a man could contemplate? Perhaps death was awaiting him as his reward.

He grasped the knob. He took a step back and opened the door.

Dynamite pierced his eyes, exploding. After a while he opened them fearfully to an awesome wasteland glaring in the noonday sun. As far as he could see, with the exception of the horizon, there was not a single shadow. To the extent that he could peer into the dark sky, not a single cloud. A hot dry wind blew past, stirring up a dust storm.

"Aah. . . It's just as though the horizon line in one of my designs had become the landscape itself. Aah. . ."

The chalk hadn't resolved anything after all. He still had to create it all from the beginning. He had to fill this desolate land with mountains, water, clouds, trees, plants, birds, beasts, fish. He had to draw the world all over again. Discouraged, Argon collapsed onto the bed. One after another, tears fell unceasingly.

Something rustled in his pocket. It was the newspaper he had bought on that first day and forgotten about. The headline on the first page read, "Invasion Across 38th Parallel!" On the second page, an even larger space devoted to a photograph of Miss Nippon. Underneath, in small print, "Riot at N Ward Employment Security Office," and "Large-scale Dismissals at U Factory."

Argon stared at the half-naked Miss Nippon. What intense longing. What a body. Flesh of glass.

"This is what I forgot. Nothing else matters. It's time to begin everything from Adam and Eve. That's it—Eve! I'll draw Eve!"

Half an hour later Eve was standing before him, stark naked. Startled, she looked around her.

"Oh! Who are you? What's happened? Golly, I'm naked!"

"I am Adam. You are Eve." Argon blushed bashfully.

"I'm Eve, you say? Ah, no wonder I'm naked. But why are you wearing clothes? Adam, in Western dress—now that's weird."

Suddenly her tone changed.

"You're lying! I'm not Eve. I'm Miss Nippon."

"You're Eve. You really are Eve."

"You expect me to believe this is Adam—in those clothes—in a dump like this? Come on, give me back *my* clothes. What am I doing here anyway? I'm due to make a special modeling appearance at a photo contest."

"Oh, no. You don't understand. You're Eve, I mean it."

"Give me a break, will you? Okay, where's the apple? And I suppose this is the Garden of Eden? Ha, don't make me laugh. Now give me my clothes."

"Well, at least listen to what I have to say. Sit down over there. Then I'll explain everything. By the way, can I offer you something to eat?"

"Yes, go ahead. But hurry up and give me my clothes, okay? My body's valuable."

"What would you like? Choose anything you want from this cookbook."

"Oh, great! Really? The place is filthy, but you must be pretty well fixed. I've changed my mind. Maybe you really are Adam after all. What do you do for a living? Burglar?"

"No, I'm Adam. Also an artist, and a world planner."

"I don't understand."

"Neither do I. That's why I'm depressed."

Watching Argon draw the food with swift strokes as he spoke, Eve shouted, "Hey, great, that's great. This *is* Eden, isn't it? Wow. Yeah, okay, I'll be Eve. I don't mind being Eve. We're going to get rich—right?"

"Eve, please listen to me."

In a sad voice, Argon told her his whole story, adding finally, "So you see, with your cooperation we must design this world. Money's irrelevant. We have to start everything from scratch."

Miss Nippon was dumbfounded.

"Money's irrelevant, you say? I don't understand. I don't get it. I absolutely do not understand."

"If you're going to talk like that, well, why don't you open this door and take a look outside."

She glanced through the door Argon had left half open.

"My God! How awful!"

She slammed the door shut and glared at him.

"But how about *this* door," she said, pointing to his real, blanketed door. "Different, I'll bet."

"No, don't. That one's no good. It will just wipe out this world, the food, desk, bed, and even you. *You* are the new Eve. And we must become the father and mother of our world."

"Oh no. No babies. I'm all for birth control. I mean, they're such a bother. And besides, I won't disappear."

"You will disappear."

"I won't. I know myself best. I'm me. All this talk about disappearing—you're really weird."

"My dear Eve, you don't know. If we don't re-create the world, then sooner or later we're faced with starvation."

"What? Calling me 'dear' now, are you? You've got a nerve. And you say I'm going to starve. Don't be ridiculous. My body's valuable."

"No, your body's the same as my chalk. If we don't acquire a world of our own, your existence will just be a fiction. The same as nothing at all."

"Okay, that's enough of this junk. Come on, give me back my clothes. I'm leaving. No two ways about it, my being here is weird. I shouldn't be here. You're a magician or something. Well, hurry up. My manager's probably fed up with waiting. If you want me to drop in and be your

Eve every now and then, I don't mind. As long as you use your chalk to give me what I want."

"Don't be a fool! You can't do that."

The abrupt, violent tone of Argon's voice startled her, and she looked into his face. They both stared at each other for a moment in silence. Whatever was in her thoughts, she then said calmly, "All right, I'll stay. But, in exchange, will you grant me one wish?"

"What is it? If you stay with me, I'll listen to anything you have to say."

"I want half of your chalk."

"That's unreasonable. After all, dear, you don't know how to draw. What good would it do you?"

"I do know how to draw. I may not look like it, but I used to be a designer. I insist on equal rights."

He tilted his head for an instant, then straightening up again, said decisively, "All right, I believe you."

He carefully broke the chalk in half and gave one piece to Eve. As soon as she received it, she turned to the wall and began drawing.

It was a pistol.

"Stop it! What are you going to do with that thing?"

"Death, I'm going to make death. We need some divisions. They're very important in making a world."

"No, that'll be the end. Stop it. It's the most unnecessary thing of all."

But it was too late. Eve was clutching a small pistol in her hand. She raised it and aimed directly at his chest.

"Move and I'll shoot. Hands up. You're stupid, Adam. Don't you know that a promise is the beginning of a lie? It's you who made me lie."

"What? *Now* what are you drawing?"

"A hammer. To smash the door down."

"You can't!"

"Move and I'll shoot!"

The moment he leaped the pistol rang out. Argon held his chest as his knees buckled and he collapsed to the floor. Oddly, there was no blood.

"Stupid Adam."

Eve laughed. Then, raising the hammer, she struck the door. The light streamed in. It wasn't very bright, but it was real. Light from the sun.

Eve was suddenly absorbed, like mist. The desk, the bed, the French meal, all disappeared. All but Argon, the cookbook which had landed on the floor, and the chair were transformed back into pictures on the wall.

Argon stood up unsteadily. His chest wound had healed. But something stronger than death was summoning him, compelling him—the wall. The wall was calling him. His body, which had eaten drawings from the wall continuously for four weeks, had been almost entirely transformed by them. Resistance was impossible now. Argon staggered toward the wall and was drawn in on top of Eve.

The sound of the gunshot and the door being smashed were heard by others in the building. By the time they ran in, Argon had been completely absorbed into the wall and had become a picture. The people saw nothing but the chair, the cookbook, and the scribblings on the wall. Staring at Argon lying on top of Eve, someone remarked, "Starved for a woman, wasn't he."

"Doesn't it look just like him, though?" said another.

"What was he doing, destroying the door like that? And look at this, the wall's covered with scribbles. Huh. He won't get away with it. Where in the world did he disappear to? Calls himself a painter!"

The man grumbling to himself was the apartment manager.

After everyone left, there came a murmuring from the wall.

"It isn't chalk that will remake the world. . ."

A single drop welled out of the wall. It fell from just below the eye of the pictorial Argon.

BAD COMPANY

Yasuoka Shōtarō

Translated by Kären Wigen Lewis

Yasuoka Shōtarō's characters are all clumsy, bumbling individuals who masochistically persist in challenging themselves even when they realize there is not the slightest chance they will ever succeed at anything. Failure has been such a consistent trademark for Yasuoka that he has had a great deal of difficulty coping with his enormous success as a writer. In the delight he takes in playing the failure, Yasuoka resembles Dazai Osamu, while in the earnest purity of his characters' endeavors, he is reminiscent of Shiga Naoya. Unique to his work, however, is a distorted critical sense that allows Yasuoka to view all the ridiculous acts of his characters with a wry, detached humor.

Yasuoka was born in 1920 in the island town of Kōchi, but most of his youth was spent in transit, following his army veterinarian father on transfers between Manchuria and various spots in Japan. The idea of a home is thus absent from Yasuoka's work, and the embarrassment his mother felt being married to a "horse doctor" was conveyed undiluted to her son. The many failures of his father's life, and the dotage of his mentally unstable mother, are important motifs in Yasuoka's fiction, and his finest work, the short novel Kaihen no kōkei *(A View by the Sea, 1959; tr. 1984), is a moving examination of the shattered relationships between these three family members.*

During the war Yasuoka was drafted and sent to Manchuria to fight, but he contracted a respiratory disease and had to be hospitalized for the duration of the conflict. Even after the war, Yasuoka had to spend six years in bed with Pott's Disease, a painful affliction that bends and constricts the spine. From his sickbed, Yasuoka began writing agonizingly funny stories about characters not unlike himself who were total disasters as human beings. He won the Akutagawa Prize for two such stories in 1953: "Inki na tanoshimi" (Cheerless Pleasure) and the story translated here, "Warui nakama" (Bad Company).

Since his early autobiographical success, Yasuoka has written with wry perception about his war experiences in the novel Tonsō *(Flight, 1956), which anticipated the "M.A.S.H." view of war by a couple of decades. With the stirring success of* A View by the Sea *Yasuoka began to turn from purely humorous examinations of failure to more probing studies of the breakdown of human relationships. A pair of novels on this subject,* Maku ga orite kara *(After the Curtain Falls, 1967) and* Tsuki wa higashi ni *(The Moon Is to the East, 1970), were followed by a translation into Japanese of Alex Haley's* Roots. *Most recently Yasuoka has produced his own* Roots *saga,* Ryūritan *(A Tale of Wandering Ancestors, 1981), a quest in Japanese history for the home that was denied him, which received the Grand Prize for Japanese Literature.*

* * *

The China Incident was just beginning to be one more commonplace episode in our lives when my friends and I began to see our faces clearing at last of acne, that plague of the middle school years. It was our first summer break after advancing to college prep school. I had turned down an invitation from a classmate, Kurata Shingo, to visit his home in Hokkaido and, having no plans of my own, had decided to kill time by signing up for a summer session French class in Kanda.

One day I walked into the classroom to find someone else's belongings spread out on the front-row seat I always took. The desk hadn't been specifically assigned to me, but I moved the books to the next empty seat anyway and sat down, then went back out to the hallway for a cigarette. But when the teacher came and I returned to the classroom, a small kid in a blue shirt was sitting in my chair. He looked like a sissy, with his skinny neck and an oversized shirt of a pastel shade that belonged on a woman's apron, but his looks only made his insolence all the more striking. I walked up to the desk and deliberately snatched my textbooks out from under him, but he didn't bat an eye. He simply sat with his wan face turned to the front, irritating me more than ever with the profile of his large, unsightly nose. I had no choice but to take another seat—not the empty one next to him, however, but one as far away as possible.

Presently the teacher began to call roll. Each student was supposed to answer with the French "*présent.*" When our teacher, a thin blonde named Mademoiselle LeFolucca, looked up at the class over her spectacles and read off "Monsieur Fujii," the boy in the blue shirt shot up and practically shouted in a drawn-out, high-pitched voice,

"*Je—vous—réponds!*"

Then with a feminine flourish he sat down again. . . This queer response shattered the harmony that normally reigned in the classroom. The backs of the boy's ears turned bright red as he shrank in his seat and hid his face like a baby bird on its perch. "Idiot!" I muttered to myself. Fujii Komahiko told me later that he had been trying to flirt with Mlle. LeFolucca that day. I was stunned. She was an ugly, mean-tempered woman.

One day on the train home from school I happened to end up in the same car with Fujii. To my horror, as soon as he recognized me he came over with a big grin on his face and sat down next to me. My nostrils were immediately assaulted by a strange, abhorrent smell. He greeted me like an old friend, but with large, exaggerated gestures; as he warmed up he started flapping his arms around like wings, exposing in the process a pair of cuffs blacker at the wrist than any I have ever seen, and giving off even more of that horrible stench. Wondering how long it would be before I was rid of him, I asked,

"Where do you live?"

"Shimo-Kitazawa."

My luck—the last stop before mine. The whole way there he talked in a steady stream, telling me how his family was from Shinuiju in Korea; how he was now staying in his brother's apartment by himself, while his brother—who was a medical student—was home for vacation; how this was his first time in Tokyo (his high school was in Kyoto); and so on, and so on. At the least response from me he would scoot forward and excitedly rub his thighs together, sending up a new wave of that rotten onion smell each time. . . By now I had quite forgotten my irritation at his having taken my chair in class the other day; all I wanted was to get away from that smell. Just as we came within one stop of Shimo-Kitazawa, he changed the subject and asked,

"What do you know about Kurt Weill?"

I was somehow flattered. In those days there wasn't anything that could have made me feel as proud as being asked a question like that. I immediately launched into telling him all about the man who had composed *The Threepenny Opera*. Despite the fact that he was now on the listening end for a change, Fujii's mannerisms remained as exaggerated as before. He nodded his head up and down emphatically at every word, and leaned so close to me he nearly rammed his ear into my mouth. But this time I wasn't dying to make my escape from an embarrassing situation. Besides, I wanted to show off my *pour vous*, rare items in those parts, and the programs and stars' photos I'd been collecting since junior high. So when Fujii started to get off at his station I invited him to come home with me. His answer was not what I expected.

". . . I'd be embarrassed, going to your house." His cheeks and eyelids flushed red, and he laughed weakly. Then he said, "Why don't you come to my place instead? It's that one, there," and he pointed to an apartment visible from the window. I didn't know what to make of his attitude, but I agreed to visit him later that afternoon.

I didn't take this promise to Fujii very seriously. When I reached home, a cousin from Den'enchōfu had come to visit. Now that she was engaged she hardly ever dropped in any more, unlike before. She also seemed to have started looking more like a lady. To tease her I did mocking imitations of her fiancé's Tōhoku accent, as well as of his table manners, his way of greeting people, and other quirks of his. Though I didn't quite understand why, the more this seemed to fluster her, the more I enjoyed my little game. . .

The next day, as soon as I walked into the classroom, Fujii bounded to my side and demanded, "Where were you yesterday?"

I said nothing. "I bought apples and bananas and sat there waiting for you," he said, staring straight into my face. . . The whole scene was somehow comical. But when I tried to laugh, no laughter came. There was something in his eyes that I couldn't identify, something I hadn't noticed until now. Mouthing a wordless reply, I realized that for the first time in my life I had let down a friend on account of a girl. "My old lady got sick and I couldn't come," I said.

That afternoon—perhaps out of guilt for having lied to him—I went straight from school to Fujii's apartment. Oddly enough, from that day on I was never again put off by his overpowering smell.

From our first get-together Komahiko and I quickly became close friends. With my father away, Komahiko seemed to feel less uncomfortable at my house than he had expected. I for my part was intrigued by his independent life in a one-room apartment, where inkwell, school cap and books lay side by side on a shelf with the frying pan and coffee pot. . . When I went to the apartment early in the morning, Komahiko would thrust one naked arm out from between the rumpled sheets and beg a cigarette. When I handed him the cigarette and matches, he'd open his puffy eyelids to a slit, look at me, and smile. . . At such times I found myself unconsciously acting out love scenes from books and movies. Komahiko was slight of build, and except for his nose being too big, his face had a kind of clear-eyed beauty. . . Not that I thought of him as a weakling. He had a measure of bravado that I just didn't have; I noticed it when he talked to his landlord or his neighbors. I had also seen him sit, unfazed, in a tiny, filthy restaurant and calmly—even with seeming enjoyment—proceed to eat a piece of fish that was covered with flies. . . But none of this had particularly impressed me yet.

There came a day, though, when I had to be surprised. The two of us were walking down the street together when we found ourselves saying how hungry we were. In the fanciful mood that camaraderie seems to conjure up, we started talking about *kuinige*—skipping out of a restaurant without paying the bill.

"Want to give it a try?"

Komahiko was already pushing open the door of a restaurant on a side street when he put this to me, though at the time I had no intention of actually going through with it. For me, eating away from home itself counted as an adventure, *kuinige* or otherwise. Moreover, in this kind of formal, European-style restaurant my head was soon swimming with such problems as whether to tuck my napkin in at my chin or lay it across my lap. . . The dining room was fairly crowded. The waiters hurried back and forth but always gracefully, flitting about like white butterflies. The two of us chose a table overshadowed by a large, hairy hemp plant, ordered two dishes, and had our meal. When we had finished, Fujii smiled and said, "Ready?" "Sure," I answered absentmindedly. Then Fujii took hold of one strand of the hemp plant and struck a match.

Suddenly there was a burst of light in front of me. In a flash the trunk of the hemp plant was a pillar of flame. Pandemonium broke loose. All the patrons were on their feet at once, and instantly the place was transformed into a classic fire scene. . . Dazed, I leaped up from my chair when above the din of breaking crockery I heard Fujii's voice at my ear and, snapping out of it, I dashed after him full speed toward the exit.

The whole thing had turned out so unexpectedly that I thought I must be dreaming. But what really amazed me happened after we lost sight of each other running down crowded back streets and became separated. . . As soon as I was by myself, I was seized with fear; this on top of the excitement and the running had my chest pounding alarmingly. I wandered restlessly in circles, not knowing where to go or what to do, greatly agitated, setting out to find Komahiko one minute and wanting to take to my heels again the next. The sunlight glared harshly off the concrete sidewalk, and though my back and chest were pouring sweat, a chill ran through my body. Hounded by fear and remorse, I had almost completely given in to my guilty conscience when at last I saw, up ahead, the familiar oversized blue shirt: it was Komahiko, the sun behind him as he strolled down the broad avenue toward me. . . My mood swung right around: I now felt flushed with triumph.

"Hey!" I could have hugged him.

"Hey!" he called back.

Full of my own excitement I started telling him all about the crowded streets I had run through, when I noticed a large mysterious package in one of his hands. "What's that?" I demanded. He mumbled nonchalantly, "Oh, miso, dried sardines. . ." I was shattered. Here he was telling me that within minutes of doing something as dangerous as that he had calmly stepped into a grocery store to do his evening's shopping. My sense of high drama was dashed. What had been a terrific adventure for me had been a purely practical affair for him.

I had always been intimidated by restaurant workers before, thinking of them as nasty "etiquette police"; but after this episode, I saw them instead as people just grown malicious from scurrying around serving other people for too long.

One day toward the end of our summer vacation, I went to Fujii's apartment to find wire, wire cutters, nails and whatnot strewn about the place and Fujii himself facing the window hard at work. . . As he fiddled with a hand-held shaving mirror, Fujii explained that he was setting up a periscope for seeing into the bathroom of the house diagonally across from his flat. I was thrilled with this idea, and let out a loud exclamation. Fujii reproved me. Then he asked, "Didn't you have a mirror at your place that was a little bigger than this?"

"I think so," I said, perking up again, and dashed out of the room. But when I got back with the larger mirror, the wire and the wire cutters were gone, the whole mess cleaned up, and Fujii himself was acting deliberately nonchalant. . . At a loss for anything else to do, I set about constructing a reflecting device of my own.

"Forget it. It's too dark to see anything now."

Something cold in his tone made me bristle. Fine then, I'll do it myself, I thought, and without a word I continued with my work. But sure enough, as the sun began to set, the light in my mirror all but went out; the bath, lit only by a single bulb, was also barely visible; and before long all I could tell was whether someone was in there or not. When I refused to give up even then and continued fiddling with the mirror, Fujii said tauntingly from where he lay,

"Do you really want to see it that much?"

"What about yourself?" I retorted.

"Why, me. . ." Fujii began, and then broke off with a snicker. I persisted. He said, ". . . Well, you know, until two or three days ago I could see straight into the bath right across the street. Shame they had to go and close the window."

I was furious.

"Why didn't you say something sooner!"

At this Fujii, still slumped across the bed, crossed his legs which had been spread wide toward me, let out a simpering laugh, and said, "I . . . I couldn't, especially not to someone like you."

In a flash of intuition I knew then that Fujii had had a woman. . . In that split second my image of Komahiko was turned on its head—a hidden something inside him, a secret domain so vast that the eye could not take it all in, suddenly stood bared before me. Feeling as embarrassed as if I had strayed by mistake into a stranger's house, I completely clammed up. . .

The truth is that I thought constantly about women. Whenever I daydreamed about the future, whenever I imagined myself in the kind of role I wanted to fill someday, inevitably there was a woman beside the hypothetical "me"; in addition, I entertained various sexual fantasies about women. But in spite of all this I had never once thought of approaching a woman in real life. To me, women were too distant to be anything but objects of fantasy. My several female cousins were somehow in a class apart from the rest of womankind, and all my other relationships with women were on the order of passing encounters on a bus or train: I could see them but I was cut off from them. . . So now, though Fujii lay right in front of me, I felt a sharp difference separating us. He was a man from an unknown world.

I went home that evening and thought about nothing else all night. In my exposure to Komahiko during the short space of this summer vacation, I had felt an attraction stronger than anything I'd ever experienced before. If I was still unable to go into the dingy restaurants he frequented, it was not out of any great scruples about nutrition or hygiene, but because the dark, damp gloom of the place scared the wits out of me. Likewise with prostitutes: it was more than a question of disease or morality; it was something harder to overcome that made me avoid even the thought of going to them. Nevertheless, now I was coming to believe that I would have to learn to love precisely these things that I had always avoided. . . Just as a man begins to perceive the woman he loves as mysterious, I began to think of Komahiko as a boy with awesome powers. The smallest detail of his way of life seemed to take on a whole new splendor. With the logic of a child who imagines a miniature orchestra inside a phonograph, I began to see a woman inside my friend. . .

From the next day on I tried on various pretexts to get him talking on the subject of women, but Fujii remained elusive, and I only grew more perplexed. Unfortunately, at this point I had no power to pressure him with. It wasn't until the day before he was to go back to Kyoto, as we walked the streets together that night, that I finally persuaded him to talk. It was the first time I had consciously played on his vanity.

"Listen, it's an incredible bore," Komahiko warned me. "You're bound to be disappointed, so I'd drop it if I were you." It turned out, however, that since coming to Tokyo Komahiko had gone to amuse himself several times without my knowledge.

Autumn came.

When Kurata Shingo, back from his family home in Hokkaido, first saw me at the start of the new term, he was taken by surprise. He seemed not to know how to respond to my subjects of conversation, my vocabulary, even a lot of my gestures and mannerisms. To me, on the other hand, this old friend and classmate seemed as dumb as a mule. . . It bored me to death now to sit around with Kurata, listening to records and nodding stupidly to the beat, or hearing him brag about his tennis. He talked eagerly, gesturing emphatically with his long neck, but I turned a deaf ear to almost everything he said.

Suddenly, at one of my mumbled replies, Kurata turned his long, sunburned face straight toward me. The conversation broke off as his voice trailed away. I too was silent. From the opening of his short sleeves came a scent like the sweet smell of dry hay. . . This was the smell of virginity, I thought, and that odor I noticed when I first met Fujii must have been the smell of experience. . . Which smell did I have now? I wondered. The day after I had said good-bye to Fujii, I had found my way, following the directions of a famous novelist who had written about the place, to a brothel across the river.

The shock I had received at Komahiko's hand was now to be passed on to Kurata. . . Only half aware of what I was doing, I began to retrace the course Fujii had marked out over the summer. *Kuinige*, stealing, voyeurism. . . The difference was that my actions were marred by something that smacked of revenge, something that wouldn't be satisfied until I had forcibly shaken him up. With *kuinige*, for instance, the way I handled it was not to let him in on it ahead of time but to spring it on him out of the blue and force him to make a run for it. The only time I was a hundred percent successful was when I stole a spoon from a restaurant on the main strip of the Ginza. That time Kurata's admiration was spontaneous. . .

The pattern on this particular restaurant's teaspoons was an unusual combination of straight lines and circles, and I took a fancy to it. As we stood up to leave I pocketed mine. But as we were on our way out, the waiter ran up behind us and said, "Excuse me, sir, I believe you have one of our teaspoons. . . ?"

I turned slowly around. "You mean I'm not allowed to take this?" I asked taking the spoon out to show him. . . The waiter was flustered. Blushing, he waved me away, saying, "No, go ahead," and he actually went away beaming as if he had brought his customer some forgotten belonging. Kurata, who I thought was standing next to me, must have fled at some point, for the next thing I knew he was about eight yards away and staring at me wide-eyed. When we were outside the restaurant, he let out a sigh like a man confessing, and applauded my calm, saying, "That was superb." It was the first time I had impressed Kurata without contriving the effect. Just how impressed he was became clear as early as the next day, when he pulled the same stunt himself at a cafeteria near the school. His performance there was so good that the waitress ended up giving him a cutlet knife almost as big as a butcher's. This unwieldy token of her admiration was too large to fit in his pocket, and he couldn't very well ditch it by the side of the road, either.

In short, there was no mistaking that Kurata too felt an inexplicable fascination for adventures of this sort. Now the most important of these by far was undoubtedly my trip to the quarter across the river. But when this subject arose, the urge to advertise what I had done became entangled with my desire to lead him on yet awhile through a net of enigmas, so that in the end, every time I looked at Kurata, I couldn't help hesitating. . . True, perhaps I had been disappointed on returning from the other side of the river, as Komahiko had predicted. But "disappointment" in Komahiko's sense was precisely what I had set out to find. The indefinable dissatisfaction I felt had nothing to do with that. I had in fact had more than enough of this kind of letdown: for two or three days afterward, I couldn't look at a female without being overcome by the absurdity of it, so much so that I nearly found myself in trouble. . . But this wasn't what I'd had in mind. What I had been hoping for was some kind of token. Nothing visible to strangers, but something I could recognize as a sign—that's what I thought I would come away with. But if I had, it must have been stuck to the middle of my back, or hanging behind my ear. Though I followed in Fujii's footsteps, I was totally on my own. . .

"You really want to see it that much?" Sitting in the front row at the Asakusa Revue, I was planning to turn to Kurata and say this to him. But somehow when I was about to open my mouth it seemed that I was the one who wanted to see the show. . . What would Fujii have done in a situation like this? Wanting to make the same impression as he had that time, I rehearsed his glance and other mannerisms in my head. But nothing I tried would make me sound like that. This only made me more and more irritated, until I finally blurted out,

"Let's go. This is boring."

My saying this for no apparent reason when the show had barely begun, especially after I'd insisted so adamantly on bringing him here, made Kurata angry, but he didn't want to say we should stay, either, so he had no choice but to follow me out. . . When I finally recovered my own good humor, it was ironically through doing what I could to coax Kurata out of sulking over the bind I had put him in in the first place.

In short, the whole time I was with Kurata I thought only of Fujii. The more progress Kurata made from mulishness to normality, the more I became like Komahiko, or so I thought. So I took care not to treat Kurata like a dumb animal. . . Once in a while, however, though I was sure Komahiko was in Kyoto, I would be tormented by the nightmarish possibility of Kurata and Komahiko somehow meeting. If that happened, what would become of the image of myself that I'd been at such pains to plant in Kurata's mind?

This nightmare came true. Roused from sleep one morning by the maid, I went downstairs to find Kurata and Fujii standing together at the front door. They just happened to have taken the same train. Fujii had nothing with him except the raincoat he had thrown over his shirt.

"I was getting fed up with Kyoto—thought I'd come up here for a while," he said.

Yet this coincidence turned out to be not the disaster I had imagined, but a totally unexpected joy. The atmosphere was festive, and soon the three of us were feeling like old chums. The odd thing was that Kurata, who was generally withdrawn and rarely said a word to someone he had just met, acted as if he'd known Fujii for years. For he had already become familiar with another Fujii, the one inside me.

The conversation between the three of us was animated to an alarming degree. Now that the real Fujii had appeared, I had no doubt faded to a pale shadow in Kurata's eyes. This meant that at the same time that I was struggling for Fujii's approval, I also had to work to shore up the image Kurata had of the Komahiko in me. And what with Kurata and I outdoing each other to ingratiate ourselves with Fujii, he had to talk twice as much as usual in order not to lose either friend. . . With all of us trying to impress each other this way, the boasts grew by the minute. Finally, hoping to dump Kurata, I proposed that we go to the other side of the river.

As a scheme to upset Kurata, this completely backfired. Contrary to my expectation that he would blush and have to mull it over first, he immediately joined in. . . Thinking back on it, I can see now that this was the last thing I should have done. Kurata was like a man in a blazing house: he had that freak strength to perform incredible feats without feeling any pain. I had thrown away my most valuable trump card. And the worst of it was, I didn't have a bit of fun once we got there. What happened was, the three of us split up when we reached the place to seek our respective adventures, but almost as soon as I started walking I was picked up by a policeman on a juvenile delinquent beat. This after I had been trying to pass myself off as an old hand in front of Kurata.

Finally released from the police box three hours later, I ran across the street and was heading for a dark corner to hide in when someone called out,

"Hey. Over here."

It was Kurata and Fujii. My initial joy at returning to the fold was short-lived. It turned out that these two had stood in the shadow of a yakitori stand at the side of the road and watched for over an hour as I bowed to the crowd of policemen surrounding me, or raised my arms against threatened blows and pleaded for mercy. . . They told me all this with an air of the utmost concern.

Fujii left again for Kyoto. But I could not go back to treating Kurata like a mule. . . Fujii had stayed only two nights in Tokyo, but those two nights had been like two years of ordinary time, if not more. Like a guide on some whirlwind tour, he had led us from one place to another, seeking out his favorite spots—specialty seafood restaurants, coffee houses, theaters; we would hop in a cab to go some ridiculously short distance, and then traipse along on foot for hours and hours around a particular district that he liked. We needed no alcohol to intoxicate ourselves. Three abreast we strode through the back streets of the Ginza, Fujii in the middle, firing off our automatic lighters like pistols. . . The third day ended with the fanfare of a carnival.

Komahiko's image only grew larger as he receded. In Kurata's eyes I was now but a shadow of Fujii—even the incident with the spoon now seemed a mere imitation of Fujii's exploits. At first this was unbearable. But as the days passed each of us came to feel a certain pleasure in bringing out the Komahiko in the other. We walked the streets we had walked with Komahiko, we went into the coffee shops we had visited with Komahiko, we made a leapfrog game out of taking turns playing the part of Komahiko. . . We imitated even completely trivial things like the way Fujii held a coffee cup to his mouth. He never picked up a cup by the handle, but would always take hold of the cup itself, lift it slowly to his mouth, press it to his thickish lips, and then, extending his tongue slightly as if to lick the rim of the cup, let the coffee dribble slowly down his throat. It made him look greedy, as though he were trying to suck the last bit of flavor from every drop. Another thing was we both started unconsciously stooping our shoulders. Fujii, who was short, always walked erect, his chest thrown out and his head back, but in our efforts to imitate him, the two of us found ourselves doing just the opposite, rounding our backs. Again, while both Kurata and I had always been finicky eaters, now we outdid each other by eating anything Fujii had pronounced good. My mother couldn't work out why all of a sudden with the arrival of fall her son should develop an appetite for tomatoes. . . In all things Kurata and I served as each other's inspectors. Neither would allow the other to copy Komahiko directly. If Fujii had worn a pair of socks embossed with a fish design, for example, that specific design was out of bounds. A bird or butterfly pattern was the loyal as well as tasteful choice in a case like this.

The letters between Tokyo and Kyoto flew thick and fast. . . These letters were everything to us. With all the stunts we pulled, the thrill of the act itself was nothing to the pleasure of writing about it afterward. Fujii always compared and rated the letters from the two of us in Tokyo. His letters from Kyoto were invariably addressed in both of our names, and mailed to each of our houses by turns. When we showed them to each other, each of us would secretly judge the thickness of the letter sent to the other's place.

In this way our mental image of Komahiko grew more idealized every day. Even in our striving to outdo each other Kurata and I were united. And at every turn we'd think, "If only Koma were here." A bus crammed with passengers might break down in the middle of the road and be unable to move, and we'd look at each other and think, "If only Fujii were here. . ."

In Kyoto Fujii was killing himself with this correspondence. Almost every other day he had a letter to write. At least if his correspondent had been a woman, the work of letter writing wouldn't have been so grueling. All you have to do to satisfy a woman's interest is write down the same old things you've been doing every day of your life. With another man, though, it doesn't quite work that way. . . The letters arriving from these two friends one after another raised Fujii to a dizzying height before he knew what was happening. Looking about him, he could hardly find any explanation for it. In this precarious, intoxicated state, like walking on clouds, the one thing that was clear was the importance of stringing along for as long as possible the fellows who were helping to induce it. . . But Fujii was soon trapped by a misleading suggestion he himself had thrown out. To wit, like Kurata and I, he too started believing that the true source of beauty in his life was his intimacy with women. The result of this was that Fujii started making a veritable religion of frequenting the red-light districts. And all to stir up inspiration for his letters to us. . .

One day I arrived at Kurata's house in Harajuku to find him clearing his father's gold trophies off the ornamental shelf at the front of the hallway.

"What's going on?" I demanded, but he seemed highly agitated and wouldn't answer, hurling the cups one after another into a closet on top of his little brother's toys. "What's going on?" I demanded again, but looking into Kurata's troubled face, I suddenly felt like laughing out loud.

So it's getting to him, too, I thought. Kurata's family was much like mine. My father had gone off to North China with the military; his father was an executive in a munitions company, and toured the country to inspect regional plants. As a result, both of us were largely free to do as we pleased from one day to the next. But recently I had started to find my house somehow constraining, confining. It wasn't that anything in particular had changed at home, but that the pact between the three of us was starting to bind me even there. For instance, it wouldn't do to hesitate or be scared when you came in late at night. That was definitely a disgrace. It was also against the rules to wash your hands after going to the bathroom. There were a host of new injunctions like this binding us. Since the goal in all things was to achieve "beauty" (beauty being defined by Fujii's way of life), this outcome was inevitable. . . I had no choice but to be a complete slob at home. I happily let my clothes and my room get as dirty as I could. It was as if I were trying to bury the household mores I now found so oppressive in a heap of junk and garbage. . . But Kurata had another kind of pain to bear. While all I had to do was sit back and watch as dust and cobwebs covered the photographs of starlets I had pasted on the wall, Kurata's room was decorated with skiing equipment, a tennis racket, the tail of a broken glider, and even a sterling silver model of a naval bomber that he had secretly taken from the guest-room mantelpiece in his father's absence. These things had once been his pride and joy. Recently, however, like Jean Valjean's troubling tattoo, they had become a daily torment for him.

Now, to make his humiliation complete, in order to escape his friend's judging eyes he had come secretly to return the bomber to its original spot. . . His pent-up rage had finally exploded, and he had lashed out even at the trophies in the hall.

Once you start doing battle against a parent's hobbies like this, there's no stopping. Every inch of the house is their territory. . . For me, it started with my father's sword, which had been placed on display in the decorative alcove; then the hanging scroll and the flower vase began to irritate me; soon I reached the point where I couldn't tolerate things I had never even noticed before—down to the pattern on the sliding paper doors and the cracks in the pillars. Especially the food: it came to be downright ridiculous. Everything on the table irritated me. Even when I had my mother fix up a separate dish of something I had liked when I ate it with Fujii, it seemed to lose all its taste as soon as I took a bite of it at home.

Needless to say, both Kurata and I began to spend less and less time at home. We passed the better part of each day in a dingy little coffee shop. As our allowances tended to be on the low side for regular eating out, we came up with halfway measures such as spreading butter on baked potatoes we bought on the street, and this was the sort of thing we lived on.

In those days, Japanese society as a whole was behaving every bit as eccentrically as we were. Everyone in the country was suffering from a whole array of factitious observances which had their basis in the moral code of a "new" era. Once, for instance, when a line of people waiting to see a performance by some famous movie star had wound all the way around a certain movie theater, someone decided the crowd was being unnecessarily frivolous and turned a fire hose on them. Periodically troops in the signal corps could be seen riding around in the streets—more for display than for lack of any other place to practice. Suffering miserably under the heavy copper coils wrapped around their chests, all they managed to do was obstruct the traffic. . . Apparently on some kind of orders from somewhere, our school would hastily assemble the students on the playground for a lecture from the principal. The principal, wearing pale yellow gloves and standing like a bronze statue, would say something like, "The way to train a monkey to dance is to take it when it's still young and make it walk on a red-hot sheet of iron. When it feels the heat, the monkey begins to prance about. This is the meaning of discipline. Now the same goes for you boys. . ." A number of us would be fighting hard to keep from laughing out loud. . . The idea of us being little monkeys! The deeper symbolic meaning of this story was utterly beyond us. Nobody—the principal included—had any idea what the sheet of iron stood for. . . Afterward, many of the students who had heard this speech were wounded or killed in combat. Among those who suffered burns was none other than the principal himself.

Already it was getting to the point where a person could be publicly reprimanded for anything at all. Surprisingly, it happened more often in reputable places like the coffee shops that sold nothing but pastries, places frequented only by the quietest students, than to those wandering through the red-light districts. Dim-witted students who had been spotted in front of a pool hall during school hours would be hauled off to the police station to get paddled and come back blubbering. . . We were completely in the dark about when this sort of thing would happen and what form it would take. The one thing we could be sure of was that when the day-to-day tedium was starting to kill us, when we began to get the feeling that we'd left something undone but were completely helpless to remember what it was—then these things would suddenly spring out at us. For when we fell into a mood like that (which we called "stagnation"), we were itching to pull something off ourselves.

We hit stagnation pretty often. Naturally the thrill of a dare wore off after the first time around; as the repetitions mounted, stagnation was sure to follow. The arbitrary punishments already mentioned helped us out at first. That topsy-turvy state of affairs had grown more remarkable with every passing day, until even the military police were drawn in to help round up juvenile delinquents. For us, the effect of all this was exactly the same as sitting in a chair and "traveling" by watching a panorama go by. . . But as these disciplinary actions, too, became commonplace, we gradually lost our nerve. Both Kurata and I skipped most of our classes, but we had no desire to do anything else, either, and we fell to spending whole days sitting in that grimy downtown coffee shop, staring at each other and feeling as if we were starting to rust away. Seeing Kurata huddled like an old man over the damp-smelling charcoal brazier, I would automatically think of Komahiko. I'm sure I provoked the same thoughts in Kurata. . . We would start in animatedly on the subject of our plans for a new round of adventures, knowing all the while that it was mostly a lie. But that too would as suddenly break off. . . For the figure of a soldier with a bayonet—on the prowl for some runaway comrade—had passed across the darkened window like the silhouette of evil.

The letters from Kyoto became more and more frenzied. Unaware that the pair of us in Tokyo were stooping to gross exaggeration in our competition to impress him, Fujii—determined not to be outdone himself—was pushing himself to the limit. . . His letters were full of wildly idiosyncratic theorizing, replete with dogmatic pronouncements, morbid images developed to an extreme, and nearly indecipherable leaps of logic, all written in an eccentric style. Then one day in the dead of winter came a letter bearing the following enigmatic poem.

> Desolate as when I came—
> Taking leave of Kyoto at springtime.

This was accompanied by the news that he had been expelled from school, was seriously ill, and was thinking of going back to his home in Korea.

The letter had come to Kurata first. Kurata arrived at my house in Setagaya panting like a post-horse, his breath a white vapor in the cold.

One look at the letter left me so dazed I could barely think. I was too afraid to read the whole thing through. Kurata was undoubtedly in the same state. Hastily we left the house. Trancelike, we walked for some time, stopping in the middle of nowhere, occasionally making loud, meaningless attempts at conversation. . . I didn't know what to do with myself. All our escapades of the past half year had seemed to take place in a dream. In fact, a real human life had been at stake in all these "dreams" of mine. . . And all the while, Kurata and I had been having a ball.

Is it because this is all too frightening that I actually feel cheerful? I speculated. The truth was, however, that another part of me refused to acknowledge that I was rejoicing at my friend's misfortunes. . . I was, at least, aware that there was something despicable in my reaction. I thought therefore I was saying the opposite of what I "really" felt, but paradoxically I spoke the truth when I cried out,

"We ought to celebrate. Let's go out and have a feast."

Kurata replied with apparent relief,

"You're right. Today Fujii sets out on his greatest adventure of all."

Together we picked the fanciest restaurant we could find. I decided that in a formal place we were likely to be so preoccupied with wielding our forks and knives properly—cutting a piece of meat without sending it flying off the plate, or carefully winding slippery spaghetti onto a fork—that we wouldn't have time to think about anything else. As we soon found out, however, self-inflicted suffering while dining did nothing to alleviate our inner pain.

"Let's at least send a telegram to congratulate him," I said, emerging from my private misery to make another jaunty suggestion.

"Good idea," Kurata answered.

But when we left the restaurant we went to the usual dingy coffee shop and sat there until closing time without any plans to do another thing. Until we separated that evening, not another word about the telegram passed between us.

That night I was upset—not over the business with Fujii but over Kurata's inscrutability. . . It was perfectly clear that if we carried on much longer the way we had been, we too would soon share Fujii's fate. I dreaded that prospect. Not that I would have known how to answer if asked to explain my dread. I could only have said that I was terrified of the uncertain, insecure future I imagined. . . Regardless of whether I had any intention of deserting Fujii in the end or not, I at least wanted to bring it up for discussion—though the only possible motive for doing so was in fact a desire to turn traitor.

Kurata was by nature the more withdrawn of the two of us. From the next day on, while paying lip service to Fujii's character and outlook on life, I began dropping hints here and there about the misery that awaited Komahiko in the life he was likely to lead from now on. . . If I could somehow maneuver Kurata into saying he was going to desert him, my plan was to follow in his footsteps.

The scheme worked. More than there being any particular force behind my warnings, the fact was that something in Kurata was waiting to hear them. . .

In the growing frenzy as final exams approached, deals were being made all over the classroom for the swapping of notebooks. "I hear more guys flunk the first-year exams than any of the rest." "Yeah, and they say if you fail the first time around you're stuck for good, too. . ." In our present state of mind this kind of talk, even from a crowd we normally despised, was enough to get through to us.

"Shall we go to F's grave and pay our respects?" I asked Kurata cynically. Every year on the birthday of the school's founder, the whole student body paid a visit to his grave; tradition had it that anyone who didn't go along would fail his exams. The two of us had been absent that day, as usual.

"Yeah, let's go," Kurata said, brightening. . . The day was clear, and it felt good to walk through the cemetery. Hoping to boost the effect still further, I worked to put him in a genuine class-outing mood. Before I knew it I was feeling like a regular doctor treating a sick patient. In fact, the pleasure of taking the initiative for once, and the prospect of seeing Kurata again, even made me leave for school the next day in time for the first class.

Kurata was not there. The second period arrived and he still hadn't shown up. At that point my suspicions started working on me. It dawned on me that Kurata was probably somewhere with Fujii. Sitting in my iron-legged chair listening to a boring lecture, I wished that I had slipped out before class had started. But as each lecture ended, I had a feeling Kurata would show up for the next one, so I passed up my chance and stayed in the room. Kurata didn't come to a single class even in the afternoon. . . I had never felt this impatient waiting for Kurata before. But then, was it really for his sake that I was waiting here? If I really wanted to see him, surely it would have been faster to go to his house, or to the café where we always hung out. Was I staying in the classroom only out of solicitude for my patient, Kurata?

When I returned home there was a note from Fujii. "Came up to see you before I go back to Korea. Staying at a flophouse in Asakusa. . ."

So I was right, I thought, with a touch of self-satisfaction at having guessed correctly, and not particularly surprised. A map in Fujii's distinctive handwriting accompanied the letter. I took a cold and cursory look at it. (It's too bad about him. But if I sit here feeling sorry for him, I'll end up going right down the hole after him.) By this time I had put Kurata quite out of my mind. . . Having sat around waiting all day already, I felt as if I were the one who had been betrayed by my friends. And since I thought I had fulfilled my obligation to the friendship in that gesture, I felt clean and clear, as though my demon had been exorcised.

I dare say this change of heart, this resolve to shape up and fly straight, was merely a matter of convenience. The proof of this came the next morning when I had already begun to backslide. In other words, my real desire—to take the easy way out—showed its true colors. Arriving in the middle of rush hour at the station where I had to change trains, I sat on a bench and let one train that would have taken me to school go by. As I smoked a cigarette there, I had a frighteningly vivid image of the cold iron chairs and concrete floors of the classroom, and let the next train, too, pass by. . . My attendance record was bad in the extreme. It was possible that missing today's class would mean I would fail for sure. These hours were far too precious to squander. But for that very reason, idling this time away became a special pleasure. . . When I had watched the last train that would have taken me to class on time pull out of the station, still full of commuters, I stood up and muttered to myself, "What's the difference, it's just one more day."

I myself couldn't see my treacherous heart for what it was. Like a habitual liar who believes his own lies even as he tells them, I too failed to see just what I was doing. Or more precisely, I made no effort to see it. . . Having given up the idea of going to school, I went instead to our usual café. The place was completely deserted this early in the morning, and smelled like a rotting kitchen drainboard. There was a dazed, vacant feeling to the place, like that of a man who hasn't had enough sleep. I tried to burrow my way into that state by sitting in the farthest corner chair and staring at the soiled curtains or the stains on the wallpaper, merely marking time. . . What was I doing there? Maybe a certain doglike element in me, the loyalty to run after a master even when left behind, was sustaining the way of life I had been living until a short week ago. But the rational part of me didn't notice that at all.

When it got close to noon, I started thinking about lunch, and though I wasn't hungry, I was just wondering what to have when suddenly I heard familiar voices advancing across the street toward the shop. . . It was Fujii and Kurata. I shot up as if yanked out of my chair, and as soon as I came to my senses I dashed out the back door and up a different street. The first thing I felt was an unspeakable terror. Discomfort and humiliation brought on by ruminating on my own cowardice followed soon after. . . While my mind wavered between retreat and return, my feet took me further and further away.

What had terrified me so? Like an overcoat lining exposed by the wind, the intentions I had been hiding from myself had appeared in a flash as soon as I heard their voices. If I turned back now, there might still be a chance. But fast on the heels of this thought was another one, that they were probably talking right now about my betrayal and about those intentions I had just seen exposed; it was now this fear that made it impossible to go back.

Walking blindly from street to street wherever my feet led me, stepping in the broken tiles and the puddles of washtub water that were strewn across my path, I tried to forget the two voices that still rang in my ears. . . They were not easily erased. Then I knew why: that was the last time I would ever hear them speak. . .

When I had come far enough to think I really couldn't go back, I stopped and looked over my shoulder. . . If I hadn't heard those voices, if they hadn't approached the coffee shop talking so loudly, I would still have been sitting in that chair. And if that had happened, the three of us would undoubtedly have become good friends again as before. . . I was sure of it—for something hidden in my heart was waiting for just that to happen.

In fact, the final act of my betrayal was yet to come. This was not to take place until evening, after I had gone home. As long as I stayed in the city, there was still some connection between us.

That night a woman in a black kimono jacket appeared at our house. It was Mrs. Kurata, Kurata's mother. . . My mother answered the door, then called me.

Mrs. Kurata had been worried sick about her son, who had left the house two days ago and had not been seen since; and today she had opened a dresser drawer to discover that the family's bankbook was missing. Besides that, two Boston bags, her husband's duck-hunting cap, a tiepin set with a precious stone, and even a large sum of cash were all gone. . . Searching through the diary and memos on her son's bookshelf and through the mound of letters, she had understood the gist of this appalling situation.

"I wonder where he went," I sighed, not without envy. Mrs. Kurata, however, interpreted this as the most obvious sort of subterfuge. . . She had suspected me from the start.

"Come on, I want the whole truth now. . . Where has my Shingo gone off to?"

I could only answer that I didn't know. At this, Mrs. Kurata suddenly broke into a strong Kyushu accent and lashed out at me, saying the basic fault was mine. A bead of spittle gathered at the corner of her clay-colored mouth. . . The woman's words only increased my determination. I looked over at my mother. She looked back at me. After the wasted, embittered face of Mrs. Kurata, I could hardly miss the flush of triumph on my mother's round face, the beaming pride of one whose son has been compared with another and won.

Seeing this, I knew it was safe to excuse myself.

"Well, I guess I'll go out and look for him then," I said, and after locking up my bookcase, just to be on the safe side, I left the house.

Night had fallen. Naturally, I had no intention of tracking my friends down, despite my promise to Mrs. Kurata. When, out of habit, my feet began to turn toward the coffee shop, I changed direction and walked down unfamiliar streets. I didn't know where to go or what to do with myself. A warm wind blew from a starless sky. . . On an impulse I stopped a cab and gave the name of one of the red-light districts across the river. Maybe I would run into them there. So I said to myself. But of course that wasn't what I was hoping for.

As the cab started up, I was lured by the car's speed into a heightened, sentimental mood. Looking at the lights reflected in the window as they went past, what I saw were the flickers, deep in my heart, of feelings from the time when I had loved my friends. . . But as the car picked up speed, the sheer joy of moving obliterated everything else.

Each time we crossed one of the numerous bridges, the midsection of the girders would float into view in the headlights, as soon to be buried again under the body of the car. . .

At some point I rose half out of my seat, put both hands on the back of the driver's seat, and slipped into a fantasy that I was moving under my own power. . .

That winter, a new group of nations joined the war against Japan.

EGGS

Mishima Yukio
Translated by Adam Kabat

Mishima Yukio (1925–70) was the first Japanese writer to achieve an international reputation almost paralleling his career at home. The English translation of Shiosai (The Sound of Waves) *came out in 1956, only two years after the novel's original publication, and seven years after Mishima's spectacular literary debut. This was followed by English translations of eleven books during the remaining fourteen years of Mishima's life, a record yet to be equaled. One clue to Mishima's success abroad may be his ability to combine a finely honed Japanese aesthetic with Western-style literary tradition, making his writing both sufficiently exotic and easily approachable. This eclecticism is also evident in the story translated here. While "Tamago" (Eggs, 1953) is, in Mishima's own words, "a farce in the manner of Edgar Allan Poe," the egg creatures recall the faceless goblins of Japanese legend.*

Mishima's samurai-style suicide in 1970 brought him another kind of fame, and his work came to be used as a pyschological tool to explicate the mystery of his life and death—an ironic outcome for a writer who spurned the Japanese tradition of autobiographical fiction. Even almost twenty years after his death, fascination with Mishima the man inevitably gets in the way of a more objective appraisal of his writing, and a new generation of Japanese readers approaches his work with a guarded skepticism similar to that in the West. These same readers, however, are often surprised to discover a very different Mishima behind their preconceptions. A pre-

cisely controlled romanticism, an almost religious respect for language, and a painfully accurate dissection of the human psyche are qualities in Mishima's writing that will endure.

"Eggs" was chosen for this anthology to show a comic side of Mishima not often seen in translation. Although the piece has received scant critical attention, it was a personal favorite of the author, who included it in a 1968 short-story collection. Mishima wrote at the time that "one can choose to interpret 'Eggs' as a parody of the authorities pronouncing judgment on the student movement, but I was aiming at nonsense beyond satire. Rarely has my pen aspired to such extremes of 'pure silliness.'"

* * *

More than anything, Chūkichi, Jatarō, Mōsuke, Satsuo, and Ingorō were determined to have fun. The five college students were big and gangling and boisterous, and much too lazy ever to attend classes. They were members of the same boating team who simply went on living their lives as though they were at training camp. They shared the expenses for one huge twenty-mat tatami room at a private boarding house. The story goes that the late owner had contracted elephantiasis and had built on this parlor out of fear that his gradually expanding body would no longer fit into an ordinary-sized room. The five competed to see who could sleep the latest, and made it a hard-and-fast rule never to put away the bedding.

Chūkichi had the bad habit of appropriating his friends' belongings, in a drowsy-eyed sort of way. He'd seem to be taking a nap, but the next thing you knew the big box of chestnut sweets under his roommate's desk would be empty. There was one edifying incident when he put on a friend's school uniform by mistake and, surprised by the unusually large sum of money in the billfold, delivered it to the police, mistakenly concluding that he had purloined somebody's wallet when he was drunk.

Jatarō was an incorrigible womanizer. Even more impressive was the fact that he never let them get away from him. One evening he chased a young woman as far as the entrance to the imperial grounds. Unfortunately, the guard refused to let him through the gate, so he dived into the moat and swam across to the stone wall. As he climbed over, he spotted the girl in question heading inside the Imperial Palace. He followed her even more doggedly. He could make out the Empress in her bedroom, frowning as she extended her royal white foot from the bed. The young woman took out a pair of tweezers and relieved the Empress's pain by gently removing a splinter from the royal foot. The woman turned out to be a lady-in-waiting sent out to buy the tweezers. As she was returning to her quarters, Jatarō grabbed at her from behind the bushes; but she threatened him with the pair of tweezers, which looked as big as pruning shears, and the cowardly Jatarō ran off as fast as he could.

Mōsuke was a simpleminded youth who took delight in telling lies. His lies were quite incredible. "The sun rises in the east and so does the moon—it's true, you know, 'cause I saw it with my own eyes," he would cheerfully assert. Or, "Today I saw an old man and guess what—he was old! It's true, you know, 'cause I saw it with my own eyes." None of his friends believed him any more, but they would all listen and smile, pretending they were taken in. Just the other day Mōsuke had brought up an amusing anecdote he'd read in Plutarch's *Lives*. "Antony and Cleopatra went fishing. Antony couldn't catch a thing. So he secretly ordered a fisherman to go underwater and attach a fish to his line. Unfortunately, he pulled it up rather too quickly, and Cleopatra caught on to the ruse. She praised him lavishly at the time, but the following day she quietly arranged for a diver to attach a pickled fish to Antony's line. When he hauled that in, everyone laughed hysterically!" Mōsuke's four friends, however, knew enough to realize you could read Plutarch's *Lives* from cover to cover and never find this story in it. Exchanging knowing glances, it was all they could do to stifle their own laughter.

Satsuo was a violent sort who loved to get into knock-down, drag-out fights. In primary school he was hospitalized with typhoid fever, and given nothing but rice gruel to eat. So he waited for the nurse to go off to chat, then crawled out of bed, grabbed at a sparrow by the window, and roasted it against his own feverish body. After he had eaten a dozen of these, he quickly recovered. In junior high school, first drawing energy from a mouth-watering sukiyaki dinner of snakes caught in the woods near school, he set off on a heroic mission to sneak in on the irascible old headmaster while he was asleep. His plan was to rub gunpowder onto the man's bald head, stuff Roman candles in both of his deaf ears, and light them all at once. People still talk about the breathtaking spectacle of the sparks hissing and swirling about the principal's head, and the fireworks as they burst from his ears in the shape of huge multicolored chrysanthemums. Oddly enough, thanks to this rough-and-ready treatment, tufts of black hair sprouted on his head, his deafness was instantly cured, and Satsuo ended up receiving a certificate of merit.

Ingorō was a prodigious drinker. When he was a small child, he fell into a vat of saké at the family brewery. He was in danger of drowning until he started draining the saké inside the vat. Within seconds he was able to stand up, the saké reduced to about the level of his stomach. By choosing drinking over drowning, the child saved himself quite easily.

With these five living together, one can imagine the confusion and annoyance they caused in the neighborhood. There was nothing they feared. They had no time for dreaming like the weak; no time for thinking like the wise. They believed, all five of them, that the world consisted of nothing but boats and their own bodies. As for women, drink, and food, these belonged to another realm and, like household deliveries, could simply be ordered as necessity demanded. Beyond this conviction, the world had no significance. If these five self-assured youths looked up at the blue sky and together opened their mouths in laughter, the sun, shaken by such a display of confidence, would probably drop down in shock and fall into the mouth of one or the other of them, burning his tongue.

That wasn't all. In order to maintain the tempo of their cheerful antics, they took care not to neglect their physical condition. Accordingly, it was their practice to drink a raw egg for breakfast each day.

The mistress of the boarding house would bring them breakfast served on a large low table in the middle of the room. The five of them, pushing aside their bedding with their feet, would then gather around in the best of spirits. Sitting there facing their breakfast, they looked ready to consume the very table itself.

While the landlady dished out their bowls of rice, Chūkichi would scratch his back with the tip of his chopsticks, Jatarō would dip his chopsticks in the miso soup and compose some outrageous graffiti on the table, the unsophisticated Mōsuke let his droop from both sides of his mouth pretending they were tusks, Satsuo would use them to kill flies on the table, and Ingorō looked as if he had absolutely no interest in rice.

They all took part in a strange custom. Shouting together a ceremonious "Dig in!" in their raucous voices, in unison they would crack the eggs in front of them against the edge of their bowls and drink them down in one gulp. Before this ritual began, the landlady, who was getting on in years and was concerned about her poor turn-of-the-century eardrums, always fled downstairs.

By now the neighbors had got fairly used to it, but when the five first moved into the boarding house, some dashed out of their houses when the terrifying roars and subsequent detonations occurred just before noon. The barbarous racket from this daily egg ritual echoed for miles in all directions.

Chūkichi would drink his egg without uttering a word.

Jatarō, licking his lips, would moan, "It's as soft as a woman!"

Mōsuke would claim, aptly, "Chicks are born from eggs—it's true, you know."

Satsuo would snicker and announce that "living things taste delicious."

And Ingorō would always pout: "I want some eggnog."

With expressions of utter satisfaction the five would then open wide the clattering warehouse doors of their mouths and shove in as much breakfast as they possibly could. Afterward they lay down wherever they pleased, thrusting their hairy legs up to the ceiling. Those smoking cigarettes would use the forehead of the friend beside them as an ashtray.

One evening the five were invited to dinner at the home of an older member of the boating team. After gorging on rare treats such as elephant with sesame seeds, raw minnow, fried cat, a delicate consommé of black goldfish and hornwort garnished with beetles, and giraffe neck cut in thick pieces and boiled in syrup, they consumed ten bowls of rice each; and feeling in even better spirits than usual they headed home, their arms linked around each other's shoulders, singing boisterously. Of course alcohol had thoroughly permeated their bodies, much the way the sap of an olive tree seeps into the very tips of the leaves, or the way guerrillas infiltrate under the very beds of their enemy's headquarters. To achieve the same level of drunkenness as his four friends, Ingorō required a special infusion of alcohol. Tonight he had put away seven and a half gallons of saké, twenty-eight bottles of beer, five gallons of *shōchū*, three bottles of cognac, and five of whisky. This was all within the space of five hours. Ingorō was giving serious thought to the feasibility of hammering a nail into his stomach and hanging a bottle opener from it with a red ribbon; after swallowing various kinds of alcohol, bottle and all, he could simply remove the caps inside his stomach and let the liquids flow. Then, just as a snake vomits the shell of an egg after drinking its contents, he could disgorge the empty bottles afterward.

But Ingorō's metaphysical speculations were crushed by his companions as they burst out singing their boating song, so he too joined in, keeping time with large belches.

> Our boat is born
> Of the wrath of gods.
> Shaped like a siren,
> Her belly slick,
> She mocks the waves.
> Go swift! Dear boat of ours!

At which point Ingorō belched in tune. Everyone roared with laughter and continued singing.

> Bitter rivalry will
> Never bring her low.

Who dares to match
Her looks and speed,
Her strength and skill?
Go swift! Dear boat of ours!
Belch, belch.

Tired from the race
She reaches a quiet bank.
Bathed by the soft sun,
Refreshed, she murmurs
"I've no need of men."
Go swift! Dear boat of ours!
Belch, belch.

Laughing merrily and singing, they made their way shoulder to shoulder down a twisting hill. It had been a while since they had left their teammate's house, and it was already late at night. There was neither moon nor stars, only the light from scattered streetlamps projected onto the high stone walls on both sides. At the bottom of the hill there should have been a large road where the streetcars passed, but they could hear neither the dull echo of the trains nor the intermittent honking of automobile horns.

Since it was already two hours after the last train, the five were planning to get home by hailing some dirty old cab and intimidating the driver into lowering the fare. They were aware, of course, that too much badgering might make the driver pull into a police station and kick up a row.

The wide streetcar road seemed forever out of sight. Finally they realized that they had taken a wrong turn when they came out into an unfamiliar, dark, and dampish little street, crammed with houses on an incline. It was impossible to walk five abreast down this narrow road, so they had to break up into groups of two and three.

"Well, if we keep going, we're bound to hit the main road eventually," one of them called out.

So the five continued on their way, singing and carrying on as before.

On both sides of the path were sleepy houses arranged in complicated disarray. What seemed like lights still burning inside small windows were simply reflections from the distant streetlamps. There were signs for masseurs and gynecological clinics, but the letters were hard to make out in the dark; they could only vaguely decipher ones that said "New Patients Welcome" or "House Calls in Afternoons, Except Sundays." Typically, Satsuo felt a great urge to tear them down, but since he was sandwiched between his comrades and couldn't move his arms freely, he abandoned the idea.

One side of the small road gave way to a low stone wall, mottled with patches of moss. It smelled of mold, and the earth at their feet was unusually slippery.

"Wasn't that a police whistle?" one of them said.

"Hey, you're right."

They could definitely hear the sound of whistles. Not just one or two, but a number of them mixed together, calling to each other as they came closer. The sound of hurried, clattering footsteps turning the corner in front of them made them stop in their tracks.

Several policemen were blocking their way. Wearing their caps low over their eyes and gripping their nightsticks tightly, the officers advanced up the hill. Step by step, without a word, they made their way toward the students.

As courageous as these fellows were, they knew enough to avoid trouble, so they whirled around abruptly, seeking an escape route; whereupon they discovered that, from the rear as well, a group of policemen, caps also low over their eyes, was pressing in on them. From both sides their numbers seemed to be increasing rapidly. They could hear more panting policemen catching up from behind.

"Is there anything the matter? We're on our way back to our boarding house," said Chūkichi in an amiable, sleepy tone.

"You're under arrest," the man in charge replied, his voice sounding strangely yellow.

"But we haven't done anything wrong."

"You're under arrest!" the policeman repeated.

Chūkichi exchanged quick glances with his comrades. At this signal, the five spirited youths pounced en masse on the policemen surrounding them. The scuffle was truly spectacular: the five formed a big wheel, and proceeded to grab their enemies one by one and knock them down. The only sound that stirred the darkness was the occasional crack of something hard breaking. The ground beneath their feet became more and more slippery; losing their balance, they all fell down together, at which point they were swiftly handcuffed by their swarming opponents.

The policemen led them off arm in arm, one on each side. The road had finally become wide enough for three to pass, and the route had gradually turned uphill. In the lead, Chūkichi, by the light of a corner streetlamp, glanced at the profile of the man grasping his arm. He felt a sudden chill run down his spine and wished he hadn't looked. Like all the others, the officer's hat half obscured his face. Underneath he had no features.

Hemmed in by policemen, the group obediently made its way up the street. It occurred to Chūkichi that the reason his rambunctious comrades had quieted down was because they too had discovered, as he had, that the policemen had no faces. But surely it was a trick of the eye; recalling his intoxication of just moments ago, he resolved to wipe out this illusion once and for all.

This time he looked at the policeman on his left. The profile had neither eyes nor nose, but was a perfect, pure white oval. There was a bulge in the white skin that suggested a cheek but it was extremely hard, and the surface had a dull luster.

"My god! They're eggs!" Chūkichi realized. He now decided that if he suddenly hurled his own hard head at it, he might be able to crack the face-shell. But the egg cop skillfully averted his head, thus deflecting Chūkichi's attack.

At the crest of the hill, an imposing building on top of a cliff appeared before them. None of them had ever come across such a building in this area, although this wasn't the first time they had visited their teammate's house. The stark white construction was shaped like a baseball stadium in a modern concave style. It differed from a stadium in that it was covered with a domed roof. As if the building engineers had rebelled against this circular form, a horn-shaped structure like a watchtower extended on one side from ground level and rose into the sky at a forty-five-degree angle without any supports.

The group was pushed through heavy doors and led inside. The interior was arranged like a huge amphitheater, but it was dark and chilly. At first they couldn't see anything; they could only sense the presence of a large crowd. Instead of the sound of clothes rustling there was a noise like the shuffling of ivory mah-jongg tiles.

The group was led to the center of the circle, where they could faintly make out a stately white dais in front of them. Here three judges were seated. The gold embroidery on their black gowns glimmered. The faces of the judges were pockmarked, florid, jumbo eggs. The district attorney and defense counsel, the law clerks and court attendants who hovered about, all were eggs as well. The five students, whose eyes had adjusted to the light, realized that the thousands of spectators filling the hall were also eggs.

Without any preamble the D.A. egg began to make his case. He had no mouth to speak with, of course; his yellowish voice seemed to emanate from within.

"I demand the death penalty for the accused—these five insubordinate youths, Chūkichi, Jatarō, Mōsuke, Satsuo, and Ingorō. The accused have desecrated the honor of eggs; they have wantonly committed destructive acts against them. Not only have they used eggs as food, but through the deliberate act of cracking eggs simultaneously every morning, and by means of such sounds, they have worked to spread the propaganda that eggs are meant to be consumed. The history of the humiliation eggs have endured ever since they came to be regarded as edible objects is a long one, but there is no precedent for the heinous offense of drinking eggs with such brazen audacity. . ."

The defense-counsel egg stood up. He was a rather weakly, unappetizing specimen.

"In response to the prosecutor, I would like to point out that the shell of an egg is harder than the skin of the defendants. Thus the cracking of an egg by those with such tender skins cannot be interpreted as an act of the strong preying upon the weak; rather, it must be seen—should we say—as a mere act of unruliness."

"What is hard is brittle," the prosecutor exclaimed, his tone becoming more emotional. "Although we may be superior in form, the ideology of the accused is more highly developed. And ideology, whatever form it takes, embraces elements of violence.

"However, as you are well aware, the defendants are members of a boating team. Society at large accepts the fact that such people are incapable of adhering to any ideology. Rather, they are the embodiment—should we say—of mere brute force.

"It is precisely such brute force that is at the root of all ideology. If brute force had never cracked the shell of the first egg, who would ever have come up with the idea of eating eggs? We must regard their violence as a dangerous ideological act. Or, if you prefer, their acts of violence were committed under the guidance of this belief that eggs are to be eaten." Overcome with excitement, the prosecutor's shell turned a bright red, as if glowing from inside.

"The prosecution will demand the death penalty for the five defendants. We are seeking for Chūkichi, death by omelettes; for Jatarō, death by scrambled eggs; for Mōsuke, death by hard-boiled eggs; for Satsuo, death by fried eggs; and for Ingorō, death by eggnog."

At this statement, the spectators shook in jubilation. Rows of them clattered as they bumped against each other, and a wavelike motion was set off by the yolks rejoicing inside their shells. The students pouted in dissatisfaction; only Ingorō seemed somewhat pleased with his sentence.

"The prosecutor may demand such a sentence, but I'd like to hear just how he plans to carry out the punishment in egg-like fashion," the weakly defense-counsel egg responded. "Is he seriously suggesting that human beings contain within their bodies sufficient egg-like protein to make them suitable for omelettes?"

"Absolutely," the prosecutor insisted resolutely. "It is a scientific fact that human beings who have consumed one of us eggs each day will themselves turn into omelettes when cooked."

"Then you recognize the possibility that eggs that have been broken down inside the human body can become eggs again?"

"Naturally. And thus an egg-like execution becomes a chemical possibility."

"If that is the case, then this execution will result in a second slaughter of the reconstituted eggs by the very hands of eggs themselves. We ourselves would be guilty of the contradiction of making the same egg dishes that are designed for human consumption. Instead of the death penalty, we should resuscitate the eggs in the five defendants, and spread the good news to their survivors."

"That is utterly ridiculous!" The prosecutor, beside himself with rage, threw his head against a pillar, coming dangerously close to breaking the shell. "We demand revenge! We must have omelettes! Hard-boiled eggs! . . ."

The five students, thoroughly fed up with this nonsensical debate, were finally composed enough to take a careful look around them. Their drunkenness was beginning to wear off. Jatarō searched for a pretty girl among the spectators to make a pass at, but he was disappointed to find that, while they varied somewhat in size, the egg girls were completely lacking in individuality. Female eggs apparently sought to express their personalities through their apparel, and the motley assortment was quite astounding. One egg was wearing a classical twelve-layer kimono with a bonnet. Mōsuke, stamping his feet in boredom, was surprised that his shoes made a metallic sound as they hit the floor.

"This floor is made of steel," he whispered to his friends. They all snickered. None of them believed him, or tried stamping on the floor themselves. But when Mōsuke looked about him excitedly he realized that the narrow, protruding, tower-like section which they had seen from the front of the building was actually a corridor rising at a steep angle from the circular room where they stood. In fact, it looked just like a handle connected to the rim of the circle. Mōsuke had a revelation. He whispered to his friends in the same buoyant tone he always used when telling lies:

"Hey, look! This building is a frying pan." The four glanced vaguely toward the tower. But, seen from inside, it is hard to tell that a frying pan is a frying pan. The four were sure that the incorrigible Mōsuke was up to his usual fibs.

On the shadowy white dais, the chief-justice egg swayed slightly to left and right. He seemed to be conferring with the other judges. At last the chief justice rose to announce his verdict. The crowd of spectators became tense, and a noticeable chill spread through the hall. The chief justice pronounced sentence in the same kind of yellowish voice, but it was a solemn, dignified yellow.

"The opinion of the defense counsel deviates from the morality of eggs, and errs in the direction of humanitarianism. Therefore, as the prosecutor has demanded, I sentence the five defendants to death. The sentence will be carried out immediately in accordance with Act 82 of the Egg Criminal Code."

Instead of cheering, the spectators produced a deafening clatter by hitting their shells against each other. Ten policemen approached the students.

"What are we waiting for? Let's get them!" Mōsuke urged in a low, powerful voice. The other four decided that they had no choice but to believe Mōsuke's lie, and, still in handcuffs, they ran off together toward the tower. The connecting corridor was indeed a grooved steel gutter—unmistakably the handle of a frying pan. The five ran to the top and hung from the tip of the handle. Since they weighed an average of two hundred and fifty pounds each, an accumulated weight of over a thousand pounds was pulling down on the handle. Mass confusion reigned as the frying pan flipped over perfectly and thousands of eggs came crashing down in a horrendous explosion. The noise echoed for hundreds of miles in all directions, waking everyone up and driving them out into the pre-dawn streets. The myriad eggs were smashed to bits as they collided and hit the ground; the yolks and whites, blending as if beaten with a whisk, were transformed into a liquid mass the size of a reservoir. Just then a sparkling blue oil truck happened to be passing through the neighborhood, and as its tank was conveniently empty, the five, assuming sole ownership of the huge egg supply, feverishly filled the truck with the liquid and had it transported to their boarding house.

From that day forward, Chūkichi, Jatarō, Mōsuke, Satsuo, and Ingorō were treated to omelettes every morning. There seemed to be no end to the supply, though they gorged themselves on omelettes the size of cushions. Their neighbors had to go on listening to their regular morning roars, but they were spared the piercing shell-cracks. And though these happy-go-lucky youths were deprived of the fun of breaking an egg every morning, they resigned themselves to the fact that that was the price you had to pay when you had smashed so many all at once.

STARS

Kojima Nobuo

Translated by Van C. Gessel

Kojima Nobuo, born in 1915 in Gifu, is a solitary figure on the contemporary literary scene, a novelist who has turned a bitterly satirical gaze upon himself and his contemporaries and found them all to be "partial cripples." His novels and short stories take a dark look at ineffectual characters thrust into a vortex of relativism and contradictions that render them unable to act.

The primary literary influence on Kojima has been the writings of Gogol, the master Russian satirist whose works Kojima encountered while studying English literature at Tokyo University. The experiences of his own life have tended to reinforce the view that human life is absurd: Kojima began teaching English at the middle school level just eight months before Japan declared war on all the major English-speaking nations of the world; after he was drafted into the Japanese Army in 1942 and failed officer candidacy tests, he was sent to Manchuria, where he worked alongside Nisei intercepting and decoding transmissions from U.S. Air Force units stationed in Asia.

Since his recognition as a writer with the publication of "Kisha no naka" *(On the Train, 1948), an incisive account of the pandemonium of the early postwar days, symbolized by the masses swarming and jostling to board an express train, and the train's frantic rush toward Tokyo and a new, "modern" order; and* "Shōjū" *(The Rifle, 1952; tr. 1979), an erotic tale of an ambivalent soldier, Kojima has continued to write about morally handicapped individuals who search for, but never find, meaning in their everyday activities.* Hōyō kazoku *(Embracing Family, 1965), which won the*

Tanizaki Prize, is one of the most harrowing of modern Japanese novels in its focus on an enfeebled intellectual, while the gentler story "Amerikan sukūru" (The American School, 1954; tr. 1977) is widely admired for its humorous study of a painfully proud yet insecure teacher of English in Occupied Japan. Kojima's most recent work is a massive, fourteen-hundred-page novel, Wakareru riyū *(Reasons for Parting, 1982), which critics in Japan are already calling a landmark in the evolution of the modern Japanese novel.*

"Hoshi" (Stars, 1954), translated here, is one of the more biting chronicles to emerge from the Pacific War. Kojima has created an essentially perfect literary emblem of spiritual ambivalence in George Sugihara, a Nisei educated in America but drafted by chance into the Japanese Army. Kojima has infused this character with much of the ambivalence he himself felt during the war years. The story concerns itself with the various "stars" by which men seek stability and guidance in their lives. For George Sugihara, who goes into the army confused and uncertain, there can never be any reliable stars; but he goes on searching for them anyway.

* * *

What man wouldn't feel an unusual surge of emotion as he gazed at the lone red star on the collar of a uniform hurled randomly in his direction? I for one felt dazed at that moment. It may have had something to do with the fact that I was an American Nisei without a jot of military training who was going to have to spend the rest of his life as a soldier. That demeaning insignia—the simple, worn, tarnished star buried in some threadbare red cloth—would cling forever to my collar, invisible to me but obvious to everyone else. A curse upon the man who thought up such a cunning mark! By its nature, that unlucky token exercised far less control over me if I made no conscious effort to remember it was there. That star pinned to my collar—I wore the lowliest of them all. For everyone to see. I was made to realize this every single day.

I found that I really knew nothing about the army up until then. When I thought of the long chain leading upward from private second class to general to field marshal, my eyes swam as though I were peering up a ladder to heaven. The gulf was so incredible; one could never skip a single rung of the nearly twenty steps above. And a swarm of single stars like an ocean surrounding me. Moreover, this miserable single star acquired new life as it became two, then three stars. Suddenly on the next level a stripe was added. Then a silver stripe was joined by a silver star. Next the design changed and was given lively borders. And thereafter. . . Thus, the higher you got, the more decorative and resplendent your uniform became. I suppose a conference must have been called to decide all this. One can imagine how inspired the delegates had been by the belief that the Great Ones must be suitably adorned. "No, that's a bit too pretty." "The balance is off." "Make that one a bit more humble—the way it is, it doesn't bring out the distinction enough."

So when I joined the army, each time I noticed someone gazing at me, I angrily returned the look, feeling this would let people know where I stood. But I realized that I'd been singled out by the senior noncoms as their plaything. Until then I hadn't known how feeble a look of hatred can be. They laughed uproariously at me because my body was built like an American's, because I wasn't very agile, and because of the solemn expression on my face. Then amicably they would tell me to look in the mirror. When I turned around, the "roasting" began. When they taunted me, they referred to it as "Western-style cooking" or "American sightseeing." I had to answer all sorts of questions about California and American women. "Speak some English," they'd jeer. "Sing some jazz." If I had performed to their satisfaction, they might have dropped these demands. But I refused to answer them, angered at the malevolence of this vegetarian race. Once I adopted that attitude, they shifted the direction of their interrogations. No longer did they treat me like a jester; now they were looking for excuses to beat me up. "Western-style cooking" came to mean frying me alive, and "American sightseeing" meant watching me double over in pain.

As a result, I became even more averse to looking in the mirror. I stopped even using one to shave.

A soldier named Hikida slept in the bed next to mine. He too was viciously beaten and abused. I stood by and watched while he was pummeled, and surprised myself by experiencing feelings of pleasure. He had done nothing to deserve this kind of treatment. Frankly I enjoyed watching him being beaten because I couldn't bear his ugliness. I realized then that I felt not the slightest affinity with him, and that I too was abusing him in my own special way.

His ugliness had little to do with his awkward posture, or the fact that his uniform was always in disarray because his spare time was all devoted to receiving upbraidings for his idleness. Rather I felt that the measly single star on his collar deserved a better setting than his tiny eyes and his long, pale, downcast face with its three moles. Indeed his looks were an insult to that star. Even one star was too exalted for him. He made me wish that someone had invented an even humbler insignia.

I couldn't bear thinking about the way others viewed me. But vaguely I sensed they felt that I was a disgrace to my own star, too. By insulting one star I was insulting every other star.

In our barracks once, we had a bottle of soy sauce that we'd brought over from the mess hall. Hikida asked me what he should do with it, and I told him to pour the stuff out. I thought that if we returned with what was left in the bottle, they would threaten simply not to give us any more—that was a bit of military common sense even I could figure out. Hikida did as I told him and poured the sauce down the toilet. Then we took the bottle back to the mess along with the other dishes. The cook was waiting there for us, wanting to know what had happened to the soy. Apparently, everyone from the other barracks had dutifully brought their leftovers back.

"You must have poured yours out," he insisted.

"I used it all," I replied.

"Liar! Where did you get rid of it?" He looked at me. "Hey, American! I bet you made him pour it out!" He had work to do in the kitchen and we had assignments of our own, but the cook detained us and thoroughly bawled us out. Normally I would have borne the brunt of the assault, but somehow when the cook's eyes fell on Hikida, he began stamping his feet as though in pain. From the expression on his face it was obvious he wouldn't be able to keep from attacking Hikida. I stood to one side, gritting my teeth. Hikida had his own unique way of taking a beating. Like a child, he covered his face with his hands, trying to deflect the oncoming blows from his head. Of course it would have been more natural and effective to roll with the punches. Hikida had the knack of making people want to beat him, and clearly sometimes his submissive posture only increased his assailant's anger. The cook was so inflamed as he disposed of Hikida that he forgot I was even there.

It dawned on me that if I stuck close to Hikida, it would be like wearing a cloak of invisibility. After all, there was no question that Hikida was my inferior.

Mentally I had moved up a step to some vague, undefined status. I have cited only one example, but I was gradually growing in confidence.

It may sound foolish, but I lived in fear of army horses. There were several horses in our signal corps, and we had to feed them, clean up their dung, and groom them. These were duties that had to be attended to even more scrupulously than the care of our weapons and equipment. The horses were, after all, living creatures. There was a danger we might be kicked, or contract some disease from them; mostly, though, I was afraid of their eyes. The army has a saying that goes, "Even horses can recognize rank." These creatures had been part of the battalion long before we came along, and had transported our commanding officer and our vital equipment. How could they possibly be inferior to us? In fact I was often asked, "Could *you* run with the commander on your back? Even if you could, he'd refuse to ride you. Do you think you could carry all that equipment, American? It takes four men just to lift it—five men the likes of you. Which is better—you or the horse?" As a consequence of many such interrogations, I had become convinced (though it still seemed a bit odd) that what they said was true: a horse really was vastly superior. I was amazed that it hadn't occurred to me before. But a soldier didn't have the leisure to ponder the question at length, and at the bottom of my heart I couldn't bring myself to believe that horses were so very exalted. This was borne out by the fact that horses had no stars. I knew they could give us some stiff competition, but their status as such was surely inferior. And yet, we were a sort of domestic animal ourselves, and as animals they could certainly hold their own. So, when I thought of them peering at my star with those cool eyes, that army proverb felt as sharp as the flick of a whip.

For this reason I dreaded my encounters with them even more than my associations with my human superiors. It wasn't so much the fear that they would recognize my star and just disdain me. It was more the apprehension that they would compare our relative positions and try to display their superiority by kicking or biting. Would you laugh if I confessed that I hid my collar insignia from the horses? Well, it's true.

Still, how do you keep a horse from seeing your star? Their necks are so long, they're going to get a look at it eventually.

We were not allowed to look after the commander's horse. Yet somehow one morning we found Hikida sprawled out with his chin kicked in, and it turned out to be the commander's horse that had done it. This chestnut horse, called Gorō, had made mincemeat out of Hikida and then fled unchallenged to the parade ground, where he cut a figure of enviable beauty. Whoever instructed Hikida to groom that horse must have had it in for him. All right. *I'm* the one who falsified orders and told him to take care of it. Stupidly, he didn't even know it was the commander's steed. He was actually supposed to groom the horse in the neighboring stall. Later on I was thrashed, of course; they found out I had lied. But I didn't dread beatings. I dreaded being humiliated.

I no longer feared even beatings in the middle of the night, so long as such treatment involved no humiliation. As a student in America, I was once part of a rowing team, and the experience came back to me vividly. We sat aft in the boat and had to practice several thousand strokes. As we approached, say, five thousand strokes, shouts of encouragement would pursue us agonized oarsmen. The same thing happened to me when I was beaten across the face. Every ten blows or so as we approached the ultimate goal—thirty, forty, or fifty, depending on the offense—the haunting jeers of encouragement from the onlooking soldiers seemed to swell in volume. The humiliation tortured me more than the chastisement.

In the dead of night I often passed Hikida some of my portion of bean jelly. To that end I patiently saved up some of my own rations. It gave me the creeps just being near him. And then he would start backfiring under his blanket. I ignored the demands of my own stomach and stored up my rations just so I could have the pleasure of hearing those sounds. I also gave him part of my rice. We were both singled out for hatred because of what we did, but it put me in a position of superiority over him. And over my persecutors also.

Confined to his bed after the episode with the horse, Hikida received less sympathy than he had when, in the past, a fellow soldier had knocked him down. I poured gruel down his throat and mashed up sweets to stuff into his mouth. I've never been so conscious of how disgusting a mouth can be. And performing these tasks was my sole delight in life.

The region just southwest of the village where we were stationed was surrounded by high mountains. We were sent out to climb them many times. Should the enemy ever come, they would storm down from there. Soldiers who wanted to make a name for themselves were very fond of climbing them. Even though we never fought a single battle, being the first to the summit with a heavy pack on your back was a sure way of attracting attention. I hated those mountains. I wasn't really weaker physically than the others, but I couldn't bear the thought of being in competition with soldiers who had once been woodcutters or charcoal burners. I had decided to make Hikida my hiking companion.

We set out in the middle of one night. By noon of the following day we had crossed over three large, bald mountains. Our formation crumbled, and as expected, Hikida with his short scrawny legs soon fell behind the others. I stayed with him, and before long the two of us had formed a rear guard on our own. It took no more than a glance at his pathetic figure to make me want to rip the star off his collar. It seemed so venomous, so green, so like a parasite. I began counting the number of times he stumbled against the rocks. I plucked his rifle from his hands and shouldered his along with my own. Even he knew what it meant to surrender your weapon to someone else, but he let me take it anyway.

Just an hour later Hikida was dangling upside down over a cliff.

The men who had gone on ahead had already reached the summit and were waiting there to lay into us. But when the sun began to set and we still hadn't caught up with them, they came back looking for us. There they discovered Hikida stumbling along twenty or thirty yards behind me, about to fall off the cliff. I knew what was happening to him, because time after time he had called my name: "Hey, Sugihara! Hey, Sugihara!!" If I'd felt any goodwill toward him then, I wouldn't have been able to ignore him. But I had myself to think of, which is why I stayed about thirty yards ahead of him but still behind the rest of the unit. I knew they'd beat up Hikida before they turned on me. And after all, I was carrying his rifle for him, wasn't I? Obviously he'd given up his weapon and was trying to get himself killed. There could be no greater insult to his superiors—to those majestic stars they wore. As a reward for his cowardice, two senior officers dangled him callously by his legs over the top of the cliff.

Hikida let out piteous screams before he was hoisted up and set on the back of the commander's horse. The commander himself ordered it. Naturally the horse was our old friend Gorō. Hikida hung his head, stealing occasional glances at me in the hope that I would help him.

Along the way there was a brief skirmish in which two of the enemy died. During the fighting Hikida remained on horseback, hiding behind a crag.

One of the dead soldiers, dressed in a sky-blue padded uniform, lay face down at the side of the path. One of our men nudged the body over with his foot and stared at it. There, in the same location on his neck, the dead soldier wore a single white star against the black of his collar. The meagerness of that enemy star—though it wasn't an absolute meagerness—made me feel close to the dead man. Or was it just because he was now a corpse? When I was in America, I attended the cremation of a Japanese acquaintance. As the bones were broken up and placed in an urn, I heard an American comment, "He was well built for a Japanese, wasn't he?" I'm sure I wouldn't have felt envy for my late friend if his bones had been small and fragile.

Hikida's ceremonious return to camp astride the commander's horse should by all rights have been compensated by increased abuse from the men. But instead he was taken to the infirmary with pneumonia. I ended up carrying his meals to him.

He had been an artist, the kind who paints scenes on umbrellas. When we were alone he showed me some pictures he had drawn on tissue paper, and he blew his nose in them and asked me to throw them away. His drawings of roses and morning glories were prosaic and lifeless. But the expression on his face when he sketched them was unique, and I tried not to look at him when he was that way. I had to wash out his hospital gowns. When I peeled them off him, he looked bewildered and unable to express his gratitude. It was important to me that he feel like that.

It's unfortunate, I suppose, but it never occurred to me that he might have a family. He may have mentioned it to me, but I must have forgotten, because when he asked me to bring a picture of his wife and children from his locker, I realized for the first time that he was a family man. He tried to get me to look at the picture, but I lied and said I'd already seen it. To admit that Hikida had a family would be tantamount to regarding him as a fellow human being. I wanted him to remain a domestic animal.

And so I wept when I reported to him that he was the only man who hadn't been promoted from buck private. There was no way he could have seen through my act.

What is it about getting an extra star that wields such tremendous power over the mind of a soldier? What meaning does it have to receive just one more pitiful earthbound star? Like all other ceremonies, the promotion ceremony is carried out with great solemnity. From that day forward, soldiers become more diligent than before. They want to go out in the world. Go out on a foray and display their advancement to others. But just who do they expect to show off for?

I peered into a mirror again for the first time since becoming a PFC. I only deserved one star. Now I was locked into the system. Seeing myself, I was overcome with shame.

In his infirmary room, Hikida called me, "Private, sir!" He was due to be released soon, and he had some things he wanted to discuss with me. He had been able to relax a bit here in the infirmary, he said, but if he had to go back to the unit now, he would have preferred being persecuted without a break from it. I told him I was going to be serving as a sentry now, and that while I was on duty we would be by ourselves. At that word of encouragement, he buried his head under the covers. He seemed somehow afraid of me.

"No matter what happens, Hikida, you've got to give up trying to die."

He peeped out from under the covers. "I do? I wish I'd been born a woman. No woman would have to put up with the likes of these guys. Why, they'd come running after me!" he said with regret. He seemed to have spent his leisure hours thinking about his family and about dying. A chill ran down my spine. So far the suicides in our unit were limited to men with one star; without exception they had all hanged themselves.

Hikida was indispensable to me. He was less a human being for me than a sort of star. He was an even more necessary existence to the senior officers. That much was evident, because once he was hospitalized a sense of desolation swept over the unit; the men tried unsuccessfully to turn me into their punching bag, and afterward they often inquired about Hikida's condition.

In any case, he and I ended up standing watch at the city gates. The city was surrounded by a wall two and a half miles in circumference, which had been standing for fifteen or sixteen centuries. One gate opened out at each point of the compass. We were to unbolt the rusted locks of the heavy gates at 5:30 each morning, and close them at 5:30 each evening. Once the gates were shut all traffic ceased. We began patrolling the walls after things had quieted down. When we were off duty we were frequently sent outside the city to steal melons. Without even noticing, I had started giving Hikida orders. I stood stiffly over him as I made him tear a melon off the vine, then found another ripe melon and had him pick it. He looked up at me sheepishly. This angered me and I was forced to shout at him. This had never happened to me before. When Hikida moved, I moved too. What did all this mean? When had this come about?

As sentries, Hikida and I had to check the papers of every Chinese who went in and out of the gates, and keep an eye out for forgeries. Not only were we left on our own here, but with our metal helmets on our heads and our bayonets in our hands, none dared ridicule us. Nobody even knew I was a Nisei. In a position like this, I thought, I could get to like these locals.

"What's your name? Birthplace? Age?"

"Do you have any children? How many?"

"Where have you come from, and where are you going?"

"How far away is that village?"

"Your daughter's going to grow up to be a beauty!"

I strung together what few Chinese phrases I knew and asked questions of this nature, even commenting on things that had nothing to do with my sphere of responsibility. When missionaries passed through I greeted them in English. I realized that Hikida was aping me and making all sorts of inquiries. He knew a great deal more about commerce than I, and there were many things he wanted to learn. The locals carried cotton goods, flour, bedding, household belongings, charcoal, and all sorts of other items on their backs or tied to mules. Ostensibly it was our cruel duty to jab at their packs with our bayonets, and sometimes even to dump out the contents to check for concealed weapons. Instead Hikida and I spent our time plying them with questions for our own edification.

Because these peculiar inspectors never seized any of their belongings, the Chinese always thanked us with a "*Hsieh-hsieh*" as they passed through. One evening, though, our superior officer stole up behind us, saw what we were doing, and gave me a swift kick that sent me sprawling onto the ground. I fell flat on my face like a squashed frog, still clutching my bayonet. I couldn't understand why I was singled out for such treatment, but since I was a PFC and responsible for both myself and Hikida, maybe it was to be expected. When I got to my feet I was booted to the ground again. The Chinese man who had been standing by me suddenly began showering compliments on my superior. Those who were still waiting to go through the gate cast wry smiles in my direction. They must have found it amusing that the frames of my glasses were broken and one of the lenses had fallen out. At once they seemed distant and hostile to me, accomplices of my superiors. I realize now that, in that moment, they were given a graphic demonstration of the relationship between one, two, and three stars. That alone was sufficient cause for laughter.

My dreams were shattered in that fleeting instant. I still think Hikida is the one who destroyed my illusions. After that day I ceased to feel any sense of camaraderie with the Chinese who passed before me. When I caught Hikida leering at the occasional man who went by with a pregnant woman, I signaled to him to cut it out. But he merely grinned at me. It was obvious that lately he accepted everything I told him to do, and even reveled in carrying out my orders. He trusted me, and depended on my protection. Why was it that I couldn't bear that buoyant look on his face? Was that what happened when you climbed up one step on the hierarchical ladder?

A path three or four yards wide ran along the top of the city wall. One night we patrolled that pitch-black path. Normally one soldier patrolled two of the four sides of the wall, but since we were still trainees, Hikida and I stood guard together.

During the daylight hours it was all I could do to keep from throttling Hikida. When we were on duty, though, he followed his usual practice of trotting along behind me, gazing down from atop the wall at the houses in the town. Twice he nearly slipped and fell off the wall as he did this. Enraged, I vowed he wouldn't get off so easily a third time.

The next time the fool began sliding off the edge, I grabbed him by the collar and dragged him up, then hauled him over to the parapet on the other side and pinned him against it. Forgetting my sentry duties, I shouted, "You're a soldier, you know!" and gave him a good whack. The pain he felt reverberated through my hand. It was the kind of pain, I suppose, that can only be understood by one who has been continuously beaten himself. What I had really wanted to say was, "You're the lowest of all stars, you know!"

Hikida resisted by covering his face with his hands. He had just learned during his most recent pummeling not to lift his hands to his face, but with me he did it again. I jerked his hands away and beat him further.

"Jōji! Please stop—I'll do whatever you want! I'll do your laundry—anything!"

"You think I could stand being fawned on by someone like you?"

I must have said something like that. I was caught up in the fury of my mood. Hikida turned his flat, tearstained, frantic face out away from the city, wailed bitterly, and then tried to scale the parapet and leap off the thirty-foot-high wall. Remembering how close to suicide he had seemed in his hospital room, I froze in horror. Then I dragged him down off the wall.

What had I done atop that city wall? Inside the town, the intermittent braying of mules outside the wall could be heard. From the eaves of the house just below us rose voices chanting sutras. The lives these Chinese led were wretched, but perhaps ours were even more miserable. My torment had driven me to the brink of madness, and as I clutched at the cold, ancient stones of the city wall, I saw a wreath of stars ascending from a point below me into the sky. It circled the sky and then disappeared behind the wall opposite me. For a long while I had forgotten that there were stars in the heavens.

I trembled, feeling desolation welling up within me. Hikida, still huddled on the ground, muttered petulantly, "You're not a Japanese after all. You aren't! You aren't!"

Once the unwelcome Hikida had been transferred to a unit in Southeast Asia, orders came for me to report to regimental headquarters to serve as an orderly to Captain Inoma of the district command. He was twenty-two or -three, with nothing special to recommend him aside from the fact that he was an officer. His chief claims to fame were the manner in which he could spit vigorously out his window each morning after I brought in his water, and the fact that he could drink the murky Chinese tea. He was, in short, a model officer. Bedecked in his officer's stars, he looked at least thirty years old. Strangely enough, when a man acquires two stars, his age seems to advance in concert with his promotion, as though even his years were subject to the rule of the stars.

Brought into close contact with these distant stars, I felt not hatred, but something more like adoration. I wondered if, as a result of all the anguish I'd been made to suffer in the midst of those inferior stars, I hadn't come to feel that life had greater meaning if I surrendered to the star system and regarded myself as worthless. I had indeed come to believe that stars had an intrinsic value to them—that a PFC was truly superior to a buck private, a lance corporal better than a PFC, a noncom greater than a common foot soldier, and an officer vastly more exalted than a noncom. I had become convinced that those of a higher rank than my own were an inherently different breed of human being. Particularly an officer. How could I even imagine that Captain Inoma—this lofty being for whom I washed laundry every day, delivered meals, and poured tea—belonged to the same species as myself? There was even a brief period when I embraced the peculiar notion that he was my superior by virtue of the fact that he belonged to a race of vegetarians. Perhaps I had fallen short of the mark because I had lived in America and been corrupted by the consumption of animal flesh.

More importantly, however, my advancement to two-star rank increased my faith in the stars themselves.

On one occasion the division commander inspected our regiment. When Captain Inoma barked, "Eyes right!" the soldier standing directly opposite me jerked his head toward the commander. In that instant it seemed to my apprehensive eyes that the soldier's face had stretched all out of shape. The commander marched briskly up to the soldier, placed his hand on the man's chin, gave a grunt, and moved on. The soldier stiffened his elongated face even more and stood unflinching. What had happened was that the officer had corrected the soldier's dislocated jaw in a flash. I was dumbstruck. The entire regiment wept tears of gratitude afterward, of course. Somehow the commander's majestic poise and magnanimity seemed well in keeping with the number of stars he wore. Thinking back on it now, perhaps there was nothing so special about this histrionic scene. Maybe he was just good at repairing dislocated jaws.

My duties as Captain Inoma's orderly were pretty much those of a chambermaid. If this very minute I were to bring out a captain's collar insignia and that of a PFC and ask a child to choose the better one, I have no doubt he would choose the captain's. I recognized the disparity between our positions and bowed low before Captain Inoma.

Since I had the lowest-ranking stars, I was sent to regimental headquarters to represent all the men from our office at roll call. First, however, I was supposed to put logs into five stoves, polish the twenty-odd yards of hallway and stairs with a rag, then take the captain's breakfast to him—BUT, only after I had taken him his washbasin, of course, and folded up his bedding. Even before all that, I had to go and get everyone's breakfasts and deliver them. I couldn't light the stove until I stole some coal from the kitchen. Strangely enough, I enjoyed carrying out this morning's worth of endless duties. As I scrubbed the floors, I found delight in the manner in which I wrung out the rags, and it was a challenge to try to miss all the nails in the floorboards. When I went to pick up meals for delivery, struggling to keep the slippers from flying off my feet and the soup from spilling out of the bowls, invariably a senior officer would be coming toward me in the distance, and I would have to muster a salute.

But I always experienced a pleasant afterglow as a natural offshoot of my trials. And it was somehow thrilling to be crawling along the floor with a rag in my hands and suddenly be able to stand up before the regimental flag, salute the sentry, and then return to my floor polishing. Our dust-covered flag was poised on a pedestal, guarded by a living soldier, and to it I offered my salutes.

The first time I met Captain Inoma, he wanted me to write out a *rirekisho*. Apparently he wasn't pleased that his new orderly wore only two stars and was, moreover, a second-generation Japanese-American. I'm ashamed to have to admit it, but I didn't know right off what a *rirekisho* meant.

"*Rirekisho. Rirekisho*?" I chewed the word over, until finally he explained what it was.

"Oh, you mean a 'personal history'!" I blurted out in English. That really exasperated him. But he seemed to consider it his duty to take what there was of this orderly and make a first-rate soldier out of him. In my personal history, I wrote that when I reached junior high age, I was sent back to California to be with my parents. After finishing college in the U.S., I returned to Japan to see my grandfather, and was at once drafted into the army. When he read this, the captain peered into my face as though examining some exotic animal. He admitted that I hadn't seemed completely Japanese to him, and he was kind enough to ask me all sorts of questions about California. I warmed to the occasion and began relating all manner of fond memories of the place, until suddenly he snatched up the résumé I had written, ripped it to shreds, and tossed the fragments into the stove.

"PFC Sugihara Jōji! You're going to have one hell of a time becoming a Japanese soldier. You will consider today the last time you have any past whatsoever," he ordered. He decided in addition that I was to write a daily "Journal of Self-Examination," which he would read to determine whether I was making progress toward becoming a true Japanese soldier. He also set out to teach me the fine art of Chinese poetic recitation. Subsequently he had me write out two new personal histories, but he tore these up as well. These facts were duly noted in my Journal.

If I wearied of ferreting out new material for my daily introspections, Captain Inoma did me the favor of pointing out my shortcomings.

Nothing made him happier than to see me covering sheets and sheets of paper with my self-examinings. He seemed highly suspicious that I might inwardly hold him in contempt, so I crammed my Journal primarily with rhapsodies declaring my profound respect for him. But eventually he came up with an unusual method of testing my loyalty. He had me prepare three separate collar insignia of captain's rank. While he slept at night, I was to rotate them on his uniforms every now and then. By doing that, of course, I was unable to forget even in my sleep that he was a captain. And naturally my Journal was also there to help me remember.

Perhaps because I felt humiliated as I carried out this penance of rotating his insignia, I let the notion grow in me that the captain was himself a star, and that stars had an innate grandeur about them. I had never felt quite that way before.

From my perspective now it is hard to believe that I once had such thoughts. But when Captain Inoma came walking toward me, my mind was riveted not upon him as a person, but on each of those cherished stars. The expressions on the faces of those three familiar stars were engraved upon my heart. Imagine it! Secretly I gave each of them a name. I called them Tom, Frank, and Kate, after the names of my two brothers and my younger sister. When the stars came my way, I greeted them inwardly with a "Hi, Frank!" and suchlike.

Once when I saluted Captain Inoma, I remember him asking dourly,

"Private Sugihara, what exactly are you saluting?"

"Yes, sir. I'm saluting you, Captain, sir."

"You are not to salute me. You are to salute my eyes. Write that in your Journal."

On snowy days I felt sorry for Kate.

Frank was a rowdy boy and always getting dirty.

Brother Tom was always at his best at ceremonies.

These notions could not be written in my Journal, of course, so Captain Inoma had no way of knowing what was really going through my mind.

One day when I was attending the captain in his bath, he climbed out of the tub and plopped himself down in front of me. I felt as though a powerful electric shock had run through me. I couldn't shake off the peculiar sensation that Kate was still clinging to the nape of his neck. Why should I be so stunned to see the captain nude, without his uniform? Who in fact was this naked man before me? He was muscular, to be sure, but was there such a great difference between me and this man with the close-cropped hair when both of us were in the buff? After he climbed back into the bath, he launched into one of his recitations of Chinese poetry. I sat abstractedly holding his towel and soap. The sound of his chanting reawakened in me the realization that this was indeed Captain Inoma before me, and I returned to my senses. But I had a sluggish, uneasy feeling, as though a cog had slipped out of place. I wanted to get both the captain and myself back into uniform at once.

That was the first time I'd been in the bathroom with him. After that day, I was ordered to be his regular bath attendant. But each experience left me feeling more unsettled. Most disturbing, I started thinking there was something wrong with the way he gulped his tea, the way he refilled his rice bowl, the way he snored in his sleep, and the way he spat out the window each morning. I grew pensive, something a soldier cannot allow himself to do unless he expects to be wounded or perpetrate some dreadful blunder. I began to worry that I might really put my foot in it.

One day when I accompanied Captain Inoma to Peking, I saw a string of hands across the way rise up in salute. Caught up in the movement, I too lifted my hand. Ahead of us an automobile came to a stop. The captain didn't move, so I followed his example and stood at attention, watching intently. The door of the automobile opened, and out stepped Chief of Staff Nawa. The captain at once shouted "Salute!" and I brought my hand up to the side of my head. But I was eager to see what was emerging from the automobile, so I peered out from behind the captain's back, my hand still in midair. What should appear before my eyes but a full golden galaxy more sumptuous and dazzling than a million commonplace stars! I had never seen such splendor so close at hand. To what should I compare such an array of stars? The brothers and sisters I had doted on were no longer adequate metaphors—stars of this magnitude made those everyday varieties seem wrought of base materials. This officer seemed like a queen who had deigned to grace the city with her presence. By now I had forgotten all about my right hand. In nervous excitation I watched as the queen began her procession. Chief of Staff Nawa was advancing in my direction, so I took a step or two forward, until a stentorian shout rattled in my ears. I beat a hasty retreat.

I was informed that I had been disrespectful toward the chief of staff. That seemed impossible to me, but everything went black before my eyes as the captain dragged me back to the unit. An hour later I was standing looking the captain full in the face for the first time. Although Inoma claimed we had spent every single day together for some time now, it was true that recently I hadn't looked him in the face. The base of his nose was thick. His eyes were narrow but sparkling. His chin was angular, his mouth tightly clenched—though for several minutes now it had been restlessly opening and closing. I was still in a daze, unable to make out what he was saying.

"What kind of idiot gawks at a general like he's watching a peepshow? Especially right in front of that chief of staff! I'm going to have to finish you off with my sword."

He repeated this over and over again, but all I could do was look at him in stupefaction. I was totally stunned to think that words that had such great bearing on my very life could flow so casually from his mouth. All I could think of was that today I should remove Kate and pin Frank onto his uniform. His stars were crooked. It wasn't possible. . .

My memory grows dim at this point, yet I seem to recall the fact that Captain Inoma had been a classmate of this particular chief of staff, but was two ranks behind him when they received their commissions. Inoma had distinguished himself at the front line in an attempt to close the gap, but each time he attained some merit, his rival bounced up two more ranks. The captain was bitterly disappointed.

Captain Inoma seemed to have worked himself into a rage. He stripped me naked, then energetically tore off his own jacket. He made me sit facing the east, pulled out his sword and wrapped the blade with my shirt, then stepped up to me.

"Are you ready? Don't be a coward. Cut your belly open now, and I'll chop your head off for you. Don't worry about a thing."

I didn't have the impression that he was joking. But this was all too sudden to be really happening. I didn't even have time to feel sad. I gazed down at my stomach. My belly button seemed so forlorn, so alone. As I studied my navel, I blurted out:

"Look—a star!"

"What? What's that, Sugihara?" He peered forward.

"A star. It's a star!"

"You're right. Your navel does look like a star! What a—" The captain burst into laughter so raucous that I was astonished.

If this preposterous anecdote seems to defy all credibility, the fault lies in my inability to tell it properly. When one belongs to an army whose sole aim is to destroy other human beings, a sense of the preposterous is a requisite for survival.

Blessed are they who can doubt the truth of these sentiments!

I had spoken out of sorrow—sorrow over the fact that the lowest of all stars, that solitary star which I thought I was at long last rid of, had been hiding—of all places—in the center of my own belly. I was ashamed beyond endurance that my feelings had been revealed to someone else. From his roar of laughter it seemed that Captain Inoma had given up the idea of killing me and now regarded me as a lunatic, but in fact the innermost secrets of my heart had been exposed to his gaze. I was frightened to go on living.

Frantic to cover up my belly, I hurriedly put on the shirt that had been wrapped around his sword. Captain Inoma, still apparently in a state of excitement, reached for a jacket and slipped it on. But when he looked up at me, I nearly let out a cry of incredulity. The figure standing before me was "Private" Inoma. Not once had it ever occurred to me that Captain Inoma could be transformed into a private. I should have been bewildered and embarrassed, but instead a shudder of intense pleasure ran through my body. It had been careless of him to put on my jacket, when the feel of the material and everything else about it was so different from his own. Perhaps he had lost his wits.

He seemed to sense something was wrong from my expression, and he looked himself over. Turning a bright red, he removed my jacket and tossed it to me.

"There's no need to be switching insignia any more. You're confined to your quarters. Give serious thought to your behavior." With that he stomped out of the room.

He reported to headquarters that I was suffering from nervous prostration, and confined me to my room for ten days. But who can say that Inoma himself wasn't the lunatic for trying to decapitate me just because I was standing a few degrees askew when I saluted the general? I laughed out loud at the memory of how delighted I'd been to see Captain Inoma converted into a private. Why, I'll rip Kate right off his collar! . . .

Aiming for a time when he was in the tub, I sneaked into the bathroom. Not that I was eager to continue as his bath attendant, but having performed that duty for so long, it made me feel strangely desolate to think I might be relieved of the responsibility. Previously it had been my custom to call out through the fuel hole, "How is the temperature, sir?" I felt a prick of conscience as I crept in, but I stifled it and set my sights on the collar of his jacket.

No sooner had I set foot in the room than I had the impression that Inoma was shouting at me, and I turned tail and ran. When I got a grip on myself, though, I realized that the noise hadn't been a bellow directed at me, but rather his customary recitation, which he chanted as he made waves on the surface of the bathtub:

"Nature grows all the more desolate.
Another field of battle reeking of blood."

Taking advantage of the moment, I plucked Kate from the captain's clothing, put my insignia in its place, and fled.

I opened the double doors in the captain's room and slipped behind them, making sure I returned them to their original position. There in his room I perpetrated a certain act with great haste, then waited with bated breath for his arrival.

Before long through a hole in the paper sliding door I caught sight of him running this way, gasping for breath. He wore only his underwear, and carried a jacket in his hand. He burst into the room, flinging the jacket away. As I watched all this, he seemed like a petulant adolescent. Then he saw me, and retreated several steps without saying a word. When his back struck the door, he drew himself up and bawled at me: "You bastard! Isn't th-that my formal uniform jacket?!"

I said nothing.

I have the impression that I was looking into his eyes. He had, after all, once told me to do that. I couldn't have looked at his collar even if I'd wanted to, since he had on nothing but his underwear.

I was indeed wearing his dress jacket (I had, by the way, affixed Tom to the collar). I was stunned by my own appearance.

In that fleeting instant he seemed to recover himself, and suddenly his body loomed ominously over me. He thrashed me across the face.

"You rotten lunatic! You surprise even me. Madman! If we had more like you, an officer wouldn't be able to sleep in peace. It'd be the ruin of the army! I should have killed you back when I had the chance. Do you realize what you've done, you lousy American?!"

I was silent.

"Think about why you did this. Do you know? I'm sure you don't."

I said nothing.

"It's because you were brought up in a liberal country. Who knows—someone like you could end up switching a general's stars. If you did that, I'd never make major!"

Thereupon he unjustly bound me with ropes and locked me in the unit's uniform closet. I had no idea why he'd chosen such a place to incarcerate me, or how many days he planned to keep me there. I was disheartened. I quietly maneuvered myself into a seated position and looked around. Ironically enough I found myself surrounded by veritable mountains of collar insignia. Up until then I had seldom enjoyed a peaceful night's rest, but when I snuggled down into that mound of stars, I effortlessly dropped off to sleep.

Struggling now to organize my memories of that time, it seems that at some point I jumped to my feet, edged over to the window, cut the ropes that bound me with some broken glass, removed the window and leaped to freedom. As I made my escape, I think I muttered to myself something like:

"The following morning the chief of staff went to headquarters and the staff officers came in to pay their respects. 'My word, he *is* looking seedy this morning, isn't he?' 'Wait—that isn't the general! It's a buck private!' 'What's a private doing strutting around here?!' 'But, no—better keep quiet about this.' And so everyone at staff headquarters kept their mouths shut. On the second day, the general. . ."

Assuming that I did wander about daydreaming in this way, I must have been trying to turn Captain Inoma's prophecy into reality. Just then someone behind me shouted, "Humming jazz, are you?!" and with overwhelming force tried to pin me to the ground. Clearly it was one thing to chant Chinese poetry, but quite another for a soldier to sing some jazz. I was infuriated, though that's no explanation for what I did. I sank my teeth into my assailant's hand and knocked his arm away, adding an uppercut to his jaw. It was then I realized that my attacker was Inoma.

I left him on the ground shouting something about the brute strength of a lunatic. In a frenzy I leaped a fence and came out on a road. I have no idea how long I walked, where my feet led me, what I did, or even if I was really in Peking. I had the feeling I had fallen off the planet altogether. I dropped to the ground and cried out: "Army Private Sugihara Jōji! Where are you? Get me out of here!!"

When the war came to an end, Captain Inoma announced that there was no reason the hostilities should cease. Certainly he had the initiative to go on fighting alone. And if the captain were to continue, how could I as his orderly avoid going along with him? Before too long, though, the captain declared his resolve to commit suicide. Then a short while later he announced his intention to enlist in the Chinese Communist Army, and invited me to follow suit. When you join the communists, he reported, they let you skip three ranks—a captain like himself would become a colonel, and I could end up a noncommissioned officer. The invitation was very tempting. I was ready to cast my lot in with the Reds if it meant hopping up three ranks; the fact is worth recording. After the defeat, I was ordered to do liaison work, translating communications from the interior into English so that they could be transmitted to the U.S. Marines. I knew therefore that some units in the interior had already surrendered to the communist forces without waiting for the northern advance of the Guomindang Army, and that their main motivation had been to get such promotions. Units that had refused to surrender had been annihilated.

"Do you really think I could become an NCO?" I asked Inoma, worried that perhaps only the captain would advance to colonel, and that I would be left as a common foot soldier. He seemed little interested in my problems, and replied, "Even if they don't promote you right away, I'll see to it that you get your advancement."

At that point I wore a mere two stars. But now that the war was really over, that pair of stars became as important to me as the captain's insignia were to him. They were imbued with my memories, my experiences. In that sense, I probably prized mine more than the captain did his. And because they meant so much to me, I had the strange notion that I wanted to continue living the sort of life in which stars would play a part.

Captain Inoma was directly responsible for my reinvolvement with English. One day he angrily shouted at me, "Starting today, you're going to remember all your English! Understand? No matter what it takes, you must remember every word of it. A man can do anything if he sets his mind to it."

"How should I go about remembering it, sir?" After all, it was Captain Inoma himself who had impressed upon me day and night that I was to forget every vestige of my American experience. This new command had come from the same Inoma who just a few days earlier had contemplated a one-man resistance against the enemy, then switched to a proclamation of suicide, and was perhaps even now considering the possibility of desertion.

Besides my duties as interpreter and translator, I was invested with the lofty responsibility of teaching interested officers how to converse in English. I received orders from Captain Inoma that I was not to wear my army uniform when I performed this noble function. I was told I should be happy I didn't have to wear a uniform; but I was more humiliated than I had ever been as a green recruit. I couldn't expect Captain Inoma to comprehend my humiliation. They (the chief of staff, for instance) could go on wearing their uniforms. But they insisted that I wear civilian dress. Had they let me keep my two stars on, it would have been their stars that bore the brunt of the shame. And why were they studying English anyway—a language that even I felt was better forgotten?

Once he began his English course, Inoma seemed to drop his plans of enlisting in the communist army.

In any case, they dressed me up in one of their civvy suits and forced me to sit in front of them for several hours at a stretch, for days on end. From my window I observed generals, captains, and lieutenants streaming down the tree-lined road to the headquarters building and into the conference room, each of them clutching the handouts I'd printed up for them. They still wore their swords. Soon Captain Inoma came to take me to the conference room. It was as though he had come to escort a prisoner. For the first time in my four years of army duty, I wept sloppy tears.

"I am Army Private Sugihara Jōji. It is a great privilege to teach you English conversation."

Of course, Captain Inoma took me aside after class and criticized the way I had introduced myself. "All you need tell them is the name your parents gave you—Sugihara Jōji. In fact, just plain Jōji is good enough."

Yet an unendurable sadness gripped me when I thought that, while units were at this very moment sending radio messages to report that they were surrounded by Red troops, the starry generals who controlled the fate of tens of thousands of soldiers in North China were seated in front of me like so many floor samples of the insignia of rank.

In consultation with Captain Inoma (rather, I should say it was he who composed the Japanese text), I printed up the following items in English:

—Days of the week, names of months, military ranks, names of weapons.
—"You are an American soldier, aren't you? I am Captain Inoma Goroku of the Japanese Army."
—"That is untrue. I cannot believe it."
—"Where did you hear that?"
—"Welcome. What can I do for you?"
—"You're welcome."
—"Our troops were brave. So were yours. Everything is my fault."
—"So-and-so is the guilty party."

—"X number of forces from the unit remain in x position."
—"We have provisions." "We do not have provisions."
—"Would you care for some saké?"
—"How will you deal with prisoners?"
—"I am not a war criminal."

These phrases are merely those I am able to recall now. I had them recite the sentences over and over again, correcting their pronunciation. But you can hardly expect proper pronunciation from men used to shouting everything in an officer's bark. I worked with them individually (this too on orders from Captain Inoma), drumming into them their names and ranks in English. The chief of staff couldn't for the life of him remember all the titles of military ranks.

Then Captain Inoma wailed, "I'm not letting anybody beat me at grammar," and he applied himself more diligently than anyone else. He outstripped all the others in language proficiency. In his room he produced a typewriter he had commandeered from an American merchant several years earlier, and had me teach him how to use it. He pounded away on the keys with clumsy fingers. Remarkable. In spite of all this, when he set one foot outside the classroom he became a stickler for ceremony. Even though he had become my student, he was punctilious about having me salute him. If I hesitated, he poked at my chest and berated me. Only when I wore street clothes was I impelled to speak openly, and only during that restricted period was he not on guard about my discipline. He devoted his time in the classroom to absorbing what I had to offer.

We were all promoted one rank en masse. Like fleeing bandits. Come to think of it, maybe the high command did it because they were afraid we'd be overwhelmed by the Chinese army, and all the insignia in the uniform closets would be confiscated.

I became a "Potsdam" PFC. Even now the name has a certain cynical ring to it. Cynical perhaps because we knew the absurd motivation behind the issuing of promotions at a time like that, and because we were delighted by the advancement even though we saw through the whole charade. Captain Inoma became Major Inoma. He changed his insignia himself. I was released from duty as his orderly, but everything else remained the same. Nothing could have been more awkward than this pairing of Major Inoma and PFC Sugihara.

When I went to Inoma's room to announce my promotion, he remarked, "This is good news for both of us," then asked me if I could find him a job, or see if they would take him on as a laborer on my father's farm in America—if, of course, it hadn't been confiscated by the government.

"Please don't ask that, sir. I want to go on thinking of you as a major. I can't cope with this."

"Don't you have any pity? Certainly if it were possible I would want things to continue as they are now. All right, I won't ask for your help. I've been greatly humiliated, Private Sugihara. I guess I should've killed myself, shouldn't I, Jōji?"

So saying, Major Inoma wiped away his tears with the palm of his hand.

The autumn sunlight that shone through the trees from the vast Peking sky made his platinum stars shimmer. The sight made me remember something I had forgotten for a long while—the stars and bells on a Christmas tree. I felt as though I could hear voices singing "Merry Christmas!" somewhere. What a bizarre association to make, I thought.

Despite this emotional scene, Major Inoma continued to implore me for assistance at every subsequent opportunity. When we boarded the LST for repatriation to Japan early the following year, his entreaties grew desperate.

My original unit had joined up with a Chinese Communist Army division in Shansi Province and fallen under the command of a famous Chinese general. As a result, I was sent along with Major Inoma to join a separate unit for repatriation. Our vessel was a transport ship laden with tanks. A thousand of us were crowded into the hold where the tanks were stored. We were in the prow of the ship and away from the boiler room, so we could hear the waves beating against the hull, and nearly enough water to sink the ship poured in on us. I was an interpreter, a sort of unofficial officer, but now that I was away from the officers' quarters and crouched here in the hold of a ship, I had a hard time believing that the thousand soldiers huddled around their knapsacks were being sent back to Japan in defeat. I had the deluded notion that we were setting out to Japan to fight. Before our departure, the men who were sensitive to emblems of rank had picked out and put on the highest-quality items from the uniform closets. That was only natural, since whatever remained would end up in the hands of Chinese soldiers.

Not a single man wanted to remove his uniform.

Every man wanted to return to his hometown wearing his insignia.

What was the meaning of it?

Their attitudes were both touching and disagreeable, yet I shared the same feelings. I wanted to wear my uniform back to Japan and then have it on when I showed up at my parents' home in America.

Someone tugged at my left sleeve as I was immersed in these thoughts. I looked up to see a small, scrawny soldier with no collar insignia. "Come with me. I want to talk to you for a minute," he said. The moment I saw his face I shuddered, for he reminded me of Hikida. He wasn't Hikida, of course. That soldier without a unit had probably been transferred from one division to another all over Southeast Asia until he finally died somewhere. After all, he had been the sort of fellow who made you want to do all sorts of terrible things to him; even God had forsaken him. My initial impression that this man resembled Hikida was prompted by his dark, somehow idiotic face. I followed him onto the deck, where he spoke in forceful tones unsuited to his gawky frame.

"You're an interpreter, right?"

"Yes, I am."

"We're gonna beat up all the officers on board. We don't want any Americans coming in while we're at it. You either gotta make 'em let us do it, or else keep 'em occupied."

"Why don't you wait until we land?"

"We gotta do it while they're still wearing their stars. It wouldn't be any fun doing it after we got back home. You must know how we feel, having the number of stars you do."

"If you mess around with the system, we'll all end up losers."

"Once we reach Japan, everybody'll be in a hurry to get back home, and no one'll wanna beat 'em up then."

"What's wrong with that?"

He seemed so agitated that he might make trouble for me if I put up any further resistance, so I decided to humor him and said I would go at once to talk with the staff sergeant in command of the transport unit. I had taken no more than one or two steps in that direction when he let out a peculiar laugh.

I concluded from the fact that he'd been deprived of his stars that he must have been a prison guard or the like, and that as a result he had developed a personal antipathy toward symbols of privilege. He seemed to be the ringleader in the plot to assault the officers. I couldn't imagine all the soldiers on board joining in at his bidding, but there was no telling what might happen under the circumstances.

The American staff sergeant, his feet propped up on the desk in his cabin, was more than happy to chat with me. He became incredibly cordial when I told him that I had lived in Fresno for ten years. Initially I felt comfortable with him, but then he cocked his head and remarked how unusual it was for a man with a college degree to be nothing more than a PFC. He treated me as though I were part of the American army. Before long I could clearly read in his eyes that he too had begun to look down on me. As I jabbered on, I grew increasingly incensed that even this man was caught up in the system of rank.

"Georgie, would you mind giving me your PFC insignia? I'd like to take it back with me."

"What would you do with a PFC's stars, Mister Brown? You can get as many as you want down in the hold."

"No, I want yours."

I ignored his request. "Listen, would you please let my parents know I'm all right?"

He stared longingly at my collar while I wrote down my parents' address. He stuffed the paper into his pocket. When I told him about the men's plan to attack their officers, he exploded at me as though I were its instigator.

"An officer is an officer. This absolutely cannot be permitted, Sugihara!"

Besides his fear that order would collapse among the Japanese troops, his face indicated that he had an emotional distaste for the plot. He dragged me off, ordering me to point out the soldier who had spoken to me. I was greatly disappointed in him. Staff Sergeant Brown hid himself behind me, and after he had ascertained which man was the guilty party, he snapped his fingers, disappointed that his target looked so ineffectual. He called me into his room, and told me to give the soldier some gum, chocolate, and cigarettes as a bribe, then to reprimand him. He added a warning that none of it was to be eaten on board the ship, though the cigarettes could be smoked in the WC.

I did as Staff Sergeant Brown directed. I told the soldier, "If you're not careful, you'll never make it back to Japan." He took the items, but gave no reply. From the fragile, hastily constructed WC on deck (which tipped precariously toward the ocean each time a breeze blew) came a lavender stream of smoke that was whisked skyward by the wind. The toilet had no roof, and the men stood in line to use it, so he might as well have done his smoking in the hold. I did in fact reprimand him, but inwardly I hoped he would do something or other down below. I couldn't see us landing in Japan and then dispersing without *something* first taking place. Besides, I must have longed to atone for my treatment of Hikida by hoping that the soldier would raise a riot for which I would be punished.

Major Inoma was serving as commander of the makeshift unit on board, but I stayed down in the hold trying to avoid him. He searched me out anyway. I was amazed at how delighted he was that the ship was approaching Japan, and he declared that he was going to visit my relatives there. Once again he asked me to find him a job. I hoped that a certain *something*—having nothing to do with employment—would soon transpire between the two of us, but I was saddened as I looked at the major, who suspected nothing.

I latched onto another soldier and questioned him about the man who resembled Hikida. "Him? He's a madman. Didn't you know?" was the reply. He screwed his index finger against the side of his head. "They let him run loose because there aren't any rooms to lock him up in." Feeling desolate, I climbed up on deck to look for the lunatic. He was still tamely puffing away on a cigarette in the WC. It was true—a red strip of cloth denoting a mental patient had been sewn onto the back of his cap. That, I suppose, was his star. Now that I had been alerted, I did notice that his eyes jerked about irregularly. If he was a madman, though, I had greater contempt for those considered sane.

On the morning of the second day, after we had finished off our single daily ration of gruel and slumped down on our knapsacks, five or six American marines came sauntering in with their hands in their pockets. A few were whistling and cracking jokes. They appeared to be a pleasant enough group, but from their eyes it was obvious they were planning something, so the Japanese soldiers watched them closely. They divided up and started walking through the crowds of seated Japanese. They paid no attention to where they stepped, treading on knees and ankles here and there. Before long, I realized that they had their eyes riveted on the soldiers' necks. That seemed odd, but in the next instant one of the marines ripped the insignia off the collar of the sergeant seated just beside me. Then he stepped over me and pulled off the stars of the staff sergeant behind me. He stepped back over me and came to a halt in front of the staff sergeant seated in front of me. Comparing the two insignia he held in his hand, he flung the first across the floor as if he were playing hopscotch.

"What are you doing?" I asked him.

"You speak English? We're taking these as souvenirs. We forgot to bring any back from Okinawa."

"Do the repatriates always have their stars taken away like this?"

"This is our first voyage. I don't know what anybody else does."

"Does Sergeant Brown allow you to confiscate stars?"

"He wants them more than anybody."

"What happens if this leads to trouble among our men?"

"This!" He pretended to be firing a machine gun.

I learned from this experience that badges of rank were taken as souvenirs of battle, in the same way that enemy heads and ears had once been taken as the spoils of war.

Nearly all the NCOs' stars were appropriated by this band of marines. They then lined up the stars and chose the prettiest among them. While this was going on, I spotted some Japanese who looked as though they wished it were their very selves that had been snatched from them. I could no longer bear to watch this humiliation. Amidst cheers and screeches, the marines gleefully arranged the stars in several rows down the passageway.

Finally they marched off in triumph, heading next perhaps for an invasion of the officers' quarters. Something like a sigh filled the hold. This was followed by the sound here and there of stars being yanked off uniforms. But the men seemed at a loss what to do with the plucked stars. Then one man tossed his into the air, and the others began to follow suit. Some even chuckled as they did so. I kept my eyes on the mad soldier, but he had fallen back and was staring blankly at the ceiling. His lethargy seemed to stem only partly from the fact that he had no star to toss.

Unable to endure the spectacle any longer, I stood up and shouted, "You mustn't tear off your stars. They're priceless! Stop it!!" I repeated the words again and again, until those around me stopped hurling their stars about and gathered around me. One of them cried, "Who is this bastard? I'll get his!" He lunged and ripped off my insignia, then trampled on the three PFC stars with his boot and knocked me to the floor.

I climbed up onto the fiercely rolling deck. Inoma, bereft of his stars, stood there smiling.

"George! Brown took my knapsack and boots."

In their place he wore a pair of American army boots. Suddenly I recalled that his feet were larger than average.

. . . Inoma and the other soldiers were now looking for new stars.

With a list of its prow and a blast from its whistle, the LST entered Sasebo Harbor. Hills came into view through the morning mist. Their color seemed so familiar I became almost frantic to identify it. I paced back and forth on deck, wanting to ask people, "What color is that?" Then I stopped in my tracks. I realized that the hills were the color of the khaki uniform I wore.

ARE THE TREES GREEN?

Yoshiyuki Junnosuke

Translated by Adam Kabat

Yoshiyuki Junnosuke belongs to that line of sensual writers stretching back to Ihara Saikaku in the seventeenth century and including Tanizaki Jun'ichirō and Nagai Kafū in the modern period. Generally considered by his contemporaries to have the finest-honed literary style today, Yoshiyuki has persistently focused on the physical relationships between men and women in his quest for an unsullied emotional purity. Most often that bond is discovered in the associations men have with prostitutes, relationships uncluttered by egotism and unfulfillable demands.

Yoshiyuki was born in Okayama in 1924, but raised in Tokyo. Exempted from military service by ill health, he studied English literature at Tokyo University for a time, but opted for a journalistic career midway through school. Plagued by respiratory problems (like so many of his fellow writers in Japan), Yoshiyuki was in the hospital when he received word that his story "Shūu (Sudden Shower, 1954; tr. 1972) had been awarded the Akutagawa Prize. Although a few of his novels have won recognition, including Anshitsu *(The Dark Room, 1969; tr. 1975) and* Hoshi to tsuki wa ten no ana *(The Moon and Stars Are Holes in the Sky, 1966), Yoshiyuki's best work has been done in the short story, and in a peculiarly Japanese genre of fiction known as the* rensaku*—a cycle of stories linked by theme and character but more loosely bound together than a novel. Yoshiyuki's best work in the* rensaku *form is* Yūgure made *(Toward Dusk, 1978), a Noma Prize-winning book about a middle-aged man who seeks obsessive-*

ly for an emotional rather than physical virginity in his mistress.

The present story, "Kigi wa midori ka" (Are the Trees Green?), was published in 1958.

* * *

Iki Ichirō came to a stop on the overpass, and turned to face the twilight streets spreading out below him.

Every day he would leave for work at the same time. And every day he would stand still on top of the bridge and look out on these streets.

The town was half sunk in a kind of mist. It was hard to tell whether this was a genuine mist or rather the smoke rising from the numerous tall chimneys of the area, forming a layer that covered the streets. In any case, the town was always shrouded in mist.

When he looked out on the shrouded town, he would experience two different emotions. One was a feeling of ennui at the thought of having to go down into the town. It was oppressive just to think of the monotonous work waiting for him there. How much better if he could retrace his steps from the bridge, return to his room, crawl under the bedding, and go back to sleep.

The other was a stimulus at the thought of descending into the unfathomable, shadowy depths of the mist. He would have one or the other of these feelings, varying with the day.

Whichever one he experienced would serve him as a barometer to measure his own mental state. He would, therefore, purposely come to a stop on the bridge.

Today he could barely conjure up any desire to go on into the town below. For a while Iki remained standing on the overpass.

Since the small overpass straddled high, bulldozed cliffs, the people walking on the streets below looked about the size of cats and dogs.

For the most part the scenery viewed through the mist was made up of numerous parallel and intersecting railway tracks, glistening leadenly. One rectangular freight car, as if left forgotten on a siding. Gas tankers squatting blackly in the space beyond the tracks. Countless chimneys looking as if they had been cut out of gray paper and pasted on. Further back, a faint glimpse of the sea. The twilight sun gleaming dully.

Today the scenery affected him badly. On a day like this the thought of descending the long, narrow stone steps clinging to the cliff made him uneasy. The steps formed a path to the town below. He wanted to turn back. But he started down the steps after all.

The stone steps were crumbling. Halfway down, a junior high school student was sitting, memorizing vocabulary cards. When he walked around him unsteadily, he could make out the student's mutterings as he stared at the cards.

"Con . . . gra . . . tulations, congratulations." Congratulations, hmm, *omedetō*.

Simultaneously, the faces of a group of young men and women floated before Iki's eyes. In half an hour Iki would be addressing these faces. He was a high school teacher for a night school class.

"Hey, Ichirō. It is Ichirō, isn't it? I haven't seen you for ten years."

The owner of the voice was right in front of him, thrusting out his own face and peering into Iki's. A man about fifty years of age, wearing white overalls and sandals. Iki was momentarily at a loss. But from beneath those worn and wrinkled features a younger face soon came back to him.

"Oh, Mr. Yamada. You've aged a bit."

"Life's been rough."

His brow darkened as he searched his pocket, brought out a cigarette, and stuck it in his mouth. His hands, covering the lighted matchstick while he brought it to his mouth, were trembling violently.

Iki's eyes fell on these hands. As the smoke rose from the cigarette, the man threw away the matchstick irritably and dug both his hands deep into his coat pockets. It seemed as if he was nervously trying to hide his shaking hands. The cigarette still in his mouth, he spoke as though pushing the words out.

"It's from drinking too much bad alcohol. Anyway, it certainly doesn't affect my work."

While talking, he kept staring at Iki's hatless head.

"You've turned into the spitting image of your late father. The shape of the head is the same too. That's not an easy head to work with. I was the only one who could cut your father's hair. Who's doing yours now?"

"No one in particular. I go to whatever barbershop's around."

"You can't just go to any barbershop, you know. Look how untidy your hair's become. I'll cut it for you. Why don't you come with me now? My shop's close by."

The barber looked worn out, and seeing his hands shake so, Iki felt incapable of refusing his offer.

Iki's usual route would have taken him a short way along the street below the stone steps, until he came to the station; instead he walked with Yamada in the opposite direction, cutting through the bulldozed cliffs. After covering a fair distance, they reached a spot where shops lined both sides of the road. They had already come as far as the next section of town.

The barbershop's red and blue pole was turning round and round. Yamada came to a halt in front of the shop.

On the glass front door the name HANDSOME was written in gold letters. Yamada turned and smiled in embarrassment.

"It's not a very good name, is it? The owner here chose it. Actually, he's a pretty impressive fellow. A long time ago, he even had a prince for a customer once. By the way, I'm planning on having my own shop again soon, just like before."

"I had no idea you were back. I've been living here for a while too."

"Ten years pass and I'm back near where I started. Well, come on in."

The two had both lived in the same town, but their houses had been burned during the air raids. It had been a while before they could return home.

The moment Iki sat down in front of the mirror, Yamada started vigorously combing his hair. Yamada's hand, holding the comb, was shaking as violently as it had been before. He dug the trembling comb deep into Iki's hair and then yanked it through.

Iki became uneasy. He was imagining these hands wielding a pair of scissors or a razor.

But as soon as Yamada raised the scissors in midair the trembling stopped completely. His other palm was already fluttering effortlessly around Iki's head.

"The more I look at it, the more your head resembles your father's.

The back sticks out and the top is flat. It looks just like a blimp seen from the front. I'm the only one who can cut this shape of head."

Along with the chatter of the glistening scissors, Yamada went on talking nonstop.

"How many years is it since your father died?"

"About eighteen now."

"Time goes by, doesn't it? Since he died when he was in his mid-thirties, he'd still be quite young if he was alive today. And yet he managed to do more in his life than most people have by the time they're eighty. Everyone said so at the time."

"They say he had double a man's share of food and women."

"That's for sure. Don't ask me why, but just before he died he used to invite me out specially and take me around. At that time I knew your father better than anyone. Anyway, he had quite an extravagant way of living."

Iki would sometimes—quite frequently, actually—run into people who had known his father. Each had inside him his personal image of what his father had been like. There were also people who, without ever having known him in person, had concocted their own impression of him.

Without exception, each of these images concealed a thorn of some kind. A thorn that pierced Iki.

Iki had always felt at a loss when asked what his father did for a living. From acquaintances of his he'd heard various accounts.

An artist.

A stockbroker.

Didn't I hear that he made perfume once?

A libertine.

Now the barber Yamada had described him as a man with an extravagant way of living. And as far as Iki could tell there was no hidden sarcasm behind his words.

"It's funny, isn't it? Why would somebody with all those friends end up spending his last days with me?"

He said it in a tone of simple boasting. It occurred to Iki that Yamada was somebody with whom his father would have felt comfortable. And the very fact that his father chose someone like Yamada to be his sole companion during his final days was, for Iki, a clue to the weakening of his father's spirit.

This wasn't the only thorn hidden in Yamada's portrait of Iki's father. In between the sounds of the scissors, Yamada's words rang harshly in his ears.

"Anyway, what are you doing now?"

"I'm a night school teacher."

"Hmm."

For a while Yamada kept quiet.

Iki knew exactly what the barber was thinking: "A night school teacher sounds pretty unexciting. He's nothing like his father. He's probably irritated by the fact himself." Such thoughts were a bother to Iki. The feeling of having to explain that he wasn't irritated was in itself a source of irritation. Moreover, when Iki thought that the explanation wasn't likely to be understood—how useless it was—he became all the more irritated.

There was just too big a difference between Iki's image of his father and Yamada's.

Yamada, silent for a while, started chatting again.

"How old are you?"

"Thirty-three."

"Single?"

"Nope."

"Hmm, any children?"

"One boy, in the second grade."

"Hmm. When your father was your age, you were already in middle school. Anyway, your heads are like two peas in a pod. I know how to cut your hair. When you think about it, time flashes by, doesn't it? I cut your hair from the time you were in grammar school. So, why not bring your son with you on your next visit."

While sitting in the barber's chair, Iki recalled his father's face as it looked twenty years ago, and Yamada's face too. Both seemed youthful, daring.

As a boy in grammar school, Iki Ichirō had kept his hair long, and for a certain period at that time, it had been painful even to think of Yamada's barbershop. This was directly related to his long hair.

One winter vacation, Ichirō and his father spent some time alone together at a hot spring resort situated in a countrified, backward area. It was a mystery to Ichirō why his father, who had such a restless personality, should choose to stay at this place. The whole time there his father was in a bad mood.

Ichirō, always at his side, became the perfect vent for his ill humor. All of a sudden, he started taking the boy to task for one thing or another.

"Ichirō, your hair gets in the way of your eyes. You should get a crew cut. Let's go to the town barber."

Ichirō shook his head stubbornly. His father responded in an angry tone.

"The year after next you'll be in middle school. It's the rule that all middle school boys have crew cuts, so you might as well get used to it now."

From as far back as he could remember, Ichirō had had long hair. He couldn't stand the thought of having it cut off. He continued to refuse, even more stubbornly. Then, suddenly, his father's mood changed.

"I suppose there's nothing I can do about it. I'll let it pass this time. But as soon as we get home I'm taking you to Yamada's barbershop."

In time his father completely forgot about the matter.

But occasionally he would remember. He would remember with a surge of impatience, and would try to drag him there.

A year later, in summer, his father revived the issue with a violence that Ichirō finally found impossible to resist.

Yamada held his hair between his fingers, as Ichirō sat in the high barber's chair.

"So it's finally time for your crew cut. Don't take it too hard now."

He was looking at Ichirō's face in the mirror, grinning.

"I'm fine."

Ichirō smiled back, but the smile stiffened a bit. Yamada pressed the cold blade of the hair clippers against his forehead. Then he briskly began cropping off his hair.

In five minutes Yamada had cut off all the hair on just the right side of his head. He put down the clippers and lit a cigarette. After a few long puffs, he wandered into the back of the shop.

Reflected in the mirror was a grotesque head, on the right side a blue crew cut, on the left the remaining long hair. Ichirō, feeling impatient and embarrassed, waited for Yamada's return. The barber remained out of sight.

At one end of the long mirror in front of Ichirō the street outside the shop was visible. In the street inside the mirror floated the reflection of a young girl. She was wearing sandals, and coming slowly toward him. The girl was known for her good looks, and she and Ichirō knew each other by sight. His body stiffened under the large white barber's cloth as he imagined her peeking through the window. Only his hideous head poked out above the white cloth.

If she did peer into the shop, Ichirō had resolved to stare back at her deliberately, open his eyes wide, and stick out his tongue. Clowning like this was the only means he could think of to protect himself. But Ichirō was also aware that such behavior was alien to him. He knew that he was a melancholy, introverted, unchildlike child. In the end he prayed that she wouldn't look into the shop.

Finally Yamada reappeared from the back. What remained of his cigarette was short enough to burn his fingers. He rubbed it out in an ashtray, and gave himself a good stretch.

"Well, shall I cut off the rest?"

At that moment, Yamada's pale, hollow-cheeked face was reflected in the mirror. His close-shaven beard had a bluish tinge. The words "a heartless handsome youth" floated into Ichirō's head. It was hardly an expression one expected from a sixth-grader. He had probably remembered it from some magazine story.

About twenty years had passed since that day.

As he sat in the high barber's chair, Iki noticed that Yamada's face had wrinkles that hadn't been there before. Nor was there any trace of the sharp lines that had once suggested a certain heartlessness.

Moreover, the man who had caused the young Ichirō so much suffering—namely, his father—had already left this world. But as the memory faded, he muttered to himself, "I've still got to watch my step, even if he isn't alive."

Yes, at all costs Iki had to watch his step. And yet, submerged in his memories, he had already slipped.

In between the sounds of the glistening scissors, he could make out Yamada's mutterings.

"I'll have to cut off more here."

Before Iki's very eyes his head began to take on a new, strange shape.

"Oh, I wouldn't make it too short there."

This diffident resistance was immediately crushed beneath the barber's confidence and enthusiasm.

When the clicking of the scissors stopped, Iki saw reflected in the mirror the shape of a schoolboy's head.

Iki was flustered. "How can I possibly appear in front of a class looking like this? What a mess," he muttered. But this wasn't the only reason Iki was flustered on seeing his haircut.

The other reason didn't come to him in any clear shape. Or rather, he hesitated to look directly at what it was. He only focused on the fact that his haircut didn't suit a teacher.

Yamada was energetically sharpening a razor on a leather strop. When he returned to Iki's side, he said,

"There. Now you look like two peas in a pod. So from here you're going to your night school, are you?"

When Iki stared at his face in the mirror—the face that Yamada had likened to a pea in a pod—he turned to his father and asked: "Even though you've been dead now for eighteen years, did you still want to take me to Yamada's barbershop?"

The face in the mirror rose straight to the ceiling and disappeared. Yamada had suddenly tipped back his chair.

Yamada started shaving his face.

"Your father was quite stylish. I used to shave his sideburns at a slant," he said in a nostalgic tone. Iki was annoyed at being placed in this situation. He said loudly,

"Shave me that way too. Shave my sideburns at a slant."

The nostalgic glisten in Yamada's eyes turned to an inquisitive shine. Finally, he answered dispiritedly:

"That style isn't fashionable any more, so I wouldn't recommend it. Besides, you're a schoolteacher. Anything too fancy would look strange."

When Iki left the barbershop his head felt cold. The chill went all the way down his back.

The lights were already on in the winter streets. From the loudspeaker of a radio store, music flowed out into the road. As he passed the shop, he could make out a man's voice singing.

Even though he was walking slowly, it wasn't long before he could no longer hear the music. He had only caught a small part, but he was vaguely familiar with the song.

The lyrics were fairly saccharine.

On a dark evening, a man stands alone on a cliff. Suddenly he feels a pliant breast in the palm of his hand. The flesh is so full it pushes its way between his open fingers. It is an illusory sensation. A moment later, the breast begins to melt before his very eyes, and turns into a milk-colored mist that flows through his fingers to merge with the pale twilight. The man, alone, stares at his empty palm as he stands on the cliff.

A young girl floated into Iki's mind. He shook his head in an effort to throw off the illusion.

He was moving his neck unsteadily right and left. His head felt light and cold. A clear picture of this head with its schoolboy haircut hovered before his eyes. Paradoxically, this made it all the harder to shake off the image of the girl that now clung to him.

The reason he had been so upset on seeing his head in the barbershop mirror was directly related to a girl called Kawamura Asako.

When he arrived at the school gate, the second period classes had already started.

Iki crossed the schoolyard and walked toward his classroom. The corner of the yard where people left their bicycles was too small for all the vehicles that lay scattered about. The night-class students rode to school on various vehicles they had used at their jobs during the day. There were scooters, small trucks, and even one bicycle from whose side hung a gaudy advertisement for a painting service.

As soon as Iki walked into the classroom there was a commotion among his students. Ordinarily Iki had no problem discerning the real reason for this: it came both from students who were disappointed that the class wouldn't be canceled after all, and from the more serious individuals who were annoyed that the teacher's lateness had caused a loss of valuable time.

But tonight Iki felt that the commotion was their response to his haircut.

Iki was standing alone on the dais as all the faces in the room turned in unison toward him. The experience was one familiar to every teacher, but he felt as if fate had played some absurd trick on him.

He looked down, opened the textbook on his desk, and asked one of his students to translate. As the boy began, the many eyes that had been turned in Iki's direction all looked down at their respective books.

When the boy's voice stopped, a girl suddenly got up. Iki tensed when he realized it was Kawamura Asako. She almost never came forward with a question. What on earth was she going to say? Iki waited with bated breath.

What emerged from her mouth was an ordinary question.

But once again all the eyes in the room looked up from their books and turned in Iki's direction. In fact, it seemed as if they were comparing Iki and the girl.

Until Iki had looked at his newly cropped hair from Yamada's barber's chair, Asako had been nothing more to him than a girl who had vaguely caught his eye. Or at least he had made himself believe that this was so. One could even say that he'd convinced himself that he had no alternative but to believe so.

"When you fall in love with a young girl, you want even your hair to look like a schoolboy's, do you?"

Iki found himself thinking that a voice had said this somewhere in the classroom. In fact, the voice had first come secretly to him as he was sitting in the barber's chair. The mirror image of his head had seemed to Iki as if it were his own heart laid bare.

Growing louder, the voice had clung to him, following him as far as the classroom.

Once again the fact that all the faces in the room were turned toward him forcibly entered Iki's consciousness. He found it difficult to endure.

Suddenly he felt his job no longer suited him.

It had been quite a while since Iki had known this overwhelming feeling. He had been teaching ever since he'd graduated from college; before then he had worked part-time while going to school. It had taken him twice as long as usual to graduate, and during that time he was frequently prone to such feelings about his work.

In those days it was easy for him to abandon whatever job he had and find new employment. But now he was no longer a college student working part-time. Now he had to search carefully inside himself to see whether he could simply drop what he was doing or not.

A certain scene floated into Iki's head. This small incident also focused on his dead father.

It was seven or eight years ago. At that time he was working for a small publisher.

He was outside a station, waiting for the actress Hanamura Hanae. He was wearing his black school uniform with the stiff collar. His job was to escort the actress to the hall where his publisher was holding a symposium.

Hanae was married to an American and lived in an area where it was difficult for Japanese to get in, so it had been arranged for him to meet her by the station. Since it was their first meeting, she had no way of recognizing him. It was up to him to keep his eyes open for the middle-aged actress, whose face he knew from photographs.

Hanae made no attempt to hide her displeasure when she realized that no car had been laid on. The editor of the poor publishing firm had advised him as follows: "Her husband is an American so she'll probably come by car. If she walks, then you might as well take the train."

Iki searched for a taxi, but it was almost impossible to find one in those days. Having no choice in the matter, he handed her a train ticket, apologizing profusely.

As they were going down the station stairs he realized that Hanae was pregnant. She seemed to be deliberately extending her stomach as she walked down the stairs.

Hanae's mood went from bad to worse. There were no empty seats on the train.

Iki knew something about her. He had heard that she had once been in love with his father, though it didn't seem to have been a very deep relationship. Moreover it was a long time ago. It occurred to him that if he told her he was Iki Akio's son, it might possibly touch a chord in her.

He hesitated for a while. But when he looked at Hanae's clearly angry, frowning face, he couldn't endure the discomfort any more.

He tried to make small talk, but she would answer bluntly and immediately revert to her original expression.

Finally he brought up his father's name. In matters of the heart there are things a third party cannot be aware of. There was the danger that mentioning his father's name would hurt her feelings. If that was the case, then so be it, he decided. He could no longer put up with the present situation.

Hanae's stiff expression crumbled immediately. Her attitude softened to a degree that was surprising even to him. He felt relieved and, at the same time, ashamed of having done something rather uncouth.

"Is that so? You should have said so earlier."

With the words "you should have said so earlier," he felt once again an extreme sense of failure. It was more than he could bear. And as a result he was suddenly overcome with the feeling that his work no longer suited him.

Invariably other people's portraits of his father concealed sharp thorns for him—even when these portraits were favorably drawn.

Hanae turned to look at Iki as if gazing off into the distance. She said, "Actually, you do look rather like him."

As Iki stood on the dais, her voice came back to him.

"Your heads are like two peas in a pod."

Hanae's voice overlapped with the barber Yamada's, and his recollection broke off.

Iki shook his head unsteadily right and left. His head—newly cropped by Yamada in a boyish style—was cold.

The next day, Iki stood on the windy platform, on his way to his night school class.

Three trains came heading in the opposite direction, but his still hadn't arrived.

As the wind got stronger, he felt as if his weak, malnourished body were fluttering in the wind. His head, with its new haircut, was extremely cold. He couldn't dispel the image of this haircut. For the second time, from out of nowhere, a voice came ringing in his ears. "When you fall in love with a young girl, you want even your hair to look like a schoolboy's, do you?" Iki flinched at the thought that a short time from now in his role as a teacher he'd be entering the classroom where Asako would almost certainly be sitting.

Again a train came going in the opposite direction. Its many windows, dyed yellow by the light inside the cars, flickered past him, until the train came to a halt.

The yellow light from the windows seemed warm. Without thinking, Iki got on the train. When the train started moving, he decided to visit his old friend Yui Jūji.

The company where Yui worked was located near the heart of the city. When one made one's way through the narrow streets caught between ferroconcrete buildings, and crossed a bridge, the scenery changed dramatically.

The roads were crumbling and uneven. The smell of deep-frying oil floated through the air. A group of housewives, wearing aprons and carrying baskets, stood in front of a butcher shop.

Yui's office was on the second floor of a small, wooden building sandwiched between a store selling weights and measures and a noodle shop.

Yui was working behind his desk. A young woman wearing a red sweater at the corner desk was folding paper designs out of small squares of wax paper from caramel candies. Two or three cranes, the size of peas, were lined up on her desk.

"Hey, Iki. It's been a long time."

As Yui looked up and spoke, he glanced at the wall clock.

"Already six, is it? Hey! Bring us some tea, will you."

The young woman went downstairs.

"She's new, isn't she?"

"They make me do all the piddling work, so I insisted they hire someone to help me with it."

"But don't you feel bad about it, speaking to her so roughly?"

"You've got to be kidding. Until now she's been working at some greasy spoon. She's told me herself that it makes her nervous to be treated any other way. She was orphaned by the atomic bomb, so she's suffered a lot. There's a lot of good in her. Then again, because of what she's been through, there's a lot of bad in her too."

The girl returned, carrying three steaming teacups on a black tray. She placed the teacups in front of Iki and Yui. Holding the remaining cup in the palms of her hands, she began to sip the tea, standing in her corner of the room.

Yui spoke to her.

"You can go home now. Or do you want to go back with me?"

Then he turned toward Iki.

"Whenever she's alone with a man she feels there's something wrong if he doesn't try to seduce her. It seems to be a habit with her. Once in a while I have to bring it up. Anyway, Iki, what do you think of her tits? She deliberately wears sweaters to show them off."

Suppressing her laughter, the girl started getting her belongings together. Then, out of the corner of her eyes, she glared at Yui. Her eyes had a coquettish gleam.

"Do you mind waiting thirty minutes while I finish up this work? Let's stop for a drink on the way back."

At the small drinking spot that Yui had taken him to, Iki was feeling the effects of the cheap alcohol.

"You've really changed, haven't you? You've become as tough as leather."

Yui stared at Iki for a while. A strange look flitted across Yui's face, and he flung out a reply:

"I'm just tired."

"But, for example, the way you act toward the girl in the red sweater—I'm jealous. You're so casual."

Yui looked taken aback. He seemed to have realized he had made a miscalculation.

"Hey, you're in love with somebody, aren't you? I've no idea who it is, but I'm sure it's a young girl." He looked carefully at Iki's face. "Is that why you had your hair cut like that? Is that what happens when you fall in love with a young girl?" Yui burst into loud laughter.

The words were identical to those that had been echoing around Iki's head since the night before. But Yui, in fact, was the first person ever to have said them aloud.

There was no denying that Iki was interested in Asako. Yet he had never thought that he was in love with her.

He had met the barber Yamada by accident, had felt obliged to get a haircut, and now Yui had actually come out with those very words. All this provided fuel for the passion Iki was now feeling for Asako. It was as if the love that had been hidden until now had been exposed during these last two days.

But what did he really know about Asako? Iki asked himself. The two of them had never even talked alone together.

"What kind of a girl is she?" he heard Yui's voice say.

"She works at a cheap bar."

Iki's answer wasn't a lie. Asako worked in a small bar in the old part of town. The reason Asako was going to night school was not because she was working during the day. Rumor had it that it was because she hated the family business, and if she went to night school there would be just that much less time to help out at the bar.

No, Iki's answer hadn't been a lie. What he didn't tell Yui was that Asako was a pupil of his. In this case, the word "pupil" had something unsavory, corrupt to it. Suddenly a scene floated into Iki's memory. A field in summer. He was a middle school student. By the bus stop near the fish pond a group of grammar school students had gathered. They were waiting for the bus going to the lake.

A male teacher, in his thirties, was in charge of the group. He was sitting on a large tree stump by the side of the road, holding one of the girl students on his lap. The palms of his hands were slowly stroking the girl's body, through her clothing. Just when they seemed about to reach her legs, they would return to her flat, weak chest.

The teacher's eyes were slightly bloodshot, as if he had been drinking heavily. He half closed his eyes suggestively as he continued moving his hands. From a short distance away, Iki was standing as stiff as a stick, watching the scene intently. It seemed as if the grammar school students didn't understand what was really going on. A fourth-grade boy said in a loud voice,

"Hey, that's unfair. Yōko's getting all the teacher's attention."

A faint smile hovered about the teacher's lips as he went on stroking. The girl on his lap made no attempt to get away. On her childish but rather classic features floated the gloating expression of a woman in her prime who has managed to capture the affections of a man in power.

"She works in a bar, you say? Let's go there now, then."

Yui's voice brought Iki back from the past. Iki did know the location of Asako's bar. But he felt reluctant about going there. He couldn't bear the prospect of walking into Asako's bar as a customer and having Asako wait on him. He also felt that it would be painful for Asako.

"Let's go," Yui insisted.

"Why don't we do it some other time?"

"But why? If it's because you don't have any money, I've got enough on me."

"It's nothing to do with money."

"Then why?"

Yui would never give in unless he clearly came up with a reason. Iki regretted visiting Yui. He regretted getting on the train going the wrong way. He told his friend hesitantly,

"The truth is she's one of my students."

"Your student? What difference does that make? You're probably a regular there."

"I've never been there."

Yui stared hard at Iki's face. The doubt in his look finally vanished, and he smiled faintly.

"You really are in love, aren't you? Is your heart still there?"

Yui stuck out his finger and thrust it into the left side of Iki's chest.

"I'm surprised myself. A man of thirty shouldn't feel this way."

Iki spoke in a defensive tone, as if countering an attack. When he realized how he sounded, he added somewhat disgustedly,

"But isn't it better than losing your heart altogether?"

"I haven't lost my heart. My heart is right here."

Yui lifted his arm, twisted it, and tapped his elbow.

"My feelings toward the girl are probably the same, then. My heart's in my elbow as well."

"Is that so? Well, let's go there and make sure that's the case."

Iki now felt it would be too much trouble to refuse Yui. Besides, without being dragged into the situation, he would never, in the end, have an opportunity to visit Asako and see her at work.

"Let's go."

Iki stood up with a burst of energy.

It was after ten. By this time Asako should have returned from night school and be at work.

Iki entered the bar as if being pushed inside by Yui.

"Oh, it's Mr. Iki."

The moment he stepped inside the bar, he collided with this lively voice. Iki felt flustered as all the customers turned simultaneously toward him.

More than this, it was Asako's appearance that flustered him. He had imagined her lingering in the corner of the bar, her face bare of makeup, looking indifferent and bored. But Asako danced lightly up to Iki's side. When she sat down next to him, she brought her lips close to his ear and whispered,

"What a surprise. This is the first time you've come here, isn't it?"

Her mouth was painted with a deep red lipstick that seemed to escape its borders. Her skin was completely hidden under a thick layer of makeup.

"I wasn't planning on coming. My friend lured me here."

She reacted, as if covering up for his clumsiness:

"Are you saying there's something wrong about visiting the bar where your student works? If that's the case, I'll quit school. Then you can come all the time."

Asako spoke in the manner of a bar hostess used to dealing with men. He couldn't help staring at her face.

The thick makeup didn't make Asako ugly. If anything, her face was even prettier, more charming than usual. And yet there was too much of the artificial about her. There were times when a mature expression—or, more exactly, the expression of a forty-year-old woman—seemed to flit momentarily across her face. For Iki, the face seemed an enigma, thrust right before his eyes.

Yui was silently observing Asako. His eyes were shining. Iki had no idea what Yui was thinking or feeling, either.

"Does your father have a beard, by any chance?" Yui suddenly asked the girl.

"My father died when I was in grammar school. No, he didn't have a beard. Why do you ask?"

"When I look at your face, I can't help thinking so. Hey, Iki, you know the girl in the red sweater at my company? When you look at her face, can't you see her father with a beard? With a big moustache like a paintbrush. But her father died when she was three. Her mother was killed in the atomic bombing, leaving her an orphan. But her father had died before that. I've tried any number of times to make her remember. But you know the memory of a three-year-old. She did recall something about how, when her father hugged her and rubbed his cheek against hers, it felt scratchy and hurt. But that's no good. It could be the scratchiness of unshaven stubble, and anyway, there has to have been a full moustache or else it doesn't count. A big moustache like a paintbrush. There aren't any photographs either. And there's nobody who remembers her father. Even if he didn't have one, it's better to know for certain. It's not knowing either way that makes me uneasy."

"But what does this have to do with anything?" Iki asked. Yui gave his usual weak smile.

"I'm so bothered by it, I can't sleep with her. I can't even kiss her."

Then Yui caught Asako's eye.

"I could sleep with you."

Iki, taken aback at Yui's words, failed to catch Asako's reaction. He had wanted to see whether a girlish embarrassment at Yui's unexpected, improper remark would show on her face.

As far as Iki could tell, the only expression floating on Asako's face was the look of a bar hostess fending off a customer's joke.

"You're quite a character, aren't you," she replied.

When he looked at the girl's heavily made-up face, Iki began to feel flustered again. An ominous feeling was mixed in with his embarrassment. He had fallen into this selfsame mood before. When was it? Iki groped within his memory.

He followed a faint, vague, frail thread. The face of a bar girl with heavy makeup. There was something next to her. The angry face of his grandmother, his now dead grandmother, who for many years had been confined to her bed. It was when he had turned to face her, perhaps. No, that wasn't it.

Suddenly it came back to him.

"I remember now. It was the face of a kangaroo."

"What's that about a kangaroo? Mr. Iki, you're drunk."

"No, it's about my dead grandmother," Iki corrected himself, at once surprised by what he'd said.

"Your grandmother? Is it something to do with your childhood?"

"Umm."

"They say that when you fall in love you start getting nostalgic," Yui said in a teasing tone.

Ichirō was a first-grader at the time. A circus had been set up in a nearby field. A big tent had been raised, and around it, to attract customers, various animal cages had been lined up.

A black panther with glistening eyes was crouching in the back of a dark cage; a lion was shaking its mane as it paced about.

Next to one of the cages a notice had been posted: KANGAROO BOXING FOR THOSE INTERESTED. NO ADULTS ALLOWED. Inside the cage, a kangaroo, wearing gloves on its forelimbs, was standing erect on its tail and hind legs. There were a conspicuous number of children around the cage, but none of them would come forward to box with the animal.

When Ichirō looked at the ridiculous yet unsettling figure of the kangaroo, wearing gloves and standing upright inside the dark cage, he could no longer suppress his curiosity. He hesitated for a long while, but finally resolved to take up the challenge.

A circus man, wearing a colorful uniform like a toy soldier's, put the gloves on Ichirō's hands. He was led inside the cage. When he was face to face with the kangaroo, he found the animal taller than he was. The kangaroo was just standing still. But when Ichirō thrust out his fist, the animal followed suit, waving its gloves instinctively.

Ichirō's eyes met the kangaroo's. The kangaroo's eyes were a pleasant shape. They were eyes that looked dazed, that expressed almost no feeling. One might have expected to see hatred or fear of the person striking out at it. But there was nothing beyond a dumb look of amazement. He began to feel more and more uncomfortable looking at them. The smell of the caged animal suddenly assailed him. Ichirō, in an effort to shake off this unease, desperately continued to strike, but the kangaroo simply waved its arms about.

He must have seemed just a cheerful child to the crowd outside the cage, now watching and laughing merrily. But Ichirō, as he faced the kangaroo's head, was trapped inside this sense of unease.

The feelings that floated inside Iki now, as he confronted Asako's painted face, were the same feelings he had experienced so long ago.

"What do you make of it? It's as if she's become a completely different girl from the one I know at school," Iki said to Yui after they had left the bar. "I heard that the reason she was going to night school was because she hated helping out with the family business, and she wanted to make her hours that much shorter. And yet. . ."

"She's like a fish in water in that bar," Yui answered.

"I can't understand it. Her makeup was so heavy it looked as though you could take it off all in one piece—like a mask. Perhaps she's trying to hide her real self behind that painted mask."

When Yui heard this, he gave a hoot of laughter.

"You're crazy. If you're going to be so sentimental, you'll end up getting badly hurt before long. Haven't you sobered up yet? She had the charm of a well-polished prostitute."

"I haven't sobered up at all. But it's all so pathetic."

"The ending for a man in love is always bad. Anyway, what made you fall for someone you knew almost nothing about?"

"Who ever falls in love with people they know well? It's all the fault of the guy who cut my hair."

Iki left it at that, and said no more.

Was it that Iki's love for the girl, brewing secretly all the while somewhere deep in his heart, had suddenly come floating to the surface the moment he had seen his hair cut like a boy's? Or was it, rather, that the shape of his hair, unexpectedly cut in such a style, had drawn out an illusory love for a girl who had been lurking in his memory? At this point, Iki could no longer tell.

Iki tried to remember the face of the girl he always saw in class. For the second time the face of a large kangaroo floated before him, and superimposed itself on a girl with heavy makeup.

The image of the kangaroo now led him to his grandmother and another painted bar girl. Iki's grandmother, paralyzed from the waist down and bedridden, would experience violent emotional ups and downs. For a long time she had been living apart from his grandfather. Her hair was abundant and black, and there was still a youthfulness left in her unpowdered face. People told her again and again that it must be awful to be referred to as granny. Their words were meant sincerely, but were also meant to flatter her.

In grade school Ichirō was often put out by his grandmother's sudden changes in mood. She would read to him at length from a picture book. She seemed to enjoy doing it, so the following day Ichirō would approach her with the same book in hand, feeling sure this could only cheer her up. But the old woman's temper would suddenly turn sour.

"Act your age. You can read a picture book by yourself," she would say cuttingly.

Ichirō's father was sometimes brought home in a drunken stupor by a heavily made-up bar girl. His grandmother's attitude toward the woman would be completely different, depending on the day. A few days after Ichirō boxed with the kangaroo, the bar girl stuck her hand into the lion's cage at the circus, and beckoned to it. She must have been dead drunk. The lion leaped at her hand and tore into it with its sharp claws. Apparently, white bone peeped out from the ripped flesh.

There was something indecipherable about his grandmother when Ichirō was that age. There were times when her features seemed to merge into those of the kangaroo he had confronted in the cage.

But now Iki could easily understand the old woman's capricious moods. The key was clearly in his hand. He still didn't understand about the kangaroo.

Both his grandmother and Asako were human beings. The kangaroo was a kangaroo.

"I'm going to spend more time alone with Asako," he resolved, as he walked side by side with Yui down the night-dark road.

"I've got to be careful whenever my father or grandmother reappear," he murmured suddenly. He gave his head a good shake, as if to dispel the illusion. His head, with its boyish haircut, still felt cold in the night air.

The next day in class, Asako turned to Iki, her face as usual, without makeup.

What is it about her that attracts me? Iki asked himself.

Her eyes are nice; they have a rich color.

A rich color, but what color? Shining strongly, then suddenly losing their shine—changing over and over. Sometimes they gleam pathetically. A pathetic gleam? Yui's laughter echoed loudly in the empty air.

Suddenly Iki realized that until now he had never once seen Asako laugh. Last night the heavily made-up Asako was laughing constantly. But he had yet to see the unmade-up Asako laugh.

When he realized this, Iki's desire to try approaching her alone suddenly dropped away.

After a few days had passed, Iki finally decided to pay Yui another visit at his office. He thought that he would invite him out to Asako's bar with him again. He couldn't imagine entering the bar by himself.

That evening, too, Yui was at his desk, working. The girl in the red sweater was sitting at the corner desk.

Lying about on Yui's desk were numerous, severed pieces of a nude photograph. The photograph had been cut along the outlines of the body, and then divided into any number of smaller parts. By the side of a breast lay half an arm, and beside that a thigh—all scattered about on top of the desk.

"What are you doing?"

Yui turned to him, holding a large pair of scissors in his right hand.

"She's really come apart, hasn't she? This way I do two pages of color layout for free. A poor company like this has no money to spare for layouts. How does this look?"

With the tip of the scissors, Yui moved a picture of an upper arm with a palm attached so that it joined one of an arm cut off at the elbow.

"We're going to ask the reader to fit the pieces back together properly. The plan is to print the original photograph on the reverse page."

Yui rummaged through the muddle of papers on his desk and dug out a photograph. When Iki looked at the print, he couldn't help being shocked. It was a nude shot of the girl in the red sweater, in a horizontal pose.

"It's her. She has a good body—she boasts of it herself. You see, we save money on the model's fee."

Iki looked at the face of his old friend. His profile was exactly the same as in the past. It seemed blank, devoid of all identity. One felt as if a needle would never pierce it—as if it were a big glass ball polished to smooth perfection.

Was this, perhaps, a mask which even now could be removed from Yui's face? Or had it become part of his own flesh? Iki tried to recall the Yui he had known in his student days. Even if Yui had had a face like that, it must have been a mask back then. But now. . . In the end, he had no idea.

Inside Iki's mind, as he stared at Yui, floated one more face—the face of a painted Asako laughing coquettishly. Her expression, too, he found impenetrable.

In any case, Iki decided that he had to see Asako again.

STILL LIFE

Shōno Junzō

Translated by Wayne P. Lammers

Shōno Junzō was born in 1921, the third son of an Osaka educator. He began serious pursuit of an interest in literature during his student days at the Osaka School of Foreign Languages and Kyushu University, but his first tentative efforts at writing were interrupted when the intensification of the Second World War brought an end to draft deferments.

As soon as the war was over, Shōno took up his pen again while working as a middle school teacher in Osaka, and over the next few years he was able to have several stories published in Kansai-area literary journals. In 1949, he received encouraging attention from established literary circles in Tokyo for "Aibu" *(Caresses), a story about a young housewife and the feelings of emptiness and despair she experiences as she becomes increasingly disillusioned with her husband. Following this, he produced a number of stories in a similar vein, probing the emotional and psychological turmoils of young married couples who are faced with a variety of marital and financial crises or have otherwise become disenchanted with different aspects of their lives together. When one of these,* "Pūrusaido shōkei" *(Poolside Vignette, 1954; tr. 1962), won the Akutagawa Prize in 1955, Shōno's literary future was assured; he was able to leave the broadcasting company where he had worked since 1951 to devote himself exclusively to his writing.*

"Seibutsu" *(Still Life, 1960; winner of the Shinchōsha Literary Prize) is an early work, and one of the most important, in a long series of stories Shōno has written centering on a certain family of five. It is made up of eighteen separate episodes detailing the kind of commonplace, everyday occurrences that tend, especially in fiction, to pass unnoticed or to be quickly forgotten. Since most of the highly diverse episodes are entirely self-contained, the story offers very little by way of continuous narrative development. It derives cohesiveness instead from the juxtaposition and repetition of related imagery, and from thematic associations that emerge when the various sections are read not only literally but metaphorically. The title itself is suggestive, for "Still Life" is in many ways more a picture than a story: the reader's mind must play over the episodes as his eyes would play over the objects in a painting, moving back and forth between one set of relations and another or between the individual objects and the subject as a whole. Much of the power of the work rests upon the subtle gradations of light and darkness resulting from the interplay between shadowy background and vividly highlighted foreground.*

The family of five that appears in "Still Life" and its numerous sequels is virtually Shōno's own, and the conversations and activities described are closely modeled on real-life occurrences. His work is thus rooted firmly in the "I-novel" tradition that has played such a prominent role in modern Japanese literature since the beginning of this century. Where many other contemporary I-novelists have written of the disintegration of the family, however, Shōno's concern is often with the little things in life that hold—or at least can *hold—a family together. In extraordinarily simple language and with a remarkable eye for detail, Shōno shows us the essential beauty and significance of the most mundane of human experiences—experiences that may seem trivial and meaningless but are in fact the very fiber of life.*

* * *

"Can we go to the fishing pond?" the boy pleaded.

It was a beautiful, windless day in early March, and spring seemed just around the corner.

"You don't want to go fishing," his father said. "You know you'd never catch anything."

"I do too want to. All the kids go. Masuko caught five the other day."
"What were they?"
"Goldfish."
"Oh. Goldfish." The father's voice showed his disappointment. "It's not much fun if all you get is goldfish."
"It is too fun. Some of the kids even catch big ones."
"Oh?"
"You'll catch something too, Dad. You will." The boy would be entering the second grade in another month.
"I don't know," the father said. "It'd be my first time. The only fishing I've ever done was in the ocean. I've never been to one of those artificial ponds." Even to him the excuse sounded rather feeble.
"You should try it," chimed in his daughter, soon to be a sixth-grader. "Who knows? You just might catch something. And so what if you don't? It'll be fun anyway."
"I suppose you're right," he said. "I'll never know if I don't give it a try."
"If all three of us go, maybe at least one of us'll catch something," the girl said, seeing that her father had abandoned his reluctance. She often spoke to him like this, in an encouraging tone, when he seemed hesitant or worried about something. It was a remarkable way she had with him.

On the morning of the accident so many years before, this girl had lain in the corner of the room with her stuffed dog, alone like an orphan, oblivious to the possibility that anything could be wrong. She had been just over one year old then.

"Have a good time!" the mother called after them. "Come home hungry now, all of you." The three-year-old boy had to stay behind. He was too small to go fishing.

As they left the house, the father had a pleasant feeling inside. It always felt good to set out on something he had never done before. And the children's enthusiasm was contagious.

The boy had brought along the tin bucket he used for his water projects in the yard. As they walked, the father watched it swing back and forth at his son's side. He should get out and do these things more often, he told himself. It was better to go along, to stop making excuses. It didn't really matter whether or not they caught anything. They had set out, bucket in hand—that was the important part. It seemed a little thing, perhaps, but little things often made the biggest difference.

To begin with, anything was better than just sitting around doing nothing. All he ever did on his days off was loaf about the house. He never made plans for a Sunday outing, much less went anywhere when Sunday finally came. Sometimes he felt sorry for his family. But he had been this way for a long time now, and the children had grown used to it. So far as they were concerned, holidays were for staying at home and playing by themselves. They had fun enough.

Still, it wasn't good for him to be so lazy. After all, the fishing pond was hardly ten minutes away.

Down the road, the pond came into view, surrounded by rice paddies. Beyond it rose the slope of a wooded hill. There were two ponds, actually—one stocked with small fish, for beginners, and the other with larger fish, for more experienced fishermen. As might be expected on a Sunday, both were crowded.

"One adult and one child," the father said, as if he were buying tickets for the train. He didn't know any differently, since this was the first time he had come. He paid for an hour and got two fishing poles and some bait. But the last person to use one of the poles had returned it with the line badly tangled. No doubt he had gone home in a huff after failing to catch anything. The father couldn't tell where to start, so he asked the lady at the gate to unravel it for him.

"There you go." She handed the pole back to him with a smile.

"It's fixed?"

"Yes, it should be okay now."

Too eager to wait, the boy had run on ahead, but now he was back. "C'mon, Dad, hurry up," he shouted. "I found a good spot. Over there." The place he pointed to, however, was at the pond for experienced fishermen. Not one of the people there was using the sort of flimsy pole the three newcomers had rented. It was also more expensive to fish there.

"We can't go over there," the girl said.

"But you should see. There's lots of big ones."

"No," the girl said softly. "That pond's too hard for us. Beginners have to fish here."

"Oh."

After the lady had shown him how to bait the hooks, the father joined the children at the beginners' pond. There were quite a few adults fishing there, too—men fishing alone, young married couples fishing together.

The three of them shared the two poles, but they failed to get so much as a nibble. Whenever someone else caught something, the boy ran off to have a look, and each time he would call back in a loud voice, "It's better over here, Dad."

"Listen," the father admonished. "Whether you catch anything or not, you're better off staying in one place. When somebody over there catches something, you might think it's a better spot, but it isn't really. It just seems that way. Some people are good at it and some people aren't, but even the good ones have to wait and be patient and not change places all the time if they want to catch anything. You'll never have any luck if you don't sit still."

His own words reminded him of a story he had read in English class in junior high school. It was called "Stick to Your Own Bush." As he remembered it, several children go off into the woods to pick wild raspberries. They spread out among the raspberry bushes scattered here and there, and before long shouts of "I found some! I found some!" ring out, first from one direction, then another. One of the boys, who has yet to find a single berry, races about from place to place pursuing each new shout. When all the others have filled their baskets, he has only a few berries. "You'll never get very many that way," he is told. "Stick to your own bush." And that was the moral of the story—that it's the same with everything we do.

As a boy he had found it a dull and uninspiring story. But now he was a father, and here he was, telling his own son the same thing.

The scolding put an end to the boy's shouting, but, with no change in their own luck, he still darted off periodically to examine the fish that other people caught.

From where the father was sitting he could not actually see the fish in the water. He had to admit there might not be any there. Nonetheless he stuck to his own bush.

"I guess this isn't our day," he said to his daughter beside him. "It's not so easy after all." She went on gazing at her float.

Every now and then women with shopping baskets passed along the road in front of the pond. Some of them stopped briefly to watch the fishermen. The father had been observing these movements on the road when he turned around to find his float bobbing up and down. He raised his pole with a jerk. On the end of the line was a tiny orange glimmer.

"We got one!" cried the girl.

The boy, who had been watching an older boy fish, heard her voice and came running.

"We got one! We got one!" he clamored.

"Simmer down. Don't make such a racket," the father scolded. But his face beamed. It was indeed a tiny goldfish that had come up on the end of his line, hardly any bigger than a guppy.

Now for the first time they had a use for the bucket the boy had brought along. The little fish swam about in the pail as if to belie the fact that a moment ago it had been caught on the tip of a hook.

"W-w-when they've tried it once," the elderly doctor said, "they get so they try it again and again."

"That's what I was afraid of," the young husband sighed. Never had he imagined that only three years after his marriage he would feel so beaten and discouraged.

"At least that's frequently the case."

Would it happen again? he had asked disconsolately. Was she likely to try it again?

"T-t-t-t-taking it hard, are you?" The doctor burst into a boisterous, stuttering laugh. But there was a measure of sympathy in his voice. This distinctive laugh of the doctor's had long been familiar to the young man.

"Once is enough, I suppose?"

"It certainly is."

The doctor reached for the bottle and poured some more whiskey for his guest. The young man watched as the dark liquid rose inside the glass.

"These things can happen. You just never know," the doctor said. He picked up the pitcher and mixed a little water with the whiskey. "It's like trying to find your way in the dark."

The old doctor's sitting room was an annex of sorts, built on a level slightly higher than the main section of the house. He spent most of his time alone here, apart from the rest of his family. When he needed something, he simply clapped his hands. He never left the room except to see a patient.

The two sat facing each other, the bottle of whiskey on the table between them. Somehow, the young man always felt reassured when he talked with the old doctor like this.

The young man had been born and raised in this town, and his earliest memory of the doctor's clinic went back to when he was in the third grade. One day he was playing in a field near his house with a friend, running about barefoot on the grass, when all of a sudden he stepped on a piece of wood with a large nail sticking through it. His friend rushed off to get his mother, while he sat there crying. It had seemed an eternity before she appeared at the edge of the field.

The next thing he remembered was lying on an examination table in a dimly lit room while the doctor removed the nail. Tense faces peered down at him from above.

That had been his first visit to this place.

"H-h-how's her foot coming along?" the doctor asked. "Where she burned it."

"I think it still hurts her to walk on it."

"Yes, I'm sure it does. The burn's right on the bottom of her foot."

"She claims it doesn't bother her any more though."

The doctor gave him a sympathetic smile, then lowered his eyes.

"I was practically in a state of shock myself," the young man said after another sip of his drink. "I didn't realize the cloth had come loose."

"Of course, of course," the doctor laughed with his usual stutter. "It was hardly the time you would notice something like that. Not even your wife noticed, and it was her own foot."

The young man remembered the chill he had felt when he touched his wife's arms and legs. At first he had still been able to detect a slight warmth, but gradually her body had turned colder and colder. Frantically, he had filled three hot-water bottles with piping hot water and put them in her bed: one on either side of her chest, the third at her feet.

Later he had held her—first one way, then another—for the doctor to examine her. Beads of sweat had dripped from his forehead. He couldn't tell exactly when she had been burned; the cloth he had wrapped around the hot-water bottle must have come loose when her legs moved.

The doctor reached for the whiskey and poured himself another glass. "This kind of burn can be a real problem. I've had cases before: people go to bed with a hot-water bottle and don't realize they've burned themselves until the next morning."

"So it happens often?"

"I guess if you're sleeping soundly it doesn't hurt enough to wake you up. They take a long time to heal. The damage goes a lot deeper than other burns."

In his mind the young man pictured his wife still limping a little from the accident as she made her way about the quiet house.

"'Eight-year-old Suzie died three days after coming down with the flu,'" the father read from the paper. He had found an article among the news from America that he thought the others might like to hear. They were all sitting around the breakfast table, eating.

"Suzie is a little black girl," he explained before reading on. "'Many friends and neighbors came to express their sympathy to the grief-stricken parents. The funeral service took place without incident. But then, when it came time to lower the casket into the grave—'"

"Did something go wrong?" the girl broke in.

The father answered her interruption with a sharp look that said "Let me finish," then continued the story. "'When the parents raised the lid of the casket for a final look at their daughter, Suzie opened her eyes and said, "Mommy, can I have some milk?" The entire town went into an uproar.'"

"She came back to life?" the girl asked. She seemed anxious to have her father say it in so many words.

"That's right, she came back to life."

"Weird," the older boy said, and flopped backward onto the tatami. The three-year-old promptly followed suit.

"Imagine what a shock it would have been!" the father said. He tried to form a mental picture of the small southern town where Suzie and her parents lived, though, of course, he could not really tell how the houses or streets would look. The cemetery would be on the outskirts of town, no doubt, but what was the surrounding area like?

"What an awful story!" his wife said.

"Why? What do you mean?"

"Oh, I don't know," she said, looking very ill at ease. "I mean, my goodness, the child was supposed to be dead when all of a sudden she wakes up and starts talking. If I were the mother, I'd have been terrified." Her husband stared back at her but said nothing. "Wouldn't *you* be scared?"

Suddenly a strange voice filled the room: "Mommy, can I have some milk?"

It was the girl. She had leaned back against the wall and was gazing blankly into space, pretending to be Suzie at the moment she came back to life.

What would it sound like? the father wondered: the voice of someone who had all but entered the realm of the dead and then returned suddenly to the brightness of this world.

"Ohhh, don't do that," the mother scolded the girl. "It gives me the shivers."

The goldfish from the Sunday excursion was given a place in the children's study. It swam about happily in its glass bowl on the sill of the bay window.

"What a healthy goldfish!" the mother often exclaimed. She was the one who looked after the new family pet most of the time—changing its water, feeding it little scraps of bread, and giving it a pinch of salt every now and then.

When the father and children had come home with their tiny catch in the toy bucket, she had remarked on what a nice shape it had. It was true, the father had had to agree: it might be only so big, but it did have a nice, sleek body.

An almost invisible tinge of red showed here and there on its stomach and fins as well as on its head.

"I caught it when I was looking the other way," he had said. "We'd better take good care of it."

The study held quite a few things besides desks and bookshelves for the two children who were in school. Their mother's dresser was kept here, together with her sewing machine. In one corner was a basket containing some wooden blocks, the base of a ring-toss game, a baseball glove, and several other items—the few toys the children had not yet broken. In another corner stood two large suitcases, one on top of the other. They had seldom been used; most of the time they merely took up space.

To call it the children's study, then, was something of a misnomer. It was the room where they put everything that didn't fit anywhere else.

On the wall were two pictures. The one entitled "Star Children" had been done by the girl as a vacation project several summers before. Two little girls were holding hands and floating in a light blue sky, a star made of silver paper atop each of their heads. Their clothes had been cut from scraps of leftover fabric, and bits of yellow and gray yarn had been pasted on for hair. The second picture, entitled "Cowboys on the Plain," was a crayon drawing done by the older of the boys. One of the cowboys, a rifle at his shoulder, had just shot a large bird in a tree; the other was about to lasso a runaway horse. A bull came charging toward them and a rabbit was scampering by.

Two rattan chairs had also found their way into the room. Since they would block the doorway if set side by side, they were usually stacked on top of each other. The children liked to hitch these together with their desk chairs to make a stagecoach. One of them sat on the coachman's seat and the other two would get inside. Then, with many a shout and crack of the whip and clatter of the wheels, they would be off, racing full tilt along some old highway.

Such was the room into which the goldfish had come. It hardly seemed a safe place for a fragile glass bowl filled with water. There was no telling when a ball or some other toy might land in it, or when one of the children would get pushed against it and knock it over.

But incredibly enough, nothing happened. The children were no better behaved than they had ever been, yet somehow the bowl survived. As the days went by it blended in with the other things in the room, and no one worried about it any more.

Still, the father could never quite get over the feeling that someone would break it yet, someday.

"Good night, Dad!"

"Good night, Mom!"

"Good night, everyone!"

The echo of the children's voices seemed to linger in the air. Only a short while ago they had been racing to see who could put on his pajamas and make it into bed first. Now, with the hush of night settling over the house, only the father remained awake.

He contemplated the figure of his wife sleeping beside him. This woman, lying on her side, facing him—this was the woman he had married. For fifteen years he had slept with her, in the same bed, every night.

As a child he had slept alone, and in the army he had slept alone. But from the day he was married, he had started sharing a bed with another person. Two people who scarcely knew each other had begun to sleep together, just like that.

There had in fact been a short time when they did not share the same bed. How long had it been? Three months? Not even that, probably. They had slept in separate rooms, his wife with their baby daughter, who had just turned one. But the arrangement had come to a quick end. After the accident they had gone back to sleeping together. And they had done so ever since.

Awake alone in the stillness, the father thought back to their wedding night. He remembered the bright moonlight shining through the window, illumining his wife's face as she slept quietly beside him. She had hardly seemed to breathe. There was a small ribbon in her hair.

That was our first night together, he thought to himself.

The book he had been reading slipped from his hand. He picked it up again and started looking for his place.

"Here it is," he mumbled. "No, wait, I've read this already." He turned several more pages. Was this it? No, he remembered this part too. Where could it have been?

Choosing a page at random, he forced open his heavy eyelids and began to read. Within moments they drooped shut and the book fell from his hand.

"I forget if it was England or America, but I read a story about a boy who found a duck's egg and made it hatch," the boy told his father in their evening bath.

"He *hatched* a duck's egg?"
"Un-hunh."
"Where did he find it?"
"I don't know."
"Somewhere in the country?"
"Un-hunh, in the country."
"Near a stream or pond, I suppose."
"Maybe. Anyway, he wanted to make it hatch, so he tied it to his stomach with a piece of cloth."
"Where?"
"Right here." The boy cupped his hands at his side. The father could tell that he had picked the spot arbitrarily.
"He kept it warm like that all the time for twenty days or so. Even at school, and even when he went to bed."
"For twenty days?"
"Un-hunh, something like that, I don't remember exactly. Anyway, the egg finally hatched right in the middle of class, and the teacher and everyone was really surprised."
"That's amazing," the father said. "It actually hatched during class?"
"Un-hunh."
"And it surprised everyone?"
"Un-hunh."
"Is this something you read at school?"
"Un-hunh. On the bulletin board in the hall. There's a big paper with stories from all over the world."
"Was there a picture?"
"Some of the stories have pictures, but this one didn't."
"When did you read this story?"
"A long time ago."
"Back in first grade?"
"Un-hunh."
"And you happened to think of it now?"
"Un-hunh."
The father wondered what had made him remember the story. "You'd think he would've broken it," he said. "I wonder how he had it tied."

"I bet the egg wouldn't last a day if I did it," the boy said. "I'd forget about it when I was playing. Do you think you could do it, Dad?"

"No, I doubt it. Probably not," he said. "All right, ready to get out?"

"Yep." He jumped out of the tub.

"Just a minute," the father stopped him. "Did you wash your face?"

"My face?"

"If you have to think about it, you obviously didn't."

"Yes I did."

"Ohhh no, you can't fool me. Your face isn't even wet. Since when do you take a bath without washing your face? Come on. Stop stalling."

"Okay." The boy took the lid off the soap dish and filled it with hot water.

"Hey, no playing around now. Just wash your face."

"I will, I will." He laid his washcloth over the soap dish.

"Come on."

"Just a second." With a slow and deliberate motion he rubbed soap into the washcloth. Then, bringing the cloth to his lips, he blew on it gently. A soft bank of suds began to form.

"See."

"So that's what you wanted to do."

"Watch. They'll get bigger and bigger."

"Fine, fine. They're plenty big already."

"Isn't it neat?"

"Sure."

"You wanna try it?"

"No. You've shown me your little trick now, so hurry up with your face."

"Just a little more."

The heap of suds quivered gently as it swelled. Before long the boy's face was completely hidden.

"I wonder if you remember that movie we saw," the father said to his daughter. She was sewing a blouse for her doll.

"What movie?"

"When you were in the first grade. Or was it kindergarten? No, it wasn't the year we moved, but the year after, so you would've been in first grade."

The family had moved here from another city when the girl was in kindergarten. The older boy had just begun to say a few words; the second had not yet been born. The father could still remember the long train ride and his first glimpse of their new house standing by itself in the middle of some open farmland.

The following year, in winter, he had taken his daughter to see a movie.

"The foreman at a construction site falls into a pit being filled with concrete."

"Oh yeah, I remember," the girl said.

"How much do you remember?"

She stopped stitching. "The man was a carpenter, wasn't he?"

"Well, yes, he built houses. He laid bricks, though, so I suppose you'd call him a mason. He was in Italy at first, but then he got on a ship and came to New York."

"He was really poor."

"That's right. That was why he came to America. He couldn't make a living in Italy."

They had seen the movie in a theater at the back of a short alleyway, just off the main thoroughfare in front of the station. Even with their overcoats on, it had been chilly inside.

"He was sick or something and couldn't go to work."

"I think he had hurt himself," the father said, still trying to retrieve the details from his own hazy memory. "That's right. He becomes foreman of a demolition crew tearing down an old building, but then something goes wrong between him and his men and they don't get along very well any more. First the men stop speaking to him, then they walk out on him. So he has to work all by himself. Pretty soon a wall falls over on him and his leg gets crushed."

"That's why he couldn't work?"

"Something like that."

"Oh, I remember now. It's when his leg finally gets better and he goes back to work that he falls into the hole they're filling with concrete. He screams for help but there's too much noise and no one hears him. So the concrete keeps getting higher and higher."

"And in the end only his head shows."

"I covered my eyes, it was so scary. But I couldn't help hearing his screams."

"What happened next?"

"His wife comes out with kind of a blank look on her face, and someone's talking to her."

"Right. Since her husband was killed on the job, she's supposed to get paid a lot of money. Someone asks her what she plans to do with it, but she only shakes her head to say she doesn't know. Or maybe she means she hasn't even thought about it. Do you remember anything else?"

"Unh-unh."

"No? How about the book I bought you before we went into the movie?"

"Unh-unh." She picked up her sewing and began stitching again. Her father watched the way her hands moved.

As he remembered, it was a picture book, but he couldn't recall the title. He had bought her the book to try to make up for dragging her along, on their one day off, to a movie that *he* wanted to see. Not only was it a foreign film, but the things he had heard about it suggested that it might be a bit heavy-going for a six-year-old.

The first few scenes were mild enough. One of the mason's friends at work tells him he ought to get married, and suggests a girl he knows. The mason starts seeing the girl and falls in love with her. And she falls in love with him.

"But what about a house?" she asks. "I can't marry you if you don't have a house." Her family, too, had emigrated from Italy. She knows what it's like to be poor. She knows how miserable life can be for a couple who marry without a house of their own.

The mason tells her that he has a house, believing this is the only way he can get her to marry him. The wedding is held. Immigrant families from the neighborhood gather for a joyous celebration.

Everything was fine up to this point. But then the bride finds out that the house she thought was theirs belongs to someone else. Her happy smile vanishes. She had always been a cheerful, lighthearted girl, but now she sinks into gloom.

They begin their married life in a small, shabby apartment. On the wall they carve little notches with a knife, a record of their determination, no matter what the sacrifice, to save enough money to buy a house. Then a child is born.

As the movie continued, the events unfolding on screen became more and more harrowing. Early one morning the mason comes home drunk, having spent the night with another woman. On his way up the stairs of the apartment building, he decides to punish himself. He swings his open palm down on the pointed tip of the newel-post.

No! The father caught his breath and quickly turned to look at his daughter. The book he had bought her on the way to the theater was raised in front of her face. She had instinctively lifted it from her lap, as though merely closing her eyes would not be enough to block out the scene. Clever girl, he thought, breathing a sigh of relief.

The mason continued to suffer one misfortune after another, and with each frightening scene the book on the girl's lap rose, then fell again. Each time, her father let her know when the scene was over. "It's all right now," he would whisper. "You don't want to miss this part."

Near the end, when the mason fell into the pit, the father stole another look at his daughter. Once again she was hunched tensely behind her book. This time the book remained up throughout the scene, while the roar of the falling concrete and the sound of the mason's screams filled the theater.

Suddenly the screen fell silent, and the girl peeked tremulously from behind her book. The mason was nowhere to be seen. His bereaved wife stood all alone, utterly stricken.

"Did . . . did he die?" the girl asked in a tiny voice.

"Yes," he answered.

The father recalled all this as he watched his daughter work at her sewing. That book had really come in handy then, he thought. It had helped her get through the movie without having to watch the scary scenes.

In the same way, his daughter had been spared knowledge of the accident that took place in her own home. She was still an infant at the time, and could not have known the meaning of her mother's deep sleep. An invisible hand had gently covered her eyes.

"Hey Dad," the boy said. "Tell us something that begins with S."

"Something that begins with S?"

"Un-hunh. S-T."

"S-T?"

"S-T-O-R-Y. A story."

"What about a story?"

"We want you to tell us one."

"I don't know any stories," the father protested.

"You do too."

"I can't think of any."

"How about the wild boar story?"

"But I've told you that one lots of times."

"That doesn't matter."

The father had run out of excuses. "During the summer," he began, "boars always sleep. They stay at home in their dens, lying on big soft beds made of thatch, and all they do is sleep and sleep and sleep. Thatch—that's what the old hunter who told me this story called it—is a plant that grows in the mountains. Besides using it for beds, the boars make roofs out of it, to keep off the rain when there's a storm and to shade themselves on hot sunny days. It works very nicely, both ways. So the boars just lie around sleeping in their cozy little thatched houses, day in day out, all summer long. If that isn't the easy life!" he exclaimed enviously, glancing from the older boy to the younger.

"The old hunter told me, though, that you can't eat boar's meat in the summer. It doesn't taste good. So I guess maybe it's not such a good idea to sit around doing nothing after all. You see, when they butcher a summer boar, there's always a layer of fat as stiff as a board right under the skin. In fact that's what the hunters call it—a 'board.' And they say a boar with a board isn't any good because you can't eat the meat. But actually the 'board' has a special purpose. It helps keep the boar's energy inside its body so that it can sleep the whole summer long."

"That's why badger's fat is better, right?"

"Right. Badgers are the opposite of boars. They sleep through the winter, which means they have a lot of fat then and almost none in the summer. Badger's fat is really good. If you take some from just under the skin and heat it in a pan, you get a smooth, clear oil. Oh, by the way, there's another special name the hunters use: 'cukes.' That's what they call baby boars, because they have patches of fur on their backs that look just like big fat cucumbers."

"That's kind of neat," the older boy said.

"That's kinda neat," the younger quickly repeated.

"Mmm, I thought so too. Now, one of the boar's favorite foods, of all things, is earthworms. To think that an animal that big would go for worms—when they're known to gobble up a whole patch of sweet potatoes in a single night! The old hunter was really shaking his head over this one. He never could understand why such a big eater would take a liking to little earthworms. And they like spiders and mud snails, too. They dig up the snails with their snouts, just like the worms, but it's a mystery how they eat them because they never leave any shells behind. They must either take them home to eat, or else they swallow the whole thing, shell and all. The hunter said he didn't imagine snails would taste very good with the shell on them." The father tilted his head thoughtfully, then shrugged. "Who knows what they do?"

He went on: "Hunting for boars can be pretty rough, I guess. When you walk through the snow looking for tracks, your feet get soaked and clumps of snow fall on you from the branches overhead, and after a while your stomach starts to growl. An important thing to know when you're looking for tracks is that boars always travel the same paths. Maybe they're just the methodical type, or maybe they're actually afraid of something—I don't know. But in any case they always follow exactly in each other's footsteps. So no matter how many boars have gone by it looks like only one. That's how consistent they are.

"One time a terrible thing happened because of this. At the power station in the mountains there's a sluice for the water that turns the generators, and it has a log lying across it for a bridge. One snowy morning the workers at the plant found three dead boars washed against the sluice gates. They went up along the sluice to see if they could find out what had happened, and when they got to the log they discovered there was an icy spot about halfway across. What had happened was the first boar to come along that morning had slipped on the ice and fallen into the water. Since the sluice is made of concrete and the sides go straight up and down, the boar had no place to climb out and it got swept away by the current. Then the second one came along, and, because it followed the first boar's tracks onto the log, it slipped at the same place. After a while a third one came and fell into the water just like the others. Poor things. The men couldn't tell whether the boars had come one right after the other or a long time apart, but they could see what had happened from the way the tracks ended in the middle of the log."

"They should've watched out better," the older boy said.

"They should've watched out better," his brother echoed.

"That's right, they might have been okay if they had only stopped to think, 'Hey, wait a minute. The tracks don't go all the way across.' But they didn't, I guess. Well then, let's get on with the story about the old hunter meeting up with the wild boar."

The boys leaned forward. This was the part they had been waiting for.

"When he was in the mountains one day, the hunter came across a boar's den—made of thatch, as I said. He went home and told three of his hunter friends about it, and without letting anyone else know of their plans they got ready to go back for the kill. You see, you have to have at least three or four hunters to get a boar. If you try to do it alone, the boar will always get away. On the day of the hunt—remember, this all happened before the hunter was as old as he is now—the four of them set off for the mountains early in the morning. As it turned out, there was another group of hunters that had somehow got wind of their plans and had left even earlier. But the old hunter and his friends didn't know this yet, and they hiked on and on through the underbrush toward the boar's den. They came to a small cliff, and started climbing it, when all of a sudden they heard a panting sound and *boom!*—"

Pretending he was the hunter crawling up the side of a cliff, the father jerked his head back.

"Just as the old hunter started to pull himself over the top, he found himself face to face with a giant boar. Talk about being caught off guard!

They had all assumed the boar would be fast asleep in its den! The hunter immediately ducked down and reached for the rifle slung across his back. And the startled boar retreated, too, almost as quickly."

Now the father acted the part of the wild boar, first leaning forward as if poking his head over the edge of the cliff, then hastily pulling back.

"The hunter thought the boar had decided to run back the way it came, and if he didn't hurry it would get away. He started to scramble up after it. But *whoosh*!—the boar suddenly went flying by his head, landed with a tremendous skid at the bottom of the cliff, and went crashing into the underbrush below. By the time the hunters turned around, all they could see was the broken branches where the boar had disappeared, and, farther on, the churning of the undergrowth as it ran off."

"Wow!" the older boy exclaimed.

The younger boy sat speechless, his wide eyes glued to his father's face.

"What had happened was the other hunters, the ones who had gone earlier, had already shot at the boar and put it in a panic. That's probably why it made such a desperate leap. So when the old hunter thought the boar had taken off in the other direction, actually it had only backed up a little way to get a running start for the jump." The father broke into a laugh for a moment, but then finished the story with a straight face. "The hunter said someone else finally shot the boar a week or so later. And that's the end of the story."

Their uncle came to visit them from the town where they had lived before moving to their present home. He brought with him a bag of walnuts for the children.

"What a nice gift," the father said afterward. "We couldn't spend money on nuts for ourselves—they're too much of an extravagance. But as a gift for someone with children, they're perfect. A real treat. A chance for the children to have something we couldn't normally afford."

But how would they divide up the nuts? The mother decided as follows: the girl could have seven, the older boy five, and the younger boy three. That would still leave two, so she and her husband could have one each.

The older boy went to get the hammer and quickly finished off his share. The younger boy ate all of his, too, after his mother had helped him crack them open. The mother waited to eat hers until the following afternoon when she was at home alone with the younger boy. The father slipped his into his pocket; he still had it when he went to work the next day, but lost it somewhere the day after.

The girl decided to save hers for a while. She put them in a drawer in her desk, and took them out one at a time to polish them with a piece of felt. She wanted to bring out their best shine.

A few days later she told her friends at school, but only her two best friends, about the nuts. "They were a present from my uncle when he came to visit," she explained. "Do you like walnuts? If you want, I'll bring you some tomorrow."

"Sure," they said. They both liked walnuts.

Should she give them each two, or only one? she wondered. If she gave them two, they could rub them together in their hands to make a grinding noise, and they'd have more fun with them. But if she gave each of them two, that would leave her with fewer than half of her original seven. She wasn't sure she liked that idea. She enjoyed watching the walnuts roll around when she opened the drawer, and it just wouldn't be the same with only three nuts left. To give two would be better, of course. There was no question of that. But even one was better than nothing.

When she was getting ready for school the next day, she took four walnuts from the drawer and dropped them into the pocket of her skirt.

At school she ran into one of her friends. "I brought the walnuts," she said, reaching into her pocket. She still hadn't made up her mind whether she would give one or two.

"Here." She held out a single walnut.

"Thank you," her friend said gratefully.

That afternoon she walked home with her other friend, Ikuko. As they passed through the school gate she handed her a walnut.

"Thanks," said Ikuko.

"Try this. It's fun," she said, taking the other two nuts from her pocket and rubbing them together.

"That's neat," Ikuko said. The girl lent Ikuko one of her walnuts. Ikuko rubbed the nuts together for a while as they walked, then gave back the one she had borrowed.

"Not very long after that," the girl later recounted to her father, "we went by a place where some men were working on the road. We still had the nuts in our hands, but I guess I wasn't really paying attention because all of a sudden Ikuko said, 'Hey, you dropped one of your nuts.' So we turned around to look for it right away, and guess what. We hadn't gone back more than five or six steps when one of the construction workers said, 'I bet you're looking for your walnut, aren't you?' and started laughing. He said he'd already eaten it and showed us the shell broken right in half."

"And the nut was all gone?" her father asked.

"Un-hunh."

"Was he still chewing?"

"No, he wasn't. He'd already swallowed it. It couldn't have been more than a couple of seconds."

"Mmm."

"What I want to know is how could he have cracked that hard shell? With his teeth? We told him he was mean and just came on home, but we were really mad."

"I can imagine," her father nodded. After a pause he said, "I guess the nut must have rolled right in front of him—right where he happened to be looking."

The goldfish seemed to have grown since it first joined the family. Its stomach had filled out; the faint patches of red were now a deeper hue; and with each passing day it looked more and more like an adult fish. Everyone enjoyed watching it dart briskly around its bowl on the sunny windowsill.

"I don't think I've ever seen such a peppy goldfish before," the mother said.

"Yes, we should count ourselves lucky," the father replied. "Let's hope he stays that way."

Every other day the mother changed about half of the water and sprinkled in a pinch of salt, and every third day she gave the fish some bread crumbs or pieces of crackers or cookies. When the children wanted to feed it, she made them take turns, and she kept track of the days to ensure they didn't feed it too much or too often.

The father did not help with the fish, but from time to time he would go into the children's study and watch it move about in its bowl. Such poise! he marveled. With the slightest flick of its fins and an occasional twitch of its tail, the fish could hold itself perfectly still, going neither forward nor backward, for as long as it wished.

He and the children had recently made a second trip to the fishing pond. This time, however, the little tin bucket proved useless, for they failed to catch even a single fish. Nor were they the only ones to come up empty-handed; nobody else's luck appeared any better, at either of the ponds.

As evening approached, the air over the pond grew heavier and heavier.

"This time it looks pretty hopeless," the father sighed. "No one's getting anything." Even changing the bait seemed a waste of effort. Still, he stuck it out at the same spot until the hour they had paid for was up.

The fish he had caught the last time now became more precious than ever. There was a big difference between catching one fish and catching none at all. To have hooked that one fish almost began to seem like a special meeting of fates.

An old man wearing a hunter's cap started to put his gear away. "I should've known better than to come today," he muttered grumpily as he left. "Fishing's never any good when the wind's out of the east."

A few minutes later they were all given a start. Over at the other pond, a boy who had been watching his father fish fell into the water with a loud splash. Everyone turned to see the fisherman pulling his son out. The child, soaked from the neck down, looked about ten years old.

A gentle wave of laughter spread among the few people remaining at the pond. The incident dispelled the oppressive mood that had descended over the place, and everyone relaxed again.

Frustrated and tired from an afternoon spent in vain, the man had apparently started to doze off. When he leaned over against his son, the boy had lost his balance and tumbled into the water.

Having retrieved his son—instead of a fish—from the pond, the man could hardly go on fishing. The sun was low in the sky as the two left for home, the hapless boy sloshing awkwardly along behind his father.

"I wonder what's wrong with this thing," the father mumbled to himself. "It manages to flower all right, but it always looks so straggly."

On Sunday morning he had stepped out into the yard to take a closer look at the lilac bush. His eyes moved from the long, spindly branches, to the clusters of tiny, purple flowers, and to the ground underneath the bush.

The bush had been planted in the spring five years before, the year after they had moved to this house. But once it had reached a height slightly taller than he was, it had stopped growing. It never developed a main trunk; instead, it had split at the base into a mass of skinny branches that fanned out toward the sky.

He had originally hoped it would grow large and full enough for the children to hide behind when they played games of hide-and-seek. This no longer seemed likely.

He was still contemplating the lilac when he saw a band of street musicians come into view down the road. The man at the head of the troupe pranced about nimbly in time with the music, turning first one way, then the other.

He keeps people's attention that way, thought the father. If he walked along normally, there wouldn't be anything to watch.

From where he stood inside the fence, the father continued to follow the dancer's movements as the band moved closer. Suddenly he saw that the dancer was not a man at all, but a woman, a rather skinny woman dressed in men's clothes and made up with white greasepaint.

Behind her came a second dancer in a similar outfit, only this one actually was a man. Third in line was a woman in a black beret playing the clarinet. Next came the drummer, beating with exaggerated flourish on the rack of gongs and tom-toms strapped to his chest. A trumpet player wearing a radioman's cap brought up the rear.

The procession came to a halt. The three musicians continued playing while the two dancers went from house to house passing out handbills.

The older boy had come out of the house to watch from the side of the road. Now the drummer approached him and said something. The boy stared back, but his lips did not move.

Why didn't he answer? the father wondered. What could the man have said?

The group slowly moved away again, and the boy came back into the yard.

"Did the drummer say something to you?" the father asked.

"Un-hunh."

"What did he say?"

"I had my fingers in my ears," the boy said, "and I was pushing them in and out to make the music sound real loud and then real quiet." He demonstrated as he explained, putting his fingers to his ears again. "So the man said if I had to plug my ears like that, I shouldn't come close, I should go somewhere else."

"I see," the father nodded.

"I guess he thought I didn't like their music," the boy grinned.

On Sunday evening the father took out his sketchbook and began to draw a picture of his daughter. She had gotten ready for bed after an early bath, then settled down on the tatami in the front room to read. She saw what her father was doing and tried her best to sit perfectly still for him.

"Are you getting stiff?" he asked her after a while.

"No, not particularly." She sat with her legs flopped to one side and the book open in her lap. The big toe of one foot peeked out from behind the other knee. Her father started sketching the toe.

"No, that's too big, I guess," he said, mostly to himself.

"What's too big?" the girl asked.

"Your toe."

"It better not be," she giggled.

"Do you remember your grandpa?" her father asked as he rubbed the toe out.

"A little," she nodded.

"I was just thinking of the time he told me to make a drawing of your feet."

"My feet?"

"Un-hunh."

"What for?"

"It was a day or two after you were born."

"Why my feet?"

"He said it'd be fun to have later on." He started outlining the toe again. "All I had with me was my address book, so I drew a little sketch in that. Just the bottoms of your feet. I suppose it got thrown out somewhere along the way."

"Too bad."

"Yes, I wish we still had it. You'd get a kick out of it. With my knack of losing things, I wonder if Grandpa really thought I'd keep it all this time. . . Hmm, I guess this hand isn't quite right either." He started to reshape the hand holding the book. "I remember how impressed Grandpa was with the hospital room. He kept saying it would make a great apartment, and that they should rent it out to us."

"Can I move my legs a little now?" the girl asked.

"Sure, go ahead. It really was a nice room. A quiet room, perfect for reading. The window faced the nurses' dormitory, and every once in a while we'd see one of them dash across the street through the rain. I remember there was a big paulownia by the front entrance. . . Why can't I get these fingers right? The more I work on them the worse they get."

The girl looked up and glanced at her father's sketchbook.

"That day," he went on, "as I was leaving the hospital, I ran into your grandpa coming through the rain, wearing a hat but without an umbrella. He was on his way to see your mother. We stepped under the eaves to talk for a couple of minutes, and do you know what he said? He had never been to a maternity ward before; he had never visited anyone who'd just had a baby. So I decided to go back to the hospital with him. Later, when we were leaving, he told me not to worry—for every day a baby lives it builds up that much more strength to survive. You see, we were having a terrible time getting you to drink your mother's milk. You kept falling asleep as soon as you got the nipple in your mouth, even when the nurse tried pulling on your ear. We didn't know what to do with you."

The girl giggled sheepishly.

"Guess what we found at school today," the girl said at the dinner table. "A mole cricket. We were digging in the flower bed, and—"

"Another mole cricket!" exclaimed her mother. "Yesterday it was your brother who found one. He comes in the door after school, and, before

I even have a chance to ask him how his day was, he dangles this ugly creature in front of my face and says 'Look, I brought you a present.'"

"You should've seen her jump," the boy said gleefully.

"Of course I jumped. How many times do I have to tell you? You can bring home anything you like as far as the front door, but I won't have you bringing bugs into the house."

"So-o-rry."

"So what did you do with the mole cricket in the flower bed?" the father asked.

"Mine was in the sandbox," the boy said.

"The sandbox? You mean you brought it home all the way from school?"

"Yep."

"When we caught the one in the flower bed," the girl said, "we held it like this and asked it, 'How bi-i-ig is so-and-so's brain?' and it would sort of wiggle in surprise and spread its front legs."

"Whoever thought *that* up?" the father wanted to know.

"We all thought it up together. When you say your own name, you say 'BI-I-IG' real loud," she said, putting extra stress on the *B*. "Then it spreads its legs way far apart, like this. But when you say someone else's name, you say the words real soft: 'How big.'" This time she lowered her voice to a whisper. "Then it only moves its legs a tiny bit." She demonstrated with her arms as she spoke.

"You've got to be making this up," her mother said.

"No, it's true, it was like the mole cricket really heard. So we started doing the same thing as the cricket, and spread our arms real wide, too, when we said our own names."

"As if the poor thing wasn't startled enough already," her father said.

The girl seemed endlessly amused by the way the mole cricket squirmed in surprise. She went through her "How bi-i-ig" antics several more times, transforming herself from little girl into mole cricket and back again, then collapsing in a fit of laughter.

"How bi-i-ig?" the older boy said, moving his arms like his sister.

"How bi-i-g?" the younger boy imitated.

"So-o big."

"So-o big."

"All right, all right," the father said when they all started doing it together. "That's enough. Let's have some quiet for a change. Please."

Even now, in the deserted schoolyard where the children had played that day, the mole crickets would be quietly burrowing their way through the sandboxes and flower beds.

Two stuffed toys, a tiger and a rabbit, shared the wide windowsill where the goldfish swam in its bowl. The tiger lay on its stomach, its legs thrust forward. Its head was tilted to one side so that its nose almost touched the ground, and it looked as if it were scrutinizing the movements of some industrious ant. The rabbit, wearing polka-dotted pants, faced the opposite direction. It lay on its back and stared up at the sky.

During the daytime, the two animals sat like this on the sill. Then, when night came, they were taken off to bed by the children. The younger boy always got the rabbit—there were never any quarrels about that. But the older boy and the girl had to take turns with the tiger, and many an argument broke out when one or the other of them would miss a day.

One night, the father was getting ready for bed in his room at the end of the hall when he heard the children's voices rise to a fighting pitch. A moment later his wife intervened: "All right, now, who had it the day before yesterday? And yesterday? No, no, you both know the rule—forgetting doesn't count."

It was their own fault if they missed a turn, she explained, as she had so many times before. They could not demand their turn the next day. If that were allowed, neither of them would be able to count on their regular turn any more, and there'd be no end to the fighting. If they forgot, it was just too bad. They would have to wait for their next turn.

How had this all started? the father wondered. How long had they been having these squabbles?

Sometimes several days went by without either of the children remembering to take the tiger to bed. Since neither of them could recall who had had it last or how long it had been, even their mother couldn't settle whose turn it should be. Eventually, to make sure this didn't happen again, she had begun keeping track by marking the calendar with the children's initials.

The father shook his head as he got under the covers. It was beyond him why they would want to take something like that to bed with them. *He* had slept alone when *he* was a child. And he had taken it for granted that everyone else did, too.

The children's dispute finally came to an end. That night, the tiger would sleep with the girl.

"Lucky stiff!" the boy grumbled loudly.

As the father picked up one of the books lying at the head of the bed, his thoughts drifted off to another stuffed toy they had once had—a puppy, neither so small nor so soft as the tiger the children had just been fighting over. He recalled the Christmas morning, more than ten years before, when he had found the puppy standing beside his baby daughter's bed. The tall, husky puppy had seemed so enormous next to the tiny figure of the baby.

Now what did she go and buy something like that for? he remembered thinking to himself.

Only a few minutes earlier, he had been equally surprised when he first awoke to find a box, neatly tied with ribbon, sitting beside his pillow. The box had contained a fedora.

Had he said he wanted one of these? He couldn't remember, but perhaps he had, sometime or other, and his wife had taken him seriously. Or perhaps he had only commented on how nice someone else's looked.

How much did hats like this cost? He really couldn't imagine. He had never considered buying one for himself, or envisioned himself wearing one to the office, so he'd never had cause to explore the hat section of the department store. His knowledge of hats was pretty much limited to the corduroy cap he got out in the summertime. But that was one of those things you could roll up and stuff in your pocket—it hardly counted as a real hat. The only other hat he had ever worn was a boater, in his student days. He remembered having to hold it with one hand on top to keep it from flying off as he raced to get on the train before the doors closed.

He knew he hadn't paid very much for that boater. But fedoras were in a different class altogether. It must have cost a small fortune. Why had his wife made such an extravagant purchase without consulting him?

She knew they didn't have that kind of money to spend.

Sitting up in bed, he tried on the new hat. He liked it, the way it gently pressed against his head. But he wasn't sure what position he should wear it in. If he pulled it down too far, his head would push out the crease on top and make it look like a bowler instead of a fedora. How did other people wear them? He would have to pay more attention from now on.

He returned the hat to its box and closed the lid.

Since it was a holiday, he could sleep later than usual if he wanted. But the surprise of the hat had left him wide awake. He decided to go ahead and get up.

The quiet of morning filled the house. Outside, clouds hung heavily in the sky.

It was then, when he poked his head into the next room to see if his wife and daughter were awake, that he had had his first glimpse of the toy puppy.

For several moments, all he could do was marvel at its magnificent size and beauty. In any display of stuffed toys, this puppy was bound to reign as king of beasts. Once you had seen it, all the other toys would look like mere knickknacks by comparison.

Clearly it had been made to last. It could probably hold a child on its back without collapsing.

But once again he wondered about the cost. Although he knew even less about stuffed toys than about hats, he could guess it had been expensive. What could his wife have been thinking, spending so much money on a toy like that? With all the daily expenses they had to worry about, she should show a little more sense.

He would have to give her a little scolding, he decided. In fact, he would do it right then and there. So what if it was a holiday? It was already later than usual and time she got started on breakfast.

He called her name, but she slept on without so much as stirring. His wife was one of those people who always looked as though they hadn't had enough sleep, and at night she was lost to the world the moment her head touched the pillow. She seldom dreamed, and was never wakeful. But when the alarm went off the next morning, or when he called her, she would be up in an instant. In all the time they had been married, he couldn't remember having had to call her twice.

"Hey, wake up," he said again, reaching over to shake her shoulder. All of a sudden he noticed that what she had on was not what she normally wore to bed.

As the father lay reflecting on that morning, he thought again of the puppy. It had proved to be just as sturdy as his first impression had suggested. The girl had played with it for a long time, riding on its back, hanging on with her baby fists clutched tightly around its soft, fluffy ears. She had started doing this even before she learned to walk. When their first son came along, he had played with it, too, bouncing up and down on its back no less gleefully than his sister. But it had still held up as good as new.

Later, when they moved to their new house, the puppy had come with them. The father remembered packing it to be shipped with the other baggage.

"The fedora was a different story, though," he sighed. *That* he had lost almost right away. At a movie theater. He had put it on his lap during the show, only to forget about it when he stood up to leave. He was all the way outside before he noticed, and by then it was too late. One of the ushers had kindly gone to retrieve it for him, but came back saying the theater was too crowded. He had had to give it up for lost.

When the boys asked for an "S" again one evening, the father told them another story about the old hunter.

"Next to hunting," he began, "the old man's favorite pastime is fishing. He became a hunter first, and he's been making regular trips into the mountains for more than forty years, since he was a young man. Then about thirty years ago, when he moved to the town where he lives now, he took up fishing. He liked the town so much, he's lived there ever since, and he's spent a lot of time at the nearby river ever since, too. He got started fishing, he says, because he found a good river-teacher there."

"A river-teacher?" the older boy laughed.

"That's right. Maybe you've only heard of schoolteachers, but there are river-teachers, too—and mountain-teachers, and even ocean-teachers. A long time ago, this river-teacher had worked as a raftsman for a lumber company. You see, when a lumber company cuts down trees up in the mountains, the logs are tied together into rafts so they can be floated down the river to the lumber mill. The raftsman is the person who steers the raft down the river, through the rapids and between all the rocks and things sticking up out of the water. It's a really dangerous job. Anyway, after this river-teacher had worked as a raftsman for a while, he decided to settle down in one of the towns along the river and become a fisherman instead. He knew that river like the back of his hand. No one could match him. He could tell you exactly how many fish there were and what they were doing or which way they were swimming anywhere along the river, even in the roughest and deepest places. If you were fishing with him and he said, 'One more,' that meant there was only one fish left in that spot. And he'd be right!"

"Wow!" the older boy exclaimed.

"Wow!" the younger boy mimicked.

"That's incredible," the first added.

"The old hunter couldn't get over it either. He said he'd never heard of anyone who knew so much about rivers and fish. The river-teacher's name was Katsujirō, but since his father's name had been Katsuzō, everyone called him Little Katsu. People still called him that when the hunter met him, even though he was an old man by then."

The older boy laughed when his father said "Little Katsu."

"The problem was that since Little Katsu depended on catching fish for his living, you could never believe what he told you. If you asked him where was a good spot, he would lie and send you off someplace he knew was lousy. The hunter got to be his best friend, and they would drink together almost every night, but he still couldn't get a straight answer out of him. For instance, he might ask if today was a good day, and Little Katsu would say, 'No.' Well, that would turn out to be a lie—the days he said 'No' were in fact the best days. So pretty soon the hunter tried doing the opposite of whatever Little Katsu said. If he said 'No,' the hunter would set out for the river. And sure enough, Little Katsu would be there."

"So he had to listen to him backward," the older boy said.

"That's right. With a teacher like Little Katsu, that was how you learned. Even then the hunter got tricked a lot, so he tried something new. Instead of asking Little Katsu directly, he would sneak up to his house and peek in to see if he was at home. If he found him puttering around the house or just taking a nap or something, he knew there was no sense in going to the river."

"'Cause he knew he wouldn't catch anything even if he did," the boy said.

"Un-hunh. Now, I said Little Katsu lied a lot, but actually there were some things he didn't lie about. Like how to cast a net so it would spread out the way you wanted it to. Or what's the best way to tie the hook to the line. Or how when you're fishing for dace and get a nibble you have to give some slack instead of pulling it in right away as most people do.

"It was lucky for the hunter that Little Katsu told the truth about these things. Otherwise he might never have learned how to cast the special sweetfish net that's used only on that river and nowhere else. It's about fifteen feet long, like a huge ribbon, and getting it to spread out just right is pretty tricky. If it goes into the water in a straight line, like this," he drew a line with his finger, "the fish will get away. They can swim right around it. To keep them from doing that, you have to make the net hit the water curved like a bow. Like this." He indicated the curve with a sweep of his arms.

"Like this?" the older boy said, making a similar arc.

"Like this?" his brother imitated.

"The reason it makes a difference, you see, is that sweetfish can't turn around very well. When they bump into the net, they just wriggle a little to one side or the other and keep trying to push ahead. That means if both ends of the net are curved back like this, then the fish are forced to swim toward the middle." The father cupped his left hand and poked at it with his right index finger to show how the fish bumped against the net and kept swimming forward until they wound up trapped in the center. The boys paid close attention.

"But if you just leave them there," he went on, "the fish eventually get turned around and find their way out. So, to make sure that doesn't happen, the old hunter swims down underwater to where the net is and breaks their spines."

"What's 'spines'?" the older boy asked.

"Right about here." The father patted the back of his neck. "Then later, after he's got quite a few, he brings them in all at once. He says he used to catch thirty, even forty, in a single night back when he first started fishing. On nights like that he wouldn't even notice how cold the water was. Until he got home, that is. Then he would start shivering like crazy. He'd take a good hot bath and jump into bed with the covers pulled all the way up over his head, and he still wouldn't be able to keep from shaking. Even in the middle of summer. But you know what? No matter how bad the shivering was, he'd be right back at the river again the very next night. It's hardly a wonder he developed so many aches and pains as he got older, but he just shrugs and says, 'That's the way it goes.'"

"Tell us about the fox," the older boy broke in again.

"Okay. That happened when he was snagging, which is another way to catch sweetfish. Instead of a net, you use a line with a lot of hooks spaced three or four inches apart, and you snag the fish by their gills. Sometimes you can catch five or six all at once. With this method, too, the best fishing is at night, especially when the river is swollen and muddy after some rain. You can haul in dozens.

"Anyway, one night when the old hunter was snagging out in the middle of the river, a fox came along the bank and stopped to watch him. For a long time it just stood there like a little statue, not moving a muscle." The father got on all fours and made a fox's face, then continued. "Now, the hunter wouldn't have minded about the fox except that his basket of fish was sitting on the bank. You see, he had two baskets for the fish he caught—a small one that he tied around his waist, and a larger one that he left on the riverbank. Whenever the small one filled up, he would go back to shore and empty it into the larger one. The problem was the fox had stopped only a few steps away from this larger basket."

"Chase him away!" the older boy cried.

"Chase him away!" the younger boy echoed.

"You can imagine the hunter got pretty nervous about the basket. He picked up a rock from the riverbed and threw it hard at the fox, thinking that would surely send it scampering. But no, the fox just ambled a few steps to one side, stopped, and turned to eye him again. Then after a few moments it sauntered back toward the basket."

"Throw some more rocks!" the older boy said.

"Right. He picked up another rock and yelled 'Beat it!' as he hurled it off. But the fox wasn't any more impressed than the first time. The old hunter said he had never seen such a lackadaisical fox. Then, just as he was trying to decide what to do next, the fox grabbed the basket in its snout and trotted away."

"Too-o ba-a-ad," the older boy said sympathetically.

"Too-o ba-a-ad," the younger boy repeated.

"Hey Mom, Ikuko and I are going to make doughnuts this afternoon, okay?" the girl asked one Sunday, a little before noon.

"It's fine with me," her mother nodded.

"She said she'd bring the ingredients."

"She doesn't have to do that."

"That's what *I* said."

"I'm sure we have everything you need."

"I know, I told her that, but she insisted."

Ikuko arrived around two, bringing with her a bag of flour and an egg. She was a cute, cheerful girl, who never seemed to stop smiling.

"Can I help?" the older boy asked.

"There you go again," his father admonished. "Always getting into other people's projects. For girls, making doughnuts is like doing homework. You'd be in the way."

"But I want to do some homework too."

"Look, there's not enough room in the kitchen for all three of you to work in there at the same time."

"Yes there is," the boy whined. He stuck out his lips in a pout. His eyes filled and a tear or two trickled down his cheek.

"All right, you can help," his mother agreed. "But don't get carried away now. Understand?"

"Oka-a-a-y," he promised. A smile had already spread across his face. The switch from sad to happy was just that quick.

The father looked on as his wife got the children started. Then, having nothing better to do, he decided to go and lie down for a while. "Make them small," he said as he stood up to leave. "They're better that way."

In the back room he folded a cushion in half to use as a pillow and stretched out on the tatami. Even from there he could hear the voices in the kitchen.

"Stop taking so much," the girl scolded the boy. It seemed he had gotten carried away after all.

Then his wife was saying something. That was the voice of the woman he had married, he thought to himself as he listened. That was how she sounded when she did things with the kids.

For some reason he was reminded of the muffled sobs he had once heard, a long time ago. When had it been? Oh yes, it was in their old house. He was taking a nap upstairs late one Sunday afternoon—he even remembered using a folded cushion for a pillow, just like now—when all of a sudden he began to hear what sounded like a woman crying. He lifted his head to listen more closely, but the sound stopped. Then, while he was still puzzling over what to make of it, it started up again.

Was something wrong? Who could it be? Why should anyone be weeping?

Going downstairs, he found their second child fast asleep on the baby bed and his wife rinsing some spinach at the kitchen sink. Their daughter had gone out to play.

"Did you hear anything?" he asked his wife.

"No, not that I noticed," she replied, turning around with a bright face.

"That's strange. I could have sworn I heard something. That's what I came down for—to see what it was."

What could it have been, then, that sound of short, broken sobs? Something being jostled by the wind, perhaps, rubbing against something else. But why had it sounded to him so much like his wife's voice?

He went back upstairs, but the sound did not return.

The father now lay on the tatami in the back room staring into space as he thought over the incident that had puzzled him so. His wife had had no cause for weeping then. And in fact she *hadn't* been weeping.

"This one's mine," the boy's voice broke through the father's thoughts. "I put a mark on it so I could tell."

A few moments later someone began to laugh. Then they all laughed.

Footsteps came running down the hall and the door slid open. It was the younger boy. "They're done. It's time to eat," he said, and went dashing back toward the kitchen.

The father got up and followed. He found the others at the low, round table in the front room, the doughnuts divided up onto several small plates. There was an extra plate for him.

"Ummm, perfect!" he said between bites. "Just as I said, the small ones are best." He finished the doughnut and sat back to watch as the others ate theirs.

"Have some more," his wife urged.

"No thanks. One's enough for me." He pushed his plate toward the children.

"That was fun," the girl said as she took her last bite.

"And delicious," Ikuko added, finishing hers.

The boy, too, was down to his final bite, when his sister suddenly cried out, "Wait! Save a little piece!" But it was too late. The last bit had vanished into her brother's mouth. "Ohhh well," she said, disappointed.

"What's the matter?" her mother asked.

"We forgot to save any for the goldfish."

The boy tapped his cheeks as if to prove that the doughnut was completely gone. Neither on the plates nor on the table did a single crumb remain.

"We listened to the *New World* Symphony in music class today," the girl said one evening near the end of dinner.

"How nice!" her mother said. "Did you like it?"

"It was beautiful."

"Yes, it really is a beautiful piece."

"But you know what? When the teacher told us he was going to play it, the boys all groaned and didn't want to listen. Only the girls wanted to hear it."

"Why? What did the boys have against it?" the father asked.

"I don't know. All they said was 'Bo-o-oring. Bo-o-oring.' I guess they didn't think it would be much fun. They must have liked it more than they expected, though, because once it started they all listened quietly."

"Do you get to choose the music you listen to?" her mother asked.

"Un-hunh. Every once in a while the teacher asks us what we'd like to hear and makes a list on the board. One time, not too long ago, a lot of people wanted the *New World* Symphony. But he didn't have it taped yet."

"Oh, so you listen to a tape," the father broke in.

"Un-hunh. He's got lots of different music on tapes."

"I see."

"Anyway, today he came in and said he'd finally had a chance to record the *New World* Symphony the other night, so let's all listen to it. But first he explained that the beginning wasn't recorded very well—he hadn't had time to adjust all the knobs before the symphony started because he forgot until the last minute that it was going to be on the radio that night; he only barely got the tape recorder set up in time. And he said there was a place in the middle where we would hear his son's voice."

"Did you?" her brother asked.

"Un-hunh."

"What did he say?"

"I couldn't tell. Something like 'Ahhh-yooo.'"

"Ahhh-yooo?"

"I couldn't really tell, it went by so fast."

Several evenings later the girl had another story.

"In Ikuko's class," she began, "they listened to *Invitation to the Dance* today. The teacher told them beforehand that the composer—I think his name was Weber—had dedicated it to his wife, and that it was a flowery sort of piece."

"So that's what you call it," her father said.

"Then after he started the tape, he explained what was supposed to be happening at each place in the music." She had begun to speak a little faster, as she always did when she neared the best part of a story. "Well, evidently there's a place in the middle where the music stays kind of low for a while and then gets high, and the teacher explained that the low part was where the men go up to the ladies and ask, 'May I have this dance?' Then when it came to the high part, he started to tell them that that was where the ladies turn all red and say, 'Ohhh, something-

or-other.' But just as he said 'Ohhh,' his false teeth came loose, and they almost fell right out of his mouth!" Unable to hold back any longer, she burst out laughing.

Her parents stared at her in disbelief.

"His false teeth?" her father asked.

"It's really true! They almost fell out!" She laughed so hard that tears came to her eyes and she had to hold her stomach. Before long her father began to laugh, too, and then her mother and the boys. They laughed and laughed, unable to stop.

Finally the older boy asked, "So what did the teacher do?"

"Ikuko said he turned the other way and fixed them in a real hurry," the girl answered.

A bagworm the older boy had been keeping in a small cardboard box disappeared.

At the time, the father did not yet know about the bagworm. No one had thought to mention it to him. It was not until afterward that he heard the story.

The boy had originally found the bagworm on a tree in their neighbor's yard when he and a friend were gathering nuts to use as pellets in their toy guns. His friend told him that if he stripped the cocoon off and put the worm in a box with some leaves and bits of paper, it would make itself a new cocoon in about three hours.

The boy brought it home and did as his friend had said. But when he peeked into the box that night, the bagworm had not moved. The next morning it still hadn't moved.

He then forgot about the worm, and three days went by before he thought to check its box again. This time it had crept into a corner and begun building a little tentlike shelter on its back. The boy poked at the half-finished canopy with his finger. To his surprise, it flipped right off.

A day or two later he found the tiny creature crawling across the floor of the study. This time, too, it had a tent on its back, about the same size as the one before. The boy carefully returned it to its box.

After that, once again, he neglected to check on the bagworm for several days. When he finally remembered, it was no longer in the box.

With his mother to help him, he scoured the floor of the study from under the sewing machine to behind the toy basket, but to no avail.

Then one evening about two weeks later, the mother went into the study and found the bagworm in a cocoon on the wall, a little way below the picture of the star children.

"Here it is!" she exclaimed in surprise.

The lost bagworm had made itself a new cocoon out of the persimmon twigs and newsprint scraps the boy had given it, plus bits of lint it had gathered on its own. Patchwork though it looked, it was a perfectly good cocoon.

Where could it have been hiding all that time? the father later wondered. Someplace no one would find it, that much was clear. Perhaps behind the bookshelf, where there was plenty of lint it could use to make a cocoon. Then, when it had finished weaving its new quarters, the worm had crawled out to a bright, sunny spot near the southern windows.

The boy was in the bath shooting his water pistol at the walls and ceiling. Caught up in his game, he had stayed in much longer than he should have.

"Dry yourself off and come on out here. We've got a surprise for you," his mother and sister called to him.

Little imagining that the "surprise" would be his bagworm, the boy jumped out of the bath and dried himself as fast as he could.

The last one to see the cocoon was the father. He had gone out that evening and did not get home until late, long after the others had gone to bed; it was the next morning before he finally heard about the bagworm from his wife.

Out of doors, he had never given bagworms a second thought. But there was something rather curious about a worm that built itself a cocoon when it was inside a house with a solid roof and ceiling overhead.

"I wonder what it has in mind," he said to his wife. "Does it intend to set up house there, do you think?"

"It certainly looks that way."

He noticed a tiny piece of bright red paper stuck to one side of the cocoon. Had his son put some bits of construction paper in the box too? Or was this something the worm had picked up in its travels around the room?

WATERSTONE'S

22/10/97 13:10 J 59 6846

1 @ 9.99 4770017081 # 9.99*

SHOWA ANTHOLOGY

SUBTOTAL # 9.99

SALES TAX @ 0.00% # 0.00

TOTAL # 9.99

TENDER CCARD # 9.99

SAUCHIEHALL STREET VAT No. GB238554836

Tel. 0141 332 9105 Fax. 0141 331 0478

At the other end of the bay window from where the two stood inspecting the cocoon, the goldfish swam quietly in its bowl. It nibbled for a moment at some moss that had formed along the edge of the water, then lost interest and turned away.

WITH MAYA

Shimao Toshio

Translated by Van C. Gessel

Once in a great while a reader stumbles across what the Japanese refer to as a "crane in a dunghill," a true gem of a writer whose work has not been widely recognized, but who obviously deserves our attention. Such a writer is Shimao Toshio, a profoundly moving author whose name was virtually unknown to the reading public in Japan until 1977, when the publication of his novel Shi no toge *(The Sting of Death) earned him every literary award that could be offered. Since that time a wealth of critical studies have appeared, some of them suggesting that Shimao may well be the finest novelist at work in Japan today.*

Born in Yokohama in 1917, Shimao graduated in Asian history from Kyushu University in 1943 and at once volunteered for service in the Japanese Navy. Given a year of training, he was then appointed commander of a suicide squad that was sent to defend the Amami Islands between Okinawa and the mainland. After nearly ten months of daily preparation for death, the orders to ready for launching finally came—on August 14, 1945. The bizarre experience of living daily life for the sake of death, and of a reprieve that was no real release from anxiety, has formed the core of Shimao's fiction. Many of his short stories deal with his war experience, such as "Shuppatsu wa tsui ni otozurezu" (The Departure Never Came, 1962), which was shaped by his suicide corps experience.

Shimao has also written a string of surrealistic, nightmarish stories in which mundane everyday life easily slides into the horrors of chaos and uncertainty; the finest of these stories is "Yume no naka de no nichijō"

(Daily Life in the Midst of Dreams, 1948). But the decisive incident of his life, which reinforced his apprehensions during wartime, came in 1954, when his wife Miho suffered a severe nervous breakdown. In response, Shimao had to terminate his teaching and writing careers for a time, joined Miho for treatment in a mental hospital, moved his family back to her native home on the Amami Islands, and converted to Roman Catholicism. Removed from the center of literary activity in Tokyo, Shimao published "Ware fukaki fuchi yori" (Out of the Depths I Cry, 1955), the first of many stories dealing with his tormented relationship with his wife. Over the ensuing twenty years, Shimao published several volumes of stories on the same theme. These were eventually brought together as Shi no toge, *one of the finest modern novels written in Japan.*

"Maya to issho ni" (With Maya, 1961) is a touching, self-conscious story set on the fringes of Shimao's personal anguish. In it Shimao writes gently of an emotionally disturbed little girl, one of the victims of family battles described in his other works. Maya is a symbol very much like the deformed baby in the writings of Ōe Kenzaburō: *a portrait of modern man, ravaged and anguished by life but unable to express in words the source of all that pain.*

* * *

The patients, who leaned against the corridor walls or sat on sofas waiting for their doctors, resembled fish that dwell at the bottom of the ocean. They wore expressions like fish that know their bodies will shatter if they come too close to the bright surface of the sea, and suffer from the sharp difference they can see between their own faces and those of fish that move in shallower waters. I felt an affinity with that look, realizing that it mirrored my own nature perfectly.

I wrapped my raincoat around my legs and folded them under me on the sofa, hoping to ward off the chill that was creeping from the soles of my feet up through my entire body. Doctors and nurses in white coats streamed down the hallway and in and out of rooms, but I had no idea what connection they might have with our appointments.

In an attempt to assert control over this oppressive waiting, I took a book out of my coat pocket and began reading. The book was made up of fragments taken from an unusual life by a novelist who was no longer living. I wanted to let those episodes pass through my mind once again, and then forget them completely.

Maya walked up and down the long hallway as though battling the winds across a vast plain. She wore the slacks we bought her after our arrival here in K City; her oversized jacket was in fact one of my wife's old coats, which had hurriedly been retailored for our trip. With half-hearted, aimless steps she would wander to the far end of the corridor, then return. On her way back, she would thrust out her chin a bit and stare with open mouth at the faces of the people standing in the hallway or walking past her. Each time she came up to me, I stroked her hair, moved over, and sat her down beside me. But she was on her feet again immediately, to continue her restless wandering. As she walked she swung the long string of her little handbag, which was decorated with clusters of colored glass beads. She was tall for her age, but gave an impression of frailty and slenderness that was exaggerated by the threadbare coat.

The nearest exit was a glass door down the corridor; through it, the row of square windows in the white building across the street was distorted in the rain. One could see only a small portion of the building even through the large windows here in the clinic. Maya flattened her nose and cheeks against the glass door and stood there for what seemed an eternity. I finally got up from the sofa and went over to her.

"What can you see?" I put my hand on her shoulder and peered through the glass, but she looked up at me without responding. The pupils of her eyes were immobile, and her face revealed no emotion. Still, I recognized this as a look of trust.

I could see the two-dimensional shapes of cars and people moving in various designs along the broad, rain-soaked asphalt far below.

"Is it interesting?" I tried to inject some enthusiasm and makeshift cheer into my voice, but her answer was a simple "Nope," the negative phrase that all the children in our island village used with their peers.

"Are you cold?"

"Nope."

"Do you hurt anywhere?"

"Nope."

I changed my tactics. Touching her abdomen, I asked, "Is your tummy all right?"

Finally she laughed, as though I had tickled her.

"What are you up to? You really worried Daddy. You were wandering around with a really funny face, and then all of a sudden I find you standing over here staring out the window. You tell me right away if you start hurting anywhere. Don't try to keep it a secret."

I had no way of knowing whether she could understand what I was saying. Once she had told me her stomach hurt, when she was actually trying to let me know that she was hungry.

My examination was over quickly, and I was sent to a different room to have some gastric juices drawn. I put my arm around Maya's shoulders, hugging her tightly to me, and we walked down the hallway in step. My spirits were high, and I felt like whistling.

"After they take some of Daddy's stomach juices, it'll be your turn to see the doctor. We have so much to do! What do you think Mommy and your brother are doing now? I bet they're thinking about Maya. Are you worried about Mommy? You don't need to be. You're with Daddy now. Do you wish we were back on the island right this minute?"

"Nope." She gave the pat answer, but after a moment's thought she revised it to, "A little."

"You wish we were back home a little? Well, Daddy wishes we could go back now, too. Daddy likes it best when Mommy and your brother are with him."

"Maya too?"

"Of course Maya too. Mommy and your brother and Maya and everybody all together. Do you like this city?"

"Yep."

"Why?"

"Lots of everything," she answered in a soft, hesitant voice. It was easy to miss much of what she said unless you were used to that voice.

The room I was shown into was merely a cubicle with a bed, a desk, and some diagnostic equipment crammed into it. The steam-heated air carried the odor of an unfamiliar medication.

A young woman was helping a feeble old man out of the room just as I started in. Following the nurse's instructions, I lay down on the bed. It still retained a faint warmth from the old man's body.

A doctor in a white coat was in the room, and I nodded to him, but he offered no reply, and merely looked me over the way one would study an inanimate object. Without altering his expression he said something to the nurse, but the words meant nothing to me.

"It must have just slipped your mind, Doctor, that. . ."

I understood the words in the first part of her remark, but the rest seemed to involve some private matter. The two halves of the phrase came together, skittered across my body, and were gone.

The doctor spoke only a word or two and then left the room. All they were going to do here was extract some of my gastric juices, so he probably didn't need to be present. The nurse had removed her white cap. She looked like an office girl who didn't care much about anyone but herself. I didn't like the idea of having this young woman work on me, perhaps because the image of gastric juices was unpleasant. Thanks to her makeup and the steam that filled the room, her cheeks were dyed an unnatural red. She rolled a cart up beside my bed. On it were several test tubes and some rubber tubing. Maybe it was just my imagination, but she seemed to dislike this particular procedure.

"Please turn this way." She helped me turn over, held out the rubber tube to me and said perfunctorily, "Swallow this down to the white line."

I sat up and looked over at Maya. Seated on a round chair in the corner of the room, she had taken a tiny doll out of her bag and, with lowered head and pursed lips, was avidly dressing and undressing it.

"You keep playing over there, Maya. Don't touch any of the machines." I swallowed the rubber tube.

The odor of rubber was like the smell of entrails seeping from somewhere deep underground. When the cold metallic tip of the tube poked the walls of my throat, I gagged and coughed it back up.

"Can't you get it down?" the nurse asked reproachfully.

I moved my jaw in a chewing motion as I reflected that she had probably never tried to choke down a rubber tube. Though it threatened to come up again several times, the tip eventually worked its way down toward my stomach. It left me feeling trapped and anxious; it was like wondering what would happen if you were in the middle of surgery when an earthquake struck. The tears that spilled out and moistened the corners of my eyes did nothing to settle my nerves. I took a handkerchief from my pocket and dabbed at my eyes.

"Are you in pain?" the nurse asked. I tried to say a word in reply, but again I felt like retching and kept silent. She ought to have known, having done this so many times, that it was difficult to speak. Yet she seemed disappointed when there was no answer. The faintest ripple of cruelty stirred within me, and the comfort of knowing I had shut myself off from an outsider flickered through my mind. I thought of the doctor's apathy and the nurse's hard, businesslike manner, and felt I understood them to some extent.

When the wave of nausea subsided, I lay back and rolled onto my side, where I remained motionless. The end of the rubber tube poking out of my mouth was pinched off with a clip and hung over the edge of my pillow. I stared at the procession of alien substances from my own stomach that was passing before my eyes.

Maya, apparently absorbed in her doll, was not making a sound. I supposed that when she finished changing its clothing, she would comb its hair, styling and restyling it.

Another doctor came in, but unlike his predecessor he spoke in a loud, confident voice, using a dialect I had difficulty understanding. He babbled on to the nurse about some sort of party for a colleague, then went out again. Neither doctor had even seemed to notice Maya. I couldn't imagine how they could miss seeing a little girl playing with dolls right next to the person they were treating.

The nurse moved all around the room, busy with what seemed to be a variety of chores. At intervals she removed the clip from the end of the tube, guided the tip into a test tube, and carefully examined the fluid that poured out.

Though it was a part of me, I was disgusted at the sight of this heavy, viscous liquid that came from deep within my body. It tickled the walls of my esophagus as it made its lukewarm way to the outer world. Yet the nurse did not seem disturbed. I marveled that she didn't seem to react even when some of the fluid spilled onto her fingers as she fiddled with the tube. If it had been me, though the juices were my own, the nerve ends in my fingertips would have recoiled. But the tips of her fingers casually came in contact with this gastric fluid. I had difficulty reconciling her initial distant manner with the movements of her fingertips. I avoided her face and instead concentrated on her hands. As she worked, the tepid air inside my abdomen was displaced repeatedly by the cool outer atmosphere.

"If you're bored, you're welcome to read your book."

I doubted my ears. But I pulled out the book I had stuck under my pillow and began reading where I had left off. Unlike the hallway, where the cold had worked its way up from the bottom of my feet, reading here on the bed in a room softened by warm steam, I had no desire to skim over the words. Instead I was able to relax as I read, allowing my mind to formulate whatever associations it wished between the lines. As a result I experienced a story I had read before in a totally new light, and when I occasionally came across familiar passages, I felt as though I were reaffirming my own past in the pages of the book.

Maya quietly slipped around the foot of the bed and tugged on my sleeve until I looked in her direction.

When I shifted my eyes from the book to Maya, she held out a piece of candy nestled in the palm of her hand.

"She gave me," Maya said, glancing toward the nurse.

I was gratified that the nurse had acknowledged our situation. From the time that Maya's speech became garbled and she stopped talking loudly enough for most people to hear, she had, in fact, spoken less frequently; instead she resorted more and more to attempts to communicate with her body. If she walked up to you, it meant that she wanted something. If she could not get her message across, though, she would leave without a word. Even after she was gone, her ungratified desires seemed to drift in the vacuum she left behind. Gradually I would come to realize what it was she wanted, and the more brittle layers of my heart would crumble. But Maya seemed to have no inclination to press her requests and thereby expand her sphere of influence.

Once an array of light and dark fluids had been gathered in the test tubes, Maya and I left the room.

Time ticked by relentlessly; already it was near noon. Although an entire morning had been peeled away from my life, I felt I had attended to something that needed doing. The morning was done. Now there was only an afternoon to get through, as swiftly as possible.

We went to the neurology clinic for Maya. There I stiffly set forth the circumstances of her affliction, as I had done so many times in the past. I was drained by a fear that I would leave out something significant and by the weariness of repeating the familiar story. Sometimes I volunteered every detail, sometimes not, depending on the responsiveness of the doctors and my own state of mind. There were times when I was unable to muster any enthusiasm at all, knowing that this first encounter could well be our last. I could not shake off the suspicion that once something went wrong with a person mentally or physically, that malfunction could never be corrected. The fact that any number of doctors who had examined Maya had been unable to diagnose the cause of her speech impediment only etched that doubt more blackly on my brain. It was reassuring, all the same, to meet specialists who would listen to my pleas and undertake some form of treatment for Maya's symptoms. They would try to get her to say a word or two, but she would tilt her head, look up at me imploringly, and make no attempt to respond to the doctors' requests. That was the inevitable outcome; not once in the course of an examination had a doctor persuaded her to speak or even move her tongue. When they tapped her knees with a rubber mallet, had her pull one leg up to her chest, thumped on her legs, or made her walk around, she would turn a coquettish look on them and then intentionally move her arms and legs in an awkward way. It seemed as though Maya had planned out a perfect mime of the behavior they expected her to display.

As we waited in the empty, drafty room, a young woman staffer dressed in a white lab coat came in.

"Why don't you and I have a little talk?" she said to Maya, taking her and sitting her down by the desk in a corner of the room. "Has she ever had an IQ test?" she asked me.

"I think they probably did one at her school. But I'm afraid I don't keep track of things like that, so I can't say for sure."

"Her name is Maya, isn't it?"

"That's right. Maya."

"Well, Maya," she said, turning back toward my daughter, "there's nothing to be afraid of. I'm not going to give you a shot or anything like that. You and I are going to study together, okay? You answer the questions I ask you. If you don't know an answer, it's all right to say so."

She set something out on the desk and showed it to Maya.

"What's this? I bet you know, don't you? Tell me—what is it?"

As usual Maya turned around and glanced at me bashfully.

"This is an easy one. Please tell me. Don't you want to say it? Well then, take this pencil and write it down on the paper. You can do that, can't you? What is it? That's right! It's a little mouse. See, I knew you could tell me what it was. That was terrific! Now, how about this?"

The crude, businesslike desk and couch took up the greater part of the room. From my perspective in the corner, the two of them seemed to be inside a compartment partitioned off by diagonally arranged screens. The desk was near the window, and looking at them against the light and at an angle from behind, their forms seemed to shimmer. It was oddly moving. The woman leaned forward to ask Maya questions, and Maya, unwilling to default on an answer, seemed almost in pain as she cocked her head and twisted her body in the effort to respond. Eventually she began to utter a phrase or two in that small, hesitant voice. She's let down her guard! I thought, and inwardly I mumbled encouragement to her: "Loosen up! Loosen up!" Maya seemed even younger than ten years old as she darted her eyes about, thrust out her chin, and opened her mouth vacantly. It was a shock to consider how profoundly different she was from other girls her age—shrewd, robust, competent girls who were beginning to display a touch of worldly wisdom. Like a fragile piece of machinery, Maya in all her workings was delicate, and seemed unable to tolerate even the most imperceptible exchange of emotions.

Still, I could sense in her a ready sympathy and tenderness that spoke directly to my heart. Which of her physical or mental processes had ceased to function normally? She was virtually unable to do any sort of mathematical calculation, but her memory for everyday matters was the most vivid in our household. We were amazed by her precise recollection of appointments her parents had forgotten, or of places where we had tucked away coin purses and the like. When we lost something, Maya would nonchalantly announce its whereabouts in sparing phrases, then silently lead us to the spot.

Bathed in the light from the window, the features of the two grew indistinct, but their profiles stood out in bright relief, evoking a quiet, harmonious excitement in me. Even though Maya was tongue-tied and taciturn, my head was filled with images of an incorrigible chatterbox. I imagined that her face sparkled, something that almost never happened during an examination. Tense with anxiety and fear and bewilderment, Maya was focusing all her energies on trying to accommodate herself to the unpredictable new situations that were presenting themselves one after the other. Grief invariably followed on the heels of resignation each time she abandoned the effort to communicate, but Maya was content to bear the consequences, and made no unreasonable demands on herself.

The rain continued, and as we stood at the door of the hospital, for the briefest moment a white emptiness overcame me. My mind tends to be in disarray when I'm on a trip, and though there were several places I needed to go to, I didn't feel like going to any. A number of destinations flickered through my brain—places too distant to walk to and too close to ride to. Only the knowledge that we had hotel reservations saved me from giving up entirely. The ricocheting drops of rain left pockmarks inside my head and stomach and combined with the chill air to enshroud us both in misery.

I had come to K City primarily to take care of some business. With that completed, my next objective was to have Maya examined. Getting my stomach looked at was a lesser priority. Over the last year or two Maya's speech impediment had become obvious. In the beginning it had been so subtle we wondered if she were feigning the disorder, but soon there was no room for doubt. At the country clinic on our tiny island, the doctors could detect no cause of her problem. For some time we had wanted to have her examined at the well-equipped general hospital in K City, a city many times larger than our island village, but somehow the opportunity had never arisen. Now our hopes had been realized. But we could hardly expect them to come up with a precise diagnosis during the brief time I was here on business. I was told they would not be able to arrive at any conclusions until they had observed Maya for a fixed period of time and had conducted certain tests. But circumstances and my own lack of resolve would not permit us to remain here very long. We had already had the doctors do everything within their power at the island clinic. Other new tests had been administered here, but the results were no more illuminating. They could suggest no better treatment than continuing the pills she was already taking.

I raised my hand and hailed a passing taxi, hoping to dispel the numbness that had come over me.

I had not made up my mind where I wanted to go, but as I sank into the cushions in the back of the cab, the name of a destination pushed its way between my lips.

It was a place where I still had work to complete. Basically I had finished my business here, but there are always those extra tasks to perform, so I was never without something to occupy my time. Maya waited motionless in a chair beside me, while the adults engaged in their dull conversations. As a child, I occasionally accompanied my father on business visits and despaired of the grown-up chatter, never knowing when it might come to an end. Bored beyond endurance, I would tug on my father's sleeve, only to be stabbed by a sharp glare from his eyes. Though Maya squirmed in her chair, gnawed by tedium, the hard crust I had acquired as a façade kept her from pulling at my sleeve.

Maya and I finally left after five, past the end of working hours. The rain was now a misty drizzle, not heavy enough to soak us. The sun had already set, and the city was preparing itself for the labors of the night.

Whenever I travel away from home, I am tormented by a concern that what I'm doing may prove, at any given moment, to have been a mistake. That feeling intensifies abruptly in the evenings, when I've been released from my duties at work. Inevitably I end up thinking that I've made an inexcusable blunder simply by being somewhere far away from my family. I know I have left them to look after a home in a place quite surrounded by water and separated from me by overwhelming distances. If some frightening, unforeseen calamity should occur in my absence, I could not rush to their aid. Before word of the mishap could reach me, a legion of futile hours would have slipped away. No one would know where to contact me from the time I left my hotel in the morning until I returned at night. Even if news reached me quickly, the ocean stretching between K City and our island was a daunting barrier. Were I lucky enough to make the ferry connection just as it sailed from the dock, I would still have the crossing to contend with: fourteen or fifteen hours of slow, eddying time. The simple effort it took to imagine such things all but tore my emotions out of the realm of reality.

My anxiety was alleviated somewhat on this trip by having Maya with me. She observed my every action, giving me the reassurance that my entire day's activities were being recorded on film within her dense, enclosed world, where feelings were not shared with anyone outside. From now on I would probably take Maya with me no matter where I went. The moment I imagined myself beyond the range of her gaze, I felt darkness close in with its morbid black shadows.

At such times a nightmare appeared before my eyes: I saw my wife and son suddenly plunged into a lunatic frenzy, while the villagers all walked quickly along, their bodies bent slightly forward, their mouths tightly clenched. I had no idea where they were going, but they continued to walk, half stumbling, crossing each other's paths from the left and right, with no sign that they intended to stop. There was no escaping these visions, even with Maya at my side. I was gripped by an urge to abandon my work and the doctors' examinations and race home on the first available ship. None of my business in town seemed so pressing any more. If there was one responsibility I had, it was to keep the four members of my family together, and never leave our island.

As I waited in the long hospital corridor for someone to call my name, I realized that this period of waiting was full of possibilities.

I had no notion when I would be called, or what sort of schedules the doctors kept. Since the time until my summons (no matter how long or short) was left to their whims, I had to remain where I was. But I was free to pursue some simple, fulfilling projects while I waited. I had my reading, and Maya had her strolls up and down the hallway. The best use of my time was to find a story I had already read in one of my books. Since I had nothing else to do, I could read it again without distraction, trapping and holding whatever power and resilience it had.

Eventually the door of the room in front of us would open and the doctor would call my name.

On one side of the hallway was a glass door that looked down onto a square courtyard. In one corner of that shadowy, unused space, scraps of paper tossed from the hospital windows lay dirty and stained, exposed to the elements.

Maya was desperately tired. I wanted to let her rest at the hotel, but I couldn't bear leaving her there alone. We had to do everything together. I had dragged her along with me to the city office, to the homes of acquaintances, and to dinner parties. Perhaps that was why her eyes swam unsteadily, like those of a sleepwalker. More frequently now she would drop off to sleep with her mouth gaping open.

"Maya, do you hurt anywhere?"

As always, her answer was "Nope."

"Be sure to tell me if you do hurt. You must tell Daddy."

"Um-hmm."

"I wonder why you're so jittery?"

"Don't know."

"You're tired, aren't you? Oh dear. When we get through here, we'll go right back to the hotel, okay? Now, let's see a smile for your dad."

Maya curled her lips into a little grin, which quickly gave way to a look of exhaustion.

"I'm sleepy," she sighed.

"Sleepy? Well of course you are. You were up late again last night. We shouldn't have gone to that party. Your daddy hates parties too. But I had to go to that one. Everybody there really thought you were cute, though. That made it fun, didn't it? Come over here and lie down. You can put your head on Daddy's lap and go to sleep."

I placed her head on my lap. She stretched out on the couch while I stroked her hair.

She lay with her mouth propped weakly open, but her eyes did not shut, so I stroked her eyelids closed with my fingers, repeating softly: "Go to sleep, go to sleep."

My wife had often put our young children to sleep that way. "Close you eyes, and go to sleep."

But Maya could not sit still. Before long she lifted her head. "Go to sleep, go to sleep," I insisted, pushing her head back down, my hands stroking her soft, red-tinged hair. Her eyelashes and the hair at her temples were long. There was a full-blown femininity in her face, the look of a grown woman in miniature. We had lived in Tokyo until she entered elementary school. There she had been a vigorous child and spoke a crisp Tokyo dialect. She would go everywhere by herself, and even tried to retaliate on her brother's behalf when he lost a fight with another child. There was no trace of that nimble spirit in Maya now.

I held her down lightly to get her to sleep. She closed her eyes, apparently giving in, but her eyelids continued to flutter. Finally she seemed to abandon the attempt and tried to sit up again.

"Are you okay, Maya? Do you hurt anywhere?"

"Go pee-pee," she answered.

"Pee-pee? Oh dear. Can't you wait? I suppose you can't hold it, can you? Daddy has to stay here. . . I have an idea. Can you try to go by yourself?"

"Uh-hmm."

"You'll be okay, won't you?"

"Uh-hmm. Okay."

"Daddy doesn't know where the bathroom is. Can you find it by yourself?"

"Can find."

"Well, you go ahead then. Come right back. Remember now."

Maya took a few steps, then returned and asked, "Can I buy chew gum or something?"

"Of course. You can buy chew gum or anything you like. Do you know where the snack bar is?"

"Uh-hmm. Know," she said lightly.

Maya was surprisingly good at remembering routes she had taken, the faces of people she met, and where things had been put. She may have seemed flighty and unobservant, but it was as if she had been blessed with a special talent for accurately recalling circumstances involving herself. Before I knew what was happening, I had let her go off alone. But she was scarcely out of sight before I began to squirm with the anxious fear that I had made a bad mistake.

The door in front of me remained closed. I still had no idea when it would open and my name would be called. I was nervous about missing my turn, so I couldn't bring myself to leave my seat. I shifted my eyes to the words in the book I was reading, but my gaze merely stroked the surface of the written symbols and left me with no sense of their meaning.

I realized at some point that my eyes were dreamily chasing after the characters printed on the page, an indication that I was nodding off to sleep. I lifted my head instinctively and looked around. Maya was nowhere to be found. The shock that she had not returned increased my fear. It seemed as if a long time had passed since Maya had left me, but having no watch I could not be sure. During that time my eyes had skated over a succession of words. Though I could not grasp their overall meaning, I had a clear sense of the gist of each individual phrase. Perhaps Maya had been confused by the layout of this large hospital, where all the wards looked alike. In my imagination a vision of Maya's face quickly took shape—the face of a girl falling into a black despair because she could not find her father. There was little chance that Maya could even find the words to explain her dilemma to someone else. And even if she made a decisive effort to express herself verbally, there was no guarantee she would be understood. Perhaps fear would make her lose her mind.

I had piled blunder on blunder. In trying to impose some sort of order on the petty details that swam about in my head, I had paid too little attention to more important matters. I could not rid myself of the image of a member of my family being driven to distraction as a result.

Aimlessly I stood up from my chair and thrust the book into my pocket. My hand brushed against something. I pulled it out to find the wrapper from some chocolate I had bought for Maya. When had it got stuffed in there? I was as startled as if I had suddenly seen Maya's ghost. My heart began to pound, and in distress I hurried to the end of the corridor. But all I could see was the familiar figures of hospital employees and patients scattered at various points along the hallway. My eyes could not find what they were looking for.

A feeling of irretrievable loss swept over me. I did a quick about-face and retraced my steps, but the odds of finding Maya there were very slim.

Inexplicably, I had a vision of Maya collapsed and bleeding beside a white porcelain toilet. That image overlapped with one of my distraught wife. I decided it was unwise to torment myself needlessly, and abandoning the course on which an impulse had led me, I turned back to check once more in the direction Maya had disappeared. As I turned the corner, I saw her coming toward me in a crowd of people.

How haggard she looked!

Surrounded by other people, her bewildered expression was grotesquely conspicuous, and darkness pressed in on me. I searched her face in vain for a trace of her usual blunt inquisitiveness. Instead she seemed resigned to being under constant surveillance herself.

She wore the same top and slacks I put on her every morning. Her clothes were rumpled, badly in need of starch and a good pressing. The elastic waistband on her pants had stretched out of shape and dangled limply. When she saw me she did not react; it was as though she were looking at a stranger. Wandering was second nature to her now; in need of none of my feeble protection, she was setting off alone for a destination far beyond my reach.

"You were gone a long time, weren't you, Maya? Where did you go? I thought maybe you didn't know the way back. Did you find the bathroom? Did you go pee-pee?"

Maya nodded.

"It took you a long time, didn't it? Daddy was really worried. Did something happen?"

"Nothing. Got my underpants a little dirty. Okay? You mad?"

"Of course not. Don't worry. Nobody came in, did they? You didn't fall down in the bathroom, did you?"

"Nope. Nobody came. Didn't fall."

"That's good. I guess you didn't get your underpants off far enough and so you got them wet. Well, nobody's going to get mad at you. Daddy was afraid you'd fallen down in the bathroom and couldn't get up. Your underpants aren't very wet, are they? If they are, you'll have to take them off."

"Not very wet."

"Will you be all right until we get back to the hotel? You will, won't you? We'll change them as soon as we get back there."

I stared intently at Maya. Something bothered me—a fear that she would go off somewhere beyond my power to do anything for her. Apparently she had gone to the snack bar: melted chocolate rimmed her mouth like whiskers.

"Here, turn your head this way. You've got chocolate on your mouth. Hold still and I'll wipe it off. Maya. You mustn't stare at other people like that, with your mouth open all the time. You've got to control your feelings. If you don't, people will think you're an idiot."

Since Maya could not give a detailed account of her actions and feelings, I had to rely on the fragments I gleaned to get even a rough idea of how she felt. As the days passed here in K City she had obviously grown more and more exhausted. I should have kept a careful watch on her, but being away from home I ended up pushing myself until personal concerns were forced into the background and dealt with only in half measures. And Maya was forced to take part in it all with me. I could not imagine leaving her alone in the hotel room.

It was nearly noon when my name was called and I entered the black-curtained room. We had spent much of that day in the hospital corridor. In the darkened room I swallowed some barium, and afterward the doctor rubbed, patted, and poked my abdomen with supple hands. The entire procedure did not take long. Strangely, when I climbed onto the X-ray platform, the dull ache in my stomach disappeared. I felt as though I had hoodwinked the doctor, but the palms of his hands had transmitted his concern for my afflicted area, and that stirred a pleasant rhythm within me.

Maya was very tired, so we took a taxi, and I put her to bed as soon as we got back to the hotel. She went to sleep without dinner that night.

Since she was still asleep the next morning, I let her rest. Her soft hair looked like seaweed at the bottom of the ocean.

Near noon she opened her eyes and said she was hungry. I gave her an apple. She seemed to have revived, so I suggested, "Why don't we go and have something to eat at a department store?"

She smiled her approval.

That put me in high spirits, and I said, "What would you like to eat? Name anything you want."

"Sushi."

"Great. We'll have sushi. What else?"

"Ice creams."

"Daddy'll have some ice creams too."

"Wanna buy a present."

"That's right, we do have to get some presents. Should we go home if there's a boat tomorrow? I really want to see Mommy and your brother again."

"Teacher too."

"What should we get for your teacher?"

"Pencil is nice. Wanna look at lots of things."

"Well then, we'll make today our present-buying day. How do you like that?"

"Great!" she grinned. Exhaustion must have led to yesterday's incident. A good sleep, and she was back to normal now. I called the shipping line to confirm the sailing schedule for the following day, and then we set off cheerfully for the department store. We had our sushi and "ice creams" at the restaurant and went looking for presents. I didn't venture any opinions as we walked around, letting Maya choose what she wanted to get. It was not long before I felt as though I were out shopping with my wife.

There was still a little time before sunset when we came out of the department store, so I finally gave in to Maya's entreaties and took her to a movie theater. She insisted that she wasn't tired and wanted to see the film, so I had no reason to refuse.

The film involved several lively exchanges between two cheerful sisters in an American family, and each time something funny happened, Maya laughed out loud.

I breathed a sigh of relief, and the waves of anxiety that still surged faintly within me had nearly subsided when I felt Maya leaning against me. At first I thought it was because she could not control her laughter. But it seemed a little peculiar for her to be laughing, since the scene had changed to a conflict between the sisters over some man. I really hadn't been paying much attention to her, until I realized that her laughter had nothing to do with the images on the screen. I looked at her in surprise, to discover that she was staring at the floor with a handkerchief crammed tightly in her mouth.

"Maya. Maya!" I shook her, but she would not take the handkerchief from her mouth. She had been crying, not laughing, but I had no idea why. I hurriedly got up from my seat and took her out of the theater, with my arm around her shoulders.

The handkerchief was soaked with saliva, and her flushed face and even her hair were wet with tears. Her eyelids were puffy and swollen. Remorse hit me like a sudden blow to the pit of the stomach, destroying my lively mood. We grabbed the nearest taxi.

Maya buried herself in the seat cushions and continued to sob. She looked like a tiny wife burdened with grief.

"Maya, why did you start crying? You were laughing so hard at first. What was sad?" I knew what her answer would be.

"Don't know."

"Was it because you felt sorry for them?"

"Don't know."

"Was it because it was sad?"

"Don't know."

"Was there something scary? Or did you remember something scary?"

"Don't know."

In resignation I stopped interrogating her. As I wiped her face and hair with my own handkerchief, I was aware that some incomprehensible fate hovered over her.

When we got out of the taxi, Maya tugged at my elbow and said, "Always." I had no idea what she was talking about, and asked her two or three times to repeat it.

She thought about it for some time, and after groping for a way to express her feelings, she finally spoke in tones meant to convey the enormous weight of the words she had hit upon: "I always cry when I see movies."

I had not made Maya take a single bath since our arrival in K City. Mounting exhaustion had drained her of the inclination to bathe. Once the agitation that overcame her in the movie theater subsided, my anxiety dissipated, and I began to treat Maya in the usual manner. I decided it would be nice to have a bath before we went back to our island, so I took Maya with me to the public bathhouse.

When I had finished washing her, conscious of the willowy form that was growing taller without seeming to add a pound of weight, I shifted my attention to my own body. A short time later I glanced around, to find Maya with her head totally submerged in the soaking tub, while she vigorously pretended to wash her hair.

Horror surged through me like a flash of light, and I called out in an unexpectedly sharp voice, "Maya!"

Slowly she lifted her head, peered up at me from an angle, and smiled a tentative smile.

"What are you doing, Maya? Are you trying to tease me?"

I softened my tone, reminding myself that I mustn't get excited, and waited for a response. I had to remain calm and consider things carefully.

Hesitantly she answered, "Maya felt funny. All confused."

"And did it make you feel better to wash your hair?"

"Don't know."

"Maya, look Daddy in the face. Are you dizzy? Why did you wash your hair there in the tub?"

"Don't know. Got confused."

"Maya, where are we?"

"The bath."

"Do you know who I am?"

"I know."

"Let's get out, okay?"

I cut my bath short and took Maya straight back to our hotel room. I put her in a nightgown that I had finally bought her here in the city after many requests. As I dressed her, changing the several layers of underpants that my wife had told me to have her wear, I found they were soiled. I could hear her at the hospital again saying, "Got my underpants a little dirty. Okay?" I had wanted to keep a close watch on Maya during this trip, to make sure that I never deserted her. Yet at every turn something like this happened, bringing the inadequacy of my supervision into stark focus. I was now confronted with direct evidence of a time when my gaze had wandered. As I struggled to deny my negligence, I noticed that some clotted blood was mingled with the stain.

"Maya, do you remember going to the bathroom by yourself at the hospital? Did you just go pee-pee then? Or did something else come out?"

"Don't know."

"You said you got your underpants dirty. How did you get them dirty?"

"Thought I just needed to pee-pee. But my stomach hurt and went b.m. too."

"And you put your underpants back on dirty?"

"I wiped!"

Inscribed at the back of my brain was a vivid picture of Maya walking down the hospital corridor in a state of near collapse. I had not been sensitive to the feeling of abhorrence that must have enveloped her when she was left all alone to take care of the clothing she had soiled in the bathroom. Somehow I could not bring myself to imagine Maya coping with the predicament herself. I found myself wondering if Maya didn't in fact know everything that was going on, and when she was away from us and around other people, if she didn't speak quite clearly and bustle about like a hardworking housewife.

Her torso swayed precariously as she stood there in her nightgown, so I quickly made up her bed and laid her down.

"Do you hurt anywhere?"

"Nowhere."

"Does your tummy hurt?"

"Not hurt."

But I continued to inquire, refusing to take her at her word.

"Does your head hurt?"

"Hurts a little."

"Which part?"

"Hurts right here."

"How does it hurt?"

"Hurts a little."

"Does it always hurt there?"

"Um-hmm."

"When did it start?"

"Lots of people together. Daddy's friends. One was nice to Maya. Maya tried to go bathroom, fell down. Hit head."

I had been busy talking with some acquaintances and had no recollection of Maya, who nearly always stayed right beside me, leaving the second-floor meeting hall and going downstairs to the bathroom. Here was yet another piece of evidence that my supervision was inadequate. I had difficulty visualizing just how Maya was able to recover in that moment of despair. In places unknown to me, Maya had been falling down or soiling her underpants, but my head was filled with images of her that were strangely unreal. Even so, I had to conclude that what I had found was bloodstains. But I hadn't the slightest notion whether that sort of thing could possibly happen to a girl not yet in the fifth grade. Perhaps it was some presentiment of its onset. I looked down at Maya. I wanted to hurry back to the island and report this to my wife, and discuss it with her.

"Go to sleep now, Maya. There's nothing to worry about. Go fast asleep."

THE MONASTERY

Kurahashi Yumiko

Translated by Carolyn Haynes

Kurahashi Yumiko was born in 1935 in a rural area surrounding the city of Kōchi, which has been a remarkable breeding ground for modern writers (others include Yasuoka Shōtarō and Ōhara Tomie). Initially Kurahashi planned to pursue her father's career in dental hygiene, and she received her license to do so, but she had become interested in French literature on the side and enrolled in that department at Meiji University. In this she has something in common with another contemporary experimental writer, Abe Kōbō, who turned to the writing of fiction as soon as he received his medical degree.

In 1960, the year she graduated from Meiji University with a thesis on Sartre, Kurahashi published the short story "Parutai" (Partei; tr. 1982) and created a literary sensation comparable to the discovery of Ōe Kenzaburō just two years previously. From the outset of her career as a writer, Kurahashi has been influenced by Sartre, Camus, and Kafka, and her declared intention is to be an anti-realist. This she achieves marvelously through a blend of native sensitivity and a strikingly rich and fluent experimentalism. She may, in fact, possess the most fertile literary imagination in Japan today. But it is an imagination that has been tempered by accusations of "plagiarism," a year of creative writing study in Iowa in 1966, and a period of silence following the publication of her most interesting works to date: Sumiyakisuto Q no bōken *(The Adventures of Sumiyakist Q, 1969; tr. 1979),* Yume no ukihashi *(The Floating Bridge of Dreams, 1971), and* Hanhigeki *(Anti-tragedies, 1971). More recently she has returned to active participation in the literary world with the publication of* Otona no tame no zankoku dōwa *(Cruel Fairy Tales for Adults, 1984).*

The present story, "Kyosatsu," was written in 1961 and is a product of Kurahashi's early, somewhat indecisive experimentalism, but her intriguing views of reality and unreality and the fluidity of human relationships are expressed in this story with the same vigor and skill to be found in her other works.

* * *

The early walk Father and I take along the flagstone path was interrupted today by the unanticipated arrival of K. The sloping path we were about to descend, winding from one building to the next, was aglow in the still dormant light of the summer morning when K, the traveler K, came bounding up with that extravagant agility of his. He presented my father with a letter of introduction from some university. I cannot describe his vacant but intoxicating looks, which have a quality one sees in dreams; I cannot even say from what planet this traveler might have come. According to his own account, which is of course unverifiable, K is a scholar of art just recently appointed to an educational institute. Even more dubious is his claim to be a poet—dubious because of the ambivalence of that term itself. In spite of this, or perhaps indeed because of it, Father ushered K into our temple with a startling burst of scathing comments—both witty and self-mocking—and a familiarity bordering on enmity which seemed inappropriate in a priest of our sect. My hand, extended in greeting, was clasped in K's, which trembled with enthusiasm, a chilly excitement, and in that moment my eyes were seared by the fire in K's rude gaze. Taking this in with the acuity of his years, Father approached me and, as if in ridicule, muttered that name—your name, my betrothed. I am not sure whether the giddiness I felt was caused by the worn familiarity of that name or by the flicker of passion I had discerned in K.

I suppose K will stay at Temple H.

Having promised to see him again despite complex reservations, I served today as K's cheerful, intimate guide. We embarked on an enthusiastic tour of the monastery buildings, from the reliquary pagoda to the winding verandas and on to the ancient wooden storehouse. Drawn by some mysterious attraction, we walked behind the old abandoned belfry and took a small path that twisted and turned like a labyrinth through the grove. We seemed to be following the tracks of time, spiraling down into the interior of our spirits. Despite the encroaching heat, the grove had trapped cool, green air in its web of foliage. We wandered along the wooded path, avoiding the menacing sun which shone like an old bronze dish above us. The thicket of maple and beech trees interlocking above a cover of hawthorn and andromeda ended shortly, and we entered a wood of cedars rising perpendicularly. Hundreds of parallel shafts of sunlight streamed through the trees to pierce our bodies. I kicked off my shoes to let the moss caress my feet, and, shaking off K's admonishing voice which rang with shrill foreboding, I ran between the cedars like a snake through grass. K ran after me. We kept up this strange game, drawing together only to lose sight of one another, the thread of pursuit becoming more and more entangled, until we were suddenly greeted by two limpid springs. They were seductive traps the earth had laid for us, staring blue eyes our bare feet wounded as we scurried over the shifting pebbles. In silence we endured the permeating cold. After a long interval, K and I abruptly thrust out our hands in an act of plunder until they intertwined, my hand with K's, and from this moment of plantlike union we surrendered to the artifice of our burning fingers, that through our hands' embrace each might draw the other into the greedy receptacle of his own being.

This afternoon I sought refuge from the violence of the midday heat. My bare legs stretched at full length on the floor of an old pavilion in the dense green shade. I gave in to the numbing lure of drowsiness, and with the distorted precision of a hallucination, I relived from the previous day the still vivid imprint of K's caress, an embrace and connection that was purely spiritual—the contact of our hands no more than the inevitable closing of a circuit.

In the same way that it is hard for me to remember your body, I cannot even attempt a faithful description of K's physical form. I know only that your imposing, convex figure is an entity more solid than the very buildings of this monastery, the central pillar of my existence; whereas K's concave figure, an almost defiantly meager presence, seems merely hollow, the negation of a soul possessed of such ill-fated magnetism.

Until now I was the pure and innocent daughter of this kingdom, the mistress of a vast monastery—the great and small halls and the winding galleries that connect them, the scores of temples with their earthen walls, the gates, the storehouse, the grove concealing innumerable springs and streams. Yet had I ever truly seen them before? My walks with K these past few days have shown me this. I am now seeing this temple complex through K's eyes. Emulating K, sharing his sentiments, I am tying myself to this place with bonds of affection, tasting the delight of a pilgrim from a foreign land. Yet this sharing of covert pleasure is very like the uncertain solidarity of traitors.

Despite the cruelty of the afternoon sun, I set out for the spring that lies deep in the grove, to join K in a scheme he shyly proposed several days ago. He was already at the spring, standing like a ghost bathed pale in the fairy-tale light of midday. But the sight of me invariably turns K transparent and makes him drip with sweat. I clasped his hand, a hand like a bunch of red-hot rays (I can find no better words to describe this mundane contact, which is so ruinous for K, so like a secret rite to me), and we undressed in the shade of the moss-covered rocks. Then, urged on by the accord each read in the other's eyes, we set off like brave stallions on our expedition to the cave, an adventure presaged days before. Eagerly tracing the course of the water that bubbled from the spring, we struggled to breathe air heavy with the fragrance of summer grasses, until we found the funnel-shaped depression leading to a subterranean river which we had come upon the other day. Here water from the spring lapped gently against the rocks before being sucked into the bowels of the earth.

Standing at the rim of the funnel, I watched K slide into the passage, leaving an unearthly, startled cry in his wake; then I too slid my naked body into the opening in the rock, colder to the touch than reptilian skin.

The pain of rocks scraping my belly blotted out the fear I felt at crossing this threshold into the unknown. The chill gloom of the nether world hung in the air. We walked along a narrow arcade formed by columns and ledges of rock. The sound of dripping water was everywhere; the subterranean waterway coursed through its channel like a gentle vein, swollen by a host of tributaries. Our excited voices rang out in the dark as we sought to pierce the suffocating gloom; our cries were like the shrieks of bats in flight, rising to a thin pitch of fear and fascination—pathetic screams tearing at the membrane of our souls. Suddenly the cavern was filled with a faint glow. Concealed beneath the high vaulted ceiling, a mosaic of waters in every shade of blue had formed a small, mysterious lake, and a shaft of silver light, seeping through a crevice in the vault, now cleft the surface of the pool. With an inner luminescence, the stunning color of the water seemed to dye even the air of the cavern the same lustrous hue; in chill ecstasy we clasped our arms about our bodies, which had themselves become a plantlike blue. Then, without warning, K dived like a fish into the water and disappeared. The calm was shattered, and the pool, disturbed by K's agitated movements, dissolved into a thousand glittering mineral flakes and scattered its radiance throughout the cavern. I realized that I was biting my lips violently, chilled by the water which sent a shuddering but agreeable sensation through my body. Then K bared his white teeth in a shout and pulled me into the water. His arms sought my body, slippery as a fish, in a fierce, defiant embrace. Obsessively he caressed my hair, which floated like strands of seaweed on the water, but the next moment I was swimming, guided by the light, toward the opening to the world outside.

Our eyes were momentarily blinded by the light, and then we saw an awe-inspiring scene. The water flowed slowly out of the cavern and trickled in a narrow cascade down a perpendicular cliff. From its base stretched a distant world etched in hieroglyphs of rocky precipices and barren valleys, a desolate, bizarre world unmistakably not our own. I stood with my fingers twined in K's, caught in a trance yet wanting only to flee. But K's white body heeded its own impulse and scrambled down like a lizard toward this world of fierce sunlight and stone. It was a forbidden zone to me, and I was left to return despondent, plunging more recklessly than a madman back into the darkness of the cavern and on to the haven of the monastery.

I am ill. But I am confident that by your return this illness will have left me. Ultimately, my steady progress toward recovery will mean a closing of the doors for me, as I resume my life as daughter of this monastery. I cannot bring myself to forsake the inheritance of this kingdom's worldly objects, you among them. There remains only one seed of anxiety—my sorrow in knowing that K, that rootless wanderer, would also confine himself here.

Your carefully announced arrival—though it should have been an eagerly awaited homecoming—seems to have dealt a harsh blow to the sentiments that K has bottled up inside him. The first chivalrous encounter between you and K occurred, according to some exquisite, unconsciously devised scheme, at the middle gate early this morning. No visitors had yet come to the gallery where K and I stood ringing the wooden pillars playfully with our fists. My father had sent you off as his representative, and now you were returning with the fruits of your mission packed in a mundane leather case. Still clad in your dazzling black robes, you approached at a near gallop from the massive main gate, sounding the flagstones on the path as you came. As you neared us K, despite ample foreknowledge of your return, was thrown into a panic at this sudden meeting and dashed his head against the glass wall of formality that stood between you, heedless of the injury he caused himself, and scattering brilliant fragments on the ground. Like a sister trying to gloss over her younger brother's blunder, I reddened in confusion, and as I reached for your heavy case, I tossed a mocking remark in K's direction.

My cruelly lighthearted introduction must have been more painful for K than the most violent condemnation. Let it be so . . . I am satisfied for your sake. You, my betrothed, with your pendulous fleshy earlobes like the stone Buddhas, a priest epitomizing the perfect fusion of transcendence and ego, you who are to succeed my father after our marriage and become abbot of this vast temple complex—throughout my introduction you stood confronting K, that incarnation of irrefutable reality, and bit by bit you undermined his already tenuous existence. I too reverted in your presence to an unwarranted condescension toward K, acting as if he were a mere traveler, or an effete and possibly bogus artist. All the while K used this opportunity to take in my hair, my neck, especially my eyes with avid glances; but this you must not mind, for the fruits of his admiration are for you, not I, to savor.

In any event, it is natural that K should feel respect and goodwill toward you, since you are my betrothed. You both are satellites revolving in opposite orbits around the magical power that I am privileged to wield.

K will not leave the temple. Like one seeking a site for some unspeakable crime, he spends day after day probing every inch of this labyrinthine complex, every corner of its rotting buildings, its temples and refectories, the white walls of the bathhouse, the maze of paths and streams in the forest. I am no longer his guide; K's remoteness precludes the resumption of those summer walks which so resembled pilgrimages, but this stems no doubt from the good-natured jealousy he feels toward you. K seems bent on spiriting away this enormous kingdom piece by piece, absorbing its three dimensions—nature, human artifice, and power combined—through his wide-open eyes. He has even decided not to return to his research position in the autumn. So now he is nothing. I cannot explain from what world K came to intrude on ours, or imagine what will become of this oddly childlike trespasser. . . That is something only you can know, because you are a peerless gentle seer, who understands the web of karmic relations.

As the summer wanes, tilting its chalice of light with increasing swiftness, K's presence here has dwindled into insignificance as we sit behind our walls of calm conventionality; but I wonder if it isn't nurturing some dangerous cancer all the same. Precisely because I want more than anything to abandon resistance to that destiny he has set in motion here, I fear that it will continue slowly to decay, poisoned by the curse it bears within itself, until it ends in catastrophe.

I am dazzled by the sovereignty over you and K that my sex bestows on me. When the two of you have placed me at the heart of a conversation, addressing each other in silver tones while your eyes duel venomously, I conduct the swelling strains of the dialogue with a counterpoint of queenly majesty and innocent coquetry. Then why do you still refuse to acknowledge the iridescent, unplumbed bond of sympathy that has begun to grow between myself and K?

You know, you should kiss me in front of K. He wants to see it, too.

The days, each indistinguishable from the next, consume the autumn sunlight. An interminable drought has dried up almost all the springs on the temple lands; only the underground river that K and I explored that summer day supplies the secret cavern with a shallow flow of water. The sun adheres to its daily round, leaving a masterpiece behind—an arc of melancholy yellow that makes the cluster of wooden halls and the shroud of dust raised by visitors shine like gold in the autumn sky.

K has left the temple—for the time being; which is to say that he and I have a tacit understanding that his absence will last only as long as it takes us to contrive some mutually desirable scheme. He will definitely return, summoned by the mesmerizing bell on the big clock, like a traveler plunging into the snare that destiny has set for him.

As autumn enters its swift, inevitable decline, I cannot check my own descent, each day a little deeper, into a singular anguish. K's absence has become too painful, like a gaping hollow inside me. You must surely have noticed: when I look into the mirror I am startled by the morbid gray circles beneath my eyes.

In consultation with Father, you have advanced our wedding date by five months, presumably so that this change of plans and the busy days before the ceremony should redeem me.

This entire monastery is run as a single administrative unit, and it is you who are to head it next. And I am to be your wife. You will never fully possess me, though; at most you will have only that half of me which has already hardened. The vessel you know as me—unfailingly cheerful but visibly transparent—contains absolutely nothing, as befits a vessel of misery. For the present it is imperative that I have your practical concern, your affection (though no one knows better than I that you love me), and your constant touch.

K will miss the wedding. . . I set out today for the sacrifice like a maiden sent to consort with the statues that have stood in that great hall, absorbing the debris of time, for a thousand years. That was the pact we made for the sake of this great monastery.

Matrimony and its attendant rites of the flesh have worked no change in me. The void inside me is too immense, a void that cries out for another, false partner, the husband of my fantasies.

Then today K returned, coated in fatigue, to complete that obscure circuit. It must be passion that has caught him in its net. If you would give your blessing, the three of us could share a love so abundant that none need ever go hungry; yet K does not want that.

I am at a loss how to receive this bridegroom in funeral dress.

K told me this: that both he and the light of the spell that controls his fate dwell in my eyes.

You and K toss the concept of death back and forth between yourselves like a bouncing ball in a child's game. This constant dialogue on death—of course it is death by one's own hand that is at issue—is harmless and even wholesome for you, but it is mortal sport for K. Each time you toss him that smooth ball, K's whole body is stabbed by deadly thorns invisible yet as painful as if he had embraced a cactus. Again today, in the face of your eloquent refutation he pursued this passionate debate on death. I shudder with a sweet anxiety.

Still halfheartedly stirring the embers of yesterday's strange discussion on the aesthetic suicide, you and K were busy sorting through the storehouse collection of old scrolls and rare *gigaku* masks, urns fashioned as dragon heads, and swords. Shoulder to shoulder you toiled like the most amicable of twins. Recklessly I put on one of the large demon masks and wedged myself between the two of you, digging my hands into the dust. My hand brushed a sensitive fork of flesh, but whose fingers they were I couldn't tell. . . At this point K grasped the plain blade of a sacred sword. Turning to you with savage, icy composure, he made a request you could not deny him: that he be allowed to borrow this sword to protect himself on his journey.

You know, don't you, that I do not want to set K free. The cool, damp caverns of K's existence are now one more force protecting the equilibrium necessary to keep me bound to you. As if draining a cup, I have swallowed the absurd fantasy that K is my younger brother, or that I will marry him off to a friend in order to keep him close to me.

You will be tolerant, I know, and permit me these foolish dreams. And yet you scrutinize me with your contemptuous eyes, deliberately silent about my feelings for him, as if you wanted to underscore his existence and suffocate me by assiduously avoiding sarcasm.

You were instructed by my father today to take part in the secret rite of penance for the sins of the world. On this occasion, as on every other, K occupied a symmetrical position, with me as your axis (I inevitably pretend not to see your well-suppressed indignation at the impropriety of this, but would you yourself prefer that he be allowed between us?); and with only a hint of irony he presented his congratulations as though he were a perfect stranger. You returned his salutations with an air of polished cordiality: the perfect priest personifying the world and its canon of conduct. Forced into the armor of this deceitful goodwill, K treats you with brutal respect. If I radiated an almost hostile cynicism then, it was not directed at you. You have every right to display those civil, antagonistic teeth in your smiling face.

I finally passed sentence on K; with only some faint justification, I condemned him to desist indefinitely from any visit when he might possibly run into us. . . Raising his exhausted, yellow face, K listened to my decision, shreds of despair still lodged between his teeth. Then he lashed out at me, brutally, incoherently, arming himself with all the polished craft and cunning of his crime. Volleying word after word of stinging praise, he reiterated his unshaken admiration for your genius for theater and my acting skills. While this bitter barrage flew from his tongue, I threw back my head, swallowing like a lethal dose of some powerful drug his claim that you and I are in league against him.

K is still away today.

You are performing the rite of repentance. I cannot see you, either.

There was still snow on the ground at noon, but I was bathed in an unseasonably abundant February sunlight when I went to the refectory to observe your ritual meal. Milk-white light streamed over the seats of the eleven ascetics, and strict silence reigned from the ringing of the bell, when a white-robed monk began to serve the simple fare, to the blessing that signaled the end of the meal. With your glasses you stood out as the freshest, handsomest figure among those men assembled in prayer, but the tiny glint they gave off alarmed me, for it was then that I caught sight of K, standing motionless outside the hall.

From dusk onward, an incredible number of spectators and groups of foreigners began swarming about the Kannon Hall. I stood below in the tall forest of pillars supporting the veranda, in a spot where my hair and eyes risked being scorched by flying sparks, and awaited the beginning of the fire ceremony. As if in keeping with this esoteric drama, which has been repeated for a thousand years, heavy, gentle snowflakes began to fall. At the same moment, the ascetics gave an unearthly cry—reverberating from antiquity down through the ages—though in their midst one could detect the boyish timidity of the younger monks. Then they thundered wildly up the steps and into the hall. On their shoulders they bore great torches of fiercely burning cedar. The eleven torches, thrust one after another beyond the railing, blazed in cones of fire and light, swirling above my head in a dance of savage; frenzied spirits. The dance described an unfinished ring of fire, scorching the dark sky. I opened my mouth and disgorged all self-awareness so that I could drink in the sparks that rained around me. It happened then: a hand like an electrically charged hook seized my neck from behind—and instantly, in a jumble of recognition, I knew it to be K. Turning, I pressed my lips against his, lips salty as a bewitching wound glistening with blood; but still the violent shower of snow and fire cooled my face and singed my hair as if to prevent the breach before betrothal, the estrangement before union of these two insubstantial souls. I had not seen K's face, for my breasts had ripened amorously in a sudden rising of sap, and our exchange of poisonous fluids had drowned me in an intense, almost mortal pleasure. This, the entire beginning, was the end.

You see it all now, don't you: the kiss K and I shared last night, the fine tapestry of saliva lingering on my lips, the mysterious bond that brings two people's lips together. With mouth agape I await the final act.

When the black hand of night had come to rest over the monastery and gray mist began to rise from the springs and river, a messenger from K suddenly appeared. He was a novice from Temple H, and he handed you K's note. You eyed me gravely, arresting the cry on my lips and the flood in my eyes with your almost comical self-possession, that icy composure of yours. The message it bore . . . I knew was word of his fatal departure. But you cold-bloodedly tore it up, instructing me in a voice more ponderous than the tolling of a bell to bring the short sword to the messenger. Those words sent the battlements around me crashing to the ground, yet you turned to the novice with a ruthless smile—still innocent, it seemed—and asked him to convey your wishes for the safety of K's journey. The ancient sword vibrated in my palm with a metallic sound—three lines, perhaps, of delicate musical notation. My teeth chattered like dozens of rattling stones, so loud you turned in disbelief. With a cruel effort, I clenched my trembling teeth and mutely handed the novice the murder weapon, in obedience to your calm behest.

You took it all in, didn't you—my face swollen to bursting point with its burden of tears and choked sobs, my eyes sunk deep in sharply creviced flesh. . . I turned my face abruptly away, so violently it almost broke my neck. A low moan escaped my clenched jaws like a drop of despair, a single, concentrated bead of emotion, and I fled the room. In the bedroom, imprisoned by modern walls and oppressive curtains, I flung myself onto the bed, bent over double—I did not weep, for what solace could gentle tears of self-pity bring my charred spirit?—but my body stiffened unawares, deadened by the curse that had already begun to envelop K. Time made its faint footsteps echo inside my sensitized skull, pacing threateningly back and forth, and drew me little by little into abstract numbness.

In a shuddering trance I dreamed of K ripping himself open with a blade of transparent ice. Offering me his lips, where the traces of that blasphemous kiss still lingered, K mutilated his own white flesh, severing that consciousness which burned like blood in a rose-colored blaze. . . Suddenly I heard a long drawn-out cry, followed by the sad tremolo of a soul plummeting from this world.

Soon the abbot of Temple H, drawn to the discovery of K's act by that intolerable cry echoing around the globe, came with his face distorted by shock to tell you of the tragedy. Without a sound I paled and collapsed before you, yet I managed a faint satisfied smile at this blow which seemed a vengeance on you.

Rushing to Temple H, we found K lying senseless in a pool of blood. No hand could save him now. His ashen face was masked in this atrocious, pagan death. Beneath the burden of dense nothingness his dying spirit sought its final release, spewing in a cone of red mist through the hole gouged in his throat, whistling like the strains of a flute more plaintive than the sorrowful ocarina.

Suddenly a voice rising in prayer froze me to the spot. It was you; you stood motionless, a statue of hardened, bitter salt, chanting a spirited sutra in your sonorous voice.

Funeral arrangements were summarily completed; the ceremony was little more than a purging of the violent death of a sinful outsider. While the corpse was being washed according to Father's instructions, I too was washed in salty, bitter tears. The innumerable wounds held for me an attraction even greater than the flesh surrounding them, and I covered the white corpse with imaginary kisses. The pallbearers passed through woods frozen the color of white bones and out through the rear gate, drawing away into the distance unaccompanied by even an attendant monk or relative. Behind the slow procession of gravediggers and professional mourners trailing their attenuated shadows, the last spasmodic throes of the sun dyed the evening haze blood red, and presently the procession was engulfed like the intermittent line of a river on the distant, undulating horizon of dust-colored sand and stones.

UNDER THE SHADOW OF MT. BANDAI

Inoue Yasushi

Translated by Stephen W. Kohl

Inoue Yasushi is one of the established deans of modern Japanese literature, a "dean" being defined as the owner of a house around which Japanese newspaper reporters gather like vultures once every year before the Nobel Prize for Literature is announced in Sweden. Inoue certainly can boast of one of the most enduring and successful careers in modern letters in Japan, and the variety of his work has earned him many devout supporters in his country's literary circles. He chaired the international meeting of the P.E.N. Club in Tokyo in May 1984, and was elected an international vice-president of that organization.

Inoue was born in Asahikawa on the island of Hokkaido in 1907. His father was an army surgeon, and the frequent transfers that his parents endured contributed to their decision to send him off to live with his grandmother, an experience that finds literary expression in scores of his isolated heroes. Although Inoue had difficulty dedicating himself to his studies as a youth, the single-minded devotion he displayed for physical and spiritual discipline in pursuits such as Judo was later mirrored in his near-scholarly passion for literature. Inoue kept himself aloof from the many philosophical disputes of the 1930s; aesthetics was his main interest when he enrolled at Kyoto University. After graduation in 1936, Inoue joined the staff of reporters on the Mainichi. *He was drafted a year later, but illness forced him to leave his army division in North China after only a few months. When he returned to the* Mainichi, *Inoue was assigned to cover religious and artistic news, a task that gave him the opportunity to deepen his knowledge of Buddhism and the classical arts, two realms that play a central role in his fictional writings.*

By 1947, Inoue had attracted attention not only as a poet, but as the author of two exquisitely poetic short stories, "Tōgyū" (Bullfight) and "Ryōjū" (The Hunting Gun, tr. 1961); the former was awarded the Akutagawa Prize for literature. Within three years, Inoue had resigned from the newspaper and was devoting all his time to his creative endeavors. His journalistic eye for detail and sense of audience enabled him to produce a string of popular novels, but Inoue did not find his niche until he began publishing historical works, many of them set in China. A succession of novels such as Tempyō no iraka *(The Roof Tile of Tempyō, 1957; tr. 1975) and* Tonkō *(Tun-huang, 1959; tr. 1978) set the tone for Inoue's literature—the examination of the faintest ripples of cultural interchange between Japan and the outside world, ripples often created by lonely individuals who remain essentially nameless and faceless in the annals of official history. Most recently Inoue has returned to that examination of cultural interplay in* Wadatsumi *(God of the Sea, 1977), a detailed study of Japanese emigration to the United States. In 1981 he published* Honkakubō ibun *(Papers Left by the Priest Honkaku), a sensitive, ghostly account of the death of the medieval tea master, Sen no Rikyū. "Kobandai" (1961), translated here, is one of the most prominent of many Inoue stories combining meticulous historical research, a restrained, scholarly style, and an empathy with the muted details of human tragedy which are often lost amidst the larger calamities of nature.*

* * *

In those days the road from Kitakata to Hibara was a journey of some fifteen miles. By leaving Kitakata around eight o'clock in the morning and proceeding at a leisurely pace, one could be in Hibara by two or three in the afternoon. On the way, however, one crossed the Ōshio Pass just beyond Ōshio village. For some distance on both sides of the summit there was a difficult stretch that wound its way through sharp outcroppings of rock. Yet teamsters with pack animals passed this way in both directions virtually every day, and for these sturdy working men the trip was no hardship. The road, called the Yonezawa Highway, went from Wakamatsu through Kitakata and Hibara and on to Yonezawa. Now that the railroad has gone through, the highway has been largely abandoned. But in the last years of the nineteenth century, in fact, on July 13, 1888, when I set out from Kitakata to make the journey over the mountains, the road was rather crowded. Horses and travelers were frequent because of the many sawmills around Hibara which cut wood that was then hauled to Wakamatsu for use in the lacquer trade. The number of freight wagons carrying logs for that purpose alone was increasing daily, it seemed to me.

Though traveling on official business, we were not in a hurry, and from the very outset our excursion had a festive, holiday air about it. At the time I was working as a tax collector. Of course everyone supposes a tax collector is someone who goes around extorting money from poor people, but that was not really the case. Today we would call someone with my job a tax assessor or a surveyor of crop production.

Ours was the county office responsible for collecting taxes, and every year we were required to survey the amount of land under cultivation by the villages within our jurisdiction and to assess taxes on any land that had been cultivated since the previous year. Making that assessment was my job . . . but perhaps first I should explain that the town called Kitakata did not yet really exist. Instead, there were only the villages of Odatsuki and Koarai, which were separated by the Tazuki River; I worked for the county office located in Odatsuki. Back then the work we did was called "land production surveying." On the trip I am describing, our purpose was to survey the north flank of Mt. Bandai, which fell within the administrative district of Hibara village. My job was to survey the land that was being farmed by the many tiny villages scattered about the region popularly known as the "back side" of Mt. Bandai.

I was accompanied on the journey by two assistants, Tomekichi and Kinji. Tomekichi was of an age where his hair was beginning to be flecked with white. He was in his late forties, thin, and very serious. He walked with his kimono tucked up behind to allow greater freedom of movement. His spindly legs gave the impression that he was a pretty weak traveler, but in reality none of the rest of us could match him when it came to trekking through this wild north country. Kinji was a reticent young man of thirty who tended to be rather gloomy. He also wore his kimono tucked up and straw sandals on his feet. I was the only one of the group dressed anything like a modern tax assessor. I had dark blue work pants and a windbreaker, but like the others I wore straw sandals and had an extra pair tied to my belt.

Although I was the leader of the group, at age twenty-eight I was also the youngest. From the time I was twenty I had worked as a customs inspector for foreigners in Yokohama, so I had some knowledge and experience in the work of assessment; which is probably why, even at my age, I had become a person of authority in this rural county office. Tomekichi was not a professional assessor; he had originally come to the county office as a part-time employee, but over the years he had helped with the business of assessment and eventually joined the staff of the assessor's office. I believe he felt quite satisfied with the position he occupied. Kinji was a clerk who had only recently been employed in the Kitakata office. His handwriting was very neat and clear.

Our trips were usually scheduled to last ten days and we always made certain we had plenty of spare time. On our first day we planned to follow the familiar route from Kitakata to Hibara, and since it would hardly impress the villagers if we arrived in Hibara too early in the day and just lazed around, we made a point of loitering at tea shops along the road, and even paused for a nap under the shade of the trees once we reached the pass. Our clerk Kinji, who had only been married for about a month, dozed every time we stopped to rest, and was teased endlessly by Tomekichi.

The weather grew very warm and sweat bathed our bodies the moment we started walking, but whenever we paused to rest, the dry wind on our skin felt refreshingly cool. This was indeed the best time of the year to be traveling in this part of the country. The rainy season had been late and it was early July before we had any days that were completely cloudless. The weather was quite unusual that year and some people were concerned about the effect this would have on the crops. Since the weather had only just cleared, we had been accustomed to seeing a dull, overcast sky for days on end. But now the vital, green vegetation covering the mountains, the clean air that settled the dust, and the cloudless, deep, translucent blue sky all greeted us as we set out on our trip. We looked forward eagerly to days of pleasant traveling.

On that first day we finally arrived in Hibara around four o'clock. On the way, there was an incident so trivial it is probably not worth mentioning, except that I had reason to remember it afterward. We were walking along the bank of the Hibara River after coming down from Ōshio Pass when we met a woman going in the opposite direction, a woman dressed as a pilgrim making the rounds of the Sixty-six Holy Sites. For a moment she stood in silence blocking our way, until we saw that she appeared to be trying to say something. We clustered around, peering intently at her face and trying to catch her murmured words. She was muttering some sort of warning to us, saying "Go back. Go back. You will be in danger if you go any further." The woman appeared to be about forty and was dressed in the gray clothing typical of a pilgrim. A gray knapsack was on her back and she wore leggings and mittens to match. In one hand she carried a small bell. Her complexion was dark and made even darker by the liver spots of advancing age. She seemed to be a strong-willed and ill-tempered woman. She gazed steadily at us when she spoke, and I noticed that her eyes glittered with an unnatural brightness. She was no ordinary person.

Kinji and I both pushed past the woman, ignoring her words, but when Tomekichi tried to follow, she moved left or right several times, blocking his way, until finally he had no choice but to shove her aside. Having done that, he hurried to catch up with Kinji and myself, muttering, "Crazy woman! How unpleasant!" Nevertheless, Tomekichi seemed to have been disturbed by what the woman said, for as we walked along he turned back two or three times to look in her direction, and seeing that she was still watching us, he murmured something about this encounter being a very unlucky sign.

So, this was one of our experiences, but we were on the first day of our trip and were relieved at not having to face the drudgery of our usual office duties, and our spirits remained high. Later that day we felt several mild earthquake tremors. Once a jolt came just as we were crossing a bridge. It was not a suspension bridge, but the support beams began to creak, and we could see cracks appearing where the boards joined together. "It's an earthquake," said Tomekichi, and even before he spoke,

I knew it was a strong one. Over the course of the previous month we had become quite familiar with earthquakes. Even in the region around Kitakata it was common to have two or three tremors a day that were sharp enough for a person to feel, so we had grown used to them and saw no cause for alarm.

Thinking about it later, it occurred to me that the warning the mad pilgrim woman had given us should not have been laughed off. Indeed, if we had listened to her and turned back at that point, most likely we would each be leading our appointed lives without ever having experienced the tragedy and sadness that soon befell us. When you come right down to it, man's intellect is a pretty shallow thing, and we never know what the future holds. So, as it turned out, we continued on our way, taking ourselves step by step unwittingly toward the gates of Hell.

Hibara, as I said earlier, was a village of some fifty houses located along the Yonezawa Highway. In earlier times it had been called Hinoki Yachi. The village was surrounded by groves of cypress called *hinoki*, so the original name of the place meant "valley choked with *hinoki*." The village lay in the shadow of Mt. Bandai, to the west of Mt. Azuma, and on the flank of Mt. Takasone. It was surrounded by mountains, and not only was there very little level ground in the region, hardly any of what was level had been brought under cultivation. In that sense, it was not a productive area. The people of the villages there preferred to make their living cutting wood or stripping bark for use in making paper, or by driving their packhorses over the mountains.

There were three inns in the village. Were one to continue along the road from Kitakata directly northeast and cross the pass at the county border, in another seven miles one would reach the village of Tsunagi; and from there it was another seven miles or more to Yonezawa. Hibara was indeed a tiny mountain settlement, but it was situated on a corridor used, much more then than at present, to spread the new Meiji enlightenment, and just four or five years earlier a troupe of Sumo wrestlers had passed through this region on their way to Yonezawa and Yamagata. We were guided by the village headman to the entry hall of an inn where we removed our traveling sandals. I noticed the inn sported an enormous sign announcing that it was here that the Sumo tour had stayed. Apparently the sign had been made soon after the wrestlers' visit.

It was our plan on the following morning to leave the Yonezawa Highway on which Hibara was located. We were to turn due south and follow the Nagase River through the forests that covered the lower slopes of Mt. Bandai. About four miles from Hibara was a hamlet of seven houses called Hosono, and a couple of miles further on was the village of Ōsawa, consisting of some twenty houses. At Ōsawa one stood directly beneath Bandai. It was only a couple of miles from Ōsawa to the hot spring resorts of Nakanoyu and Kaminoyu, located midway up the slope of Mt. Bandai; the road went straight up the side of the mountain. Several miles from Ōsawa toward the northeast flank of Bandai stood the village of Akimoto, which was composed of twelve households.

Our job on this trip was to survey these three villages—Hosono, Ōsawa, and Akimoto. We had postponed our survey in Hibara, thinking that since there was a village headman living there, we could conduct it any time. We decided to survey the three small villages buried deep in the mountain forests during the brief period between the end of the rainy season and the onset of really hot weather in midsummer.

That night, by previous arrangement, we had a meeting at our Hibara inn with the people from the village headman's office. We received support for our plan from the three members of the headman's staff, namely, Shuntarō, Kume, and Shinshū. Shinshū, of course, is an odd name, but everyone kept calling him "Shinshū, Shinshū," and soon I was following their example. Both Shuntarō and Kume were men in their sixties. Shuntarō was a rather reserved, aristocratic man, with large ears and a cheerful expression. Kume was quite the opposite, being somewhat impulsive and loud by nature. He had sunken eyes and prominent cheekbones. Shinshū was a small, intelligent man who managed all the details of the office work with a voluble tongue and vivid gestures. It was difficult to judge his age from his features; he might have been in his thirties or forties.

These three men were eager to have the land survey carried out and agreed to accompany us to the actual survey sites. Barely twenty years had passed since the Meiji Restoration and many local citizens thought we were trying to cheat them when we described the system of levying land taxes. And so we had to marshal a force of workers at least this large to persuade a mere forty households to consent to the annual survey.

Early the following morning, July 14, the six of us were ready to depart. The three local men, Shuntarō, Kume, and Shinshū, had the skirts of their kimonos tucked up like Tomekichi and Kinji. We all wore leggings and straw sandals and used towels to protect our faces from the sun. Just as we had all assembled in the earthen-floored hallway of the inn to set out on our journey, we felt the first earthquake of the day. This was the most severe of the many tremors we had experienced recently, and all of our group as well as the maids at the inn quickly spilled out into the road.

As we were leaving the village, we came to a bridge and from there proceeded along the left bank of the Nagase. Here the road curved gently in a southerly direction and passed through an open area of stony ground. No sooner had we come to that rocky place than we felt another tremor. This one was milder than before and we supposed it was merely an aftershock of the previous jolt. None of our party made any comment, but it did give us reason to pause. I noticed that the ground was littered with small stones and the morning sunlight touched these stones, glinting off the blades of grass that grew between them. Even though it was still early, the sunlight sent up shimmering heat waves which promised a hot day ahead. To be watching something as insubstantial as this haze of heat and at the same moment to feel the ground begin to tremble filled me with uneasiness, as though even the earth itself were not to be relied upon. But the tremor passed in an instant, like the shadow of a bird sweeping over the ground, and though an ominous feeling flickered through my mind, as soon as the trembling stopped I forgot all about it.

After leaving the flat land along the river we found ourselves confronted by the three massive peaks of Daibandai, Kobandai, and Akahani. Gazing at these lofty summits, we were deeply impressed by their grandeur. I had often heard people speak of the beauty of this region in the shadow of Mt. Bandai, and I now realized that it was in fact more magnificient than I had been told. From the lower slopes of the great mountain down to the river plain stretched large natural forests of cypress, oak, zelkova, and maple, which gave a dark, almost gloomy aspect to the landscape. The slopes of Bandai itself were covered with stands of red pine, white birch, and other sorts of trees. From where we stood on the riverbank the whole view was one vast wooded panorama. It was hard to believe that the three villages we planned to visit were somewhere out there beneath that sea of living trees. Indeed, it was a bit frightening to think that people spent their whole lives beneath the canopy of that seemingly endless forest.

Just before reaching Hosono, the road forked. One branch went along the lower slopes of Mt. Naka Azuma, and the other, the road we would follow, led in the direction of Mt. Bandai. We took the fork to the right and soon came to a long, log bridge that crossed over to the right bank of the Nagase River.

As we passed over the bridge, the clerk, Shinshū, noticed a swarm of toads moving beside the river.

"Look at all the toads down there among the stones. They must be migrating." Shinshū's comment prompted the rest of us to notice that what appeared to be stones beside the river was in fact a vast army of toads on the move. They followed one leap with another without a moment's pause, and since the ones behind kept surging forward, those in front had no choice but to keep moving. There was an odd single-mindedness in this moving, living mass. I had the feeling they were all intent on a single goal, allowing nothing to divert their attention.

We all commented on this remarkable sight and stood for a time entranced by it. Shinshū said that in the spring when the snow begins to melt he had seen groups of toads mating, but this was the first time he had ever seen so many of them migrating. Kume replied that once, about ten years ago, he had seen toads fighting in this area. Apparently one group had a dispute with another group from further up the river, and they had waged a toad battle to settle the issue by force. He was sure that was what these were up to as well.

"Come on! Let's get going. We'll never get our survey done if we just stand here," said Tomekichi. At this the rest of us turned away from the toads and continued on our way.

Around ten o'clock we reached the village of Hosono. I call it a village though it consisted of no more than seven households. They were nice, sturdy houses clustered together on a narrow piece of land closed in on the east and west by the peaks of Hachimori and Tsurugigamine. The encroaching hills seemed to crowd into the village on both sides. This was truly a mountain hamlet. The main work of the men there was logging, and each of the houses had a small shed attached which looked something like a chicken coop. Here the family kept a wood lathe or two. The farming was left to the women, and when we arrived at the village there was no sign of them because they were all out in the fields.

Tomekichi was taken by one of the villagers to the mountains behind the settlement so that he could get a view of the layout of the fields, while the rest of us passed the time in desultory conversation with an old man who had once been a logger. There was another small tremor during our talk.

While waiting for Tomekichi to return, we met some of the men of the village and made preliminary arrangements for the survey we would be conducting during the next few days. Having accomplished that much, we left Hosono and headed on. Beyond the village the land suddenly opened out into low, rolling hills. A broad plain spread east and west, and standing in the middle of it we had an unobstructed view of Mt. Bandai.

After leaving Hosono our route turned away from the river we had been following for so long. Ōsawa was a couple of miles further along this road, which ran through virgin forests. Actually the path was so narrow it could hardly be called a road. We passed places called Kiyomogihara and Ōfuchi, but they were merely names, for we did not see a single dwelling. At Kiyomogihara we met a group of people, including some women, who were coming down from one of the hot spring resorts on Mt. Bandai. The group consisted of a man and his wife who were in their fifties, their youngest son who was fifteen or sixteen, the wife's younger sister who was in her thirties, and two young men from the village of Shiobara near Hibara who were serving as guides to the group.

The man was a merchant from the Niigata region who had gone to the resort of Nakanoyu for a month's treatment, but they had cut short their visit by a full week and were now hurrying down the mountain, having formed the uneasy impression that the mountains were somehow different from usual.

The husband had the sallow complexion one associates with the chronically ill and he remained silent in a sullen, bad humor. The woman's face was tight with emotional strain of the sort seen in hysterical people, and she rattled on like a person unable to stop talking. According to her story, four or five days earlier they had been surprised to find that the amount of hot mineral water flowing down from Kaminoyu had dropped off significantly. Also, the quantity of steam that issued from among the rocks had inexplicably increased in both volume and pressure. Although Nakanoyu still had plenty of water for the baths, in the past couple of days it had become so hot no one could bathe in it. In addition, the mountain had been rumbling for the past four or five days and the rumbling had grown more ominous each day. This morning the sound was so fierce it seemed the mountain itself might burst. Then, of course, there had been the tremors. The woman said they made a habit of coming to this resort every year, but this was the first time anything strange had occurred, and they thought something alarming was going to happen.

In concluding their story the wife said, "There are many other people besides ourselves who are frightened and leaving the mountain. And now we meet a group like yourselves going in the opposite direction. I suppose it takes all kinds." She estimated that there were still some thirty guests at the Kaminoyu hot spring and about twenty each at Nakanoyu and Shimonoyu.

One of the young guides from Shiobara said that for the past ten years people had often predicted that Mt. Bandai was about to blow its top, but it never had. Still, given the recent events, he thought it might blow this year after all. Last night there had been a light sprinkling of rain on the mountain, but today on the way down he had noticed that the small lake at Numanotaira had completely dried up. His view was that this sort of thing could be a frightening sign if one chose to interpret it that way, and yet it might not mean anything at all. On Mt. Bandai he felt that such signs were cause for alarm. The young man explained all this to us falteringly in the local dialect. Judging from what he said, he might have had reason to be worried, and then again, maybe not. But his fear was evident in the inconclusive way he spoke. He finished by saying, "What can one do, anyway?" Motioning for the rest of the group to follow, he led them quickly down the mountain. The young man had used the odd phrase, "blow its top," suggesting that it might erupt, but in the local dialect this literally meant that the whole top of the mountain would blow off.

We were a bit disturbed by these stories from the family from Niigata, but we did not feel all that uneasy about getting any closer to the mountain they were fleeing. After parting with the merchant and his family, the normally reserved Shuntarō said, "In all my life I have never seen so many snakes as we've seen today. I, too, believe something odd is going on." I had also noticed the snakes, but since this was my first trip to the area, I thought perhaps this was just a place where they were unusually common. After leaving Hosono we saw any number of them crossing the road with their heads raised. Every time we stopped to rest and looked around before sitting down, we saw something long and thin slither off silently into the bushes. The fact that Shuntarō, a local resident and a man not much given to expressing his opinions, commented on the matter seemed to be all the more significant. Then, in response, Kume tilted his head to one side and said, "I haven't been aware of the snakes particularly, but I have noticed that the doves and pheasants seem upset. I've hunted for years, but I've never seen birds as worked up as this." Kinji, who had hardly said a word all day, had a frightened look on his face, and in ominous tones said, "Yesterday, we met that pilgrim just below the pass. Do you remember what she said?" He turned to Kume as he spoke.

At the same moment, from the other side Tomekichi said, "Kinji!" ordering him to be quiet in a surprisingly harsh tone of voice. "Don't talk about that rubbish!" This outburst was strange coming from the usually taciturn Tomekichi.

Shinshū was the only one in the group who appeared to be totally unaffected by the atmosphere of tension that had developed. "Sometimes the mountains rumble and the snakes and birds move about. What's wrong with that? If you start letting yourself get excited about every little thing you'll have another stroke, Shuntarō. And you, Kume, to hear you talk, one would think you're getting senile as well as bald." He made a joke of the situation, but what he said had been instructive as well. I realized for the first time that Shuntarō's usually phlegmatic attitude toward things was due to the fact that he had once had a stroke. As for

Kume, I had thought he kept his head shaved, but after Shinshū commented on his baldness, I noticed that in fact he had small wisps of hair growing here and there on his head.

It was one o'clock when we arrived in Ōsawa. The village was composed of several parts with names such as Oshisawa, Osusawa, and so on, and there was no way of knowing for sure which was the original name. Various people had from time to time made different entries in the county register, calling the place by different names. I suppose it didn't much matter what its real name was, since everyone within the boundaries of the forest, whether they lived in the village itself or elsewhere, referred to it simply as Ōsawa. There were twenty houses and some two hundred people living there. They had a splendid view of Mt. Bandai from dawn to dusk.

We asked the people there to provide us with lodging for the night, and then, since the sun was still high in the sky, we set out for Akimoto, which was a couple of miles further on to the northeast. We had planned to begin our survey there the following morning, so we wanted to have a look at the site today and talk a bit with its inhabitants. Just beyond Ōsawa the Nagase River turned sharply east, making a wide sweep around the base of Mt. Bandai. As everyone knows, this is the river that flows into Lake Inawashiro on the front side of Mt. Bandai. In the area where we found ourselves, the river was flanked on both sides by broad, flat plains. After leaving Ōsawa we followed a road upstream along the river. About a mile from the village we came to the spot where the Ono joined the Nagase. From that point onward, the Nagase became a wide stretch of water. Another mile further on was the confluence of the Ogura. Akimoto consisted of a dozen houses located several hundred yards from where the two rivers ran together.

The lower slopes of Mt. Bandai between Ōsawa and Akimoto were carpeted with thick forests broken occasionally by high meadows and rolling hills. A clump of white birch crowned one hill, and here and there were broad open spaces overgrown with dwarf bamboo and reeds taller than a man. These open, brushy spaces created striped patterns across the flank of the mountain.

As we traveled from Hosono to Ōsawa, the peak known as Kobandai was directly in front of us, while on the right and left were Akahani and Daibandai. These three together formed the massif known collectively as Mt. Bandai. The peaks had towered before us for a long while, but when we reached the village of Akimoto, the view of Mt. Bandai had assumed a new aspect. Up until then Kushigamine, which was actually some distance to the left, seemed quite close to the three peaks of Bandai and appeared to be a fourth in the group, but from Akimoto we could see that there was a considerable distance separating them, and that Bandai was a different mountain entirely. It was, at any rate, a beautiful view.

At Akimoto we were served tea at one of the farmhouses, and while enjoying this new view of Mt. Bandai we made arrangements with the local people to begin our survey the following morning. As we sat together on the long veranda of the house discussing these matters, we felt the jolt of yet another earthquake. The old farmer who owned the house thought it was perfectly natural that the people of Ōsawa were upset by so many earthquakes. He suggested that we would be safer if we finished our work in Ōsawa as quickly as possible and came here to his village.

It was from this farmer that we learned for the first time that the wells of Ōsawa had gone dry and that the tremors had been especially sharp there, with the rumbling of the mountain reaching unusual proportions. The people of Ōsawa had been living in constant fear, and had not been able to work in their fields for the past ten days, wondering among themselves whether they should evacuate their homes or not.

Akimoto and Ōsawa were both in the shadow of Mt. Bandai, but there were several long swales running north of the mountain in such a way that they set Ōsawa apart. It was a common belief that whenever anything strange happened on the mountain, Ōsawa alone felt the effect of it. The people of Akimoto were quite unconcerned, treating Ōsawa's misfortunes as though they were standing on one bank of a river watching a city burn on the opposite shore.

When we heard all this, we did not feel much like spending the night at Ōsawa, and wondered how the people there must feel at having to provide hospitality for us while they themselves were frightened for their lives. Still, we had already asked them to arrange lodging for us for that night, and the following day we would be free to make other plans, so with this in mind we decided to return.

On reaching the place where the Nagase and Ono rivers met, we came across a young man and woman dressed much more fashionably than other people in the region. Even seeing them from afar we could not imagine they were locals, and since we were walking at a faster pace we soon overtook the pair. They were probably in their early twenties and everything about them suggested the sophistication of city-dwellers. At first glance the man appeared to be a student of some sort; he was wearing casual Western clothing and carrying a Western-style umbrella. The woman had a pale complexion and a round, feminine face. Her head was covered by a shawl, and judging from her hairstyle and elegant, striped kimono we could only suppose that she came from a fashionable Tokyo neighborhood.

When I asked the pair where they were heading, the man mentioned the Kaminoyu hot spring, but the only luggage they had was a single cloth-wrapped bundle which the woman carried. Although they were obviously travelers, it seemed unlikely that they were typical guests at a local spa. Shinshū asked when they expected to reach Kaminoyu, yet neither of them could reply. In fact, they did not know where exactly Kaminoyu was, or which road to take, or how far it would be; they seemed to be just strolling casually about the fields and meadows on the lower slopes of Mt. Bandai.

I all but insisted that they spend the night with us at Ōsawa. Under the circumstances it appeared to be the only solution, since they seemed almost in a daze. The woman hesitated and looked as if she wanted the man to refuse, but he seemed rather weak-willed and finally, as though making a concession to me, he agreed to go with us.

The young couple were considerably slower than we were, so I paused from time to time to let them catch up. As I waited I had occasion to inspect the woman. She was extraordinarily attractive. Though she was not strikingly beautiful in the traditional sense, there was a purity and innocence in her face, in the way she walked and in the smallest movement she made, that impressed me more deeply than any other woman I had seen.

Eventually we made our way back to Ōsawa along with our two new companions, and Shinshū had no trouble arranging accommodation for them as well. As it turned out, I stayed in one house with the young man and woman while the other five stayed across the road. The village well had dried up so we were not able to have a bath that night, but otherwise we were treated with remarkable hospitality by the people of the village.

As we had learned in Akimoto, the people here were frightened by the earthquakes and the rumbling of the mountain and were all ready to flee, but our hosts seemed to take courage from our presence and from having additional people to share the house with them.

Both the house where I was lodged and the one where Tomekichi and the others stayed were occupied by large, extended families which included people of several generations. Not just in Ōsawa, but in Hosono and Akimoto as well, there were many households with large numbers of children; apparently eight or nine per family was normal around here.

All the homes were built in the same pattern, having a large room with a sunken hearth and wooden floor that faced a dirt-floored hallway. Beyond the room with the hearth was a smaller living room, and beyond that a wooden door which led to a back room. The living room looked out on the front garden, and the back room faced the rear gate; both were bordered by a small veranda. It was decided that I would sleep in the living room, the young couple would have the back room, and all the members of the large family would sleep together in the room with the wooden floor and sunken hearth.

After deciding who would sleep where, the young couple and I joined the rest of the family around the hearth where we were served dinner. As we ate, the farmer and his wife told us of several unusual happenings. This year's snow had been deeper than usual but had melted off early, and recently the people from Tsuchida had gone into the swamp to cut walnut trees. They had heard a loud report like the sound of a tree trunk snapping, but it had come from deep within the earth so the people had been frightened and had run away. Also, at about nine o'clock in the evening on April 15, a pale blue flame had flared from the peak of Mt. Bandai and flashed across the sky, followed a few moments later by a great rumbling sound. As the parents related these stories, the children sat in a cluster gazing intently at their faces, and whenever I interrupted with a comment, they all turned in unison to stare at me. I noticed that the young man and woman hardly said a word all evening, and they seemed so preoccupied with their own thoughts I was worried about them. They replied in monosyllables when spoken to, but they never initiated a conversation.

As we were eating dinner, another guest arrived at the house. He told us he had set out from Hibara at about noon that day. Sitting on the edge of the raised floor by the hallway unlacing his straw sandals, he spoke with great animation, saying this was the first time he had made the trip from Hibara and that he had found the road bad and it had been farther than he thought, and that altogether he had had a rough time of it. He was completely uninhibited as he talked on and on. When at last he approached the hearth where the rest of us were seated and the light of the lamp fell on his face, he appeared to be a salesman of some sort, about forty years old, with surprisingly pleasant features.

Somehow we all knew right away that he would end up telling us the story of his life even though no one asked to hear it. He said he came from a certain village on the front side of Mt. Bandai. As a young man he had left home and gone to Osaka where he had been successful in the fish-cake business. Over the years he had saved a little money, and now for the first time he was on his way back to his village for a visit. He planned to sponsor an elaborate memorial service for his parents who were now dead, but his real purpose in returning to his birthplace was to surprise the people there, and to watch their mouths drop open in amazement when they saw how successful he had been.

Since his home was on the other side of Mt. Bandai, the normal route would have been by way of Inawashiro, which was closer and easier. But he was not taking the usual road, and indeed the fact that he had decided to approach the mountain by way of Hibara and make a surprise return to his village seemed typical of a small-time entrepreneur who had achieved some measure of success. He was clearly easy prey to flattery and somewhat proud and boastful, but hardly to the point of being disagreeable. There was also a good side to his nature and I found it admirable that he had been thrifty and industrious enough to save some of his money for the sake of this trip.

Until this man's arrival the people of the household had told us only the most gloomy and discouraging stories about Mt. Bandai, but once this lively character appeared, the tone of the conversation changed completely. From that point on sounds of laughter burst out time and again from the group gathered around the hearth. And yet even while we were talking we felt one slight tremor and heard the mountain rumble twice. The tremor was very mild, but it filled our hearts with dread nonetheless, and the small children clung desperately to their parents with frightened faces and began to cry. The other sounds I merely took to be the wind, and when I learned they came from the mountain, I realized that I had already heard them several times that day. The rumbling of the mountain was quite different from the earthquake tremors in that the children neither cried nor clung to their parents. Rather, I thought I could detect signs of extraordinary intensity in their innocent faces as they strained to follow the sound as it died away somewhere deep within the earth. It seemed cruel that these youngsters had to endure such dread and anxiety.

That night, after we had finished dinner, all of us including the family members retired to bed early. The fish-cake merchant from Osaka ended up sleeping in the living room with me and we arranged our quilts side by side. No sooner had his head touched his pillow than he was sound asleep and snoring loudly.

I also was soon asleep, but I slept lightly and was awakened a short time later. The moment my eyes opened I heard the faint noise of the shutters being slid open in the back room. The sound lasted only a moment, then stopped, but after a brief silence it was repeated. I had an idea that these cautious noises had been going on for some time. I strained my ears trying to hear what was happening in the back room and presently I heard footsteps and the rustle of clothing. Judging from the sounds, I determined that the young couple were leaving the house by way of the veranda. Somehow, ever since going to bed I had had a feeling that something like this might happen, and I realized why I had been sleeping so lightly. In any case, now that I was aware of what was going on, I knew I could not simply ignore the situation.

Without hesitation I threw open the shutters of the living room and stepped down into the garden in my bare feet. The moonlight made the scene outside as bright as midday. I could clearly make out the leaves of the nandina bushes at the bottom of the garden. I went around the side of the house to the back and followed a path that passed beside the well and came out in a corner of a field that was terraced up one level higher than the garden. The wild plants and the tassles of the pampas grass shone silver in the moonlight, stretching away into the distance. Far across the field I could make out the figures of the young couple as they walked away from the farmhouse.

The situation did not seem critical enough to require that I dash after them, so I merely quickened my pace and began to catch up. When I got within fifty yards of them they turned around and I called out, "Don't be fools! Where do you think you're going?" I tried to make my voice sound as loud and peremptory as possible. The woman looked as if she was ready to break into a panicky run, but quickly gave up with a slump of resignation. She hid her face behind her sleeve and began to weep. The young man seemed utterly incapable of doing anything, and from the moment I called out, he just stood there dazed.

The woman was dressed in a different kimono from the one she had worn earlier. It was of a deep purple fabric, and in the brilliant moonlight her pale face contrasted sharply with its color. I had a suspicion that she had had death in mind when she put on her finest clothes.

Her face was tear-stained as she looked up and said, "Neither of us is prepared to go on living." I ignored her and merely told them to go back to the house, setting out in that direction myself. When we reached the well at the rear I stopped to wash my feet. They both followed my example and washed theirs too. Since I had no shoes to put on, I entered the house through the back room and from there returned to my own bed in the living room. For a while I heard the woman softly sobbing, but I paid no attention to this and was soon asleep.

The following day, July 15, I was woken by a loud rumbling in the earth. It was shortly before six o'clock. I knew the time because the fish-cake merchant also rose from his bed at the same moment. From somewhere on his person he produced an enormous, gold pocket watch, and holding it up to a ray of bright sunlight that had slipped through a crack in the shutters, he announced the time.

Since neither of us could get back to sleep again, we opened the shutters and seated ourselves on the veranda, where we each smoked a cigarette and felt the cool morning air on our skin. As we sat there, we heard the shutters of the back room and the room where the family had slept being opened. Apparently everyone had been woken by the sound of the mountain, though of course this was not such an early hour for a farming family to be getting up. It looked as though the people in the house across the road had been awake for some time. I saw Tomekichi and Shuntarō in the front garden discussing something as they laced up their traveling sandals. Moments later Kume, Kinji, and Shinshū also appeared; they were getting ready to start the survey. Since I still had to eat breakfast I decided to delay my departure and set off a little behind them.

I was watching their movements without really paying much attention when Tomekichi happened to look over in our direction. Apparently he caught sight of me, for he waved. He gestured to indicate that they would go on ahead, and I watched as they set out from the garden and disappeared from sight: Kume, Shuntarō, Tomekichi, Shinshū, and Kinji, in that order.

About thirty minutes after the others had left the house across the road, I started after them with the fish-cake merchant and the young couple. The woman was dressed in the same purple kimono she had worn the night before, which led me to suspect that they had not yet given up the idea of taking their lives; the thought irritated me.

"I'm going on to Akimoto from here," I said to the couple. "You had better come with me. I can find someone there to accompany you as far as Inawashiro."

The man nodded slightly in acknowledgment, but the woman kept her eyes on the ground and said nothing. From their expressions I had the feeling that the man had already abandoned the idea of suicide and that it was only the woman who was still determined to carry out their plan. Perhaps, I thought, the man had never really been interested in killing himself and had only been led unwillingly to these alpine meadows by his companion. If that were the case, the woman's desire to take her life seemed especially poignant.

We set out along the river, the same road I had taken to Akimoto the day before. Just as on the previous day, the sky was delightfully clear: a limpid, pale blue unmarred by clouds. A short distance out of the village of Ōsawa the road crossed a small stream flowing down from the Kobuka marsh. Just beyond the stream the road forked, one branch going to Akimoto and the other to Kawakami and Nagasaka.

There the merchant parted company with us and went off along the upward sloping road, half hidden by the scrub bamboo. All we could see of him was his white shirt, the cloth bundle in which he carried his spare clothes, and a small knapsack. He walked away from us with disagreeable swiftness, and soon even his white shirt was lost from sight.

Accompanied by the silent couple from the city I set off toward the confluence of the Ono River. After parting from the merchant, we had hardly gone any distance at all before we saw about ten children from the village standing on an outcrop at the top of a low hill that flanked our road. The youngest was perhaps five or six and the oldest about ten years old. Apparently they had come from the village looking for a place to play. There was certainly no school playground in such a remote village, and no doubt once these youngsters were a little older they would be busy doing chores around the house, but they were not yet old enough for that. It was just the height of the silk-making season, and to keep them from being underfoot, the younger ones were sent out every morning to play by themselves in the open fields.

They stood clustered together on the outcrop above and solemnly gazed at us as we passed along the road below. I looked up at them and wondered if any of them belonged to the family in whose home we had spent the night. All these farm children looked more or less the same to me; they were the same faces I had seen masked with fear as they sat around the hearth when the earthquake had struck, the same faces I had seen straining to hear the receding sound of the rumbling mountain. I could not distinguish the children of one family from those of another, but felt that if any of the group had been in our house, I would like to call out some word of greeting.

It was at that precise moment that everything happened. At exactly 7:40 the earth gave a great heave and shudder. This was different from the tremors we had felt before, much more violent, and I was knocked to the ground. I could not tell if it came from the mountain or the ground beneath me, but I heard the most terrifying sound issuing from the bowels of the earth. I saw the young woman lose her balance, stagger, and fall to her knees. I scrambled to my feet only to be thrown down again by a second violent jolt. This time I used my right arm to brace my body against the bucking earth. I glanced up at the outcrop to see if the children had also been thrown down, but there was no sign of them. All I could see was a swirl of dust slowly rising in the air.

By this time I knew better than to try and leap up again, but after the second quake subsided, I carefully rose to my feet. Beside me I saw that the young man had reached out a hand and was helping the woman up as well.

At the same moment, I saw two or three small heads poke up above the edge of the outcrop. Soon all the heads appeared in a row and I heard one of the children cry out in a loud voice, cadenced almost as though he were singing, "Blow, mountain, blow! Give it all you've got!" Soon several of the others joined in, shouting with all their tiny might, "Blow, mountain, blow! Give it all you've got!"

Their chant—or scream of defiance, whatever it was—was scarcely finished when in thunderous answer a roar came rolling back over the earth. It was a blast so powerful that I was lifted off my feet and hurled to the ground several yards to my right. On and on went the roar while the earth heaved in convulsive spasms. Later, when I tried to recall the exact sequence of events, I was never sure just when it was that I happened to catch sight of Mt. Bandai, but I know I saw a huge column of fire and smoke rising straight up into the clear tranquil sky; like one of the pillars of Hell it rose to twice the height of the mountain itself. The whole mountain had literally exploded and the shape of Kobandai was blotted out forever. It was only much later, of course, that I realized what had occurred.

I cannot say with any certainty how I survived the explosion. The entire north face of Mt. Bandai came avalanching down in a sea of sand, rocks, and boulders. I remember it now as a nightmare vision, as something so terrifying as to be not of this world. The avalanche obliterated the forests that covered the lower slopes of the mountain. The wall of debris swept down with terrible speed and force. I saw the purple kimono swirl up in the air like a scrap of colored paper, and in a flash it was swept away in that tide of mud. I do not know exactly where or when it was that the kimono disappeared from sight. The air was so thick with clouds of ash and pebbles I could not tell whether it was day or night. I staggered along the bank of the Ono River and sought refuge on the high ground north of Akimoto. That alone saved my life. If I had fled in any other direction I would simply have been whisked away without a trace.

Within an hour of the time Mt. Bandai exploded, the villages of Hosono, Ōsawa, and Akimoto were all swept away, and whatever remained was buried under yards and yards of stone. As most of my readers will know, it was not just the north slope that was affected; many villages on the east side of the mountain also met the same tragic fate.

Many accurate and detailed studies and reports have been published regarding the eruption of Mt. Bandai, and I certainly have nothing to add to them. My intention here has been quite different, for it was a personal experience of the eruption that I wanted to relate.

What remains indelibly burned upon my memory and ringing in my ears is the defiant challenge—"Blow, mountain, blow! Give it all you've got!"—uttered by those brave children, who could do nothing else in the face of the mountain's awesome power.

And one more thing: officially, 477 people died that day, but for the sake of accuracy I believe at least three more casualties should be added to that number. Although their names are not known, I feel that when we honor the victims of this disaster we must also mention the departed souls of that young man and woman and the fish-cake merchant from Osaka as well. Today Hosono, Ōsawa, and Hibara are all buried beneath the large lake that formed when the stones and mud of the eruption blocked the Nagase River. Akimoto lies at the bottom of another such lake. Though I have related this story in some detail, the fact is that I have never gone back to visit the area, and it is unlikely that I ever shall. The region today, they tell me, is noted for its pristine alpine lakes, but who can say what terrible memories would revive if I were to go there again and gaze upon them. No, I shall never revisit the countryside that lies in the shadow of Mt. Bandai.

MULBERRY CHILD

Minakami Tsutomu
Translated by Anthony H. Chambers

Minakami Tsutomu's career as a writer did not really get under way until he was forty. During the first thirty-nine years of his life, he went through thirty-six different occupations, ranging from Buddhist acolyte to clerk in a geta shop, peddler, manager of a mahjong parlor, and journalist.

The second son of a shrine carpenter, Minakami was born in 1919 in the village of Okada, Fukui Prefecture, which is the setting for "Mulberry Child." When he was ten years old, his parents, desperately poor and eager to reduce the number of mouths to feed, sent him to the famous Zen monastery of Shōkokuji in Kyoto, where he took his vows in 1930. In 1937, a layman once again, he was enrolled briefly at Ritsumeikan University and began his multifarious succession of careers.

After the war he studied with the novelist Uno Kōji (1891–1961), under whose influence he wrote his first novel, the autobiographical Furaipan no uta *(The Song of a Frying Pan), in 1948. But Minakami was unable to support himself by writing until 1959, when he published an extremely popular mystery entitled* Kiri to kage *(Mist and Shadow). In 1961 he won the Mystery Writers' Club Prize for* Umi no kiba *(The Fangs of the Sea), which deals with Minamata Disease, caused by environmental pollution.*

Dissatisfied with his reputation as a writer of social-problem mysteries, however, Minakami turned to the experiences of his youth for Gan no tera *(The Temple of the Wild Geese), which brought him the Naoki Prize in 1962. In* Gobanchō Yūgirirō *(The Yūgiri House in Gobanchō, 1962), he treats the burning of the Golden Pavilion from a different point of view than Mishima Yukio had in his* Kinkakuji *(The Temple of the Golden Pavilion, 1956), that of a young prostitute from the Japan Sea coast. The element of local color becomes even stronger in* Echizen takeningyō *(The Bamboo Doll of Echizen), which won high praise from Tanizaki Jun'ichirō in 1963.*

An exceptionally prolific writer, Minakami has published a number of historical novels, biographies, travel accounts, and autobiographical essays. His biography of his mentor Uno Kōji won the Kikuchi Kan Prize in 1971, and his study of the fifteenth-century Zen master Ikkyū was awarded the Tanizaki Prize in 1975.

"Mulberry Child," written in 1963, demonstrates Minakami's characteristic blending of autobiographical elements with Buddhism and local color in a sweet-sad portrayal of the lives of the very poor in rural Japan.

* * *

"Do you know the story of the mulberry child, the child born out of a mulberry patch? It's probably nothing new to a writer like you. In the poor villages of the north country, only so much land is available for fields and paddies, and when there get to be too many children, well, all the people can do is abandon them, starting with the third or fourth boy. 'Thinning,' it's called, and it was tolerated until about 1900. Mothers would come right down to the police station and report, 'It was a boy, so I wet a towel and covered his mouth, and killed him. Please don't be too hard on me.' Well, the officer would pretend he didn't know anything, and arrange it so the higher-ups never found out. In the village where I was born, too, a lot of thinning went on."

This is how old Tarokichi began his story.

Every year, in the Second Month by the old calendar, a curious observance called "Shaka Shaka" took place in the Ōi District of Wakasa Province.

Wakasa is a narrow strip along the Japan Sea coast between Echizen and Tamba. The towering mountains on the border of Shiga Prefecture send a series of ridges, like the teeth of a comb, down toward the sea, where they end as promontories and peninsulas. The coastline looks like the blade of a saw, so that the highway from Tsuruga to Maizuru passes through one short tunnel after another and skirts the coast so closely it is showered with spray from the waves. The villages that nestle in the valleys running from the sea into the mountains are isolated from each other by the ridges between them. Each village has its own customs and dialect.

Ōi District, where Tarokichi was born, was in one of these valleys; and the observance of "Shaka Shaka" survived only in the hamlet of Okada, at the far end of the deep valley. It was a remarkable custom, one not to be seen in any other village.

Well, "a remarkable custom" may sound a little pretentious, Tarokichi added. This is how he described it.

After midnight on the fifteenth of the Second Month, all the village children from six to fifteen would gather before the Kannon Hall, deep in the forest behind the village. At the first light of dawn they formed a procession and walked through the village, rapping softly at the door of each of the sixty houses. In groups of three, four, five, and six, the children rapped on the doors at dawn. As they went they called "Shaka, Shaka-a," over and over.

"Shaka Shaka" probably refers to Lord Shakyamuni—the Buddha—and Tarokichi thought that the observance might be a demonstration of faith in the temples in the area. In any case, the children went from door to door, knocking and crying "Shaka, Shaka-a." At each house, someone would get out of bed and open the door just enough for a hand to pass through.

"Who is it?" a grown-up voice would ask from inside.

The children would give the hereditary names of their houses and their personal names. In Ōi District, most of the house names ended in "-zaemon" or "-emon," and so a child would identify himself by shouting something like, "I'm so-and-so from Taroemon's." Thereupon the grown-up, hiding behind the door, would thrust out a hand and say, "Open your bags."

The children would loosen the strings on their large cloth sacks, pull the mouths open, and hold them toward the crack in the door. The grown-up's hand would shoot out and drop sweets and roasted beans into the bags.

By the time they had made the rounds of all sixty houses, the children would barely be able to stand up any longer, and their bags would be swelling with all manner of sweets and beans.

All of this took place early in the morning. That night, the men and women over sixty gathered at the Kannon Hall, where a votive lamp had been lit. The hall was equipped with a sunken hearth, in which pine roots and large branches were burned. The old men and women would spread mats around the hearth and, with the oldest ones nearest the fire, pray to Amitabha and talk through the night. The children sat with them.

Among the old people there were some who chanted "Shaka, Shaka-a," which suggests that this gathering, too, had to do with Shakyamuni.

Tarokichi didn't know what the fifteenth of the Second Month signified in Buddhism, but he said he had a feeling that it was the date of the Buddha's death and Nirvana, and that the activities of the children and the old people were by way of a memorial service for his soul.

Each household, then, as it prepared sweets and beans and put a handful in each child's bag, was performing in its own way the ceremony known as *Segaki*, or "Feeding the Hungry Ghosts." And for their part, the children—who are often called *gaki*, or "hungry ghosts"—accepted the food offerings that day in deference to Lord Shakyamuni. Likewise, when the old men and women gathered at the Kannon Hall to light a fire and pray to Amitabha, they were comforting Shakyamuni's soul. In the snow country, lighting a fire was the warmest form of hospitality. And so the old people entertained themselves around the fire with stories of the departed who had gone to join the Buddha.

Tarokichi was born in the hamlet of Okada, in a house known as Katsukichi. Katsukichi had been his grandfather's name, and was assumed in turn by his father. Tarokichi turned six that year and joined in the Shaka Shaka observances for the first time.

Tarokichi couldn't sleep on the night of the fourteenth. He was happily anticipating the hour when he would finally be able to join the other children and walk in the Shaka Shaka. A child of five could not join them; but when he turned six his parents would tell him, "Now you can go with the others in Shaka Shaka." Thus from the age of five—or even four—children waited eagerly for their day to come.

It snowed on the fifteenth of the Second Month. In Wakasa the snow was heaviest during the Second Month; at times it would fall steadily for a week. The houses had steep, triangular roofs of thatch, from which the snow slid to form high walls around each house. Reeds that had been cut and stored in advance were stretched around each house to soften the fierce winds, rendering the interiors still darker.

Tarokichi waited sleeplessly for morning. At about five o'clock, he heard a child's voice at the entrance to the Katsukichi house: "Shaka, Shaka-a."

"Who is it?" asked Tarokichi's mother.

"It's Yasuke from Kanzaemon's," came the voice from outside.

"All right," said Tarokichi's mother, opening the door a crack.

The wind came in, bearing white, powdery show. His mother, wrapped in a short robe, felt the icy blast on her knees. Exclaiming at the cold, she took a handful of roasted beans from a bucket she had ready by the door. "Here, for Yasuke from Kanzaemon's," she said, and gave the beans to the child as he waited in the blizzard with his bag open.

Yasuke from Kanzaemon's was seven. Pulling the string to close his round-bottomed bag over the roasted beans, he said, "Hey, Tarokichi. Tarokichi, where are you? Do you want to come with me?"

Tarokichi was up and ready to go, without even washing his face. The strap was around his neck and the bag dangled against his chest as he concentrated on tying the cord of his baggy cotton pants.

"Yasuke from Kanzaemon's. Will you take him with you?" his mother asked.

"Yes," came the reply.

Hearing this, Tarokichi was at the door in a flash and bounded out into the driving snow.

"Yasuke, take me with you for Shaka Shaka."

"All right, follow me. When I say 'Shaka Shaka,' you say it too."

Yasuke was one year older than Tarokichi. Walking along the village roads in the snow, he called "Shaka, Shaka-a." In no time the two children were white with the powdery snow.

Oddly enough, the child one accompanied on one's first Shaka Shaka always became a close friend. Tarokichi became Yasuke's friend. If Tarokichi had waited silently at the door when Yasuke called his name in the snow, then Yasuke would have had to go on by himself. Yasuke had invited Tarokichi with friendship in mind, and Tarokichi had agreed; and so they made the rounds together.

For two hours, Tarokichi and Yasuke ran through the snow-covered village, filling their bags. When the Shaka Shaka was over, they played together all day and promised to go together to the Kannon Hall that night.

The Kannon Hall was the village community center. The tile roof that covered it was just adequate to ward off the elements; the walls had collapsed, and the posts and beams had begun to tilt. A large stone, on which visitors left their footwear, lay in front of the square building, and just inside was a large, plank-floored room. Facing the entrance was an altar, containing a small, boxlike shrine. The doors of the shrine were opened only on this day; in the dim interior stood an image of the Bodhisattva Kannon, about three feet tall and covered with dust.

There was nothing unusual about the image, except that the gold leaf had fallen off, exposing the grain of the wood. One arm hung to about the navel; the other was bent at the elbow, the thumb and forefinger joined to form a circle. On the candlestand in front of the image flickered a "one-pound candle." Mats had been spread over the planks, and a fire had just been lit in the hearth. Smoke billowed from the damp wood. That year there were thirty-two men and women over the age of sixty in the village of sixty houses, but several who had passed ninety were unable to negotiate the snowy path to the hall. Those who could walk with the aid of a staff would join the assembly. But when Tarokichi and Yasuke arrived, the hour was still early, and only old Shōza from Kamimura was there.

"Shōza" was short for Shōzaemon, the name of his house. When Tarokichi and Yasuke looked inside they saw old Shōza seated by the hearth, poking at the smoldering wood.

"Has it started to burn?" they asked as they stepped inside.

The old man was popular with the village children. They liked some of the old people of the village and disliked others. Shōza was one of their favorites. He often had strange stories to tell them.

"Who's that? Ah, Tarokichi from Katsukichi's, and Yasuke from Kanzaemon's."

Rubbing his bleary eyes, he glared in their direction. He was past seventy and hard of hearing.

"Yes, Tarokichi and Yasuke," replied Yasuke.

The two boys sat at the hearth. Shōza eyed them.

"The mulberry child from Kanzaemon's," he said out of the blue.

Yasuke was startled. "What's a mulberry child? What's a mulberry?" he asked.

Tarokichi pricked up his ears, too. What a funny thing for Shōza to come out with, he thought.

"You don't know what 'mulberry child' means, Yasuke? Tarokichi? You're the child of a mulberry patch, Yasuke. You were born from a hole in a mulberry patch."

Old Shōza grinned broadly; his one or two remaining teeth were a grimy yellow, and his gums showed purple. He fixed his sunken eyes on Yasuke. Tarokichi could not look Shōza directly in the face. He was frightened. Though he didn't know what the old man meant, he thought that Shōza was insulting his new friend Yasuke by calling him a mulberry child.

"I wasn't born from a hole in a mulberry patch. I was born from my mother," shouted Yasuke, about to cry.

"Yasuke, you don't know," said Shōza, trying to explain. "You're a mulberry child. You'll understand when you grow up. You were born from the mulberry patch."

Yasuke was on the verge of tears, but he fought them back. He didn't want the young Tarokichi to see him cry, and he was loath to give in so easily to old Shōza, who said such scornful things about him. Stoically he clenched his teeth.

The old people began to gather in front of the hall. Removing their wooden geta and boots and shaking the snow off their hoods and blankets, they came inside. Seeing old Shōza poking at the fire, they would say, "Good work, Shōza. So it was your turn to build the fire this year. Thank you."

Proceeding to the shrine, each one would pull from his sleeve the incense sticks he had brought, light the tips at the candle, and push the sticks into the damp ashes that filled the incense burner. Then each would join his hands and begin to chant the prayer to Amitabha:

> Nan Amida Butsu, Namu Amida Butsu,
> Namu Amida-a Butsu, Namu Amida Butsu.

The chanting of the old men and women swirled with the smoke toward the low ceiling of the Kannon Hall. Tarokichi and Yasuke, oppressed by the heavy odors of hair oil and perspiration, soon went outside.

It was snowing. From the hall came the voices of the old people praying to Amitabha. Tarokichi walked ahead. Behind him, Yasuke said quietly, "Mulberry child. . ."

Tarokichi looked back; Yasuke was glaring at him furiously. Tarokichi saw contempt in his face. Feeling a surge of anger, Tarokichi began to run, kicking the snow as he went.

Why had Yasuke changed so, after old Shōza called him a mulberry child? Tarokichi did not understand until he had grown up.

They had become friends by doing Shaka Shaka together, but from that day on Yasuke never came to play with him. It was very strange.

"Only recently did I understand why Yasuke looked so dejected and angry." Tarokichi continued his story.

"Yasuke was Kanzaemon's third boy. They were a poor family. That makes it sound as though my family was rich, but we were poor, too. The difference is that Yasuke's family had a lot of children. There are extra expenses when you have a lot of children, and so they were that much poorer. Yasuke's father, Kanzaemon, and his mother—her name was Okane—were both hard workers. Yasuke was born in the late autumn of 1899. Okane was busy one evening, harvesting beans on a terrace in the farthest fields at Tanida, when her term came full and she began to feel labor pains. Farmwives used to go on working right up through the last month—they weren't able to check into a clinic and give brith with the help of a nurse or a midwife, as they do nowadays. When Okane felt the pains, she held her stomach and started back toward the house at Okada. The house was empty—Kanzaemon was a carpenter and had probably gone off to help on a construction job somewhere. On her way home, Okane, still holding her stomach, met up with Shōzaemon.

"Seeing Okane covered with oily sweat and her veins bulging as she walked toward him, he asked, 'Is it the baby, Okane? Is the baby moving?' Without answering, Okane fell to her knees at the side of the road. The pains were getting worse.

"'Okane. What are you going to do with so many children?' asked Shōzaemon. 'You have two boys. This will be your third. How do you think you can raise it? Shall I help you? Let it be a mulberry child. Let it be a mulberry child, and pray for its happiness on the other side.'

"There were no passersby that evening on the mountain road. Okane must have thought of Shōzaemon as the Buddha himself, as he helped her up from behind.

"'Shōza. Please help me. Just do what you think is best.' Okane was groaning with pain as she spoke.

"Shōzaemon nodded and said, 'All right.' He helped her lie down on the grass at the roadside, loosened her sash, and began to rub her stomach. The baby came right away. It gave a big cry. Okane, clutching some plantain roots by the road, had exhausted her strength and fainted. When she came to, much later, Shōza and his wife had put her to bed in the storeroom at home. The baby she had given birth to was nowhere to be seen. When he saw that Okane had opened her eyes, Shōza spoke.

"'It's a mulberry child now. I left it in a mulberry patch. If it isn't alive tomorrow, I'll bury it. Don't worry, Okane. I'll take care of everything for you.'

"I wonder when the custom started. Around that time, many of the families were raising silkworms for the extra income, and mulberries grew in most of the fields at the edge of the village. I remember from my childhood that, when the leaves were full, the fields would be covered in green; and when the leaves fell, the mulberry fields would look like Needle Mountain in Hell. Okane gave birth to Yasuke in late autumn, when the big mulberry leaves were swaying in the ocean breeze. I went into the mulberry fields many times. When the red fruit ripened—in May, was it?—I would stuff myself with mulberries. The village children would roam the fields from morning to night, hunting for the tastiest berries. Once I came across a hole, and it gave me a fright. As I recall, it was in the middle of a field, at the farthest point from the surrounding walkways.

It was shaped like an urn; the sides had been carefully tamped with a mallet. At first glance, the place looked as though an urn *had* been buried there. The hole was about a foot across, and quite deep—I had to lie down and peep over the edge to see the bottom. I could make out lots of something that looked like rope, all glistening and slimy. Most likely it was weasels and rats that had gone down to drink the rainwater that collected there, and died, unable to climb up the hard-packed sides. There was a peculiar smell—yes, like the smell of a dead cat or dog. The children were afraid of these holes. When they saw one, they'd say, 'A tochinampin hole!' and run away. A *tochinampin* is a giant flying squirrel in our dialect. When I saw that hole in the mulberry field, I asked my parents, 'What's that hole for?' 'It's a tochinampin hole,' they told me. 'The tochinampin stores dead mice and cats in there to eat in the winter. Don't go near it. If you fall in, you'll never get out. You'll be eaten by the tochinampin.'

"All the children in the village ate mulberries, and all of them asked their parents about the frightening holes. When they did, they were told that those were tochinampin holes.

"The sad truth is that Okane, with Shōzaemon's help, had put her third boy out as a mulberry child. In other words, he was left in a tochinampin hole."

"But that's not the end of the story. As I said at the beginning, a 'mulberry child' was a child *born out of* a mulberry patch. That's right: it's a child who crawled out of the hole he had been left in. The day after a newborn infant had been left in a hole, someone from the family would go to make sure it was dead; and they say that sometimes there'd be a strong child who had crawled out of the hole and was found crying under the dew-covered mulberry leaves. A very strong and lively child, that must have been. When a baby was found still alive the next morning, they would take it home and rear it. I suppose the people figured that such a strong child would be sure to grow up into a good worker who could help with the family business.

"Yasuke from Kanzaemon's was born at the roadside and abandoned by old Shōza; but the next morning, when Shōza went back to the mulberry patch to look, he was sleeping peacefully under the mulberry leaves. It was remarkable. The grown-ups said that Yasuke was a prodigy, the first 'mulberry child' in the village, and they gazed at him in astonishment.

"That night in my sixth year—on the fifteenth of the Second Month, at the hearth in the Kannon Hall—when old Shōza called Yasuke a mulberry child, he wasn't being insulting.

"He was saying to Yasuke, 'You are the strongest boy in the village.' Come to think of it—early one morning, about ten days after I joined in Shaka Shaka for the first time, before the snow began to melt, when the village saw blizzards day and night, old Shōzaemon suddenly died.

"The old man's words—'mulberry child'—still ring in my ears; but Yasuke, the mulberry child, died of cholera when he was thirteen. It's hard to forget your childhood friends. Yasuke was taller and stronger than I was; his pug nose was always running, and he called 'Shaka, Shaka-a' in the blizzard as he led me by the hand, walking through the village to get our sweets. I can see him even now."

ONE ARM

Kawabata Yasunari

Translated by Edward Seidensticker

In his Nobel Prize acceptance speech of 1968, Kawabata Yasunari (1899–1972) wrote: "The snow, the moon, the blossoms, words expressive of the seasons as they move one into another, include in the Japanese tradition the beauty of mountains and rivers and grasses and trees, of all the myriad manifestations of nature, of human feelings as well." This ability to fuse the distinctions between the human realm and the domain of nature is a distinctive and intoxicating feature of his writings. In renowned works such as Yukiguni *(Snow Country, 1948; tr. 1956) and* Yama no oto *(The Sound of the Mountain, 1954; tr. 1970), Kawabata displays a true poetic genius for describing the human situation in terms of the subtle movements of flora and fauna, of mountain rumbles and winter landscapes bathed red by fires and passions.*

These elements have endeared Kawabata to the Western reader, who recognizes in him a prolongation and fulfillment of the traditions of classical Japanese literature. That aspect is indeed strong in Kawabata. Equally forceful, however, are the insurmountable distances that Kawabata places between his characters. Often it seems as if the men and women in his stories belong to opposing magnetic fields: however much they may think they want one another, something in their basic natures always drives them apart. Yet this very unattainability (or at times an unconscious desire to be alone) creates that element of unsullied purity which hovers over many of the women characters. Yōko in Snow Country*—first seen not* directly*, but in a mirrored reflection—retains her attraction for Shimamura because* *he can never obtain her. Kikuko in* The Sound of the Mountain *preserves both her purity and her fascination for Shingo because she is his daughter-in-law. These distant encounters can be traced all the way back to Kawabata's "maiden" work, "Izu no odoriko" (The Izu Dancer, 1926; tr. 1955).*

Another aspect of Kawabata's writings which figures prominently in stories such as "Kataude" (One Arm, 1963) is a strong element of surrealist fantasy, a product of Kawabata's early training as a modernist. Indeed, with all of Kawabata's late fascination with makai *(the demon world), madness, and bizarre use of imagery, "One Arm" could be called one of the more typical examples of his work as it is known in Japan.*

* * *

"I can let you have one of my arms for the night," said the girl. She took off her right arm at the shoulder and, with her left hand, laid it on my knee.

"Thank you." I looked at my knee. The warmth of the arm came through.

"I'll put the ring on. To remind you that it's mine." She smiled and raised her left arm to my chest. "Please." With but one arm, it was difficult for her to take the ring off.

"An engagement ring?"

"No. A keepsake. From my mother."

It was silver, set with small diamonds.

"Perhaps it does look like an engagement ring, but I don't mind. I wear it, and then when I take it off it's as if I were leaving my mother."

Raising the arm on my knee, I removed the ring and slipped it on the ring finger.

"Is this the one?"

"Yes." She nodded. "It will seem artificial unless the elbow and fingers bend. You won't like that. Let me make them bend for you."

She took her right arm from my knee and pressed her lips gently to it. Then she pressed them to the finger joints.

"Now they'll move."

"Thank you." I took the arm back. "Do you suppose it will speak? Will it speak to me?"

"It only does what an arm does. If it talks I'll be afraid to have it back. But try anyway. It should at least listen to what you say, if you're good to it."

"I'll be good to it."

"I'll see you again," she said, touching the right arm with her left hand, as if to infuse it with a spirit of its own. "You're his, but just for the night."

As she looked at me she seemed to be fighting back tears.

"I don't suppose you'll try to change it for your own arm," she said. "But it will be all right. Go ahead, do."

"Thank you."

I put her arm in my raincoat and went out into the foggy streets. I feared I might be thought odd if I took a taxi or a streetcar. There would be a scene if the arm, now separated from the girl's body, were to cry out, or to weep.

I held it against my chest, toward the side, my right hand on the roundness at the shoulder joint. It was concealed by the raincoat, and I had to touch the coat from time to time with my left hand to be sure that the arm was still there. Probably I was making sure not of the arm's presence but of my own happiness.

She had taken off the arm at the point I liked. It was plump and round—was it at the top of the arm or the beginning of the shoulder? The roundness was that of a beautiful Occidental girl, rare in a Japanese. It was in the girl herself, a clean, elegant roundness, like a sphere glowing with a faint, fresh light. When the girl was no longer clean, that gentle roundness would fade, grow flabby. Something that lasted for a brief moment in the life of a beautiful girl, the roundness of the arm made me feel the roundness of her body. Her breasts would not be large. Shy, only large enough to cup in the hands, they would have a clinging softness and strength. And in the roundness of the arm I could feel her legs as she walked along. She would carry them lightly, like a small bird, or a butterfly moving from flower to flower. There would be the same subtle melody in the tip of her tongue when she kissed.

It was the season for changing to sleeveless dresses. The girl's shoulder, newly bared, had the color of skin not used to the raw touch of the air. It had the glow of a bud moistened in the shelter of spring and not yet ravaged by summer. I had that morning bought a magnolia bud and put it in a glass vase; and the roundness of the girl's arm was like the great, white bud. Her dress was cut back more radically than most sleeveless dresses. The joint at the shoulder was exposed, and the shoulder itself. The dress, of dark green silk, almost black, had a soft sheen. The girl was in the rounded slope of the shoulders, which drew a gentle wave with the swelling of the back. Seen obliquely from behind, the flesh from the round shoulders to the long, slender neck came to an abrupt halt at the base of the upswept hair, and the black hair seemed to cast a glowing shadow over the roundness of the shoulders.

She had sensed that I thought her beautiful, and so she lent me her right arm for the roundness there at the shoulder.

Carefully hidden under my raincoat, the girl's arm was colder than my hand. I was giddy from the racing of my heart, and I knew that my hand would be hot. I wanted the warmth to stay as it was, the warmth of the girl herself. And the slight coolness in my hand passed on to me the pleasure of the arm. It was like her breasts, not yet touched by a man.

The fog yet thicker, the night threatened rain, and wet my uncovered hair. I could hear a radio speaking from the back room of a closed pharmacy. It announced that three planes unable to land in the fog had been circling the airport for half an hour. It went on to draw the attention of listeners to the fact that on damp nights clocks were likely to go wrong, and that on such nights the springs had a tendency to break if wound too tight. I looked for the lights of the circling planes, but could not see them. There was no sky. The pressing dampness invaded my ears, to give a wet sound like the wriggling of myriads of distant earthworms. I stood before the pharmacy awaiting further admonitions. I learned that on such nights the fierce beasts in the zoo, the lions and tigers and leopards and the rest, roared their resentment at the dampness, and that we were now to hear it. There was a roaring like the roaring of the earth. I then learned that pregnant women and despondent persons should go to bed early on such nights, and that women who applied perfume directly to their skins would find it difficult to remove afterward.

At the roaring of the beasts, I moved off, and the warning about perfume followed me. That angry roaring had unsettled me, and I moved on lest my uneasiness be transmitted to the girl's arm. The girl was neither pregnant nor despondent, but it seemed to me that tonight, with only one arm, she should take the advice of the radio and go quietly to bed. I hoped that she would sleep peacefully.

As I started across the street I pressed my left hand against my raincoat. A horn sounded. Something brushed my side, and I twisted away. Perhaps the arm had been frightened by the horn. The fingers were clenched.

"Don't worry," I said. "It was a long way off. It couldn't see. That's why it honked."

Because I was holding something important to me, I had looked in both directions. The sound of the horn had been so far away that I had thought it must be meant for someone else. I looked in the direction from which it came, but could see no one. I could see only the headlights. They widened into a blur of faint purple. A strange color for headlights. I stood on the curb when I had crossed and watched it pass. A young woman in vermilion was driving. It seemed to me that she turned toward me and bowed. I wanted to run off, fearing that the girl had come for her arm. Then I remembered that she would hardly be able to drive with only one. But had not the woman in the car seen what I was carrying? Had she not sensed it with a woman's intuition? I would have to take care not to encounter another of her sex before I reached my apartment. The rear lights were also a faint purple. I still did not see the car. In the ashen fog a lavender blur floated up and moved away.

"She is driving for no reason, for no reason at all except to be driving. And while she drives she will simply disappear," I muttered to myself. "And what was that sitting in the back seat?"

Nothing, apparently. Was it because I went around carrying girls' arms that I felt so unnerved by emptiness? The car she drove carried the clammy night fog. And something about her had turned it faintly purple in the headlights. If not from her own body, whence had come that purplish light? Could the arm I concealed have so clothed in emptiness a woman driving alone on such a night? Had she nodded at the girl's arm from her car? Perhaps on such a night there were angels and ghosts abroad protecting women. Perhaps she had ridden not in a car but in a purple light. Her drive had not been empty. She had spied out my secret.

I made my way back to my apartment without further encounters. I stood listening outside the door. The light of a firefly skimmed over my head and disappeared. It was too large and too strong for a firefly. I recoiled backward. Several more lights like fireflies skimmed past. They disappeared even before the heavy fog could suck them in. Had a will-o'-the-wisp, a death-fire of some sort, run on ahead of me, to await my return? But then I saw that it was a swarm of small moths. Catching the light at the door, the wings of the moths glowed like fireflies. Too large to be fireflies, and yet, for moths, so small as to invite the mistake.

Avoiding the automatic elevator, I made my way stealthily up the narrow stairs to the third floor. Not being left-handed, I had difficulty unlocking the door. The harder I tried the more my hand trembled—as if in terror after a crime. Something would be waiting for me inside the room, a room where I lived in solitude; and was not the solitude a presence? With the girl's arm I was no longer alone. And so perhaps my own solitude waited there to intimidate me.

"Go on ahead," I said, taking out the girl's arm when at length I had opened the door. "Welcome to my room. I'll turn on the light."

"Are you afraid of something?" the arm seemed to say. "Is something here?"

"You think there might be?"

"I smell something."

"Smell? It must be me that you smell. Don't you see traces of my shadow, up there in the darkness? Look carefully. Maybe my shadow was waiting for me to come back."

"It's a sweet smell."

"Ah—the magnolia," I answered brightly. I was glad it was not the moldy smell of my loneliness. A magnolia bud befitted my winsome guest. I was getting used to the dark. Even in pitch-blackness I knew where everything was.

"Let me turn on the light." Coming from the arm, a strange remark. "I haven't been in your room before."

"Thank you. I'll be very pleased. No one but me has ever turned on the lights here before."

I held the arm to the switch by the door. All five lights went on at once: at the ceiling, on the table, by the bed, in the kitchen, in the bathroom. I had not thought they could be so bright.

The magnolia was in enormous bloom. That morning it had been in bud. It could have only just bloomed, and yet there were stamens on the table. Curious, I looked more closely at the stamens than at the white flower. As I picked up one or two and gazed at them, the girl's arm, laid on the table, began to move, the fingers like spanworms, and gathered the stamens in its hand. I went to throw them in the wastebasket.

"What a strong smell. It sinks right into my skin. Help me."

"You must be tired. It wasn't an easy trip. Suppose you rest awhile."

I laid the arm on the bed and sat down beside it. I stroked it gently.

"How pretty. I like it." The arm would be speaking of the bedcover. Flowers were printed in three colors on an azure ground, somewhat lively for a man who lived alone. "So this is where we spend the night. I'll be very quiet."

"Oh?"

"I'll be beside you and not beside you."

The hand took mine gently. The nails, carefully polished, were a faint pink. The tips extended well beyond the fingers.

Against my own short, thick nails, hers possessed a strange beauty, as if they belonged to no human creature. With such fingertips, a woman perhaps transcended mere humanity. Or did she pursue womanhood itself? A shell luminous from the pattern inside it, a petal bathed in dew—I thought of the obvious likenesses. Yet I could think of no shell or petal whose color and shape resembled them. They were the nails on the girl's fingers, comparable to nothing else. More translucent than a delicate shell, than a thin petal, they seemed to hold a dew of tragedy. Every day and every night her energies were poured into the polishing of this tragic beauty. It penetrated my solitude. Perhaps my yearning, my solitude, transformed them into dew.

I rested her little finger on the index finger of my free hand, gazing at the long, narrow nail as I rubbed it with my thumb. My finger touched the tip of hers, sheltered by the nail. The finger bent, and the elbow too.

"Does it tickle?" I asked. "It must."

I had spoken carelessly. I knew that the tips of a woman's fingers were sensitive when the nails were long. And so I had told the girl's arm that I had known other women.

From one who was not a great deal older than the girl who had lent me the arm but far more mature in her experience of men, I had heard that fingertips thus hidden by nails were often acutely sensitive. One became used to touching things not with the fingertips but with the nails, and the fingertips therefore tickled when something came against them.

I had shown astonishment at this discovery, and she had gone on: "You're, say, cooking—or eating—and something touches your fingers, and you find yourself hunching your shoulders, it seems so dirty."

Was it the food that seemed unclean, or the tip of the nail? Whatever touched her fingers made her writhe with its uncleanness. Her own cleanness would leave behind a drop of tragic dew, there under the long shadow of the nail. One could not assume that for each of the ten fingers there would be a separate drop of dew.

It was natural that I should want all the more to touch those fingertips, but I held myself back. My solitude held me back. She was a woman on whose body few tender spots could be expected to remain.

And on the body of the girl who had lent me the arm they would be beyond counting. Perhaps, toying with the fingertips of such a girl, I would feel not guilt but affection. But she had not lent me the arm for such mischief. I must not make a comedy of her gesture.

"The window." I noticed not that the window itself was open but that the curtain was undrawn.

"Will anything look in?" asked the girl's arm.

"Some man or woman. Nothing else."

"Nothing human would see me. If anything it would be a self. Yours."

"Self? What is that? Where is it?"

"Far away," said the arm, as if singing in consolation. "People walk around looking for selves, far away."

"And do they come upon them?"

"Far away," said the arm once more.

It seemed to me that the arm and the girl herself were an infinity apart. Would the arm be able to return to the girl, so far away? Would I be able to take it back, so far away? The arm lay peacefully trusting me; and would the girl be sleeping in the same peaceful confidence? Would there not be harshness, a nightmare? Had she not seemed to be fighting back tears when she parted with it? The arm was now in my room, which the girl herself had not visited.

The dampness clouded the window, like a toad's belly stretched over it. The fog seemed to withhold rain in midair, and the night outside the window lost distance, even while it was wrapped in limitless distance. There were no roofs to be seen, no horns to be heard.

"I'll close the window," I said, reaching for the curtain. It too was damp. My face loomed up in the window, younger than my thirty-three years. I did not hesitate to pull the curtain, however. My face disappeared.

Suddenly a remembered window. On the ninth floor of a hotel, two little girls in wide red skirts were playing in the window. Very similar children in similar clothes, perhaps twins, Occidentals. They pounded at the glass, pushing it with their shoulders and shoving at each other. Their mother knitted, her back to the window. If the large pane were to have broken or come loose, they would have fallen from the ninth floor. It was only I who thought them in danger. Their mother was quite unconcerned. The glass was in fact so solid that there was no danger.

"It's beautiful," said the arm on the bed as I turned from the window. Perhaps she was speaking of the curtain, in the same flowered pattern as the bedcover.

"Oh? But it's faded from the sun and almost ready to go." I sat down on the bed and took the arm on my knee. "This is what is beautiful. More beautiful than anything."

Taking the palm of the hand in my own right palm, and the shoulder in my left hand, I flexed the elbow, and then again.

"Behave yourself," said the arm, as if smiling softly. "Having fun?"

"Not in the least."

A smile did come over the arm, crossing it like light. It was exactly the fresh smile on the girl's cheek.

I knew the smile. Elbows on the table, she would fold her hands loosely and rest her chin or cheek on them. The pose should have been inelegant in a young girl; but there was about it a lightly engaging quality that made expressions like "elbows on the table" seem inappropriate. The roundness of the shoulders, the fingers, the chin, the cheeks, the ears, the long, slender neck, the hair, all came together in a single harmonious movement. Using knife and fork deftly, index and little fingers bent, she would raise them ever so slightly from time to time. Food would pass the small lips and she would swallow—I had before me less a person at dinner than an inviting music of hands and face and throat. The light of her smile flowed across the skin of her arm.

The arm seemed to smile because, as I flexed it, very gentle waves passed over the firm, delicate muscles, to send waves of light and shadow over the smooth skin. Earlier, when I had touched the fingertips under the long nails, the light passing over the arm as the elbow bent had caught my eye. It was that, and not any impulse toward mischief, that had made me bend and unbend her arm. I stopped, and gazed at it as it lay stretched out on my knee. Fresh lights and shadows were still passing over it.

"You ask if I'm having fun. You realize that I have permission to change you for my own arm?"

"I do."

"Somehow I'm afraid to."

"Oh?"

"May I?"

"Please."

I heard the permission granted, and wondered whether I could accept it. "Say it again. Say 'please.'"

"Please, please."

I remembered. It was like the voice of a woman who had decided to give herself to me, one not as beautiful as the girl who had lent me the arm. Perhaps there was something a little strange about her.

"Please," she had said, gazing at me. I had put my fingers to her eyelids and closed them. Her voice was trembling. "'Jesus wept. Then said the Jews, Behold how he loved her!'"

"Her" was a mistake for "him." It was the story of the dead Lazarus. Perhaps, herself a woman, she had remembered it wrong, perhaps she had made the substitution intentionally.

The words, so inappropriate to the scene, had shaken me. I gazed at her, wondering if tears would start from the closed eyes.

She opened them and raised her shoulders. I pushed her down with my arm.

"You're hurting me!" She put her hand to the back of her head.

There was a small spot of blood on the white pillow. Parting her hair, I put my lips to the drop of blood swelling on her head.

"It doesn't matter." She took out all her hairpins. "I bleed easily. At the slightest touch."

A hairpin had pierced her skin. A shudder seemed about to pass through her shoulders, but she controlled herself.

Although I think I understand how a woman feels when she gives herself to a man, there is still something unexplained about the act. What is it to her? Why should she wish to do it, why should she take the initiative? I could never really accept the surrender, even knowing that the body of every woman was made for it. Even now, old as I am, it seems strange. And the ways in which various women go about it: unalike if you wish, or similar perhaps, or even identical. Is that not strange? Perhaps the strangeness I find in it all is the curiosity of a younger man, perhaps the despair of one advanced in years. Or perhaps some spiritual debility I suffer from.

Her anguish was not common to all women in the act of surrender. And it was with her only the one time. The silver thread was cut, the golden bowl destroyed.

"Please," the arm had said, and so reminded me of the other girl; but were the two voices in fact similar? Had they not sounded alike because the words were the same? Had the arm acquired independence in this measure of the body from which it was separated? And were the words not the act of giving itself up, of being ready for anything, without restraint or responsibility or remorse? It seemed to me that if I were to accept the invitation and change the arm for my own I would be bringing untold pain to the girl.

I gazed at the arm on my knee. There was a shadow at the inside of the elbow. It seemed that I might be able to suck it in. I pressed it to my lips, to gather in the shadow.

"It tickles. Do behave yourself." The arm was around my neck, avoiding my lips.

"Just when I was having a good drink."

"And what were you drinking?"

I did not answer.

"What were you drinking?"

"The smell of light? Of skin."

The fog seemed thicker; even the magnolia leaves seemed wet. What other warnings would issue from the radio? I started toward my table radio and stopped. To listen to it with the arm around my neck seemed altogether too much. But I suspected I would hear something like this: because of the wet branches and their own wet feet and wings, small birds have fallen to the ground and cannot fly. Automobiles passing through parks should take care not to run over them. And if a warm wind comes up, the fog will perhaps change color. Strange-colored fogs are noxious. Listeners should therefore lock their doors if the fog should turn pink or purple.

"Change color?" I muttered. "Turn pink or purple?"

I pulled at the curtain and looked out. The fog seemed to press down with an empty weight. Was it because of the wind that a thin darkness seemed to be moving about, different from the usual black of night? The thickness of the fog seemed infinite, and yet beyond it something fearsome writhed and coiled.

I remembered that earlier, as I was coming home with the borrowed arm, the head and tail beams of the car driven by the woman in vermilion had come up indistinctly in the fog. A great, blurred sphere of faint purple now seemed to come toward me. I hastily pulled away from the curtain.

"Let's go to bed. Us too."

It seemed as if no one else in the world would be up. To be up was terror.

Taking the arm from my neck and putting it on the table, I changed into a fresh night-kimono, a cotton print. The arm watched me change. I was shy at being watched. Never before had a woman watched me undress in my room.

The arm in my own, I got into bed. I lay facing it, and brought it lightly to my chest. It lay quiet.

Intermittently I could hear a faint sound as of rain, a very light sound, as if the fog had not turned to rain but were itself forming drops. The fingers clasped in my hand beneath the blanket grew warmer; and it gave me the quietest of sensations, the fact that they had not warmed to my own temperature.

"Are you asleep?"

"No," replied the arm.

"You were so quiet, I thought you might be asleep."

"What do you want me to do?"

Opening my kimono, I brought the arm to my chest. The difference in warmth sank in. In the somehow sultry, somehow chilly night, the smoothness of the skin was pleasant.

The lights were still on. I had forgotten to turn them out as I went to bed.

"The lights." I got up, and the arm fell from my chest.

I hastened to pick it up. "Will you turn out the lights?" I started toward the door. "Do you sleep in the dark? Or with lights on?"

The arm did not answer. It would surely know. Why had it not answered? I did not know the girl's nocturnal practices. I compared the two pictures, of her asleep in the dark and with the lights on. I decided that tonight, without her arm, she would have them on. Somehow I too wanted them on. I wanted to gaze at the arm. I wanted to stay awake and watch the arm after it had gone to sleep. But the fingers stretched to turn off the switch by the door.

I went back and lay down in the darkness, the arm by my chest. I lay there silently, waiting for it to go to sleep. Whether dissatisfied or afraid of the dark, the hand lay open at my side, and presently the five fingers were climbing my chest. The elbow bent of its own accord, and the arm embraced me.

There was a delicate pulse at the girl's wrist. It lay over my heart, so that the two pulses sounded against each other. Hers was at first somewhat slower than mine, then they were together. And then I could feel only mine. I did not know which was faster, which slower.

Perhaps this identity of pulse and heartbeat was for a brief period when I might try to exchange the arm for my own. Or had it gone to sleep? I had once heard a woman say that women were less happy in the throes of ecstasy than sleeping peacefully beside their men; but never before had a woman slept beside me as peacefully as this arm.

I was conscious of my beating heart because of the pulsation above it. Between one beat and the next, something sped far away and sped back again. As I listened to the beating, the distance seemed to increase. And however far the something went, however infinitely far, it met nothing at its destination. The next beat summoned it back. I should have been afraid, and was not. Yet I groped for the switch beside my pillow.

Before turning it on, I quietly rolled back the blanket. The arm slept on, unaware of what was happening. A gentle band of faintest white encircled my naked chest, seeming to rise from the flesh itself, like the glow before the dawning of a tiny, warm sun.

I turned on the light. I put my hands to the fingers and shoulder and pulled the arm straight. I turned it quietly in my hands, gazing at the play of light and shadow, from the roundness at the shoulder over the narrowing and swelling of the forearm, the narrowing again at the gentle roundness of the elbow, the faint depression inside the elbow, the narrowing roundness to the wrist, the palm and back of the hand, and on to the fingers.

"I'll have it." I was not conscious of muttering the words. In a trance, I removed my right arm and substituted the girl's.

There was a slight gasp—whether from the arm or from me I could not tell—and a spasm at my shoulder. So I knew of the change.

The girl's arm—mine now—was trembling and reaching for the air. Bending it, I brought it close to my mouth.

"Does it hurt? Do you hurt?"

"No. Not at all. Not at all." The words were fitful.

A shudder went through me like lightning. I had the fingers in my mouth.

Somehow I spoke my happiness, but the girl's fingers were at my tongue, and whatever it was I spoke did not form into words.

"Please. It's all right," the arm replied. The trembling stopped. "I was told you could. And yet—"

I noticed something. I could feel the girl's fingers in my mouth, but the fingers of her right hand, now those of my own right hand, could not feel my lips or teeth. In panic I shook my right arm and could not feel the shaking. There was a break, a stop, between arm and shoulder.

"The blood doesn't go," I blurted out. "Does it or doesn't it?"

For the first time I was swept by fear. I rose up in bed. My own arm had fallen beside me. Separated from me, it was an unsightly object. But more important—would not the pulse have stopped? The girl's arm was warm and pulsing; my own looked as if it were growing stiff and cold. With the girl's, I grasped my own right arm. I grasped it, but there was no sensation.

"Is there a pulse?" I asked the arm. "Is it cold?"

"A little. Just a little colder than I am. I've gotten very warm." There was something especially womanly in the cadence. Now that the arm was fastened to my shoulder and made my own, it seemed womanly as it had not before.

"The pulse hasn't stopped?"

"You should be more trusting."

"Of what?"

"You changed your arm for mine, didn't you?"

"Is the blood flowing?"

"'Woman, whom seekest thou?' You know the passage?"

"'Woman, why weepest thou? Whom seekest thou?'"

"Very often when I'm dreaming and wake up in the night I whisper it to myself."

This time of course the "I" would be the owner of the winsome arm at my shoulder. The words from the Bible were as if spoken by an eternal voice, in an eternal place.

"Will she have trouble sleeping?" I too spoke of the girl herself. "Will she be having a nightmare? It's a fog for herds of nightmares to wander in. But the dampness will make even demons cough."

"To keep you from hearing them." The girl's arm, my own still in its hand, covered my right ear.

It was now my own right arm, but the motion seemed to have come not of my volition but of its own, from its heart. Yet the separation was by no means so complete.

"The pulse. The sound of the pulse."

I heard the pulse of my own right arm. The girl's arm had come to my ear with my own arm in its hand, and my own wrist was at my ear.

My arm was warm—as the girl's arm had said, just perceptibly cooler than her fingers and my ear.

"I'll keep away the devils." Mischievously, gently, the long, delicate nail of her little finger stirred in my ear. I shook my head. My left hand—mine from the start—took my right wrist—actually the girl's. As I threw my head back, I caught sight of the girl's little finger.

Four fingers of her hand were grasping the arm I had taken from my right shoulder. The little finger alone—shall we say that it alone was allowed to play free?—was bent toward the back of the hand. The tip of the nail touched my right arm lightly. The finger was bent in a position possible only for a girl's supple hand, out of the question for a stiff-jointed man like me. From its base it rose at right angles. At the first joint it bent in another right angle, and at the next in yet another. It thus traced a square, the fourth side formed by the ring finger.

It formed a rectangular window at the level of my eye. Or rather a peephole, or an eyeglass, much too small for a window; but somehow I thought of a window. The sort of window a violet might look out through. The window of the little finger, the finger-rimmed eyeglass, so white that it gave off a faint glow—I brought it nearer my eye. I closed the other eye.

"A peep show?" asked the arm. "And what do you see?"

"My dusky old room. Its five lights." Before I had finished the sentence I was almost shouting. "No, no! I see it!"

"And what do you see?"

"It's gone."

"And what did you see?"

"A color. A blur of purple. And inside it little circles, little beads of red and gold, whirling around and around."

"You're tired." The girl's arm put down my right arm, and her fingers gently stroked my eyelids.

"Were the beads of gold and red spinning around in a huge cogwheel? Did I see something in the cogwheel, something that came and went?"

I did not know whether I had actually seen something there or only seemed to—a fleeting illusion, not to stay in the memory. I could not remember what it might have been.

"Was it an illusion you wanted to show me?"

"No. I came to erase it."

"Of days gone by. Of longing and sadness."

On my eyelids the movement of her fingers stopped.

I asked an unexpected question. "When you let down your hair does it cover your shoulders?"

"It does. I wash it in hot water, but afterward—a special quirk of mine, maybe—I pour cold water over it. I like the feel of cold hair against my shoulders and arms, and against my breasts too."

It would of course be the girl again. Her breasts had never been touched by a man, and no doubt she would have had difficulty describing the feel of the cold, wet hair against them. Had the arm, separated from the body, been separated too from the shyness and the reserve?

Quietly I took in my left hand the gentle roundness at the shoulder, now my own. It seemed to me that I had in my hand the roundness, not yet large, of her breasts. The roundness of the shoulder became the soft roundness of breasts.

Her hand lay gently on my eyelids. The fingers and the hand clung softly and sank through, and the underside of the eyelids seemed to warm at the touch. The warmth sank into my eyes.

"The blood is going now," I said quietly. "It is going."

It was not a cry of surprise as when I had noticed that my arm was changed for hers. There was no shuddering and no spasm in the girl's arm or my shoulder. When had my blood begun to flow through the arm, her blood through me? When had the break at the shoulder disappeared? The clean blood of the girl was now, this very moment, flowing through me; but would there not be unpleasantness when the arm was returned to the girl, this dirty male blood flowing through it? What if it would not attach itself to her shoulder?

"No such betrayal," I muttered.

"It will be all right," whispered the arm.

There was no dramatic awareness that between the arm and my shoulder the blood came and went. My left hand, enfolding my right shoulder, and the shoulder itself, now mine, had a natural understanding of the fact. They had come to know it. The knowledge pulled them down into slumber.

I slept.

I floated on a great wave. It was the encompassing fog turned a faint purple, and there were pale green ripples at the spot where I floated on the great wave, and there alone. The dank solitude of my room was gone. My left hand seemed to rest lightly on the girl's right arm. It seemed that her fingers held magnolia stamens. I could not see them, but I could smell them. We had thrown them away—and when and how had she gathered them up again? The white petals, but a day old, had not yet fallen; why then the stamens? The automobile of the woman in vermilion slid by, drawing a great circle with me at the center. It seemed to watch over our sleep, the arm's and mine.

Our sleep was probably light, but I had never before known sleep so warm, so sweet. A restless sleeper, I had never before been blessed with the sleep of a child.

The long, narrow, delicate nail scratched gently at the palm of my hand, and the slight touch made my sleep deeper. I disappeared.

I awoke screaming. I almost fell out of bed, and staggered three or four steps.

I had awakened to the touch of something repulsive. It was my right arm.

Steadying myself, I looked down at the arm on the bed. I caught my breath, my heart raced, my whole body trembled. I saw the arm in one instant, and the next I had torn the girl's from my shoulder and put back my own. The act was like murder upon a sudden, diabolic impulse.

I knelt by the bed, my chest against it, and rubbed at my insane heart with my restored hand. As the beating slowed down a sadness welled up from deeper than the deepest inside me.

"Where is her arm?" I raised my head.

It lay at the foot of the bed, flung palm up into the heap of the blanket. The outstretched fingers did not move. The arm was faintly white in the dim light.

Crying out in alarm I swept it up and held it tight to my chest. I embraced it as one would a small child from whom life was going. I brought the fingers to my lips. If the dew of woman would but come from between the long nails and the fingertips!

THE DAY BEFORE

Endō Shūsaku

Translated by Van C. Gessel

There was a time when the name of Endō Shūsaku (1923–   ) was invariably introduced to Western readers as "the Japanese Graham Greene." Recently, however, enthusiastic critical reactions to translations of Endō's works into a dozen languages have prompted a critic to suggest that, by the twenty-first century, Greene may consider himself fortunate to be labeled the "British Endō." Six novels, a play, a short story collection, and a contemplative life of Jesus have been translated into English and many other languages, establishing Endō as the most accessible of contemporary Japanese novelists, not only because he deals with questions of Christian faith and human weakness that transcend national boundaries, but also because he writes with a simplicity and an eye for detail and structure that are rare qualities among his contemporaries in Japan.

Endō was baptized a Catholic at his mother's instigation when he was eleven years old. The influence of a strong but forgiving maternal figure has remained central to his writings and to his conception of God, as the critic Etō Jun has pointed out. This Madonna-Jesus figure was first sketched out in a series of short stories that Endō wrote after a long hospitalization in the early 1960s; his collection Aika *(Elegies, 1965), from which "The Day Before" (Sono zenjitsu) is taken, is filled with preliminary sketches for the larger themes Endō would paint with bolder strokes in novels such as* Chimmoku *(Silence, 1966; tr. 1969) and* Samurai *(The Samurai, 1980; tr. 1982). Even clearer portrayals of Christ as a compassionate mother figure may be found in the story "Haha naru mono" (Mothers, 1969; tr. 1984) and Endō's* Iesu no shōgai *(Life of Jesus, 1973; tr. 1978). The* fumie *that is a central image in "The Day Before" is yet another image of Christ—in this case, a copper or wooden likeness of Mary or Jesus which the Japanese authorities in the seventeenth century used to ferret out suspected Christians. Those who would trample on the sacred image were released, whether or not such an action reflected their true inner feelings. The* fumie *for Endō thus represents the dichotomy between outward behavior—cowardice, betrayal—and internal aspirations.*

After studying French Catholic fiction at Keiō University, Endō spent two and a half years in France, beginning in 1950 when he traveled to Europe aboard a merchant vessel in one of the first groups of Japanese students to go abroad after the Second World War. In Europe, the conflicts between Eastern and Western cultures, between Oriental pantheism and Occidental monotheism, seared his conscience and led him to write his first fiction, Shiroi hito *(White Man, 1955), which was awarded the Akutagawa Prize. Endō followed this initial account of betrayal and brutality in occupied France with a study of moral corruption set in Japan,* Kiiroi hito *(Yellow Man, 1955), and created a sensation with his castigation of the Japanese moral conscience in* Umi to dokuyaku *(The Sea and Poison, 1958; tr. 1972).*

Endō is also widely known in Japan as the author of lighter "entertainment" novels, many of which, like Obakasan *(Wonderful Fool, 1959; tr. 1974), combine a comic exterior with a deeply compassionate, fundamentally religious core. The entire range and variety of Endō's literary output may, in fact, be viewed as a manifestation of his cautiously optimistic belief that the "mud swamp" of Japan may be transcended through acts of selfless charity, accompanied by a pained but bemused smile—the sort that the narrator of "The Day Before" is also to muster just before he faces possible death.*

* * *

For some time I had wanted to get my hands on that *fumie*. If nothing else, I at least wanted to be able to see it. The image was owned by Fukae Tokujirō of Daimyō village, Sonoki, in Nagasaki Prefecture. A copper engraving of the crucified Christ was set in a wooden frame eight inches wide by twelve inches long.

It had been used during the fourth siege of Urakami, the final persecution of Christians in Japan. Use of the *fumie* was supposed to have been abolished by the U.S.-Japan Treaty of 1858, but apparently it was used again in this suppression, which occurred after the signing of the accord.

My desire to obtain the *fumie* was aroused when I read in a Catholic tract about Tōgorō, a villager from Takashima in Sonoki District, who apostatized during the fourth siege. The tract fascinated me. Its author of course confined himself to presenting the historical facts surrounding the suppression and said very little about Tōgorō, but my interest was riveted on him.

Father N, a friend from my school days, happened to be in Nagasaki at the time, so I wrote to him about my feelings concerning Tōgorō. In his reply he mentioned the *fumie*. Daimyō village was in his parish, he noted, and a Mr. Fukae from the village owned a *fumie* from the period. It seems that some of Fukae's ancestors had been among the officials who had carried out the supression

The day before I was due to have my third operation, arrangements were made for me to see the *fumie*. My friend Father Inoue was supposed to go to Nagasaki and bring it back with him. This was not merely for my benefit, of course; his assignment was to deposit the image in the Christian Archives at J University in Yotsuya. That was a disappointment to me, but I conceded the necessity of preserving such precious objects. Father Inoue telephoned my wife and let her know he would be allowed to give me a brief look at it before he turned it over to the university.

I dozed off in my hospital room as I waited for Father Inoue. Christmas was approaching, and I could hear a choir practicing on the roof—probably students from the school of nursing. Sometimes I would open my eyes a slit and listen to those voices in the distance, then close my eyes again.

I sensed someone softly opening the door to my room. It might be my wife, I thought, but she was supposed to be running around making all the arrangements for my massive surgery tomorrow. So I couldn't imagine it would be her.

"Who's there?"

A middle-aged man dressed in a fur jacket and a mountaineering cap peered in. I did not know him. I glanced first from his dirty cap to his fur jacket, then lowered my gaze to the large lace-up boots he was wearing. Ah, it must be someone from Father Inoue, I thought.

"Are you from the church?"

"Huh?"

"Father sent you, didn't he?" I smiled, but his eyes narrowed and a strange expression crossed his face.

"No. I asked 'em over in the ward, and they said you might wanna buy."

"Buy? What?"

"You get four for six hundred yen. I got books, too. But I didn't bring 'em today."

Not waiting for me to respond, he appeared to twist at the waist and pulled a small paper envelope from his trouser pocket. Inside the envelope were four photographs with yellowed borders, a result no doubt of cheap developing. In the shadowy prints the dim figure of a man could be seen embracing the indistinct body of a woman. A single wooden chair stood beside the bed in what appeared to be a dreary hotel in the suburbs.

"You don't understand. I'm being operated on tomorrow!"

"That's why I brought these." He had no words of sympathy to offer. Scratching the palm of his hand with the photographs, he continued, "Since you got an operation coming up, you can buy these as a good luck charm. Buy 'em and the operation's bound to be a success. How about it, captain?"

"Do you come around to this hospital often?"

"Sure. This is my territory."

It may have been a joke, or perhaps he meant it seriously, but he made the declaration to me with all the bravura of a physician talking to one of his patients. I took a liking to the man.

"No, no. These pictures don't interest me."

"Well. . ." He looked rueful. "If you don't like these, what sort of pose do you want, captain?"

He lit up a cigarette from the pack I held out to him and began to chatter.

Nowhere does a person get more bored and develop a greater desire to look at pictures and books of this sort than in a hospital. No location was more suitable to peddle such goods, since the police would never suspect. This fellow had divided up the territory with his colleagues and made the rounds of the city hospitals.

"A few days back, the old boy in Room H took a look at these shots before his operation, and he says, 'Ah, now I can die happy!'"

I laughed. I found him a more welcome visitor today than the relatives who tiptoe through hospital-room doors with pained looks on their faces. When he had finished his cigarette, he stuck another behind his ear and left the room.

For some reason I felt in high spirits. This peddler had come instead of the priest. Bringing pornographic pictures in place of the *fumie*. Today should have been a day for me to think about many things, to put various affairs in order. Tomorrow's operation would be unlike my first two; the doctors anticipated massive hemorrhaging and danger because my pleurae had fused together. The risk was so great they had left it up to me whether or not to go through with surgery. Today I had intended to put on a face so bland it would seem that cellophane had been stretched over it, but that porn peddler had nipped that plan in the bud. And yet, in their own way, those murky photographs with their sallow images were proof of God's existence.

When the officers of the feudal domain raided Takashima, the villagers were reciting their evening prayers. They naturally had lookouts posted, but the police were already storming into the farmhouse chapel when the sentries rang the warning bell.

In the light of the moon that night, ten men—including two leaders of the peasant association—were hurriedly transported to Urakami. Among them, for good or ill, was Tōgorō. From the outset his comrades had the uneasy foreboding that Tōgorō would apostatize. He had been such an irksome anomaly in this village of fervent faith. Despite his massive stature, Tōgorō was a coward.

On past occasions Tōgorō had been lured into quarrels by the young men of neighboring villages. Though he was twice the size of an average man, there were times when he skulked back to Takashima clad only in his loincloth, having been thrown to the ground and stripped of all he had. Fear of his opponents rather than a Christian resolve to turn the other cheek prevented him from offering any resistance at such times. It was not long before the villagers of Takashima came to despise him. For that reason, although he was already thirty years old, he was the only young man of his age without a bride. He lived alone with his mother.

Of the ten prisoners, Kashichi held the highest position in the village. He was a man of principle, and the evening before the interrogations began at Urakami, he offered special words of encouragement to Tōgorō. "Deus and Santa Maria will surely grant us strength and courage. Those who suffer in this world are guaranteed a place in heaven," Kashichi reassured him. Tōgorō studied the others with the terrified eyes of a stray dog, but at their urging he joined in the chanting of the Credo and Pater Noster.

Early in the morning on the following day, the interrogations began at the office of the Urakami magistrate. The prisoners were bound and dragged out one by one to the cold, gravel-floored interrogation room, where the officers brought out the *fumie*. Those who would not recant their faith were beaten severely with an archer's bow. But before the bow had even been raised over Tōgorō, he ground his soiled foot into the face of Christ in the image. With sad, animal-like eyes Tōgorō darted a glance toward his comrades, who were disheveled and covered with blood. The officers then drove him out of the magistrate's headquarters.

"We're going to shave you and get a blood sample now." This time a nurse came into my room, carrying a metal tray and a hypodermic. Her job was to shave the fine hairs from the area targeted for surgery tomorrow and to determine my blood type for transfusions.

When she removed my pyjama top the chilly air cut into my skin. I raised my left arm and did my best not to giggle as she moved the razor along my armpit.

"That tickles!"

"When you bathe, be sure to wash really well back here. It's all red."

"I can't wash there. It's been very sensitive since my last operation. I can't scrub it."

There is a large scar on my back, cut at a slant across my shoulder. The area is swollen, since an incision was made twice in the same place. Again tomorrow the cold scalpel would race across that spot. And my body would be soaked with blood.

After Tōgorō's desertion the remaining nine men stubbornly refused to apostatize. They were placed for a time in a Nagasaki prison, and the following year—1868—they were loaded into a boat and sent to Tsuyama, near Onomichi. Rain fell that evening and drenched the open boat, and the prisoners, having only the clothes they were wearing, huddled together to ward off the cold. As the boat pulled away from Nagasaki, one of the prisoners, Bunji, noticed a man dressed like a dockworker standing at the edge of the water.

"Look! Isn't that Tōgorō?"

From far in the distance, Tōgorō was peering toward them with the same sad, appealing eyes they had seen when he apostatized. The men lowered their eyes as though they had gazed upon something filthy, and no one uttered another word.

The prison for these nine men lay in the mountains some twenty-four miles from Tsuyama. From their cell they could see the officers' hut and a small pond. At first there was little harassment, and the officers were lenient. Even the food they received twice a day was something for which these impoverished farmers could be thankful. The officers laughed gently and told them that they could eat better food and be given warmer clothes if they would merely cast off their burdensome religion.

In the autumn of that year, fourteen or fifteen new prisoners arrived unexpectedly. They were children from Takashima. The men were surprised at this strange move by the officials, yet pleased to be able to see some of their family after so long a time. But soon they were forced into the realization that this move was part of a psychological torture they came to refer to as "child abuse."

Occasionally the prisoners heard weeping from the adjoining cell, where their children were incarcerated. One afternoon a prisoner named Fujifusa pressed his face to the tiny window of the children's cell and saw two emaciated boys catching dragonflies and stuffing them into their mouths. It was obvious that the children were being given scarcely anything that could be called food. The other men listened to this report and wept.

They begged the officers to take even half of their own "good" food and share it with the children, but this was not allowed. They were told, however, that all they had to do was reject their troublesome religion, and they and their children would go back to their dear village pleasingly plump.

"There. All done."

The nurse pulled out the hypodermic, and as I rubbed the spot where the needle had entered, she held the vial filled with blood up to the light at eye level.

"Your blood is dark, isn't it?"

"Does it mean something's wrong if it's dark?"

"Oh, no. I was just commenting on how dark it is."

As she went out, a young doctor I had not seen before came in. I tried to sit up in bed.

"No, no. As you were. I'm Okuyama, Department of Anesthesia."

Okuyama turned out to be the anesthetist who would assist at my operation the next day. He went through the formality of placing a stethoscope on my chest.

"In your previous operations, did you awaken quickly from the anesthesia?"

In my most recent operation, the doctors had cut away five of my ribs. I remembered that the anesthesia had worn off just as the operation ended. The pain I experienced then was like a pair of scissors jabbing through my chest. I described the agony for Okuyama.

"This time, please keep me knocked out for at least half a day. That was terribly painful."

The young doctor smiled broadly. "We'll aim for that, then."

When it became clear that the men were still not going to apostatize, the tortures began. The nine men were separated and placed in small boxes, in which they were unable to move from a seated position. Holes were bored near their heads to allow them to breathe. They were not permitted to leave the boxes except to relieve themselves.

Winter drew near. The prisoners began to weaken from cold and exhaustion. In compensation, however, they began to hear laughter from the adjoining cell. The officers, being fathers themselves, had given food to the children. The nine men in their individual boxes listened silently to the laughing voices.

At the end of the eleventh month a prisoner named Kumekichi died. The oldest of the nine, he had been unable to endure the cold and the fatigue. Kashichi had had great respect for the old man and always asked his advice whenever something happened in the prison. He was therefore deeply affected by his death. Peering out through the hole bored in his box, Kashichi reflected on how weak his own will had become. And for the first time he hated the traitor Tōgorō.

Again the door opened softly. Father? No. Once again it was the porn peddler.

"Captain!"

"What? You!"

"Actually . . . I've brought you a good luck charm. . ."

"I told you I wouldn't buy any."

"Not pictures. I'm giving you this for free. Then if your operation's a success, you can thank me by purchasing the pictures and books I bring around." He lowered his voice to a whisper. "Captain, I can get you a woman. It's strictly 'no trespassing' around here. You can lock the door. You've got a bed. Nobody'll know!"

"Yes, yes."

He was clutching an object in his hand. Before he left he set it on the table beside my bed. I glanced over and discovered a tiny wooden doll, grimy from the sweat and soil of the peddler's hands.

They were taken from their boxes when winter came, but the mornings and nights continued cold. From the mountain to the rear they heard sounds like something splitting open. It was the sound of branches cracking from the cold. Thin ice stretched across the tiny pond between the prison and the officers' hut.

One day near evening, the officers came and took two prisoners, Seiichi and Tatsugorō, from the cell. They cast the two into the frozen pond and beat them with poles each time their heads bobbed above the surface of the water. When they lost consciousness from the painful torture, Seiichi and Tatsugorō were carried back to the prison in the arms of the officers. The six remaining men joined their voices with Kashichi's and recited the Ave Maria over and over again. But many were choked with sobs during the final benediction, "Holy Mary, Mother of God, pray for us sinners now and at the hour of our death."

Just then, through the cell window Kashichi caught sight of a tall, thin man glancing about him restlessly like a beggar. The man, whose hair and beard grew wantonly like an exile's, turned toward him, and Kashichi involuntarily shouted, "It's Tōgorō!"

An officer came out to drive the intruder away, but Tōgorō shook his head and seemed to be making some sort of fervent plea. Eventually the first officer summoned another, and the two spoke together for a few moments. Finally they took Tōgorō to the only empty cell in the prison.

"He's one of you," the officers announced, confusion written on their faces. When they were gone, the eight prisoners sat in silence and listened to the sound of Tōgorō shuffling about in the dark.

"Why did you come?" At last Kashichi asked the question in all their minds. He felt vaguely uneasy. It had occurred to him that Tōgorō might be a spy for the officers. Even if he weren't a spy, his presence might further dampen the already weakened spirits of the others. Kashichi had heard from the dead Kumekichi that the officers employed such cunning devices.

Tōgorō's reply was unexpected. In a soft voice, he told them that he had come here and surrendered on his own.

"You?! . . ."

When the men jeered at him, Tōgorō tried to stammer out a defense. Kashichi silenced them.

"Do you realize that you'll be tortured here? If you're going to make it harder for the rest of us, you'd better go back home."

Tōgorō remained silent.

"Aren't you afraid?"

"I'm afraid," Tōgorō muttered.

Then he blurted out something very strange. He had come here because he had heard a voice. He had most certainly heard a voice. It had instructed him to go just once more to be with the others. "Go to them in Tsuyama. And if you fear the tortures, you can run away again. Go to Tsuyama," the tearful, pleading voice had said.

That night the only noise that broke the stillness outside was the sound of branches splitting on the mountain. The prisoners listened intently to Tōgorō's story. One grumbled, "A nice convenient tale for him to tell, isn't it?" To him, the story sounded like something Tōgorō had made up so that his friends and fellow villagers would forgive him for his betrayal two years earlier. "If you fear the tortures, you can run away again." It seemed just another handy way of talking himself out of difficulty.

Kashichi was half inclined to agree, but another part of him refused to believe that Tōgorō's story was a hoax. Unable to sleep that night, he listened thoughtfully to Tōgorō's body stirring in the darkness.

The following day Tōgorō was taken out by the officers and hurled into the pond. The other prisoners joined Kashichi in reciting the Credo as Tōgorō's childlike screams filled their ears. They prayed that God would grant strength to this weakling. But in the end the voice they heard nullified their entreaties. Tōgorō renounced his faith to the officers and was pulled from the pond.

Still, Kashichi was relieved to know that his suspicions about Tōgorō being a spy had been mistaken. "It's all right. It's all right," he thought.

No one knows what happened to Tōgorō after the officers set him free. In 1871, the eight prisoners were released by the new government.

Father Inoue arrived. He opened the door softly and came in, just as the porn peddler had done. Though it was cold outside, a thin layer of perspiration coated his pale face. We had been friends in our school days, and together we had gone to France, sleeping in the hold of a cargo ship among coolies and soldiers.

"I owe you an apology."

"You couldn't get the *fumie*?"

"No." Someone higher up in the church hierarchy had ordered another priest to take the *fumie* from Nagasaki to the Christian Archives at J University.

Inoue had a deep red birthmark on his forehead. He was a curate in a small church in downtown Tokyo. The overcoat he wore had frayed sleeves and his black trousers were worn at the knees. Just as I had imagined, his figure somehow resembled that of the man in the mountaineering cap. But I told him nothing of that encounter.

Inoue told me that he had seen the *fumie*. The wooden frame was rotting away. The copperplate figure of Christ, covered with a greenish patina, had probably been fashioned by a country laborer in Urakami. The face resembled a child's scribble, and the eyes and nose had been worn away until they were no longer distinguishable. The *fumie* had been lying neglected in a storehouse at Mr. Fukae's home in Daimyō.

Puffing on our cigarettes, we changed the topic of discussion. I asked Father Inoue about the Last Supper scene in the Gospel of St. John. This was a passage that had troubled me for some time. I could not understand the remark Christ made when he handed the sop to the traitor Judas.

"And when he had dipped the sop, he gave it to Judas Iscariot, the son of Simon. . . Then said Jesus unto him 'That thou doest, do quickly. . .'"

That thou doest, do quickly. Obviously referring to Judas' betrayal of him. But why didn't Christ restrain Judas? Had Jesus really cast the traitor off with such obvious callousness? That was what I wanted to know.

Father Inoue said that these words revealed the human side of Christ. He loved Judas, but with a traitor seated at the same table, he could not suppress his hatred. Inoue believed that this feeling resembled the complex mixture of love and hate a man feels when he is betrayed by the woman he loves. But I disagreed.

"Jesus isn't issuing a command here. Maybe the translation from the original has been gradually corrupted. It's like he's saying, 'You're going to do this anyway. I can't stop you, so go ahead and do it.' Isn't that what he meant when he said, 'My cross is for that purpose,' and spoke of the cross he had to bear? Christ knew all the desperate acts of men."

The choir practice on the roof seemed to have ended. Afternoons at the hospital were quiet. Sticking to my rather heretical views in spite of Father Inoue's objections, I thought about the *fumie* I had not seen. I had wanted to see it before my operation, but if I couldn't, I would just have to accept it. Father Inoue had reported that the copperplate image of Christ, set in a rotting wooden frame, had been worn away. The feet of the men who had trampled on it had disfigured and gradually rubbed out the face of Christ. But more than that copper image of Christ was disfigured. I think I understood the sort of pain Tōgorō felt in his foot as he trod on it. The pain of many such men was transmitted to the copperplate Christ. And he, unable to endure the sufferings of men, was overwhelmed with compassion and whispered, "That thou doest, do quickly." He whose face was trodden upon and he who trod upon it were still alive today, in the same juxtaposition.

Still vaguely in my mind were thoughts of the small, yellow-edged photographs the peddler had brought in earlier. Just as the shadowy bodies of the man and woman moaned and embraced in those pictures, the face of the copperplate Christ and the flesh of men come into contact with one another. The two strangely resemble one another. This relationship is described in the catechisms that children study on Sunday afternoons with nuns in the rear gardens of churches that smell of boiling jam. For many years I scoffed at those catechisms. And yet, after some thirty years, this is the only thing I can say I have learned.

After Father Inoue left, I snuggled down into my bed and waited for my wife to come. Occasionally the feeble sunlight shone into my room from between the gray clouds. Steam rose from a medicinal jar on an electric heater. There was a bump as something fell to the floor. I opened my eyes and looked down. It was the good luck charm the peddler had given me. That tiny wooden doll, as grimy as life itself.

FRIENDS

Abe Akira

Translated by Virginia Marcus

Abe Akira was born in Hiroshima in 1934, but he has lived in Kugenuma, not far from Tokyo, most of his life. As a student at Tokyo University, he majored in French literature, focusing on the works of Stendhal, and actively participated in university theatrical productions. After college he worked for a Tokyo broadcasting company as a producer of both television and radio programs. In 1971, however, he left that profession to devote himself to his writing, which had already received favorable attention in literary circles.

*Most of Abe's stories belong to that distinctive genre of Japanese literature known as the "I-novel," in which the author makes explicit his use of personal experience. He made his debut in 1962 with "*Kodomobeya*" (The Child's Room), a short story about a young boy and his retarded older brother. Abe turned to the broadcasting studio for his inspiration in such stories as "*Tokyo no haru*" (Spring in Tokyo, 1967) and "*Hibi no tomo*" (Friends, 1970). Haunted by the pathetic figure of his unsuccessful father, a veteran of the Second World War and a living symbol of a defeated nation, Abe wrote several stories and a novel,* Shirei no kyūka *(The Commander's Furlough, 1970), that deal with the final years of his father's life and his own feelings of humiliation and shame.*

Although Abe's stories touch upon such ponderous themes as insanity, suicide, and shame, the author chooses to focus on everyday events and seemingly insignificant details. He does not dwell on the mysteries of life and death, nor does he indulge in sentimentality. Yet, by weaving together the details of ordinary lives, Abe achieves a work of psychological depth and creates a world that speaks of a larger humanity.

* * *

One day Urashima dropped into my office.

"Hatori's in bad shape," he said. "I understand he hasn't been to work for some time."

"So he's back in again?" Seated at my desk, I let out an involuntary laugh. "Hatori's illness" had become a kind of password between Urashima and me.

"This time it looks pretty bad."

"Have a seat," I said. Urashima pulled up a chair. How many times had we already discussed it? I chuckled, though I didn't mean to laugh at my friend's misfortune. We tried to help Hatori, and often talked about his problem, but it was always painful. "So he's back in again?" The words echoed. It made me sad to realize that I was now capable of such an indifferent remark.

Some time ago I had seen Hatori in good spirits, though even then he had seemed a little out of sorts. He sat next to us that night, sipping a beer as we drank our whiskey. I remember that every so often he would take out some pills the doctor had given him and gulp them down.

Hatori himself was aware of his problem. "I get so nervous," he had said, "I can't talk to anyone. I listen without responding. I don't use words—I just blink. People talk to me, but I can't answer and say how I feel. Instead I stare at things. I keep to myself all the time."

No one had to tell him to go to the hospital. He went on his own. For at least a month, and sometimes for as long as three or four, he wouldn't show up at work. His disappearances came as no surprise—everyone knew about his "vacations." No doubt the other cameramen welcomed his absence, for when he was himself Hatori was considered the best cameraman at the studio.

When the three of us worked together or went drinking, Urashima and I would find ourselves bothered by Hatori's sudden silences. As his symptoms grew worse, he didn't even blink any more. He stared at us with his eyes wide open like a baby, oblivious to everything. He fixed his swollen, bloodshot eyes on one spot, as if he were a statue. We blamed ourselves, in part, for what happened. As soon as he started to withdraw, we should have let him rest; instead, we ignored his illness and took him around with us every night as we always had.

When he did come to work, we could see that he was growing more and more withdrawn. Once when we were working with him on a documentary, he started taking pictures of strange objects. He had gradually lost interest in the people we were sent to film. With the utmost care he shot one roll after another, focusing his camera on everything but the subject at hand—the hollow of a gnarled, rotting tree, a broken drainpipe, a child's old, abandoned tricycle, leaves fluttering in the wind.

Some of us expressed sympathy for him, but no one had much hope for his recovery. Those who once envied Hatori's reputation and skill were now given the chance to succeed him. His illness provided them with the perfect opportunity. Gradually he was taken off the important shows. "He's not himself," they reasoned, giving him insignificant jobs more suited to a novice. Veteran cameraman that he was, Hatori had trouble accepting his demotion. We could see that humiliation and anxiety were slowly eating away at him.

Although he had no special assignments, he would leave for the office early in the morning and spend precisely eight hours at his desk. He sat there staring off into space as he puffed away on a cigarette. His face had become swollen. He hardly uttered a word to anyone. There wasn't so much as a single sheet of paper on his desk—not a speck of dust. He would return from his "vacations" before he should have, without fully recovering, and forcing himself in this way only made matters worse. At first, he went to the hospital once a year. Then two or three times a year. The space between visits grew shorter and shorter, and the number of his days off increased.

Before Urashima came by, he had called Hatori's wife to see how he was doing. I asked him what she had said.

He hesitated. "I guess she doesn't want us to visit him."

"Oh?"

"His eyes are swollen from the medicine." Urashima put his hand to his face. "It seems his face has changed, too. She said the medicine doesn't work any more." It irked me that Urashima had instinctively lowered his voice, as if he were afraid of being overheard.

"Don't you think he'd be glad to see us?" I asked.

"Maybe so." He seemed reluctant to answer and sounded dissatisfied.

In the end we didn't go to the hospital. To tell the truth, I didn't want to see Hatori's face in that condition. Besides, we had been there once before. One afternoon we had slipped away early from the office to visit him. When we left him in the evening, we decided to go out for a drink. Nothing was said, but we both knew we couldn't go straight home after seeing him like that. He had been fond of his drink, and since this was now denied him, I suppose we thought we would drink his share for him. We kept telling ourselves how depressing it had been, but even so we had a good time together.

"Do you think we've had too much?" I asked Urashima. "He'll be an invalid soon, and we'll still be here drowning our sorrows."

What could we do for him? I had no solutions. To Urashima it may have sounded as if I didn't think Hatori would ever get well. He was more optimistic than I, and he seemed free from guilt. He wanted Hatori to recover so that he could work with him again. His work wasn't quite up to par when Hatori was away.

In spite of how we felt, we both sensed that Hatori's wife did not appreciate our concern for her husband; rather, she seemed to resent us. From her point of view, we belonged to the company that had made her husband sick. As if her situation weren't difficult enough, she also had two children still in elementary school to look after. Hatori often talked about his wife to us. She seemed to be an ordinary housewife.

"It's so crowded where we live," he had once told me. "No breathing space at all. When we built the house after we got married, it was out in the middle of nowhere. One night my wife was taking a bath, and somebody peeked in the window. She screamed, and I ran outside, but he'd already gone. . . She'd tell me how lonely she got, especially during the day. The studio was new then, remember? It meant everything to us. We worked day and night. Our wives had to bring clean shirts and underwear to the office—we were never home. The first year of our marriage I traveled all the time. Who had time for a honeymoon? Before long our first boy was born. One night when I did get home, I came out of the station, and there was my wife, standing at the gate with our baby in her arms, crying. That's how bad things were. . . Anyway, you ought to come over sometime. It'd make my wife happy."

Once, on my day off, I did go to visit them. Though small in stature, Hatori's wife seemed a reliable sort of person. Looking at her, it was hard to imagine her as the young woman sobbing at the gate with the baby in her arms. I realized that Hatori had someone he could depend on, and I felt that some of the burden had fallen from my shoulders.

The moment she saw me she said, "What a fuss he's been making, ever since this morning! 'We'd better clean up the bathroom for Inoue,' he'd say, and then he'd hurry off and clean it himself. He scrubbed the hallway. He hung around the kitchen and kept asking me, 'Did you buy this? Did you buy that?' Finally I said to him, 'Just what kind of person is this Mr. Inoue?'"

She was hospitable enough, but she stared at me, looking troubled by something. Perhaps I was mistaken, but initially I detected a derisive tone in her voice, as if she envied the closeness we men had shared.

"He's always been like this. He gets wrapped up in whatever he does—his work, his friends. It almost frightens me." She sounded like an older sister talking about her sickly brother.

That night Hatori and I sat up talking by the brazier with a bottle of saké at our side. I can remember warming it in the kettle on the heater behind us. The two cats his wife had taken in loitered around us as we drank. Hatori called to them, as if he had suddenly remembered their names, and threw them a piece of dried fish. His face was flushed and he talked freely.

"You know when I first got sick? It was when we were on assignment up in a fishing village near Sendai. Yamaya was there—he's still in my section, you know. We had to shoot a story about a shipwreck, and we were staying at an inn nearby. Let's see, when was that? . . . One day after work we went back to the inn together, took our evening bath, and had a drink. The others kept on drinking, but for some reason I was preoccupied with the next day's shooting. I went down to the beach by myself to have another look at the location. I couldn't see much, though; it was night. Come to think of it, I was already starting to act strangely.

"I looked over the harbor in the dark and started back to the inn. It was more like a cheap lodging house than an inn, actually, but it did have a small garden. You could go straight to the beach from there. Just as I came into the garden, I heard Yamaya and Iwama, the lighting man, talking in the shadow of a tree. 'He doesn't work for his money! He can't even do a decent job, and he has the nerve to think he's a hotshot. He can drop dead, for all I care.' It was Yamaya. I stood there frozen, I couldn't move. I had worked hard on the beach that day. I'd worked until I thought I'd drop. My jacket and pants were soaking wet, but I'd lugged that camera around all day. And when I got back to the inn, all I could think about was the next day's work. There was no reason at all for him to say what he did. I had trusted Yamaya. I'd always done exactly as he told me, only to have him turn around and lie about me. It would've been another story if he'd said it right to my face, but he cornered someone when I wasn't there and tore into me. I was disgusted! I was miserable. I didn't want to think that Yamaya was that kind of person. Standing in that pitch-dark garden, I wished I had misheard him. But I hadn't. If only I'd come back a minute later, or a little earlier, I wouldn't have heard him say it. . . I hid in the shadow of a tree until Yamaya and Iwama left the garden. Then I crept up to my room and went to bed before anybody else." Hatori broke off at this point. He had trouble breathing, and his flushed face grew even redder.

"The next day we went to the house where the drowned fisherman had lived. We were filming his widow. Holding an infant to her breast, she clung to her husband's coffin. Suddenly I felt like it was all my fault, and I got down on my knees and apologized. I begged her forgiveness, I had to, or I couldn't have lived with myself. On my knees, I apologized over and over again.

"The tears streamed down my face, and the woman cried for me. I began to imagine that I had killed her husband at sea and that she and I were having an affair. I was so ashamed that I finally took my camera and ran out of the house in my bare feet. Apparently, I went back to the inn. After that, I can't remember. . . I think Yamaya canceled the shooting session and cabled Tokyo to arrange for our return. As I recall, he kept saying 'Hatori, don't worry. We'll be back soon. Don't worry.'"

The rest was a blank. On his way home from Sendai, apparently, he staggered off the train at Utsunomiya, lay down on the platform, and pleaded with Yamaya to set him free. The company informed Hatori's wife about this bizarre behavior, and when she saw for herself how disturbed he was, she burst into tears.

The news about Hatori spread quickly throughout the company. His "breakdown" was the butt of jokes whenever we went drinking. No doubt, Yamaya and Iwama were responsible for telling everyone what had occurred.

But was it really Yamaya who had attacked Hatori behind his back? It had happened in the darkness of a garden, and there was no way of knowing. Yamaya was considered a shifty individual, but we were all schemers to some extent. It would be unfair to presume that Yamaya was the one who pushed Hatori to the edge. It seems closer to the truth to say that the team of Yamaya and Hatori was ill-fated from the start.

The employees all had different theories about Hatori's illness. Some thought he had filmed too many tragedies. The wounded children, the distraught mothers, the helpless cripples had finally overwhelmed him. Hatori had been told what to shoot, and he earned a living at it, but the fact remained that he had seen too much unhappiness. His heart went out to the victims, and he blamed himself for their suffering. Some thought he was too sensitive for his line of work. Others wrote it off as a sign of fatigue.

But what kind of man was Yamaya? I once worked for him temporarily, and remember being five minutes late for a field trip. Yamaya knew he could count on me, so I thought he would wait. But he left without me, taking another crew member instead. He didn't give me a minute's leeway. I hurried after them only to find that, for all the rush, he hadn't even bothered to start work yet. There he sat, lounging in the sun, smoking a cigarette with the others. He was waiting for me.

When I apologized, he said, "It's okay. Don't worry." He smiled and sounded as if he meant it. But then he took me aside so that no one else could hear. "Listen, the boss came by and asked about you. I kept things under wraps." He sounded reassuring, as if it was all taken care of. And yet I found out afterward that before leaving the studio that morning he had made a point of telling the supervisor that I was late.

What a strange man, I thought—a real opportunist. What did he have to gain? Clearly Hatori was in a bad way, but Yamaya also had his problems. He kept a tight rein on his crew, but he often took days off himself. Whenever one of his own productions was broadcast, he failed to show up the next morning. Who knows, he may have felt some obscure sense of shame that prevented him from facing his colleagues.

Only a few days ago Yamaya was made section chief.

As I listened to Hatori that evening, I began to feel nervous. I knew it wasn't easy for him to restrain himself. His wife and children had gone to bed, but I remembered the look of uncertainty and caution in his wife's eyes that afternoon. She must have been afraid that her husband would spend the night talking to me.

Hatori was surprisingly calm when he finished telling me about the incident with Yamaya. He asked if I would like some soup. "The soup I make is better than my wife's," he said as he went into the kitchen. When he stood up, the two cats he had been holding were thrown from his lap. They stretched and followed him with their long tails raised high. I could hear him opening and shutting the refrigerator and chopping some scallions. I wondered if he had invited me so that he could confide in someone about Yamaya.

His youngest son's desk stood in the corner of the room, and a crayon drawing of a monster was pasted on the wall. "Dinosaur: Terasaurus; Height: 200 feet." The handwriting appeared to be the boy's. Later, when we talked about his son, Hatori opened the desk drawer and took out a piece of paper to show me. The teacher had marked the upper right-hand corner with three red circles to indicate an A. "He wrote about me at school," Hatori said. The title of the composition was "My Father."

> My father is a TV cameraman. My father and I do not see each other very much. He goes on a lot of business trips. When he comes home, he always says he is tired. When I try to ride on him piggyback, he says, "Get out of here!" But I still like my father, even though he says such things. Do you know why?

Hatori's son Kōji had innocently asked his classmates, "Do you know why?" I only had to read it once, however, to see what lay behind it. Ever since Hatori became ill, the company had tried to avoid sending him on location. Hatori's wife probably didn't want her first-grade son to know about his father's visits to the hospital. She must have told the boy that he was away on business.

When I was applying for my job at the studio, I had to take an entrance exam. I also needed a recommendation from someone who worked there. There was no one I could ask directly, but I used some connections and was introduced to a man called Hiramatsu. At that time he was serving as acting manager for the department that made commercials.

I remember the day in autumn when I went to meet Hiramatsu. I had dragged out my school uniform to wear, and as I climbed the hill to his office, I was depressed by the smell of my own perspiration. I found Hiramatsu in the annex. There were no windows in the room, and when I opened the door the air reeked of acetone from the film-splicing glue. It smelled vaguely like apples. A sixteen-millimeter camera and an editing table strewn with empty film cans filled the center of the room. A filthy couch, probably crawling with bedbugs, stood near the wall. If my memory serves me correctly, Hiramatsu was flirting that afternoon with a woman on the couch. I may be exaggerating somewhat, but, in any case, he sat sprawled out in his shirt-sleeves with a young woman beside him. The girl was heavily made up and presumably had a part in his commercials.

Speaking with a thick Kansai accent, Hiramatsu introduced me to her. "This is Inoue—top of his class at college." He didn't say anything about her. She barely acknowledged my presence, but finally said something like "Oh, is that so?" She then added in a singsong voice, "I don't like smart men." She looked at me and tried to make amends. "Oh, I'm sorry. The truth slipped out."

"That's 'cause you're not too bright," teased Hiramatsu. The woman, embarrassingly familiar with him, seemed to enjoy being Hiramatsu's plaything and began running her hands all over him. Such was my introduction to the world of television.

Hiramatsu gladly gave me a recommendation, but as I was leaving he warned me that I should reconsider. "A guy like you doesn't belong in a place like this. You won't fit in if you haven't had two or three wives, like me."

More than ten years have passed since then. Somewhere along the line I married. I have lived with my wife ever since. Hiramatsu left the studio a long time ago. He said that he didn't like working for other people. He started a business of his own, supposedly, but I don't really know what he's been doing. Several men at the studio followed his example and divorced their wives without a second thought. One even seduced a colleague's wife.

I have a feeling that an incident involving a young man named Kudō was behind Hiramatsu's resignation. Kudō took the examination and joined the company at the same time as Urashima and I, over ten years ago. He was one of about forty who started working for the studio that year. After Kudō finished the three-month training course, he was assigned to the commercial department under Hiramatsu. The summer of the following year he committed suicide.

I met Kudō for the first time on the morning of the company induction ceremony. It seemed odd that we hadn't met before. After our group interview we had been called together on many occasions for private interviews, a physical examination, and a series of training lectures that went on for a month. You would think we would have run into each other earlier, but I was sure that we were meeting for the first time.

That morning I was held up for some reason on the way in and had to hurry to the studio. Another new employee had also come late and was talking with the guard at the reception desk when I arrived. He was a hulking man with closely cropped hair and metal-rimmed glasses. He had a hearty laugh, though it was sometimes difficult to say just what he was laughing about. I had hurried to the studio because I was ashamed to be late for the induction ceremony; Kudō, on the other hand, didn't seem bothered in the least. He struck me as a disagreeable sort.

The guard directed us to a rented hall nearby, where the ceremony was being held. Kudō and I left the office together, but it was only I who seemed to feel a sense of urgency. Kudō made no effort to quicken his pace. He sauntered! He swung his shoulders and held his head tipped slightly back—perhaps to keep his glasses from falling off. He didn't utter one word to me on the way to the hall.

Yet my friendship with Kudō began that morning. He became my first friend at the studio. We had been assigned to different sections, but we would often go out to lunch together. Our comradeship was based solely on the fact that we were the only two who had arrived late for that function.

At first I found Kudō offensive. I thought that he was patronizing and I sensed a certain aloofness in his boisterous laughter. He seemed a good deal older than the rest of us who joined. He told me that after graduating from college he had taken some part-time jobs and had worked as a day laborer. He had also held a job as boiler man for the maintenance department on a U.S. Army base.

Once when I caught a cold Kudō advised me to take some salt for it. As we walked along, he explained that somehow salt thickens the blood, and that he always used it to cure his own ailments. After he died, it was our talk about salt that I remembered most about him.

Whenever we had lunch together we would go to a nearby restaurant that served fried pork. The place was run by a woman about thirty years old who had been in the business only a short time. "I'll take you to a good place," he had told me the first time we went out. I wondered why he thought so highly of it. Not so much as a sign hung outside the shack tucked away at the end of the street. It looked like a storage shed. We had to eat at a counter just large enough to seat three people. I had never seen such an awful place. The woman, who had an infant strapped on her back, was deep-frying the meat while a pale little boy played at her feet. The sullen look on her face suggested the miserable life she led. Perhaps she had lost her husband.

Even for that neighborhood, the restaurant was conspicuously inelegant, and the portions too generous. When the baby wasn't screaming beside us as we ate, the mother was giving the other child a scolding right under our noses. But how could you demand atmosphere or service when the prices were so low? And yet she had a hard time attracting customers to this filthy place. She simply didn't have enough experience to make a profit; and it wasn't long before it closed, reverting to a storage shed. Now and then I would remember and walk by to see what had become of it.

Kudō had gone to the shed every day while it remained open. He must have held out until the end as her most faithful customer. Every time we stopped there to eat he would say, "Isn't she nice?" Perhaps he was secretly drawn to this unfortunate woman who eked out a meager existence by running a tiny restaurant. He seemed to be attracted to the air of misery that enveloped her. In the whole time that I knew him, it was only when he talked about this woman that he would let down his guard and reveal the hidden desires and sorrows that his boasting belied.

Three days before Kudō committed suicide he had told Hiramatsu about his plan. Hiramatsu unexpectedly came by my office one afternoon. He didn't seem to have anything particular on his mind, he was just grumbling the way he did when someone slipped up on the job.

"He's going to do it, no matter what. I told him he's crazy—he's out of his mind. But it's no use. 'Don't stop me. Let me at least die the way I want to,' he said. I don't know what to do about him."

"Huh? What's he want to kill himself for?" I asked, letting out a laugh. But the question was ridiculous, and I realize now just how idiotic it was.

"Who knows? He didn't give me any details," Hiramatsu replied. "I have no idea what's wrong. When we go out drinking together, he's always good for a few laughs. And he does a hell of a lot better with women than I do. . ." Hiramatsu sounded as if he were annoyed with a disobedient younger brother. But it was clear to me that he was, in fact, very upset. It wasn't easy for him to accept the idea that Kudō might commit suicide—his outlook on life wouldn't allow it. I realized then that Kudō was fortunate to have Hiramatsu as a boss.

"Where is he now?" I asked.

"He's in the studio working on a commercial. Do me a favor. Go and see him."

After Hiramatsu left the room, I went downstairs. I made my way slowly to the studio where Kudō was working and poked my head in nonchalantly, as if I had dropped by merely to observe. Four or five people—probably actors or agents—were standing around the tiny set in the corner of the studio. Kudō was nowhere to be seen. When I looked up, though, I saw him in the control booth. He was sitting in the director's chair, resting his chin on his hands. He gazed down with a vacant look on his face. I couldn't tell if he saw me or not, and I left the studio without talking to him. I wondered if this would be his last assignment. Did he really plan to kill himself tonight? I stood there helpless. I was not at all proud of myself.

I don't remember what the product had been that day: one of those phony cure-alls, maybe, or a new brand of instant soup. All I know is that the day Kudō died he was working at the studio as usual.

Hiramatsu had tried his best to make Kudō change his mind. That night he took him out drinking. He must have thought that Kudō would have a few drinks, relax, and then reconsider. It was naive of him to think the plan would work, but I couldn't have thought of a more effective one.

From one bar to the next Hiramatsu fed Kudō drinks. "Please don't go through with it—for my sake," Hiramatsu begged. No doubt Kudō thought it was a ludicrous request, but he was nevertheless moved by these emotional pleas. Finally, he said haltingly, "Well, if that's how you feel, I'll think it over." Hiramatsu breathed a sigh of relief. He could let down his guard. He had been determined to follow Kudō around all night, never leaving his side. Now he was able to relax. By the time they parted on a street corner in the middle of the night, Hiramatsu felt thoroughly at ease. In fact he had fallen all too quickly into a drunken stupor, while Kudō, being younger, had kept a clear head.

In the end Kudō had outsmarted Hiramatsu. He knew that he had to go with Hiramatsu that evening. If he didn't, his boss would come barging into his room during the night and ruin his plan. Kudō went drinking with him and timed things so that Hiramatsu wouldn't learn about his death until at least noon the next day. As he must have planned all along, Kudō returned to his room during the night and crushed some sleeping pills in a mortar. Apparently he swallowed the powder in separate doses so that he wouldn't vomit and fail in his attempt. A few miscellaneous books lay beside his bed. One of them was a lengthy novel by a postwar writer, a controversial figure when we were in college. He had probably bought it at a secondhand bookstore. The covers had been torn off and the pages were frayed.

Hiramatsu had had too much to drink that night, and the following day he came to the office later than usual. He assumed that Kudō's absence meant only that he was sleeping it off. But when he hadn't shown up by noon, Hiramatsu realized his mistake. It was too late. He ran to Kudō's room. Kudō was still alive, and Hiramatsu rushed him to a hospital. I was told that he regained consciousness briefly and, with a pained expression on his face, whispered to Hiramatsu, "Why don't you leave me alone?"

When I heard about Kudō's death, my throat suddenly became very dry. I imagined the scene: a dimly lit room in the middle of the night, Kudō pushing back the metal-rimmed glasses that slid down his nose as he carefully crushed the sleeping pills. But more important, I couldn't forget the novel that Hiramatsu had told me Kudō had left at his bedside. It had never been among my favorites. At some point I may have flipped through the book, but I hadn't read it. Not a single line deserved serious attention—such was my prejudice against that particular novelist. What's more, I even disliked people who openly professed an admiration for him. My friendship with Kudō had not been a very close one, and yet I felt that in dying with that novel at his side he had somehow rejected me. He could have found an opportunity to discuss literature with me, but he never once mentioned the subject.

Can someone die for a book? The very idea seemed threatening—almost violently so. I have never owned a book that was worth dying for, least of all a novel. Could a novel bring about someone's death? It had never crossed my mind before. But wasn't I jumping to conclusions? Dying for a novel was a ridiculous notion. Kudō did not die for that book; the book did not tell him to commit suicide. All I know for certain is that he left the novel at his bedside. He didn't care that others would think he had been fond of it. In fact, he probably hadn't given it much thought. But to an observer, the tattered book lying next to the cold, lifeless body began to take on greater significance.

Kudō left no suicide note behind. Instead, on a scrap of paper he had scribbled "Don't touch me. I'll haunt you." As if enclosing instructions, he had placed the message next to what would become his own corpse, the disposal of which would present problems. But the words bore no resemblance to a suicide note. The piece of paper together with the body somehow formed a unit; the one served no purpose without the other.

I hadn't intended to write about this at all. I don't feel one way or another about Kudō. As a matter of fact, after his death no one showed too much concern. When they heard his name mentioned, few people could recall what kind of man he was—or even what he had looked like. What did make an impression on me was the way he had rushed to his death. It seems to me that when people choose to die so hastily, they make fools of those who are left behind. Their death forces us to realize how senseless it is to go on living, jotting down our muddled thoughts. To Kudō, no doubt, we appeared as niggling critics who constantly misjudged one another.

I remember the day we were told about his death. Late that afternoon, the fools all took turns visiting the department he had belonged to. When they heard the story, they walked out of the room in disbelief. But then, with renewed courage they would reconsider: "Kudō's dead? Then he won't be working any more. I guess that's one way to retire. But I'm alive—and still in good shape." I could accept this kind of unpretentious thinking: a manly attitude, I thought.

Others, however, lingered by Kudō's desk with blank expressions on their faces, smoking their cigarettes and wondering why he had done it. They pried every little detail out of a distant associate of Kudō's who had gone to his room to see the body. "How awful!" they would exclaim, and light another cigarette. Did they really mean it? Were they genuinely upset? I don't think they felt an ounce of regret. They put on a show of concern, but it was just a façade. When a colleague dies, do we go numb? Are we paralyzed by another's death? No, we aren't to blame. The deceased is at fault. It's he who makes a mockery of us all.

I was a fool too, in my own way. I thought I was different from the others. I thought I knew something they didn't know, and I held them all in contempt. How stupid they were! I wanted to scream at the top of my lungs, "Now you're upset? I knew three days ago that he would die!" I wanted to tell them as they stood there idly, "Stop it! That's enough! Go home!"

After Hatori's illness had begun, Urashima and I were assigned to different departments. Since Hatori remained in the same job, we felt as if we had deserted him. One afternoon I went for tea with Tsutsumi, a woman who had worked for the studio part-time. I was surprised when she told me that she had been to see him. I didn't think a young woman would go to that kind of hospital by herself, but I was even more amazed at my own thoughtlessness. I had forgotten to visit Hatori. As Tsutsumi spoke, she seemed to imply that Urashima and I should have been the first to visit him, but, since we hadn't, she had gone in our place.

"Hatori was so happy to see me," she said. "He says his wife hardly ever comes. He showed me his room. 'Here's where I stay. We're all friends here,' he told me when a strange group of patients came over. One wanted to show me the pictures he had drawn. Another asked if I would read a poem of his. I didn't know what to do. There was a funny smell about them. . . Hatori and I talked outside on the lawn until it got dark. At one point he took out his harmonica and played for me. He was very good at it, and I didn't mind—until he asked me to sing. He said he'd accompany me if I'd sing 'The King' by Murata Hideo. I didn't know the words but he insisted on teaching me. I hummed the tune while he taught me the lyrics. It sounded so sad I couldn't bear it. I decided to leave. It was dark and Hatori showed me to the road. Then he asked me to visit him again. Once was all right, but I'd feel awkward going again. After all, I'm not his wife—I'm nothing to Hatori. It'd be strange for me to visit him all the time, don't you think?" Tsutsumi smiled weakly.

Tsutsumi had in fact been close to Hatori. He had helped her at the studio and taken an interest in her personal life as well. Hatori treated her as his protégée and even attempted to arrange a marriage interview for her. He had spent an inordinate amount of time on the photograph for the marriage portfolio. When I went to visit him at home one day, he happened to show it to me. Hatori was a professional photographer and he had taken a fine photo, but Tsutsumi was not especially attractive and somehow she had a slightly forlorn look about her.

"Pretty good, don't you think?" he said as he showed me one splendid photo after another. He had obviously taken great care with the background and the composition.

"You did a fine job," I replied.

"She's a nice woman," Hatori added.

Of course I didn't disagree with him. Tsutsumi was a kind, straightforward young woman, though occasionally she would make a mistake at work and show very little concern over it. Urashima had once told me that she wrote in a peculiar way; for instance, she wrote the character for "shoes" backward.

Hatori's wife opposed the arrangements for the marriage interview. "It's no good—not with that girl. Absolutely no chance of a successful match." I had listened to their conversation. She seemed to feel that the young man under consideration possessed all sorts of fine qualities and that he would have no trouble finding a wife. Her voice was filled with spite and made me feel ill at ease.

"Do you think so?" Hatori asked his wife. Putting the photos away, he added, "I don't know; she's a nice woman. You don't think they'd make a good couple?"

Hatori didn't want to hurt Tsutsumi's feelings. Without mentioning the marriage interview, he had asked her to work as a model for him. She knew nothing about the complications with Hatori's wife.

I was glad that Tsutsumi had visited Hatori and that she had sung at least one song for him. When he was at work, he used to take her out for lunch or tea. After he became ill I would sometimes see Tsutsumi walking by herself. She was still unmarried. She seemed worn out. I wondered if she felt that her chance of marrying had slipped away. Perhaps she had given up any hope of finding a husband. When I bumped into her one day in the hall, I noticed dark rings under her eyes. She looked gaunt, and I asked her how she was feeling. She gave a vague reply, then added as an afterthought: "I don't know why, but I'm so tired lately."

Urashima and I got out of the taxi in front of the university hospital. As we turned to look at the white building, Hatori appeared out of nowhere. We were startled to find him standing right in front of us. The atmosphere of the place had also taken us by surprise.

A few months had passed since we had last seen him. The swelling had gone down, and at first glance he seemed to be doing well. But his hair looked a bit odd—a hospital employee had given him an unusually short crew cut—and although there wasn't a cloud in the sky, he was wearing rubber boots. He talked normally, however, and told us that he felt fine.

Hatori had phoned me one afternoon at the studio when I wasn't at my desk. Someone gave me the message: "You had a call from a fellow named Hatori. It sounded as though he'd been drinking. He was probably calling from a bar." But Hatori had phoned from the hospital. The medicine made his tongue heavy, and to a stranger it seemed as if he'd had too much to drink. When I told him this, he laughed and asked excitedly, "Really? That's what he thought?"

It was around three o'clock when we met him, and since he was convalescing satisfactorily, he had been given permission to go out. So the three of us walked around the streets near the hospital and stopped at a coffee shop to talk. Though Urashima and I had never been to the hospital before, we learned that Hatori was in a ward on the fifth or sixth floor.

As soon as we saw him he began talking nonstop. "There's someone from the university in my room. He goes around telling everyone that he's the son of a famous professor. No one knows if he's telling the truth or not. He was active in some student movement, but then he started to lose his grip. So he ended up here eventually. And now all he does is moan and groan. He says he wants to die, he can't take it any more. I'm not the only one he complains to, either—he corners just about everybody. Sits and whines all day.

"Finally I lost my temper and told him to stop acting like a baby. I even threatened him. I rolled up a newspaper and lit it with a lighter. Then I held it up to his face and yelled, 'What do you think of this, you idiot!' Then I took a razor blade and cut deep into my finger and showed him the blood. 'Take a look at this,' I screamed. 'Now don't give me any more of your whimpering!' He was trembling, but since then there's been no more wailing when I'm around."

Hatori stared at us with his eyes wide open. A bandage was wrapped around one finger. He showed us the palm of his hand. A large mark in the shape of a swastika had been drawn on it with red ink. We let him ramble on without uttering a word ourselves. As I listened to his impassioned talk, I was overcome with sadness. He had attacked a weaker patient by setting fire to a newspaper and slashing his own finger. Hatori had somehow thought he was helping him. I wondered how he had managed to get a lighter and a razor blade into the hospital ward.

"Since I've been here," he continued, "three people have committed suicide. All of them hanged themselves." Then he changed the topic again. "I became very friendly with a wonderful woman down the hall. She's older—maybe around fifty—and she's not like other women at all. She's a saint, she's so good. She recovered completely and they released her, but I want to see her again when I get out, so I asked her to write down her name and address. You should see her handwriting. It's beautiful. . . Oh, her address. I forget the number of the house. Shimorenjaku, Mitaka City. Anyway, her name is Nakamura Yaeko."

He talked on and on. Finally, he added, "I'm really much better, but I still get nervous. It's not good for me. I have to learn to relax." He had worked himself up, and he seemed to realize he should take his medicine. He took some pills from his shirt pocket and gulped them down with a glass of water.

"It must be shining," I said. But it was a bad joke. I shouldn't have been so flippant.

"Yes, it's shining—like a sword," Hatori grinned. He laughed a nervous, unpleasant laugh, and his face flushed with embarrassment.

I had been referring to an offhand remark he'd once made. He had told me there was a sword inside his head, and it either gleamed or grew dull according to his mood. I don't remember the circumstances, but I know that his face had turned red that day, just as it had now. The sword must have been shining. "I'm ready for anyone," he'd said. "Bring on your bows and arrows. I'll slash down any enemy with this sword of mine."

I realized that the weapon inside him should have been put to use. He should have pulled it from its sheath, as he'd threatened, and brandished it about. He should have lashed out at Yamaya and the others. If only he had lunged his sword at them, he wouldn't be confined like this today. But Hatori couldn't bring himself to draw the sword against anyone. He wasn't that kind of man.

It was already six o'clock, Hatori's curfew. Urashima and I were ready to leave, but Hatori didn't seem to want to go. "Please stay a little longer. It's no problem for me," he said as he stood up. He went over to the cash register to make a phone call. We heard him talking excitedly. He told them he would be having dinner out. We ate a simple meal at the coffee shop, and when we were finished Hatori began to search his pockets for money. All he had was small change—not enough to cover the bill—but we had no intention of letting him pay anyway. We left the restaurant and walked back to where he'd met us. There we shook hands and said our good-byes.

"Which one is yours?" I asked Hatori as I looked up at the white building.

"On the fifth floor—over there." He pointed to a room. The sky had already grown dark and the lights shone in the rows of windows on each floor. Actually, I never did know which room he was pointing to. Hatori did not seem at all reluctant to return to the ward.

Although he had given us detailed directions to the bus stop, we took a taxi. On the way home, as we discussed Hatori, we found ourselves wondering where we could go for a drink.

RIPPLES

Shibaki Yoshiko

Translated by Michael C. Brownstein

Shibaki Yoshiko was born in Tokyo in 1914, the eldest daughter of a dry goods store owner. She studied English at Surugadai Women's College, but went to work for Mitsubishi to support her mother and two younger sisters after her father died. In the meantime, her first stories began appearing in several minor literary magazines. In 1937 she joined the circle of writers associated with the magazine Bungei shuto; *and four years later she was awarded the prestigious Akutagawa Prize for "Seika no ichi" (The Fruit and Vegetable Market). That same year she married an economist, Ōshima Kiyoshi.*

Shibaki is perhaps best known for her series of stories depicting the lives of Tokyo's bar girls and prostitutes, beginning with "Susaki paradaisu" (Susaki Paradise) in 1954. Her next triumph was the historical trilogy tracing the lives of women in a single family from the beginning of the Meiji period to the present day. The first two parts, "Yuba" (Dried Tōfu) and "Sumidagawa" (The River Sumida), appeared in 1961. The third part was the autobiographical "Marunouchi hachigōkan" (No. 8 Marunouchi), which came out in 1962. This was followed in 1963 by "Kashoku" (Gay Lamplight) and "Konjō" (This Life), forming a trilogy within the trilogy.

In 1972, Shibaki was awarded the eleventh annual Women's Literary Prize for her most recent collection of short stories, Seiji kinuta *(The Porcelain Fulling Block). "Hamon" (Ripples, 1970) is taken from this collection.*

*　*　*

One Sunday, a short man dressed in a black suit suddenly turned up at Takako's house. If he had been a salesman, the man would have gone to the house next door, then come to Takako's and left immediately, but he had come on business. She could not tell how old he was, but from the excited look on his face Takako sensed that he brought good news even before she looked at the business card he produced. This was just the sort of extraordinary event she had been vaguely expecting; no matter what this is, she thought, she must welcome it if it would help her break through the impasse she had reached. She went to summon her mother, who was often in bed with rheumatism.

The man asked if there were only two in the family. Takako lived with her mother and worked at a university library. Her two older brothers and older sister had left home when they married, and only Takako remained. Her brothers rarely visited their mother; her sister lived in another prefecture and never even wrote. Their mother, Ritsu, said she couldn't help thinking that her children were lost to her once they married. She would look coldly at Takako, as if to ask when she too would abandon her. Since the death of her husband at an early age, Ritsu had tried her best to hang on to the family assets until her children were settled, but before she knew it, she had become a penniless old woman. She was robbed of the pleasure of giving her grandchildren everything she wished, and so was reluctant even to have them over. Her daughters-in-law came to visit now and then, but they never brought the children and usually went home early. Her oldest son lived in a public housing complex and it put him in a bad mood when she asked him for money. And when his wife sent the money, he didn't even include a note with it. Her youngest son worked with his wife and lived with her family.

Ritsu was always saying that if she had the money she would go to a nice retirement home, but Takako refused to consider it. On days when she felt well enough, Ritsu made delicious suppers, but when the sky threatened rain, she lay in bed with her eyes fixed in a gloomy expression, fretting over her daughter's late return from work.

"I can't help it; it's my job. There's no reason to get upset just because supper will be an hour late."

"No one knows what it feels like for an old woman to lie in bed alone. If I could go to a rest home—a nice one with a lawn—I'd have friends, and I'd feel so much better."

"If we ever get some money you're more than welcome to go!" Takako realized that her own peevishness was mounting. As long as she lived with her mother, it seemed, she herself would never enjoy any happiness.

Lately she had fallen into the habit of dreaming the impossible whenever she felt overwhelmed by life or by her ties to other people. In the morning, for instance, when she opened her eyes and parted the curtains, she imagined that she was living on the third floor of a large, comfortable apartment building with flowers on a sunlit terrace. Turning around, she would see a man still asleep in the dark inner bedroom: that had to be Tamura. "How wonderful," she would think, "I'm married!" She never used to eat a good breakfast before leaving for work, but now she would heat up the beet soup she'd made the night before, and sit combing her hair until the aroma of the soup awakened him. It was important to her that living above the ground floor prevented any chance intrusion. But then, she did not think her brothers, her sister, or even her mother took her marriage prospects seriously.

Only the night before, when she was with Tamura, Takako had felt awkward about evading him when he said he wanted to move to a new apartment. He asked her what she thought of "life" and told her they were too old to be meeting on the streets—and besides, it was tiresome. With a faint smile, Takako said it didn't bother her.

"You're always missing the point, aren't you? I've had it with the way things are—do you think there's a future if we continue like this?"

Tamura had become testy. He worked in a research lab and was thinking about studying in Germany, but he was beginning to feel weighed down by her. They used to meet every Saturday, but now the relationship would probably collapse if she didn't phone him. Not that Tamura would break off with her. Once he had invited her to an art exhibit, not so much to look at pictures with her, shoulder to shoulder, but because he had tickets and it was better to go with someone than no one at all. Looking at paintings by Turner, both agreed they found in them a moving, dreamlike quality, and she did, after all, enjoy herself at the time; but that was hardly enough to satisfy her. She and Tamura exchanged intellectual-sounding theories about art, but their conversation never had the intimacy that a man and a woman standing close together might have reached. Still, she had no one else but him, so she could only be evasive when he talked about the future.

As they started home after spending that Saturday evening together, Tamura let slip that his older sister was urging him to marry into a family as an adopted son and heir. If he were to do this, Takako started to say, his sister could spend her twilight years in peace, but she swallowed her words. Once that much was said, their relationship would be finished. His sister worked in a globe-fish restaurant and spent the two days each month when it was closed resting at his apartment. With her help he had graduated from college, and the only family they had was each other. He told Takako he did not want a home where his sister would be uncomfortable. Tamura's circumstances touched Takako deeply, for she herself was stuck with her mother in a life of constant quarreling. Fettered by family ties, she and Tamura shared the same fate. Even so, she was wounded by the ambivalent expression on his face when he spoke of marrying into another family.

Takako rarely went to Tamura's apartment, afraid that people would talk. Gossip was somehow quick to reach his sister's ears, and he detested that. The possibility of marrying into another family became the trump card in a relationship that had already been played out. Takako walked along in stubborn silence. Although she was annoyed that their three-year affair had reached an impasse, she did not know who was at fault or what had gone wrong. When they reached the station, Tamura bought the tickets and watched her expression as he handed her one. She dropped the ticket. "Don't be so careless!" he snapped, picking it up. Takako couldn't bear fond farewells; they were only a ruse to get away from someone as smoothly as possible. She clutched her ticket as she climbed the stairs to the platform. The train arrived before they could reach an understanding, and she got on. She gazed at him through the window as the train started moving and bit her lip: she could not, she thought, just back out of the affair as matters stood.

Few visitors came to the house where Takako lived with her ailing mother. She showed the man in the black suit into the parlor and saw that, up close, he was middle-aged—much older than she first thought. The name on his business card read "Commercial Promotions, Inc.," and his errand had something to do with Miki Seiichirō. Miki was Takako's father, who had died twelve years before. Takako had no idea what sort of business Commercial Promotions was engaged in.

"Our company develops land and sells it in lots. Right now we're developing Karuizawa and Nasu." The man produced an old newspaper clipping and showed them one of his company's advertisements. Takako's father, he announced, owned almost half an acre in Karuizawa adjacent to the property being developed by Commercial Promotions, and they wanted to know whether Miki had left any instructions concerning it.

"My husband died. . . ," Ritsu stammered in confusion as she searched her memory. "Did he have any such property? It's nice to find out that he owned land in Karuizawa, but I'll have to give it some thought."

Seiichirō, a geologist, went to Manchuria during the war, and after the surrender worked at a university in Kyushu while his wife and children remained in Tokyo. His work often took him hiking into the mountains. Though he had little contact with his family, he was a decent man who would never have purposely kept them in the dark about land he had purchased. According to the real-estate agent, the land was registered in 1942, almost thirty years earlier. The area, he told them, was not called Karuizawa then. When she heard the old name, Ritsu was faintly reminded of something.

"Now that you mention it, my husband once loaned money to someone during the war, and I remember him asking what I thought about getting some land as security, but I'm not sure what happened after that. My husband went to Manchuria. Then his acquaintance passed away, so perhaps he even forgot where he got the land from. The value of money changed when the war ended, and the money he had loaned didn't seem worth its face value. . ." Ritsu told her story just as she remembered it.

"I see. In its present state, the land slopes sharply and there are no houses on it. I heard that during the war one square yard was worth less than a pack of cigarettes. Our company decided to develop the bluff and sell it off in lots. That's when we discovered you owned the property. We'd like to discuss the matter, but . . . excuse me for being so blunt—do you have the title?"

"Hmm . . . I wonder where he put it?" Ritsu was going to say she had never come across anything like that, but stopped herself. Even so, now that her husband was dead and they had moved, she still couldn't fully believe such unexpected news.

"I might add," he said courteously but with added emphasis, "it has taken me more than three months to find you."

The owner of the land, he had learned, was not living at the address recorded in the land registry. He inquired at the ward office, but their building had burned down during the war, so they had no official documents to consult. He checked into one thing and another, but all clues to the owner's whereabouts had vanished in the war. The agent learned that the previous owner had also died, but his family reported that he had sold it to someone connected with the Investigation Bureau of the Manchurian Railway.

The Manchurian Railway Company was dissolved after the war; there was no way to find out where its former employees had scattered. The real-estate agent had been ordered by his superiors to find Mr. Miki Seiichirō. He spent day after day searching through railway company archives and, in the end, all he had to go on was the names of several men who had compiled data for the company. One had died, but another who was still alive, an old man living in retirement in Zushi, provided the name of yet another man who had once been with the Investigation Bureau. On his way to see this third man at his present company, the agent told himself: "Now I'll find out what happened to Miki."

This man told the agent that he had worked for the Investigation Bureau in Harbin. When asked about Miki, he had no distinct recollection of him, but he didn't think there were too many sections within the bureau. The path cleared again when the man came up with the names of two or three others he had worked with in Manchuria, and the agent was spurred on at the thought that this time he would unearth something definite. He interviewed several other people connected with the railway before he found out that Miki Seiichirō had not been an employee of the Manchurian Railway at all, but a scholar commissioned by them to conduct geological surveys. He was understandably excited when he first heard the words "I knew Miki." But it meant nothing to have found someone who had known Miki in the past if the man could provide no clues to his present whereabouts. The man who had known Miki, however, telephoned an old acquaintance as the agent stood by, and learned that Miki had passed away.

Elated and disappointed by turns, the real-estate agent one day heard that Miki had been living in Seijō when he died. But it was getting dark, so he returned home, looking forward to the next day. When he joined his wife and son at the dinner table, his wife laughed: "Since when did you become a private detective?" And she teased him, saying, "Look out . . . there's someone behind you!"

At first he had been angered by this tiresome, pointless assignment: it really had nothing to do with his job at the company. But now he had set his sights on locating Miki's heirs and had thrown himself into the task. Finding Miki's family had become a mission. Unlike the mundane uncertainties of buying and selling land, where only one deal in a hundred was ever finalized, he felt the excitement of the chase, of moving at full tilt. Tenaciously he pursued his quarry, and at the end of a day of wasted effort he would think to himself: "Tomorrow for sure." Soon the elusive Mr. Miki seemed to beckon to him from up ahead. He found the old rented house the Miki family had moved to from Seijō. Walking himself stiff for three months had paid off; and when he checked the nameplate on the doorpost, he smiled with relief rather than professional satisfaction. Until Takako answered the door, he all but forgot that he had come to strike a deal. "Are you the daughter of Mr. Miki Seiichirō?" At her reply he muttered to himself: "At last!"

". . . You went to all that trouble?" Ritsu, who had moved from house to house over the years and now had nothing in the bank, sighed and glanced at her daughter. Takako was amazed at the man's persistence and the intricate trail he had sniffed out, for he spoke as if he had done nothing remarkable. She doubted that the land could be worth much if her father had forgotten all about it.

"We'd be very grateful if you would sell us the land for development."

"How much do you think it's worth?"

"Well, it's a bluff, so it can't be used for anything in its present state. I imagine it's worth about five hundred yen per square yard."

Takako's eyes lit up when she calculated that their half acre was worth about a million yen. "I'd love to see it! I've never been to Karuizawa."

"It's a difficult place to find your way around in. And Karuizawa is cold now, though it's nice once summer begins. If you're willing to sell, we could pay you a million two hundred thousand yen. It's a good price."

"Even if we don't have the deed?"

"We'll be able to work something out, I'm sure."

Ritsu fidgeted happily and replied that, though she herself had no objections, she would have to get the consent of her children. Once again the man's face assumed the businesslike expression of a real-estate agent and he made a date to visit them again. As he got up to leave, he paused a moment and asked if, on his next visit, they might show him a photograph of Mr. Miki, if they had one. He wanted to see the face of the person who had kept him going for three months. Feeling kindly toward the man, Takako escorted him to the door and watched him leave.

Ritsu's health seemed to improve the more money she had on hand, and now took a turn for the better: the pain in her elbows and knees abated and she cheered up. She was buoyant even in her daughter's company, and they began to laugh together for no apparent reason. The sudden news promised an unbelievable amount of money, and Takako wondered if she could put her mother in a pretty rest home, one that had lawns and flower beds. It would be a gift from a father who had been indifferent to money. Takako hoped that her mother could then live out her years in peace.

Her oldest brother, Hideichi, and Yasuo, her other brother, hurried over to the house as soon as they heard the news. What surprised Takako was that even Namiko, her older sister who lived in distant Hirosaki, showed up. Though the seasons came and went, Namiko never sent so much as an apple, but now she left her seven-year-old child behind and raced to her mother's house. Takako didn't think she would have come so quickly even if she had been told her mother was seriously ill. Since none of them had ever heard about the land their father purchased thirty years before, they listened to Ritsu's tale in utter disbelief.

"He got the land as security for a loan and then forgot about it in the confusion after the war, is that it? I suppose it was because, like everyone else, he was in a state of shock for those two or three years."

"I guess it was something like that."

Hideichi had never spoken at leisure with his father, either when he was going back and forth to Manchuria, or later, when he went hiking in the mountains. Even when he died suddenly of a heart attack, Hideichi had not been at his bedside. Having pinned all his hopes on the Chinese continent, his father doubtless cared little about what happened to a half acre of poor ground in Karuizawa.

"It was a coup, even for Father, wasn't it?" Namiko's face broke into a smile.

"The real-estate agent certainly worked hard to find us. I hear there are unscrupulous businessmen who, given the chance, would put an unregistered deed in someone else's name." Hideichi felt grateful to the agent and savored the realization that the family owned land. "Even Mother used to complain about Father, but I'm sure she thinks better of him now."

"You know, I do believe your father did something right, after all," Ritsu said rather self-consciously, and made them all laugh.

Enjoying the lighthearted atmosphere, Takako felt closer to her family than she had in a long time. "If we do get a million two hundred thousand," she said, "it would last Mother a long time. How about going to a rest home?"

Takako's words somehow disturbed them. They all fidgeted in silence for a moment. Then Hideichi spoke: "Do you think you can put Mother in a private rest home for a million yen or so?"

Namiko, sitting next to Hideichi, took a different tack: "I gather the value of land in Karuizawa has skyrocketed. . . Shouldn't we look into it?"

The man had mentioned Karuizawa, but he told Takako that the bluff was outside Komoro and that the company was just beginning to clear the land. She didn't know whether the figure he had quoted was a suitable price for half an acre or not, but she thought perhaps they should go along with the man's offer because of all the trouble he'd gone to in locating them. It was a windfall they hadn't expected in the first place.

"Takako—did he say it was definitely a half acre that had been registered? If we have it surveyed it may turn out to be even more." Hideichi had become serious. Namiko immediately adopted the same tone as her brother:

"It might be more valuable than we think; it's no ordinary thing for a real-estate company to seek out the owner so eagerly."

"I agree with Namiko," Yasuo added. "We might take a loss if we go along with what he says and dispose of the land for the price they're offering." Yasuo had heard from his wife's family that property in Karuizawa was worth at least twelve hundred yen per square yard. Someone would have to go there and investigate.

Takako looked at her brothers. The joy of discovering that the Miki family owned land had been swept from their faces and greed had taken over. Expecting that something like this would happen, Takako had made the first move by suggesting that they use the money for their mother's living expenses or to send her to a retirement home. If they were not going to look after their mother themselves, then this windfall had to be used to support her for the rest of her life.

Takako did not mention that the real-estate agent seemed reluctant to show them the property. They decided that the brothers should negotiate on behalf of the whole family, no matter how things turned out. Hideichi and Yasuo wanted someone to examine the property before they met with the agent, and after all their wrangling decided that the slow, timid Hideichi should go. Yasuo, who by nature usually bustled about in a confident way, regretted that he had to go to Osaka on business. As they chatted about the land under development, their half acre seemed to grow larger and larger, swelling into a preposterously big plot.

"The minute I heard it was half an acre," Namiko said, "I knew it couldn't be worth less than three million yen. You've got to keep your eyes open so we don't get swindled by the real-estate company." Looking at the happy faces of her mother, brothers, and sister, Namiko added that, if it turned out to be that much money, she too wouldn't mind a small share. Then she began to complain about the daily pressures of scratching out a meager living as a clerk in a distant prefecture; her daughter's studies; the cruel fate that kept her from returning to her company's main office after their move; her daughter's talent for the piano and the cost of her lessons—on and on she rattled, mixing self-pity with self-praise.

"We all have problems," Hideichi said, turning away from her. Her brother, he pointed out, had found life rough as well. Yasuo felt constrained living with his in-laws, and joked that he couldn't go home again unless he got his share; that very morning he had left the house with a look of self-assurance on his face. The discussion took another turn when someone suggested that their father's legacy should be divided up in the legal way.

"In other words," Hideichi said, "Mother should take one-third, and we four should get one-sixth each."

Only Takako objected: "A million yen is a lot of money, but if we split it up it won't come to much. Think about that!"

"You say that because you don't know what a burden a family can be."

"In short," Yasuo said, "we'll hope for three million yen; then Mother's share would come to a million."

"Then how much would we get?" Namiko asked. "Half a million? Is that right?"

Rebuffed by her brothers and sister as they rambled on, Takako's lips trembled: she wanted to insist that their mother had a right to the entire three million. This was her mother's last opportunity to go to a rest home. And that would mean freedom for Takako as well. She could no longer keep still, knowing she was on the verge of losing Tamura. Takako looked at her mother, who seemed smaller as she sat amidst her sons and daughters with a confused look, rubbing the painful joints of her fingers.

Though her children did not come right out and demand a share of the money, Ritsu could tell what they had in mind; and though she wanted to be generous toward them all in true motherly fashion, her parental pride was wounded when they started talking in terms of sixths or thirds of the money. If they divided it up, she wondered uneasily, wasn't it likely that this great sum would spark off a family quarrel? She also understood Takako's feelings quite clearly: she was now intent on packing her mother off to a rest home. Her children were tossing around numbers in the millions, and she was concerned that the important thing—the initial offer—would be lost in the void of human avarice. Like Takako, Ritsu preferred to sell the property, with no strings attached, to the man in the black suit for his efforts. But she was hemmed in by lively talk of what half a million yen could buy.

Karuizawa is about two hours and ten minutes by express train from Ueno Station. Takako invited Tamura along, and they left from Ueno. The season for fall excursions was almost over. Several days earlier, Hideichi had gone to Karuizawa and had been able to verify the land in his father's name at the registration office; but even though he had wandered around looking for the property using the office's topographical map, he had not found it. He had returned exhausted, having only walked around an area close to what seemed to be their property. He asked Takako to go, and they decided that she should have the man from the real-estate company guide her. She spoke to Tamura, who showed some interest and joined her on the trip.

"You come from a good family," Tamura said. "A repatriate like me has no relatives to consult with, not to mention any land." He felt a little resentful toward Takako, who now had property in her dead father's name, but he nonetheless decided to go and see what sort of land it was.

"Come from a good family?" Takako mused, and took it sarcastically. She wished he had seen how her brothers and sister had wrangled over the distribution of the money. As her sister was leaving to go back to Hirosaki, she all but stuck out her hand and demanded, "When do I come back for the money?" Her brother Yasuo remarked that, if it all turned out well, he would like to travel abroad. Each of them probably wished he could have the money all to himself. Takako was happy to be going to see the property but was reluctant to face the man in the plain black suit from the real-estate company: she thought he could probably see right through them.

"How much will your brothers sell the land for?" Tamura asked.

"They seem to be thinking of two or three times as much as the man offered. Before people settle on an actual price, they like to dream about all the money they can—enough to build a house or take a trip. Out loud I say that I want to give it all to Mother, but in fact I've been thinking about you and me going to Guam. Why Guam, I don't know. . ." Takako suddenly remembered that Guam was where couples went for a honeymoon. With the promise of coming into some money, she was dreaming of being happily married.

"Guam!" Tamura said scornfully. To have a taste of a foreign country for five or six days—was that the best she could do? Whenever he got fed up with his dead-end job at the research lab, or with life on his meager salary, Tamura thought about being free and pursuing a pleasant career—as a restaurant manager, perhaps, or a bathhouse cashier. Living abroad as a vagabond was another of his daydreams. Reassuring images floated before his eyes no matter what his dream entailed; marrying into another family was one more potential avenue of escape. Of course these fantasies would all evaporate if things started going well at his present job, and Takako's money fulfilled his dreams to some extent. But just hearing about the windfall no doubt made his unfortunate sister envy or resent Takako.

It was almost noon when they reached Karuizawa. The sky was clear but a cold breeze was blowing on the heights. Tourists who had come to see the late autumn leaves had boarded their buses. Following the agent's directions, Takako and Tamura went to the branch office of Commercial Promotions. Takako felt nervous, knowing that the man would not be very happy to have them come. He had said that he worked in the Karuizawa office half a month at a time in order to show clients from Tokyo around. Fliers announcing property tours were taped up on the glass door of the narrow office, which fronted on the street. Only one employee was there, talking to another customer. He told Takako that the other agent would be back any moment. A kerosene heater was burning in the center of the room, and the other customer, a fat man who seemed to be a local, was talking to the agent about the new development.

"That mountain is a long way off," he said as the agent listened impassively, "but the view is good once you get up to the top, so I suppose the property will sell." Takako and Tamura looked at a wall map showing the post-development subdivisions. Then the fat man got up and left, and Tamura followed him out to buy some cigarettes.

Even the towns around summer resorts become deserted during the off-season. Tamura was back by the time the man in the black suit returned to the office. Small in stature, he seemed to have aged since Takako had last seen him. He greeted them cordially, but his face betrayed no emotion to these clients who had turned down his original offer on the property and traveled all the way up here to view their holding. Only when he learned that Tamura was not a member of Miki's family did he look closely at their faces.

A car finally arrived and he took them to the property. They raced down the highway, and when they had gone some distance from the town of Karuizawa, Mt. Asama appeared on their right. The first snow had fallen about five days before, the man told them, but it had soon melted. "I suppose it's what you'd call a 'light dusting,' perhaps? The mountain was pretty with just a touch of white on it. . . We say that sales slow to a halt once the first snow can be seen on Asama."

The car went through Naka-Karuizawa, around the base of Mt. Asama, then turned onto a road going back in the other direction. As they made their way up the mountain road, moving farther and farther away from Karuizawa Heights, Takako realized that the area at best was only on the outskirts of a summer resort, and that they had been wrong to object to the price. She felt ashamed of having behaved in such a self-important way in front of Tamura too. The mountain road was covered with the red leaves of late autumn, and golden foliage still clung to the branches of the trees.

They were heading up an incline when the partly developed property suddenly came into view. Workers were moving boulders and tree stumps; apparently they were going to level off a small hill with a bulldozer. A few trees were left untouched. The Miki property was a grove of small trees on the opposite side. They got out of the car and had started toward the hillside when Takako gasped. The slope was bright with sunlight and a wonderful view greeted them: directly opposite and beyond the highway below, the whole of Mt. Asama stood revealed. Tamura too had never seen the entire mountain so close, and he stood motionless beside Takako.

The agent pointed: "There's nothing quite so beautiful as Asama from this angle. The view is my treat for you. The trouble is, it's a little far away."

"I had no idea it was such an exhilarating spot," Takako said. The man smiled uncomfortably. Takako and Tamura walked through the grove of trees from one end of the property to the other as the agent pointed out its boundaries. A half acre was not as big as they thought, and being on an incline it seemed rather hazardous. But whenever they glanced up, there was the view of the mountain. When the man left them to talk with the workmen, Takako and Tamura sat down on a tree stump. The sun was warm, but with the cold breeze, they could feel the coming of winter on their ears and the tips of their noses.

"It's wonderful, isn't it," Tamura said. "It's as if someone had dragged that huge mountain right into our own yard. I've never known such luxury."

"It would be a shame to sell it."

"I'd buy it myself if I had the money. I'd build a little house and spend the whole day watching the smoke rise from the mountain—that's how lazy I am."

Takako imagined the always listless Tamura idly stretched out. She thought of having a cottage here in the mountains. Squirrels probably scampered through the trees during the summer, and she pictured pure white laundry hanging out to dry on a line between two of the trunks. Now and then Tamura would bicycle down to the bottom of the hill to buy some French bread. Her visions of happiness were always modest and sentimental. Couldn't they leave me even a tenth of an acre? she wondered. She had a right to something, however small it was.

The bulldozer started moving, turning up the black soil. Roused from its slumber, the earth grumbled as it undulated. Doubtless they would soon knock down the trees and terrace the slope where Tamura and Takako were sitting.

"This place is worth more than a million," Tamura said. "You have to admire the shrewdness of a businessman who'd try to get you to sell it sight unseen. That guy looks honest and gentle, but he's a go-getter, that's for sure. He looks stubborn too, like he wouldn't budge an inch. You were almost had."

"I'm glad we came. But how am I going to bargain with him?"

"I'd tell him 'no sale.'"

The man walked back toward them. As they watched him stagger up the hill, he looked smaller and more agile; his pants were obviously too short.

"Aren't you cold?" he asked. "There's a strong breeze."

"We were talking about building a house and living here," Takako said. "But if we sell it, then it's all over!"

"It would be difficult to bring water up here," the man explained gently. "Our company owns the water rights to this entire mountain, so it's impractical for an individual to try to build a house."

Takako fell silent with disappointment, so Tamura continued for her: "I suppose the lots will be worth a fair amount, considering the location."

"We'll price the lots when they're finished. The land is almost worthless before it's developed; it's just the side of a hill. Mr. Miki's property wasn't worth anything until we laid out the subdivisions."

No doubt that was true, but it was also a fact that this land belonged to the Miki family. Now that they had seen it, the terms under which they would let it go would have to change. The man spoke in a low voice as he pulled up some dead weeds; once it was leveled by the bulldozer, he said, the Miki land would also become expensive resort property, but it would be foolish to miss this opportunity. There was a resonance in his voice Takako had not heard before, an urgency that made her uneasy. He had been so lively, and his face had seemed so human that first day at her home; perhaps that had been his real face, peering out from the shadows of this other side.

The white smoke billowing from Mt. Asama became a single cloud that shaded the mountain. The man's face would probably not reveal any sign of distress even if she flatly refused to sell the property. His expression was determined; he was used to bargaining and would not budge. If he did, his three months of searching would lose all meaning. Takako had been led astray by her own estimation of a man who, though basically good, could turn nasty. When he urged them to start back, the cloud was beginning to shroud the mountain, leaving only a view of the valley.

The mountain road, buried under fallen leaves, had turned dusky enough that it seemed a rabbit or a fox might run out. At the bottom of the mountain, the car turned onto the main highway and headed back toward Karuizawa. Anxiously Takako realized that her brothers would probably be furious if she failed to sell the property. Tamura was silent too and gazed out the back window.

The man led them to a coffee shop by Karuizawa Station. After taking a soothing sip of her hot drink, Takako's mood also softened. The real-estate agent started telling Tamura how business on the heights slackened off with the first snow, and how his work then switched to Tokyo. As they talked, the conversation again turned to haggling over the price. The man said they would give a million and a half yen for the property, but that was their best offer. The figure seemed too low, Tamura answered; a half acre in that area would go for six million yen, but he would settle for half that. Tamura grew more and more aggressive, promising to go back to Tokyo and persuade the Miki family to agree—this despite the fact he had never even met Takako's brothers! The agent answered curtly: Their price was out of the question. He made no move to eat the sandwiches that had been brought to their table.

When the man finally announced that he could make no better offer, Takako suddenly felt that her resolve was far weaker than all of Tamura's calculations. It was easy for him to talk recklessly about someone else's property. Takako finally asked, in view of the differences between the two men, if the agent could try once more to raise his price a little. "Isn't this half acre going to bring you quite a bit of money once you develop it?" Tamura argued, but the man would not agree to a higher figure because, he said, he would lose his profit margin. For the first time he scowled. His changing expressions caught Takako's eye.

On the train back to Tokyo, Tamura was in an eager mood as he drank some beer. "The man is stubborn, but one more try should do it," he said, as if he were talking about a horse race. "Two and a half million yen for the half acre is a bit too much, but it's certainly worth four million an acre, so we'll hold firm at half that amount." He chattered on, spurred by his own enthusiasm. "How much of that would you get?" he asked. Counting on his fingers, Tamura worked out Takako's share, insisting that he had a right to join in the bargaining. "It's less than I thought, but then you've got a lot of people in your family, haven't you!" Still, there was enough for a deposit on a two-bedroom apartment, with money left over for a short trip abroad as well. Takako had never seen him so excited, but looking at him, she felt a sort of sediment collect in her heart as they laughed together. Would they split up? Would he marry into another family? Such concerns vanished in the face of a little money. She turned away from him, but his giddy talk made her feel empty: even she no longer had the heart to give up her share for her mother's sake.

Takako sometimes wondered what hopes sustained the real-estate agent. He seemed honest and gentle, but in certain respects he was as solid as a rock, and he knew how to intimidate. He led Hideichi and Yasuo by the nose into a compromise, though they put up a fuss. Even when the talks snarled, he never once suggested they owed him some consideration for the trouble he'd gone to in finding the Miki family. No doubt he lived by suppressing such human, self-centered feelings.

Namiko, who came back to collect her share of the money and returned home cheerfully, sent a chopstick box of Tsugaru lacquerware to her mother. Subsequently, a letter came asking if her mother would lend her the money to buy a small apartment, and assuring her that she would pay her back with interest. Ritsu crumpled up the letter and threw it into the wastebasket. Takako, pretending not to notice, went for a walk. While she was out, Hideichi dropped by and suggested that they build a cottage in the garden of his mother's rented house, and that his family should live with her.

"Who would live in the new addition?"

"Well, the children," Hideichi answered and blushed slightly. He said he couldn't abandon her, bedridden as she was with rheumatism. Besides, if they all lived together, she'd have no more worries. Ritsu replied that she would think it over, but realized that the six hundred thousand yen she had set aside had brought her only momentary happiness. She did not mention Hideichi's proposal when Takako came back from her walk.

A cold wind now blew through the streets of Tokyo as well. Takako exchanged a gift coupon at a department store on her way home from work on Saturday and then went to an office in an unfamiliar part of town. Commercial Promotions was located in a small office building, and when she pushed open the door, she saw a number of men sitting at desks crowded one right next to the other. She told the receptionist the name of the man she had come to see. He stood up from a desk at the back and walked over to her. Unlike the shabby-looking figure she had seen at the office in Karuizawa, here he was neatly dressed. He seemed free for the moment, so they left the office and he guided her to a nearby coffee shop.

"Is there something I can do for you in regard to the property?" He looked sincere, in an effort perhaps to give the impression that he could be relied on.

"Thanks to you, the sale of the property is settled. I'd be happier if we discovered some more land that my father had forgotten about." The man smiled vaguely, unsure of the reason for her visit. The family had sold the land for a million eight hundred thousand yen.

"Have you finished grading the land on the hill?"

"It started to snow when we were about half done. You went at a good time."

"I don't think I'll go there again, but the view of Mt. Asama was beautiful. The bank of trees was nice too; I enjoyed spending the day there. It's strange to think my father never saw it."

"You'll go again, I'm sure. Why don't the two of you go next year, for a vacation?"

Wondering what Tamura would say to that, Takako drew her parcel closer. Ever since the agent had located her family, she had been completely absorbed in selling the land, but now, finally, she was able to come and thank him. The gift was only a symbol of the gratitude that she alone seemed to feel. A look of surprise flitted across the man's face. Searching for someone for three months had been a remarkable experience, but he'd never expected any of them to make a courtesy call afterward. He gazed at the department-store package that Takako handed over.

"It was only my job."

"I think what you did was extraordinary."

"I do a lot of investigating—locating people, character references—but Mr. Miki's case was like grabbing at a cloud. I took an interest in it right from the start. I imagined that anyone willing to buy land like that would be rather indifferent to money; I thought we'd reach an agreement as soon as I found him."

He had tried coming to grips with the task of finding Miki, but hadn't known where to look. Then, just when he had reached a dead end, the name "Manchurian Railway" had turned up. "I've got it now!" he'd thought, and went to see one person after another. But the men who had worked together in the Investigation Bureau had gone their separate ways. A vague image of the man he was looking for took shape in his mind. The slender thread of clues he followed between his regular duties formed a path that, little by little, began to clear ahead, and he felt encouraged. Facing head-on the challenge of ferreting out the Miki family, he put all he had into the task. Whenever he worked himself up, telling himself "Today's the day," his son would say admiringly how tough Dad was. After doing business for more than fifteen years, with all the pressures of profit and loss, of haggling over prices, his face had become dead, inelastic, a patched-up mask that, though still a face, had ceased to be his own. The search for Miki Seiichirō had enabled him to reclaim what he had forgotten. He told Takako that it was he who should thank her for allowing him such a rewarding experience.

"I'm sure my dead father is also happy that you found us." Takao listened happily to his story. She had put a photograph of her father in her handbag, but felt it would seem too theatrical to take it out.

"It's been business as usual since I found you." The man took a cigarette from a blue pack of Patto's and lit it. This was the first time she had seen him smoke.

"Those are odd cigarettes, aren't they?"

"I've smoked Patto's for a long time. They're low in nicotine. I go to the tobacco shop in front of the Employment Security Office and buy thirty packs at a time." His features relaxed as the tension left his face. It was the most natural of his faces Takako had seen. Though thinking it was bad to keep a man away from his work, she decided to stay for a few more minutes. She would never see him again, and for her as for him, this moment seemed very precious.

THE PALE FOX

Ōba Minako

Translated by Stephen W. Kohl

Ōba Minako began her literary career in 1968 with the publication of her prize-winning short story "Sambiki no kani" (The Three Crabs, tr. 1978), which, like many of her stories, is set in a coastal town in North America. To some extent this recurrent setting is based on the author's experience of having lived for twelve years in Sitka, Alaska. In a broader and more literary sense, however, it is a setting appropriate to the themes of many of Ōba's stories, such as Kiri no tabi *(Journey through Mist, 1976). Her fog-shrouded coasts are places where people live their lives seeing things only imperfectly, drifting through random encounters with figures that emerge and disappear in the mist.*

Fog and mist are metaphors for loneliness and the need for freedom, themes that are depicted in other ways as well. Garakuta hakubutsukan *(The Junk Museum, 1975) presents an international cast of characters who have no common language, customs, or social background. Ōba's characters are routinely isolated in alien cultures, but are nevertheless tough enough to find freedom, often through creative use of memory and imagination. Her novel* Urashimasō *(Urashima Grasses, 1977) develops similar themes in greater detail and complexity.*

Other concerns complicate Ōba's misty world. Science and technology, intruding randomly and yet inevitably on the lives of modern men and women, require new kinds of human relationships and new concepts of identity. And while doing away with traditional patterns of life, these same technologies threaten the destruction of life itself. But Ōba does not shun this development. Rather, she sees it as opening new avenues of behavior for those who have the imagination and the strength to embrace this new world.

The author sometimes uses straightforward narrative but more often prefers a montage technique, especially in works of fantasy like "Higusa" (Fireweed, 1968) and "Aoi kitsune" (The Pale Fox, 1973). Both are stories of love and death full of vivid imagery that is sometimes beautiful, often grotesque. Ōba's subtle and complex literary world provides no answers, but casts a fresh and occasionally disturbing light on the human condition.

* * *

"It's been a long time," said the Pale Fox.

Seven years ago, when they were lovers, a melancholy look in the man's downcast face had reminded her of a fox. Sometimes, in the pale light of the moon, or washed perhaps by the light of a neon sign, his face took on a bluish cast, and since that time she had referred to him in her mind as the Pale Fox. His sharp, narrow chin resembled a fox—a fox pausing in a moonlit forest, head cocked toward the moon.

"These white flowers smell nice," said the Pale Fox, "but the thistles, roses, and nettles are a nuisance."

Turning away from the light, the Fox's eyes shone amber, like glowing charcoal or Christmas tree lights.

"It's been seven years, hasn't it?"

The Pale Fox was like a priest who performed the ritual with faultless precision. The priest's eyes were too far apart for a fox, and each drifted independently. For some reason she enjoyed running the tip of her finger down between his eyebrows to the bridge of his nose.

"That's a vulnerable spot. It gives me the shivers when you do that; it makes me feel I'm about to be stabbed by an assassin." The Pale Fox disliked her doing this, but was reluctant to brush the woman's finger away.

The Fox's nose was moist in the moonlight.

The woman thought: I wonder why Father says this is the grave where

Mother is buried? It is such a splendid and majestic tomb. It might have been the grave of some venerable priest clothed in rich, brocaded vestments, or a great warrior in full armor and helmet, or a grand minister of state with drooping moustaches.

The funeral must surely have been splendid, too, with much fanfare and a service carried out in the glare of footlights, attended by joyous throngs of celebrities. The choreographer of this spectacle would have been called the Priest of Heaven, and would have led the reading of the scriptures and the voluptuous sobbing of the mourners. Yes, this was the funeral it must have been.

By now, of course, the grave was encrusted with moss and lichen, and it was impossible to read the inscription carved on it. All she could make out was a single Chinese character that seemed to be the word for "great." Yet once it had been a glittering and elaborate tomb.

Though the flesh in the casket had decayed and putrefied, beautiful women had gathered in attendance. Ladies who had flinched at the smell of corruption had risked being thrown into prison. It was a grave of writhing anguish.

This was a grave that wielded power, that threw back its shoulders in pride; this was a grave that laughed arrogantly with cold eyes and a thin smile. But this was all vanity now, for the corpse had rotted and the tomb was crumbling.

The forest was heavy with gloom. When the black birds started up with a mournful cry, cold drops fell from the trees and she looked up. Far away, between the overlapping leaves, was the violet sky.

The path was slippery with mud, and fungi that reminded her of withered and broken oranges grew from the fallen tree trunks. There were others with plump, fleshy umbrellas that spread wide like patches of snow.

Each time her father stumbled, he clutched at her. His hands were cold, and the daughter felt that a corpse was touching her. Still, she was curious about this landscape of death being shown her by a corpse, and she appreciated each stop they made.

"I found Mother's grave. I looked for it everywhere and couldn't find it, but then all of a sudden I saw it, thanks to the way the light was shining."

It was like the abalone clinging to the rocks. Somewhere down among the forest of gently waving sea tangle there comes the glitter of a fish's belly, and suddenly you see it, the tight, tender flesh of the abalone enclosed in its shell, deep within the lush growth of moss.

Her father was delighted. From his youth he had been happiest gathering abalone and edible fungi. He was a metal craftsman by trade who had brought his workshop to the rocky shore of this island and devoted the greater part of each year to making metal objects. Toward the end of the year, he would take everything he had made to the city to sell; but apart from that one annual journey, he remained on the island. The children enjoyed spending several months there with their father during the summer. Stretching out like a backdrop behind the rocky shore was a pine forest where all sorts of fungi flourished.

His eyes were as sharp as an animal's when he probed for abalone trembling beneath the surface of the sea, or the thin, white stalks of fungi hidden in the forest under fallen leaves. He would find each mollusc among the seaweed and pull its living flesh from the rocks where it clung fast. The woman imagined the old man's twisted jaw and superimposed the image on the sharp jaw of the Pale Fox.

"It was a place like this, your mother's grave."

Her father had discovered the grave deep in the inner recesses of an ancient temple on the edge of the pine forest. At the back of the tomb he had found a small door leading to the crypt. He had tried to open it, but it was choked with moss and would not move. Some grass with small, white flowers grew in a crack in the stone that marked the door to the crypt. There were also ferns.

"Your mother is sitting in there. I could see her knee," said her father. "The swelling in her shins seems to have subsided. The color of her earlobes isn't good, though."

Mother had to have her ears pierced to wear the earrings that Father made for her. The daughter remembered from her childhood that when Mother's ears had been pierced, Father had disinfected them so they would not fester.

The shells of the abalone were hidden by sea moss; the tomb was covered with forest moss. When she bent to examine the moss more closely, the beauty of a microcosmic world spread out before her. The stone tomb beneath it became an illusion; the vision of elegance vanished.

Clutching his cane of polished rose root, her father resembled a gaunt, white cat. He smiled and his eyes gleamed with a small, blue flame.

"Shall we burn a cigarette instead of incense?"

Searching in her handbag, she found two cigarettes; they were all she had left. She lit one and put it on the moss. The white paper absorbed some moisture and she watched it go out, leaving only a wisp of smoke. She lit the remaining cigarette and inhaled, turning aside to keep the smoke from getting in her eyes. Then, as though her mother were a patient lying on the tombstone, she held the cigarette out between her fingers so that the sick woman could take it in her mouth. She stayed like that for a while, waiting for the ash to lengthen and fall off.

After all, it was tobacco that had killed her mother, and now that she was dead, her father frequently offered cigarettes at the family altar.

She felt as though she were playing house with her father. It was as though they had joined hands and were dancing around some ancient tomb, playing a children's game. In the shadow of the tombstone, a toad sat watching.

For seven years she had heard no news at all, then suddenly, one day, a man came to see her and it was the Fox. His arrival was totally unexpected, like waking in the morning to find a single leaf by her pillow.

The Pale Fox was smoother than the polished rose root. He believed he had a very beautiful body; he liked to stand straight and walk slowly. She realized he was probably waiting for some word of praise, but felt it was too much trouble to try and find a compliment to satisfy his vanity. At the same time, she was ashamed of her own indifference.

The Pale Fox told her that during the seven years they had been apart, he had married, lived with his wife for four years, and then left her.

"She was like one of those dolls that can shed tears. Whenever I came home, I would find her sitting in the same place, in the same position. In the end she became like a moth, the large sort that crawl around on walls."

"First you say she's a crying doll, and then she's just a dried-up moth stuck to the wall."

"Finally that's all she was, just a spot on the wall. She was the sort of woman who dreams of finding happiness in ordinary family life. She had done nothing wrong, that's why it was such a shame. I even changed my mind after we had separated, and we tried meeting several times, but we never talked about anything. We slept together each time we met, but we couldn't talk about things. I'd leave again as soon as our lovemaking was done. At that point she changed from a moth into a butterfly sitting with its wings folded. As she sat, dust would rise from her wings and make me wheeze."

He paused, then tried to explain his own silence by saying, "Some people talk a lot. I think they lose something when they talk too much."

The woman gazed with admiration at the Pale Fox, who spoke as little as possible in order not to lose anything.

He was, however, the sort of man who could never suit his actions to his words, or his deeds to his thoughts, and so he always ended up talking when the woman remained silent. Nevertheless, he apparently felt obliged to explain what he had done during those seven years.

"I was exhausted the whole time we were married. The constant weariness made my bones ache as though I was carrying a load with straps cutting into my shoulders. I always do what I want, and yet while my own life-style was selfish, I felt some responsibility toward my thoroughly unselfish partner. At the bottom of my heart I suppose what I really want is a woman who'll be a slave to me."

"I'm sure there are women in the world who'd be happy to be your slave. But if you ever encountered one, you'd start dreaming of a woman you could treat as an equal. You really would. Haven't you learned yet that the tyrant is always bound by the tyrant's debt? In your case, the only way to free yourself is to free the other person as well."

"But women all renounce their freedom; it's a way of binding their men to them." Somewhere in his heart the Pale Fox dreamed of having a slave, but in reality he could never manipulate women in that way.

Seven years ago he had asked her to marry him, saying that he intended to be a good husband. The expression on his face had revealed the pathetic determination of someone who was throwing his own freedom away. This frightened the woman and she recoiled from him.

She could imagine him saying the same thing to his former wife before their marriage, and she pitied him. To make unrealistic promises, to make promises he could not keep, could only lead to hopelessness in the long run.

It was when he was completely beaten that he dreamed of possessing a slave. If a woman chooses to be a slave, presumably the man's guilt is resolved and this allows him to behave as he pleases. The woman understood this man's fantasy very well; he wanted her to fall on her knees and embrace him, but she felt it was too much bother. Again she felt ashamed of her indifference.

"You are too fond of women. That's why it's impossible either to pledge yourself to one single woman or to treat us simply as objects. But, you know, you're probably fond of women because women are fond of men. If women were not allowed to know men, if the person you married were not allowed to know any man but yourself, she still wouldn't necessarily become the sort of woman you want. A woman can't be treated as a woman if she's lost whatever makes her one. The sort of marriage you had in mind depends too much on someone who's lost her identity as a woman."

In an encounter like this, mood is more important than logic. And so, solemnly, tenderly, they proceeded with their ritual, devoting themselves to it wholeheartedly, and when the ceremony had reached its climax and ended, they were left clinging to the altar like a pair of bats, physically and emotionally drained. Once the ceremony was over, her earlier indifference returned, and she became embarrassed by her lack of enthusiasm. In the end she compromised by telling herself that different people just have different ideas, and that it does no good to ignore other ways of thinking.

The Pale Fox dozed. His arms, twined around her waist, went limp. She could see one ugly, swollen wart on a stubby finger; it reminded her of the skin near the ears of lizards she had seen the previous day at the botanical gardens. They had kissed for the first time in seven years standing in front of a pair of lizards locked in a motionless sexual embrace. The immobile lizards looked like stuffed animals in a specimen case.

His warty finger also appeared to be stuffed. The wart seemed to spread and grow until it resembled a crater. Countless white fungus stalks grew out of this crater.

Her father called again from the island. He had called twice while she was out. Praying Mantis, the man she was living with, passed on the information that he had phoned, but she did not feel like returning his call, and left again.

Her father was in the habit of ringing his seven children one after the other, making the same call to each. The woman was usually the last to be called. She was, after all, the youngest child. Apparently he had said the rocks on the island were covered with abalone, but that was long ago, and now the rocks were covered only by moss. Whatever phase the moon was in, there was only moss that may have looked like abalone shells clinging to the rocks.

"I told her you called, but she left again in a hurry," explained Praying Mantis when her father phoned yet again. The following day, before she had decided whether or not to return his call, there was a fourth phone call from the island, and when she picked up the receiver, she heard her father's hoarse voice.

"We're having lovely weather here on the island. Why don't you come for a visit? The place is full of abalone. There's a new moon now and there are always plenty of them around then."

Unable to endure this senile fantasy, she said, "As usual, the Mantis has a guest here just now."

"I see. A guest is it? I remember in the old days your mother and I used to think up all sorts of excuses for declining our parents' invitations to visit, because we wanted to meet each other instead. . . I'll go to your mother's grave again and offer a cigarette from you. It occurs to me that you're the only one of the children who knows where that grave is, so I want you to remember how to find it." Her father hung up the phone.

Her mother had borne seven children, and not one of them had provided a monument for her grave. In her will the mother had requested that her ashes be scattered over the sea. The children had some notion that the surging waves would transform her into various shapes. But the father was disappointed by the children's devotion to their mother's will.

Soon the Pale Fox awoke. He drew the woman to him, but it was clear he did so only because he felt obliged to. Even while he longed for a woman slave, the Fox continued to treat women with respect. Understanding this pathetic dream, the woman playfully scratched his beautiful body all over and tugged at his hair.

Like a child on a visit somewhere who wants to go home, the woman longed to return to Praying Mantis. He was a strange man, devoted to that form of ecstasy peculiar to the mantis in which the male is killed and devoured by the female. He enjoyed hearing women talk about other men they had known. He was curious about women only if they displayed curiosity about men. Searching now for words that would flatter the Pale Fox, she moved about the room making gestures, throwing glances that might appeal to him. She did not have the patience for anything more; all she wanted now was to sleep, to sleep next to the Mantis with her leg thrown over his stomach. (The woman could not sleep unless her legs were slightly elevated.)

It would not do to stay with the Pale Fox until morning, and she realized that this feeling confirmed once again the reason she had recoiled from living with him seven years ago.

If he were a real fox, she could put a collar on him and fasten it to the bedpost. Yet, even then, in the morning she might find that he had disappeared, leaving only the collar lying on the bed, the chain still attached. The Pale Fox, it seemed, was always changing into something else. The woman was indifferent to the gallant youth he sometimes became; what captivated her was his true form, a fox sniffing out his prey. She liked his beautiful blue fur, his erect ears, sharp jaw, moist nose, his surprisingly long, pink tongue, bushy tail, and glittering, golden eyes. But the Fox in his true form always eluded her, escaping to the forest; she only caught glimpses of him.

Just as she was getting dressed, the Fox, too, felt a longing for his home in the forest. "We should probably be going now," he said. "I'm leaving town tomorrow," he added, "so it would be better if I went back to my own hotel tonight. I have to pack my things."

As he got up, the Pale Fox said, "Shall we go out for something to eat?" He was looking at the key that lay on the bedside table. They no longer had any use for it, since they would not be coming back to this room.

They locked the door as they went out, leaving the key behind. Outside a warm, muggy wind blew; and the large, red sun perched on the horizon directly in front of them, wrapped in a cloak of gray smog. Groups of people hurried along in the gullies through forests of tall buildings. From the expressions on their faces, they seemed to have forgotten what a dreary business it is to be faithful. In the stores where the stench of the city was blown away by air conditioners, people kept their sullen, bloated faces downturned, and shuffled aimlessly like caged animals.

The man and the woman carried on an absurd conversation. They spoke of buying a villa together on the island. Neither of them had any money, of course, and even as they talked of buying a villa, both were thinking how impossible it would be for them to live there together. As they talked, each fantasized about imaginary slaves.

While they ate their meal of raw, spiced meat, the woman saw a reflection of herself in a wall mirror. It showed a cruel, voracious insect that only slightly resembled her elderly father. The insect appeared covered with a veil of spider web, while the Fox had transformed himself into a beetle. Their wings tangled together and their conversation was meaningless.

Mother's earlobes, she remembered, had been discolored and unhealthy-looking. Had it been her sister who retrieved Mother's earrings from the ashes after the body had been cremated?

When she arrived home, the Mantis said, "There was a phone call from your sister. Something about your father. It seems something has happened. She said he was taken into protective custody yesterday by the island police. Did he seem normal the last time you saw him?"

"I didn't notice anything wrong," said the woman.

"Your sister says he should be put in an institution."

"Oh."

The father had seven children. None of those seven children was opposed to the idea of putting their father in an institution. What they had in mind was a mental hospital located on top of a hill on the island.

In its advertising, the hospital used pictures of the surrounding fields in spring, clothed in a haze of yellow blossoms. Crested white butterflies fluttered over the yellow fields, and there in the midst of them stood a white building, rising like some fantastic castle. It seemed to float above the ground; a white-clad ghost without feet.

When she awoke the next morning the woman realized she had left behind at the hotel an ornamental hairpin her father had made when he was young. Her mother had given it to her as a keepsake. It was not yet check-out time, so she hurriedly caught a taxi and set off for the hotel. When she explained to the desk clerk that she had left the key in the room and locked herself out, he rang for the bellboy, but then, remembering, said, "Oh, wait a minute. Your husband came back a little while ago. I gave the key to him."

The woman was heading for the elevator when it occurred to her that he should be at his hotel packing and that he hadn't originally planned to come back. She went to the house phone and dialed.

Soft and light as a feather, the voice at the other end was clearly the Fox's. He was not a beetle now.

"Hello, it's me. I left my hairpin there, on the shelf in the bathroom. It's silver and shaped like a fish; the eyes are inlaid bits of black coral. It's a keepsake from my mother. Could you bring it to me before you check out? Or send it by registered mail."

The woman listened carefully, straining for any sign that he had another woman in the room with him, but she heard nothing. Without a word in reply the Pale Fox put down the receiver.

Two or three days later the hairpin arrived safely in a small, registered envelope. There was not even a note to go with it.

IRON FISH

Kōno Taeko

Translated by Yukiko Tanaka

Modern Japanese fiction, particularly by women writers, is filled with descriptions of small incidents or glimpses of everyday life, the accumulation of which forms our reality. Kōno Taeko (1926–), however, does not concentrate on details in order to create an illusion of reality. A closer look at her stories reveals the fact that the various parts of her detailed descriptions do not necessarily match one another. The result is a sense of incongruity. What Kōno tries to suggest is the precarious relationship between the real and the imagined, or the objective and the subjective.

The shocking motifs of her early stories, centering around sadomasochistic fantasies, have become less obvious in her more recent works, and a new theme has emerged: the awakening of freedom. Under circumstances where the main character finds herself both physically and metaphysically imprisoned, the meaning of reality is reevaluated. The woman in "Tetsu no uo" (Iron Fish, 1976) *tries to recapture the extraordinary experience of her first husband who was killed while serving as a "human torpedo": his last moments in the ultimate confinement of an underwater grave seem to hold for her a key to understanding her own life and reality, her past as well as her present.*

During World War II the Japanese Imperial Navy made large torpedoes that carried a man inside, an aquatic version of the kamikaze pilot. Though these "human torpedoes" had very little impact militarily, they are a grimly effective reminder of the tragedy of war. "Iron Fish" *is told from the point of view of a woman who was left behind by one of these men.*

Kōno's stories have been included in anthologies of World War II fiction. Hers is the generation whose youth was spent in factories rather than schools. With the end of the war, Kōno has stated, a new sense of freedom came to her; it urged her to write. It took a little over a decade, however, before she was recognized in the Japanese literary world. With her novel Kaiten-tobira *(Revolving Door, 1970), her position was firmly established as one of Japan's most important contemporary writers, and she continues to venture into new realms of fiction writing. Recently she has also gained a reputation as a literary critic. Kōno lives with her artist husband in Tokyo.*

* * *

We were the last to leave the room. As we both slowly descended the stairs, stopping in front of the exhibit on the wall and at the display case on the landing, an attendant came down right behind us. Hardly any visitors could be seen in the rooms downstairs, and another attendant was picking up the signboard to bring inside.

"Are you closing? Is it too late to look around?" asked a person who had just come in.

"We close at four," answered the attendant.

The clock on the wall showed that it was not quite four. A few people had come into the front lobby, unaware of the closing time. Soon the two attendants, who had already changed their clothes to go home, came back to close the large front doors, leaving one door ajar as they departed.

"They're closed," a voice remarked outside the doors.

Stragglers inside began leaving one by one from the now darkened lobby. We were also walking toward the door.

"Would you excuse me for a moment?" she suddenly said to me.

"Let me hold that for you," I said, indicating her umbrella; like most women, we did things like that for each other. She seemed puzzled for a moment, then looked at what she had in her hand.

"It's not raining now, is it?" she said to herself, and handed me the umbrella. "Why don't you go on ahead. I'll join you soon." She returned the way we had come.

I left the building, trying not to look back to see where she was going. I thought I understood why she wanted to return; it had not been necessary, then, to offer to hold her umbrella. The reason we had stayed until closing time in the first place was her obvious reluctance to leave, which didn't seem unreasonable. It must have been the front lobby that she couldn't resist seeing again. She wanted to be there, to look at the place once more without my company.

When we had arrived, the rain had almost stopped; now the sky above the trees was faintly colored by an autumn sunset. I went down the stone steps to the drive, still trying not to look back the way I had come, and slowly walked along the gravel in the front garden. The narrow garden was met by a walkway. I took the walkway, turned, and continued until I came to an arrow pointing toward the building I had just left. I stopped there and neatly folded both umbrellas. The ground was covered with fallen leaves. I played with the leaves, poking them with the umbrellas, remembering that there were several pressed leaves and flowers among the various articles that had belonged to those men. They looked quite incongruous beside the rougher, more disturbing items in the display case. Their color had faded against the paper underneath, which was also discolored. In the same case I had seen several photos of young women, or perhaps I should call them girls. One of these young victims must have pressed those leaves and flowers. The paper strips cut in irregular sizes, and the manner in which the leaves and stems had been taped here and there, told of the awkward hand of a girl who used scissors to make tape in the days before the invention of cellophane tape. A few of the leaves had retained their original bright color. I too had pressed pretty leaves and cut paper tape when I was a girl. The pressed leaves I had made were consumed in that gigantic fire ignited by remote control at the end of the war. There were several years' difference between the girls in the photos and myself, which is why I had escaped the tragic death that overtook them. Their deaths seemed so extraordinary because they were caused by something controlled from a distant location: the very nature of remote control made the whole thing difficult to understand.

I heard footsteps and turned around. It was an old woman in a worker's uniform. I walked back a little way to a spot where I could see the front of the building. Both doors were closed, with the two small round handles side by side. I had not yet started to worry. I assumed that she would appear at any moment from behind a tree or the pedestal of some statue, smiling awkwardly as she put away the handkerchief with which she had just dried her tears. I looked at the side of the building, where I saw a metal door. I went to see if it would open, but it didn't move. Its resistance filled me with a sudden apprehension: I realized that the front doors must also be locked.

The two ring-shaped handles turned out to be ornamental: underneath was another more ordinary handle with double keyholes. This wouldn't turn either. I went around to the other side of the building to make sure she was not there, then returned to the main door and started pushing and pulling the handle.

"They close so early, don't they? We thought it'd still be open, too." I turned and saw an elderly couple on the steps. They must have thought I had also come too late: they sounded sympathetic.

"Yes. It's still early," I agreed absentmindedly. I pretended to be looking at the building while I waited for them to leave. Then I went back to the door. Hoping no one would come, I pulled and twisted the handle unsuccessfully and then banged on the door. Next I tried pulling the handle while I pushed on the other door, hoping to make a small crack through which I could talk. Before long I noticed that the lower keyhole was one of those old-fashioned, mushroom-shaped fixtures that are larger than a keyhole of more recent design.

On a small piece of paper I wrote both her name and mine, and pushed it through the keyhole with a matchstick. I heard a tiny flutter as the paper dropped to the floor on the other side, then realized that I had no way of telling if she had picked it up. I wrote another note and this time pushed it halfway through the keyhole.

I was certain the paper would disappear from the hole, but when it actually did, I felt as if I had witnessed the strangest thing in the world. I lowered my head and brought my eye to the keyhole. It was dark on the other side, and I couldn't see anything. Then suddenly a voice was talking to my eye.

"I'm all right. Don't worry. . . I want you to go."

"What do you mean?"

"I want you to go home."

"Then what?"

There was no answer. I banged at the crack where the two doors met.

"Please leave me to do what I want. Pretend that you don't know anything. I'll be angry if you don't. . ."

I had been afraid that she was in trouble, but now I detected something ominous and probably illicit about her behavior.

"What in the world are you. . . ?" I raised my voice. I was not sure whether I was concerned for her or simply curious as to why she was doing something clearly forbidden.

"Someday you will understand."

"Don't be ridiculous," I snapped at her.

"I'll tell you sometime, if I can. But don't do anything that will make me angry. Please. You simply have to let me do this."

I shuddered. She sounded as if there was no chance that she would tell me why she was doing this. Her words echoed deep in my ears, like the ringing of a gong struck by a monk about to undergo some particularly arduous discipline. When I realized after a time that she was not going to answer me any more, I felt dizzy; I saw the glittering blades of those swords on display, the brownish circles of bloodstains on the clothes, and the characters in the many letters written by those men in their final days—all swirling up into the air.

The rays of the sun were fast dying away, a fact I must have noticed for my own benefit. I stared at the closed door, thinking about the pink telephone I had seen inside the building. There must be a black public phone as well, I thought. She had made a call on the way here, so she had that little black address book with her; she must have looked up my number in the same book when she called me yesterday from the station. Perhaps she would weaken and change her mind; she might try to call me out of desperation. If so, I must be at home. Resolutely I turned my back on the door.

Three different images haunted me throughout that night—images of the monk and the rigors of his trial; of a criminal; and of an accident victim (I couldn't rule out the possibility that she had met with some mishap). I felt the same awful tension that people must have experienced as they prepared to lift the giant bell of Dōjōji, which Princess

Kiyo had hidden inside. The anxiety was so real my stomach actually began aching. It was not that she had broken in, I tried rationalizing; if she simply remains inside and does nothing, it isn't a crime. But if she steals an item or two that she feels she must have, I must let her know that I won't betray her. I'm not afraid of being arrested for it. As I went over all this in my mind, I realized that I ought to try and rest; I would need all my strength on the following day. It would obviously be busy.

That was four years ago. She told me later what she did that night, which I spent without sleep. The following is what I have put together from the story she told, with a few assumptions of my own.

Sometime, somewhere, her first husband had bade a last farewell to several of his close friends and had entered the belly of an iron fish before putting to sea. His wife knew nothing about this. The iron fish had destroyed itself against another great fish—or was it a small iron island, whose upper half lay flat on some distant ocean? Her husband died, destroyed with the iron fish. His flesh was torn into many pieces that drifted down to the bottom of the sea, where they must have attracted the real fish feeding there.

She had heard that her husband had been enshrined along with innumerable other men and some women who had died extraordinary deaths, though each death was different in the manner and degree of its tragedy.

She had not been to the place where her husband was said to be enshrined. They had been married less than a year when he left her to serve his country. He came back to her only twice after that to spend a night with her. Both times he neither told her where he had been nor where he was going. One hundred and sixty-two days after his second overnight visit, she was informed that her husband was no longer of this world. By counting the days she realized that she had been unaware of his death for one hundred and twenty-one or twenty-two days. Her married life had lasted less than two years.

When it was confirmed that her husband was indeed among the enshrined, she did not go to visit the spot. It was not that she was skeptical about the act of enshrinement: rather she simply did not feel like going to a place that must be horribly gloomy. Whenever people asked her why she hadn't been, or more directly told her that she ought to go, she responded that she would go someday. Inwardly, however, she had a very different feeling; it was an attitude that could only be explained with an expression she had never used before: "The hell with it."

When she thought about her reluctance to visit her husband's shrine, she realized that the gloominess of the place was only one of her reasons after all. The main reason was that it was not yet time. She wanted to experience her husband's death all by herself, to feel the loss personally. She did not think she could do so yet. Excessive public reaction was partially responsible for her attitude, but then, for many more years after the public had ceased to pay much attention to the matter, she still couldn't have his death all to herself.

The time came when she was able to feel her husband's death personally, and by then her image of the shrine was even drearier than ever. Her reluctance had now changed to rejection, and she saw no meaning in such a visit. She knew that a time would come when she would associate morbidness with the place; she also knew that she would then go there just to make sure she was right about it. Meanwhile, whenever she thought about the visit, she was somehow certain that she wouldn't be able to explore the shrine alone and at leisure; its meaning for her was greater than its association with her husband. It was something she could possess all to herself, doing whatever she wanted there.

Time went by and she remarried. Seven years had passed since her first husband's death, but it hardly felt that long. She was still only twenty-seven, however, and that at least seemed real to her. Her first marriage, the loss of her husband, and her second marriage all seemed to have come rather quickly. After the second marriage, she began referring to her late spouse as "my first husband," even to herself.

It was not only out of consideration and politeness toward her second husband that she refrained for so long from visiting her first husband's shrine. And she was reassured somehow, knowing that she would go there someday just to see for herself what a grim place it was. She was also reassured by the thought that she had not been kept from making the visit and neglected her first husband out of consideration for her second; neither had she tried to slip away to pay her respects and thereby ignored the feelings of her new spouse. It helped her decision seem more natural when she and her husband moved to a city a long way from the shrine. When she decided to visit the place on an impulse while she was away from home, with me as a companion, nearly a quarter of a century had passed since the loss of her first husband.

It was an autumn day and, unfortunately, raining. In spite of that, the site was remarkably airy and light. This surprised her, since she had always thought it would be gloomy. There were broad gravel walkways, lanes lined with large trees, areas that looked like small parks, and open spaces adorned with young trees here and there. The place was filled with a cheerful brightness which spread to every edge and corner of the vast expanse, and the autumn rain and falling leaves seemed even to enhance its lightness.

"I'm so glad," she said to herself repeatedly. If it had been as gloomy as she had imagined, she would have felt remiss in her duties to both her first and second husbands: remiss in not having visited sooner for the first and in coming after all in spite of the second. She might even have regretted coming. Things were very different from what she had expected, however, and she felt free to think whatever she wanted.

The spot where her first husband was enshrined along with many other men and some women was a building made of natural rocks, wood, and metal. There must be places he would rather have gone to stay, she thought. She wondered whether he had seen this shrine before he died. But he must have known when he entered the iron fish that he would come here after his death. He might have quite liked this cheerful place; in fact, it was the sort of spot his spirit might have wanted to revisit now and then, though not, perhaps, on this particular day.

The ornaments on the building's exterior were not inappropriate. She saw the words "Pray for the dead" hanging from the branches of a tree. On another placard was the phrase "Rest in peace." Quite a few people who knew him were still alive, so she doubted somehow that his repose was all that peaceful.

There were a few annex buildings on the vast grounds, and it was into one of these that she locked herself.

The voice from the other side of the iron doors stopped when she refused to respond. So she went straight to the iron fish in the lobby and placed her hands on the side of its body. The surface was very rusty, and her hands felt as if they were rubbing against scales. She then stepped under the wooden rail to get even closer to the thing, and lay down so that she could embrace its body with both arms. The fish was too large for her arms—it looked as if she were clinging to it. As she held it, her body was filled with the sense that she had a right and duty to be there.

Altogether over a hundred iron fish had sunk one after another. Each had been ripped apart and scattered on the bottom of the sea. Years later, one of the fish was discovered with most of its body somehow intact. It was this salvaged body that she now embraced.

Earlier in the day, when she had first seen that long tapered cylinder in the center of the lobby facing the door, she hadn't known what it was. "This is what he rode in," she'd muttered to herself as she read the explanation on the plate. "He must have entered from this hole here," she said, noticing a round opening on top that had lost its lid. She reached her arm out to touch it. Then she came back to the plate. "So it was forty-six feet long," she noted with some surprise. She could see that it was very narrow, only four feet in diameter, and to herself she acknowledged that her husband must have found it suffocating. Since one opening faced the main door through which light still shone in, she could see halfway through the empty cylinder, which was sliced in two. The light, however, did not reach all the way to the other end. She could imagine how claustrophobic her husband must have felt.

As she moved on, looking at other exhibits, she forgot about the cylinder, but it was not because she found something else that strongly drew her attention. When she remarried, she had divided most of her first husband's belongings among a few of his acquaintances. For herself she kept some pictures and a set of badges, which she knew were at the bottom of her velveteen-covered jewelry box. The exhibits in the display cases did not seem particularly valuable or significant in her eyes. She saw me walking away from one case with a sudden awkward motion: in it was a document which read at the end, "Neither debt nor guilt nor any tie to women need I feel." She noticed me turn my face away and wipe my eyes. Someone of our generation, who has lived through and yet not personally experienced the war's most tragic moments, tends to react more strongly to such relics, she thought. She looked at the exhibits, taking more time than she needed, because I was examining them carefully.

When she came back down to the main floor and stood in front of the fish-shaped cylinder, she again thought of the claustrophobia. That sensation was intensified after one of the building's front doors was closed, darkening the lobby. When she made me leave by myself, however, she had intended to follow me right away, as she had said she would. She merely wanted to be inside the cylinder in slightly darkened surroundings. She wanted a chance to experience the feeling of being in there alone, while one door of the building was still open.

Before that chance had come, it was already almost four. In two minutes the other door would be closed. She felt as if it was going to close and trap her husband in that suffocating cylinder. If she wished, she could do exactly as he had done and lock herself in. And in that attempt she had almost succeeded. Her heart began to pound.

She was still standing in the semidarkness of the lobby when the last visitor left. The way to the stairs was blocked by a metal bar, which the attendants had locked a few minutes earlier as they were leaving. While she had been waiting for the place to become totally deserted, she had pretended to be looking at some of the exhibits by the wall near the entrance, like a late visitor reluctant to leave. Now she moved slowly, checking the two doors that she had not seen the attendant lock; she found they too had been secured. At the end of the lobby was a wall of frosted glass; beyond it was a conference room with wooden desks and benches. The light coming from the small room in the back went out at four. She hid herself when she saw an old cleaning woman locking the door to that room.

It was still not very dark in the building when the old woman latched the large front door, thereby shutting her in. The ceiling of the conference room was glass, and light came into the lobby through the frosted pane. There must have been some windows by the staircase, too: some light reached down from that direction as well.

It seemed as if the iron fish were now deep in water. She noticed a very dim light rising from the bottom of the ocean.

Part of the cylinder rested on some tiny white pebbles spread in a rectangular wooden frame. The light at the bottom of the sea was the reflection of those white pebbles faintly gleaming in the darkness. It was not yet completely dark—there was enough light to tell where the pebbles lay.

At the bottom of the deep sea she touched the white pebbles; she held them in her palm, then scooped them up in both hands. Earlier in the day she had seen a child doing the same thing. As she held the pebbles, she became convinced that the flesh of her husband's dead body on the ocean floor had not been consumed by fish and become part of their bodies; he had been dispersed and scattered about like these little stones.

Her husband had been a young, fastidious man. Perhaps she thought of him in that way because she herself had been young then. He had probably seemed fastidious because he was immature, even awkward; but she, being clumsy and even less mature, couldn't think of ways to help him relax.

"We must get a move on," he often used to say. That was the only habit of his that she could remember. No doubt the prevailing mood of the times made him use the phrase, but he also seemed to have employed it as an expression of hope that they would soon become open and intimate with one another. And perhaps he was also implying that, though young, they were a married couple and must remember to behave appropriately so that others would treat them as such. Once he even used the phrase in their marriage bed. It was much later, however, that she was able to reflect on this rather comic habit of speech: at the time she had merely listened to him with the seriousness of a student being given a lecture.

There was one more expression, come to think of it: "I'd like. . ." He would say, "I'd like you to consult me in advance," or "I'd like you not to do things like this," or "If there's a movie that you want to go and see, I'd like to know." Was he trying to convey a sense of urgency in this expression, too?

"What was it that you wanted me to do, dear?" she said. Her smile suddenly turned into a sob, and she covered her mouth with her hands. "What do you want me to do now?" she asked, overwhelmed by a surge of gentle affection for him. "I'd like you to refrain from such pointless remarks," she thought her husband would have said.

She explored the slightly curved bottom of the cylinder with her hands, then climbed into the iron fish. Once inside, she slowly straightened up, but her head bumped the ceiling before she could stand straight. Her husband, who had been taller than she, would have had to bend over even more, she thought, and she stooped down a little further. Then she took a few steps, feeling the side wall. She realized that there were rings, one or two inches in diameter, set along the wall. There must have been another curved board set on the rings, she thought, and she stooped down even more. She remained in that position for a while.

"Have you thought of anything you'd like me to do for you?" she said, squatting and rubbing the bottom part of the cylinder near her feet. Her hands touched hard, fine, sharp pieces of flesh. Again she remembered seeing a child doing just what she was doing.

Had he not wanted to see the brightness of the sun again, to breathe the fragrant air, to stretch his arms toward the sky? But he wouldn't respond to her questions and tell her what he would have liked. Her husband would not speak, and she didn't know how to help him say it. She felt the two of them had not changed since those days. A fastidious person he had been, her first husband.

Her first marriage had been so very short, and soon she had spent more years with her second husband. Over the many years of her second marriage, when she thought about her first husband, she felt that his share of her life had been unfairly small. Somehow it seemed to be her own doing, but she couldn't understand why she felt that way.

Whether because of the moon, the stars, or simply cloud, the sky seen through the glass ceiling of the conference room was not completely black. She could judge the height of the ceiling, but the floor was in total darkness. She sat on a stool, which she had brought from the conference room and placed next to the iron fish, and leaned against a wooden rail behind her.

She felt that she had remarried too soon; her second husband had been only two years older than him, though it was seven years since his death. But perhaps that thought simply allowed her to feel more freedom in her present relationship. Perhaps she wanted to feel free.

Her second husband did not want to talk about his first wife; he almost never referred to her first husband, either. Once when the conversation naturally touched on him, he said, "That's because he was on his way to the front." And simultaneously the words "departure" and "war"—words she had seen so frequently in those days—loomed before her. She saw the image of her first husband superimposed on the phrase "a man on his way to the front," and it revived his memory with double intensity. That was the first and last time her second husband mentioned him, although he didn't purposely avoid the subject. "You must have been awfully good in your previous life, being picked by a man as nice as me to start marriage all over again. Although I'm not sure I picked the best sort for retraining." His joke gently implied that she need not feel uneasy about being remarried. She had never felt more grateful to him than at that time. It was for those words, spoken very early in their marriage, that she had stayed with him, she thought. There were times, however, when she felt she had been deceived by them. And it was then she felt like doing something to find out if she had in fact been led astray.

She tried to discover what sort of disillusionment or what sense of attachment her first husband might have felt toward her when he shut himself up inside the iron fish. Had they been a specific kind of emotion? Perhaps. She couldn't help regretting that more time from her life had not been spared for him.

As she thought about these things, leaning against the wooden rail in the deep darkness, she realized that the emotions she was now experiencing for her first husband had been fostered by her life with her second, and that her first marriage had made her react with keen appreciation to the comment that her current companion had made soon after their remarriage. Was there someone, somewhere, telling her this? She thought she might be able to answer this if she could see the brightness of the sun again.

PLATONIC LOVE

Kanai Mieko

Translated by Amy Vladeck Heinrich

Kanai Mieko (1947–) was born and educated in Takasaki, and published her first collection of fiction, Ai no seikatsu *(Love Life), at the age of nineteen in 1968. In the same year she was awarded a prize for her poetry, although her first book of poems,* Madamu Juju no ie *(The House of Madam Juju, tr. 1977), was not published until 1971. She has continued to write both poetry and fiction—novels as well as short stories—since. Ibuse Masuji noted, of her first collection of stories, that her fiction creates an impression similar to the feelings one has looking at an abstract painting, and her work continues to demand an active participation from her readers. In the afterword to the collection* Puraton-teki ren'ai *(Platonic Love, 1979), she wrote: "Since it happens that the people who read a work of literature delete portions as they skim over them, read into some parts words that weren't written there, and so add to the work, the person called 'the author' is not the only one who writes a work of literature." In the title story, the narrator recounts her strange relationship with the "real author" of her stories, examining the sources of creativity and exploring the dangerous shoals of self-discovery and self-definition.*

* * *

If I ever have to prove to her that I am "the author," I suppose I would have to do it by writing an essay or a book. I became acquainted with her . . . well, in this case I don't know that "acquainted" is exactly the right word . . . at any rate, our strange relationship began when I wrote my first story. I received a letter that started: "I am the person who wrote the story published under your name." Letters with the same opening sentence began to accumulate, equal in number to the things I wrote, and while I kept trying to ignore them, the truth is I found myself completely unable to do so. As long as I continued to write these stories, she was always with me. But there was no name or address on the letters, so I had no way of communicating with this "real author." The relationship between the "real author" and myself was completely one-sided. Of course, it was only "one-sided" from my point of view; if you looked at it from hers, you might not think of it that way. But still, I didn't even know if it was really a "she" who wrote the letters.

The envelopes of the earliest letters have already yellowed. They were a variety of square white envelopes of different sizes and textures, and at various times the color of the ink was green or sepia or purple. Green and sepia and purple inks have a Taishō flavor to them, and I hate them. The handwriting had practically no individuality. As with nearly everyone after the war, the handwriting was nothing like the sort of calligraphy you would write with a brush; the characters were the kind you learn when you use a printed book as a model, and could hardly even be called clumsy. In all honesty, they were just like the characters I write —reflecting an undisciplined quality that carelessly says, if it's legible you can't complain.

Perhaps the letters were from someone who had tried to write a similar story—one could easily imagine it happening. Or some young poet my own age, speaking about my first effort, might have said, "I could write something like that in a single night," and duly caught me by surprise. Just about anyone who has read one or two things that might pass as stories could do the same sort of work. On the face of it, it did seem feasible, I suppose.

Leaving aside the unthinkable case of a story with exactly the same contents, it certainly wasn't impossible that someone had written something very similar. Aren't all "literary works" essentially the same? On reading her first letter—I remember the rustling, tactile sound when I opened the neatly folded, thick foreign paper—I admit I couldn't suppress an uncomfortable feeling that must have been some lingering sense of pride, and yet I felt it really didn't matter who the author was. The conceit of "I wrote that" became repellent all the more quickly if I was, in fact, the one who wrote it. Why shouldn't I cede the "authorship" of that story to an unknown person, and become the "author" of a different story? Yes, I would declare myself the "author" of an entirely different work. . .

Every time I published a story, a letter was invariably delivered to me, and I couldn't help getting a little fed up. Still, she was undoubtedly my most ardent and essential reader, though it was authorship she claimed, and chance might even prove it true. In any event, I first came to realize that one particular story had been written (by her? by me?) as a result of a letter from her. I kept this secret for quite a while because I didn't know how to explain it, and because for some unknown reason I felt reluctant to tell anyone about her.

Yet whatever I wrote, she would doubtless insist that she had written it herself. I might ask, "When could I possibly have read what you wrote?" and with a little smile—unconsciously I was inclined to imagine her smile as beautiful—she would say, "Don't you even remember that?" Naturally I couldn't even try to ask her questions, but simply read what she wrote, as if it were a privilege I'd been singled out for. Our relationship was concerned exclusively with the writing of stories.

In a sense I was made to suffer because of her, but gradually a curiosity about her made me wish that I knew what kind of person she was, what kind of life she led, what sort of things she was attached to, what experiences she had had, what on earth she thought about. I tried to give her a body. But I was filled with doubts, including, in fact, the question of whether she was a man or a woman. Frankly, I despised my own body, and it was painful to think of the "real author's" body as something beautiful. I sang to myself like a poet in love. You have a body!—oh, the wonder of it! Suspended in my (our) dreams. . . I even thought that if she and not I had written those few slight, inadequate works (and wasn't the description itself a means of scorning her existence?), then I would have the satisfaction of knowing I had nothing to do with them. But it was my hand that had formed those characters, or remained locked in my inability to write them. I even thought of asking other writers if they had ever received letters from someone who called herself the "real author." I might have discovered that I was not the only victim of a person who played malicious, complicated, and even fairly sophisticated pranks. There was no evidence that this wasn't a vicious and persistent piece of mischief.

I don't mean to suggest, of course, that she bothered me twenty-four hours a day. I had my own life, and I was perfectly able to enjoy it. It was a commonplace, ordinary life; I was bored occasionally, but not so often that the boredom gnawed at me, and I had no interest in the experiences that seem to make reality precious only as misfortune makes it tangible. In short, I had probably grown used to getting by without the pathetic confusion to which younger, more innocent sensibilities are so susceptible; the feelings that result from encounters with a too precise and lucidly contoured world. When I feel constrained by an overbearing world in which I cannot write, am I not already trying to start to write? So, as must be the case with any writer, rather than read my own stories (but she doesn't say that: she says the stories *I wrote*), I preferred the many works of other writers I enjoyed. And this in spite of the jealousy that goes with reading them.

I decided to go to Yugawara and take along the notes for a new story I had to get started on, together with some pieces I wanted to revise for a collection; I also took several books I hadn't yet read, and a manuscript which some strange temptation had made me commit myself to write on "Discussing My Own Work." Of course there was some doubt about how qualified I was to comment on "my own work" but, leaving that aside, I had enough money from my royalties to be able to stay at a hot spring for a while. And I must admit I was drawn to the tradition of writers staying at hot spring resorts to work.

Why is it that, try as we might to avoid discussing our own work, or the work we plan to write, in the end we wind up telling all? In spite of being enjoined to silence, words emerge. . . We start with the desire to discuss the truth, and in practice we go on to speak in terms that veil the truth. What is required and anticipated in the act we call "discussing one's own work"? Perhaps it is a form of confession. And within that act that pretends to be confession, I dream of a form in which, concealed, lie books that have ingeniously turned into illusions.

In the end, I had nothing to confess. It was just that in reading my own stories I felt a curious passion. Just supposing that the story were really something she had written, it might have been exactly because I was already her reader that I felt so strong a passion. Still, I had no more than a title for the story I planned to write: "Platonic Love." And who on earth would write it? She or I?

As I expected, "Platonic Love" didn't progress a single line; there wasn't a word written in my notebook, and I spent five days just walking during the day and reading or drinking alone at night. I tried to focus "Discussing My Own Work" on some short pieces I had written three years earlier, but the words turned out to be all hers, all taken from her letters. In an effort to resist her, I tried writing about the rabbit's pelt that was nailed to the grayish brown wooden door of a grocery store in Hanamaki (exposing the skin where the spilled blood had turned to glue), or about the dream of rabbits I'd had in the berth of a train on the way to Iwate. I tried to remember the winter sky smothering the town of Hanamaki and the rows of streets, the translucent white and bloodless sky over those arteries of gray and brown and pale blue in an ordinary, characterless, provincial town. But as I feared, I wasn't sure if I had actually been there. The requisites for life, the liveliness that embodies a town, at times even the confusion, were quite removed from the Hanamaki I seemed to know, and the town disappeared in the labyrinths of my memory. The town where "the soul of the silent city made me choose the road" had lost its form, and even the untanned rabbit's pelt, which I surely must have seen, had disappeared completely. Weren't they things I had read about once in some story? It wasn't I who saw or wrote about them. No, that pelt, with the brown, red, and purple gluelike blood and fat adhering to it, was nailed up in a story I had read, wasn't it?

It was so quiet in the setting sun in that very seedy, amateurishly run inn that there seemed to be no other guests, and the mountains that used to form the view from the west windows were blocked from sight by the gray concrete building of a large tourist hotel, so of course the guest rates were cheap enough to allow quite a long stay. A clumsy picture of a crane with a sly expression was painted on the sliding door, yellowed over the years by the late afternoon sun, and a scroll with a poem about the pathos of an egret in the snow was hanging in the alcove. A small black-and-white television right in front of it, an old low wooden table, stained all over with rings from beer glasses, with a tea set on it, a mirror stand draped with a faded length of printed silk, and a clothes rack with three hangers were all the furnishings in the room. Every day I had a bath a dusk, then sadly drank alone in silence, eating the home-style cooking prepared by the landlady: sweet-and-sour pork, sashimi, and salad with store-bought mayonnaise. And if I had to say what the great virtue of eating alone is, it would simply be that if you read a book while eating, no one is offended. Shadowing me on this trip (and how many little trips have I taken alone!) was the constant recollection that I had brought along the notes for my story. I would remember to try and listen for the voice calling me to start the story I had been as yet unable to write, and in the middle of the bath, where the surface of the water shone like pink metal in the setting sun, I would be moved to tears. I would think that the absent "he" or "she" who had withdrawn from the protagonist was really the unwritten story itself, and I cried as my feelings were exposed. My body melted into the large bath, and it was already not a body, nor was it hot water that weighed upon and enveloped it, wrapping it in warm gentleness, but something other than me floating in the water that united and merged me with all existence. In the rose-colored sunlight trembling in the milk-white mist of steam and silence and stillness, time was stretched out, and the bath would begin to expand as though in a dream within a dream, and I would not be the one dreaming, but she would be the one dreaming and I just a character in that dream; and then that eerie vision would melt into the water again. Suspended in my (our) dreams. . .

After lunch one day, when I was walking along a road by a mountain stream that flowed through the park, a woman I didn't know spoke to me. In spite of her hesitant manner, she began speaking with a certain obtrusiveness. She spoke as if she knew all about me, and intuitively I realized that this very woman was the "real author." The image I had secretly cherished of her reflected an unconscious vanity and hope, and, as I wrote earlier, was associated with the word "beautiful"; but it was rude to the "real author" to look so crestfallen when I realized that it wasn't really appropriate. (Not only is it simply not my style to explain in detail how it was inappropriate, but it would be discourteous.) And then she asked me to join her for lunch since she hadn't eaten, and, unable to resist, I answered that I had eaten but would keep her company with a cup of tea or something. We sat opposite each other at a window table in a coffee shop near the park entrance, where she ordered the most expensive roast beef sandwich, and crabmeat salad and coffee; I ordered just a cup of coffee. I actually don't remember most of what we talked about, except that she discussed the as-yet-unwritten story "Platonic Love," accompanied by the crunching sound of lettuce and celery being chewed. Yes, the "real author" discussed "Platonic Love," pausing to lick off her fingers any juice that dropped from her roast beef sandwich. Not only did I miss my chance to ask her what her motives were in sending me those letters, I also had to pay the bill for her sandwich, salad, and three cups of coffee. It was about three o'clock when I returned to the inn.

I know I should have written my "Platonic Love," but now I feel no great desire nor any great need to do so.

When I got back home, there was a letter from the "real author," as I expected, but it contained no particular thank-you for the lunch; it was the manuscript of "Platonic Love" that she had spoken about then.

I've tried and tried to convince myself that I should be able to get by without reading it. It would be extremely simple to throw it in the garbage or burn it without reading it. It would be easy to stretch out my hand to the letter on my desk, with my name written in that awful handwriting (which looks exactly as if I had written it myself), and dispose of it so completely that I would never have to think it had ever existed. I could take the letters (all the letters she's sent) out into the garden, douse them with kerosene, and strike a match. I would have to fill a bucket with water and be careful to control the fire. In a very short time, flames would lick at those letters and swallow them up, sending up a pale purple smoke; and only a light pile of crumbling black ashes would remain, to be drenched with water and trampled into the ground. But I sink into my chair with the hopeless feeling that nothing would have been destroyed. In the end I will probably publish "Platonic Love." And I will probably say it is my work.

THE CRUSHED PELLET

Kaikō Takeshi

Translated by Cecilia Segawa Seigle

Kaikō Takeshi was born in Osaka in 1930. His keen sympathy for the human condition has its origins in his own suffering and starvation in postwar Japan and the pressure of having to feed his mother and sisters at the age of fourteen after his father's death. But it was also those physically and spiritually deprived years that laid the ground for his development as a tough, vigorous, and sensitive writer.

Although he barely attended Osaka City College, taking one odd job after another, he did manage to get a law degree before joining the Suntory Whiskey Company and setting up its advertising department almost single-handedly. After receiving the Akutagawa Prize in 1958 for his Hadaka no ōsama *(The Naked King, tr. 1977), he left his job and concentrated on writing short stories and novels on large-scale sociological themes. In early works such as* Rubōki *(The Runaway, 1959; tr. 1977),* Nihon sanmon opera *(A Japanese Threepenny Opera, 1959), and* Robinson no matsuei *(The Descendants of Robinson Crusoe, 1960), he deliberately avoided an autobiographical approach both in terms of material and emotional involvement, achieving an objectivity that resembled that of a social historian. Kaikō was sent by one of Japan's leading papers to Israel to cover the Eichmann trial as a special correspondent, but it was his participation in the Vietnam War in 1964–65, a veritable purgatory for him, that proved a turning point and provided new material he could treat with passion. For virtually the first time, he was moved to reveal himself in his work, and in* Kagayakeru yami *(Into a Black Sun, 1968; tr. 1980) and* Natsu no yami

(Darkness in Summer, 1969; tr. 1973), both prize-winning novels, his involvement with his subject matter is sharply personal. The first is a brilliant exposition of corrupt Saigon and its ordinary people caught between "the devil and the deep blue sea" and patiently coping with the difficulties of daily life—a journey culminating in the novelist's shattering experience of the battle front. The other is about a writer who, devastated by his Vietnam experience, escapes to Europe. Reviving his affair with a former girlfriend, another Japanese exile, he slowly heals and recharges himself only to return to Vietnam. Kaikō is a master of the word picture employing all the sensory elements—smell, taste, sound, touch—to evoke an intense and accurate atmosphere. This uncommon skill and the power of his compassionate observation have won him several prizes in the field of reportage alone.

The present story, Tama kudakeru *(The Crushed Pellet, 1978), delves into the question of artistic freedom in a dictatorship, and was awarded the first Kawabata Yasunari Prize in 1979. It shows Kaikō's ability to embrace human beings as they are, and his sensitive reaction to a great writer's death and to a friend's grief over it. The curious title is symbolic. The character for* tama *(ball or pellet) in Chinese* (yü) *also stands for jade, or something precious. The two characters in the title together form a compound word suggesting a heroic, crushing death, a term familiar to Japanese of the war generation. The fact that the ball in this case is only human skin seems to hint at the fragility of the human being.*

* * *

Late one morning, I awoke in the capital of a certain country and found myself—not changed overnight into a large brown beetle, nor feeling exactly on top of the world—merely ready to go home. For about an hour I remained between the sheets, wriggling, pondering, and scrutinizing my decision from all angles until it became clear that my mind was made up. Then I slipped out of bed. I walked down a boulevard where the aroma of freshly baked bread drifted from glimmering shop windows, and went into the first airline office I encountered to make a reservation on a flight to Tokyo via the southern route. Since I wanted to spend a day or two in Hong Kong, it had to be the southern route. Once I had reserved a seat and pushed through the glass door to the street, I felt as though a period had been written at the end of a long, convoluted paragraph. It was time for a new paragraph to begin and a story to unroll, but I had no idea where it would lead. I felt no exhilaration in thoughts of the future. When I left Japan, there had been fresh, if anxious, expectations moving vividly through the vague unknown. But going home was no more than bringing a sentence to a close, and opening a paragraph. I had no idea what lay ahead, but it aroused no apprehension or sense of promise. Until a few years ago, I had felt excitement—fading rapidly, perhaps, but there nonetheless—about changing paragraphs. But as I grew older, I found myself feeling less and less of anything. Where once there had been a deep pool of water, mysterious and cool, I now saw a bone-dry riverbed.

I returned to the hotel and began to pack, feeling the familiar fungus starting to form on my back and shoulders. I took the elevator to the lobby, settled my account, and deposited my body and suitcase on the shuttle bus to the airport. I tried to be as active as I could, but the fungus had already begun to spread. On my shoulders, chest, belly, and legs the invisible mold proliferated, consuming me inwardly but leaving my outer form untouched. The closer I came to Tokyo, the faster it would grow, and dreary apathy would gradually take hold.

Imprisoned in the giant aluminum cylinder, speeding through a sea of cotton clouds, I thought over the past several months spent drifting here and there. I already felt nostalgia for those months, as though they had occurred a decade ago instead of ending only yesterday. Reluctantly, I was heading home to a place whose familiarity I had hated, and therefore fled. I went home crestfallen, like a soldier whose army has surrendered before fighting any battle. Each repetition of this same old process was merely adding yet another link to a chain of follies. Unnerved by this thought, I remained rigid, strapped to my narrow seat. I would probably forget these feelings briefly in the hubbub of customs at Haneda Airport. But the moment I opened the glass door to the outside world, that swarming fungus would surround me. Within a month or two, I would turn into a snowman covered with a fuzzy blue-gray mold. I knew this would happen, yet I had no choice but to go home, for I had found no cure elsewhere. I was being catapulted back to my starting point because I had failed to escape.

I entered a small hotel on the Kowloon Peninsula and turned the pages of my tattered memo book to find the telephone number of Chang Li-jen. I always gave him a call when I was there; if he was out, I would leave my name and the name of the hotel, since my Chinese was barely good enough to order food at restaurants. Then I would telephone again at nine or ten in the morning, and Chang's lively, fluent Japanese would burst into my ear. We would decide to meet in a few hours at the corner of Nathan Road, or at the pier of the Star Ferry, or sometimes at the entrance to the monstrous Tiger Balm Garden. Chang was a prematurely wizened man in his fifties, who always walked with his head down; when he approached a friend, he would suddenly lift his head and break into a big, toothy smile, his eyes and mouth gaping all at once. When he laughed, his mouth seemed to crack up to his ears. I found it somehow warm and reassuring each time I saw those large stained teeth, and felt the intervening years drop away. As soon as he smiled and began to chatter about everything, the fungus seemed to retreat a little. But it would never disappear, and the moment I was the least bit off guard, it would revive and batten on me. While I talked with Chang, though, it was usually subdued, waiting like a dog. I would walk shoulder to shoulder with him, telling him about the fighting in Africa, the Near East, Southeast Asia, or whatever I had just seen. Chang almost bounded along, listening to my words, clicking his tongue and exclaiming. And when my story was over, he would tell me about the conditions in China, citing the editorials of the left- and right-wing papers and often quoting Lu Hsün.

I had met Chang some years back through a Japanese newspaperman. The journalist had gone home soon afterward, but I had made a point of seeing Chang every time I had an occasion to visit Hong Kong. I knew his telephone number but had never been invited to his home, and I knew scarcely anything about his job or his past. Since he had graduated from a Japanese university, his Japanese was flawless, and I was aware that he had an extraordinary knowledge of Japanese literature; and yet, beyond the fact that he worked in a small trading company and occasionally wrote articles for various newspapers to earn some pocket money, I knew nothing about his life.

He would lead me through the hustle of Nathan Road, commenting, if he spotted a sign on a Swiss watch shop saying "King of Ocean Mark," that it meant an Omega Seamaster; or stopping at a small bookstore to pick up a pamphlet with crude illustrations of tangled bodies and show me the caption, "Putting oneself straight forward," explaining that it meant the missionary position. He also taught me that the Chinese called hotels "wine shops" and restaurants "wine houses," though no one knew the reason why.

For the last several years, one particular question had come up whenever we saw each other, but we had never found an answer to it. In Tokyo one would have laughed it off as nonsense, but here it was a serious issue. If you were forced to choose between black and white, right and left, all and nothing—to choose a side or risk being killed—what would you do? If you didn't want to choose either side, but silence meant death, what would you do? How would you escape? There are two chairs and you can sit in either one, but you can't remain standing between them. You know, moreover, that though you're free to make your choice, you are expected to sit in one particular chair; make the wrong choice, and the result is certain: "Kill!" they'll shout—"Attack!" "Exterminate!" In the circumstances, what kind of answer can you give to avoid sitting in either chair, and yet satisfy their leader, at least for the time being? Does history provide a precedent? China's beleaguered history, its several thousand years of troubled rise and fall, must surely have fostered and crystallized some sort of wisdom on the subject. Wasn't there some example, some ingenious answer there?

I was the one who had originally brought up this question. We were in a small dim sum restaurant on a back street. I had asked it quite casually, posing a riddle as it were, but Chang's shoulders fidgeted and his eyes turned away in confusion. He pushed the dim sum dishes aside and, pulling out a cigarette, stroked it several times with fingers thin as chicken bones. He lit it carefully and inhaled deeply and slowly; he then blew out the smoke and murmured:

"'Neither a horse nor a tiger'—it's the same old story. In old China, there was a phrase, '*Ma-ma, hu-hu,*' that meant a noncommittal 'neither one thing nor the other.' The characters were horse-horse, tiger-tiger. It's a clever expression, and the attitude was called Ma-huism. But they'd probably kill you if you gave an answer like that today. It sounds vague, but actually you're making the ambiguity of your feelings known. It wouldn't work. They'd kill you on the spot. So, how to answer . . . you've raised a difficult question, haven't you?"

I asked him to think it over until I saw him next time. Chang had become pensive, motionless, as though shocked into deep thought. He left his dumplings untouched, and when I called this to his attention, he smiled crookedly and scratched something on a piece of paper. He handed it to me and said, "You should remember this when you're eating with a friend." He had written "*Mo t'an kuo shih,*" which means roughly "Don't discuss politics." I apologized profusely for my thoughtlessness.

Since then, I have stopped in Hong Kong and seen Chang at intervals of one year, sometimes two. After going for a walk or having a meal (I made sure we had finished eating) I always asked him the same question. He would cock his head thoughtfully or smile ruefully and ask me to wait a little longer. On my part, I could only pose the question, because I had no wisdom to impart; so the riddle stayed unsolved for many years, its cruel face still turned toward us. In point of fact, if there were a clever way of solving the riddle, everyone would have used it—and a new situation requiring a new answer would have arisen, perpetuating the dilemma. A shrewd answer would lose its sting in no time, and the question would remain unanswered. On occasion, however—for instance when Chang told me about Laoshê—I came very close to discerning an answer.

Many years ago, Laoshê visited Japan as leader of a literary group and stopped in Hong Kong on his way back to China. Chang had been given an assignment to interview him for a newspaper and went to the hotel where Laoshê was staying. Laoshê kept his appointment but said nothing that could be turned into an article, and when Chang kept asking how the intellectuals had fared in post-revolutionary China, the question was always evaded. When this had happened several times, Chang began to think that Laoshê's power as a writer had probably waned. Then Laoshê began talking about country cooking, and continued for three solid hours. Eloquently and colorfully he described an old restaurant somewhere in Szechwan, probably Chungking or Chengtu, where a gigantic cauldron had simmered for several centuries over a fire that had never gone out. Scallions, Chinese lettuce, potatoes, heads of cows, pigs' feet—just about anything and everything was thrown into the pot. Customers sat around the cauldron and ladled the stew into soup bowls; and the charge was determined by adding up the number of empty bowls each person had beside him. This was the sole subject that Laoshê discussed for three hours, in minute and vivid detail—what was cooked, how the froth rose in the pot, what the stew tasted like, how many bowls one could eat. When he finished talking he disappeared.

"He left so suddenly there was no way to stop him," said Chang. "He was magnificent. . . Among Laoshê's works, I prefer *Rickshaw Boy* to *Four Generations Under One Roof*. When Laoshê spoke, I felt as though I had just reread *Rickshaw Boy* after many years. His poignant satire, the humor and sharp observation in that book—that's what I recognized in him. I felt tremendously happy and moved when I left the hotel. When I got home, I was afraid I might forget the experience if I slept, so I had a stiff drink and went over the story, savoring every word."

"You didn't write an article?"

"Oh, yes, I wrote something, but I just strung together some fancy-sounding words, that's all. I wouldn't swear to it, but he seemed to trust me when he talked like that. And the story was really too delicious for the newspaper."

Chang's craggy face broke into a great wrinkled smile. I felt as though I had seen the flash of a sword, a brief glimpse of pain, grief, and fury. I could do nothing but look down in silence. Evidently there was a narrow path, something akin to an escape route between the chairs, but its danger was immeasurable. Didn't the English call this kind of situation "between the devil and the deep blue sea?"

Late in the afternoon of the day before my departure for Tokyo, Chang and I were strolling along when we came to a sign that read "Heavenly Bath Hall." Chang stopped and explained.

"This is a *tsao t'ang*, a bathhouse. It's not just a soak in a bath, though; you can have the dirt scraped off your body, get a good massage, have the calluses removed from your feet and your nails clipped. All you have to do is take off your clothes and lie down. If you feel sleepy, you just doze off and sleep as long as you like. Obviously some are better than others, but this one is famous for the thorough service you get. And when you leave, they'll give you the ball of dirt they scraped off you; it's a good souvenir. How would you like to try it? They use three kinds of cloth, rough, medium, and soft. They wrap them around their hands and rub you down. A surprising amount of dead skin will come off, you know, enough to make a ball of it. It's fun."

I nodded my consent, and he led me inside the door and talked to the man at the counter. The man put down his newspaper, listened to Chang, and with a smile gestured to me to come in. Chang said he had some errands to do, but would come to the airport the next day to see me off. He left me at the bathhouse.

When the bathkeeper stood up I found he was tall, with muscular shoulders and hips. He beckoned, and I followed him down a dim corridor with shabby walls, then into a cubicle with two simple beds. One was occupied by a client wrapped in a white towel and stretched out on his stomach, while a nail-cutter held his leg, paring skin off his heel as though fitting a horseshoe. The bathkeeper gestured to me, and I emptied my pockets and gave him my billfold, passport, and watch. He took them and put them in the drawer of a night table, then locked it with a sturdy, old-fashioned padlock. The key was chained to his waist with a soiled cord. He smiled and slapped his hip a couple of times as though to reassure me before going out. I took off all my clothes. A small, good-looking boy in a white robe, with a head like an arrowhead bulb, came in and wrapped my hips from behind with a towel and slung another over my shoulder. I followed the boy into the dark corridor, slippers on my feet. Another boy was waiting in the room leading to the bath, and quickly peeled off my towel before pushing the door open onto a gritty concrete floor. A large rusty nozzle on the wall splashed hot water over me, and I washed my body.

The bathtub was a vast, heavy rectangle of marble with a three-foot ledge. A client just out of the tub was sprawled face down on a towel, like a basking seal. A naked assistant was rubbing the man's buttocks with a cloth wrapped around his hand. Timidly, I stepped into the water and found it not hot, nor cool, but soft and smooth, oiled by the bodies of many men. There was none of the stinging heat of the Japanese public bath. It was a thick heat and heavy, slow-moving. Two washers, a big muscular man and a thin one, stood by the wall, quite naked except for their bundled hands, waiting for me to come out. The large man's penis looked like a snail, while the other's was long, plump, and purple, with all the appearance of debauchery. It hung with the weight and languor of a man with a long track record, making me wonder how many thousands of polishings it would take to look like that. It was a masterpiece that inspired admiration rather than envy, appended to a figure that might have stepped from the Buddhist hell of starvation. But his face showed no pride or conceit; he was simply and absentmindedly waiting for me to get out of the tub. I covered myself with my hands and stepped out of the warm water. He spread a bath towel quickly and instructed me to lie down.

As Chang had told me, there were three kinds of rubbing cloths. The coarse, hempen one was for the arms, buttocks, back, and legs. Another cotton cloth, softer than the first, was for the sides and underarms. The softest was gauzy and used on the soles of the feet, the crotch, and other sensitive areas. He changed the cloth according to the area, tightly wrapping it around his hand like a bandage before rubbing my skin. He took one hand or leg at a time, shifted me around, turned me over, then over again, always with an expert, slightly rough touch which remained essentially gentle and considerate. After a while, he seemed to sigh and I heard him murmuring "*Aiya. . .*" under his breath. I half opened my eyes and found my arms, my belly, my entire body covered with a scale of gray dead skin like that produced by a schoolboy's eraser. The man seemed to sense a challenge and began to apply more strength. It was less a matter of rubbing than of peeling off a layer of skin without resorting to surgery, the patient task of removing a layer of dirt closely adhering to the body. Talking to himself in amusement, he moved toward my head, then my legs, absorbed in his meticulous work. I had ceased to be embarrassed and, dropping my hands to my sides, I placed my whole body at his disposal. I let him take my right hand or left hand as he worked. Once I had surrendered my body to him the whole operation was extremely relaxing, like wallowing in warm mud. Soap was applied, then washed off with warm water; I was told to soak in the tub, and when I came out, again warm water was poured over me several times. Then he wiped me thoroughly with a steamed towel as hot as a lump of coal.

Finally—smiling, as though to say "Here you are!"—he placed a pellet of skin on my palm. It was like a gray ball of tofu mash. The moist, tightly squeezed sphere was the size of a smallish plover's egg. With so many dead cells removed, my skin had become as tender as a baby's, clear and fresh, and all my cells, replenished with new serum, rejoiced aloud.

I returned to the dressing room and tumbled into bed. The good-looking boy brought me a cup of hot jasmine tea. I drank it lying in bed, and with each mouthful felt as though a spurt of perspiration had shot from my body. With a fresh towel, the boy gently dried me. The nail-cutter entered and clipped my toes and fingernails, trimmed the thick skin off my heels, and shaved my corns, changing his instruments each time. When the work was completed, he left the room in silence. In his place, a masseur entered and began to work without a word. Strong, sensitive fingers and palms crept over my body, searching and finding the nests and roots of strained muscles, pressing, rubbing, pinching, patting, and untangling the knots. Every one of these employees was scrupulous in delivering his services. They concentrated on the work, unstinting of time and energy, their solemn delicacy incomparable. Their skill made me think of a heavyweight fighter skipping rope with the lightness of a feather. A cool mist emanated from the masseur's strong fingers. My weight melted away and I dissolved into a sweet sleep.

"My shirt."

Chang looked at me quizzically.

"That's the shirt I was wearing until yesterday."

When Chang came to my hotel room the next day, I pointed out the dirty pellet on the table. For some reason, only a twisted smile appeared on his face. He took out a packet of tea, enough for one pot, and said that he had bought me the very best tea in Hong Kong; I was to drink it in Tokyo. Then he fell silent, staring blankly. I told him about the washer, the nail-clipper, the boys, the tea, the sleep. I described everything in detail and reveled in my praise of these men, who knew one's body and one's needs so thoroughly, and were devoted to their work. One might have called them anarchists without bombs. Chang nodded only sporadically and smiled at whatever I said, but soon fell to gazing darkly at the wall. His preoccupation was so obvious that I was forced to stop talking and begin packing my suitcase. I had been completely atomized in the dressing room of the bathhouse. Even when I had revived and walked out of the door there seemed to be some space between my clothing and my flesh. I had felt chilly, and staggered at every sound and smell, every gust of air. But one night's sleep restored my bones and muscles to their proper position, and a thin but opaque coating covered my skin, shrouding the insecurity of stark nakedness. Dried up and shriveled, the ball of dirt looked as if it might crumble at the lightest touch of a finger, so I carefully wrapped it in layers of tissue and put it in my pocket.

We arrived at the airport, where I checked in and took care of all the usual details. When only the parting handshake remained before I left, Chang suddenly broke his silence. A friend in the press had called him last night. Laoshê had died in Peking. It was rumored that he was beaten to death, surrounded by the children of the Red Guard. There was another rumor that he had escaped this ignominy by jumping from the second-floor window of his home. Another source reported that he had jumped into a river. The circumstances were not at all clear, but it seemed a certainty that Laoshê had died an unnatural death. The fact seemed inescapable.

"Why?" I asked.

"I don't know."

"What did he do to be denounced?"

"I don't know."

"What sort of things was he writing recently?"

"I haven't read them. I don't know."

I looked at Chang, almost trembling myself. Tears were about to brim from his eyes; he held his narrow shoulders rigid. He had lost his usual calm, his gaiety, humor, all, but without anger or rancor; he just stood there like a child filled with fear and despair. This man, who must have withstood the most relentless of hardships, was helpless, his head hanging, his eyes red, like a child astray in a crowd.

"It's time for you to go," he said. "Please come again."

I was silent.

"Take care of yourself," Chang said and held out his hand timidly; he shook mine lightly. Then he turned around, his head still downcast, and slowly disappeared into the crowd.

I boarded the plane and found my seat. When I had fastened the seat belt, a vision from long ago suddenly returned to me. I had once visited Laoshê at his home in Peking. I now saw the lean, sinewy old writer rise amid a profusion of potted crysanthemums and turn his silent, penetrating gaze upon me. Only his eyes and the cluster of flowers were visible, distant and clear. Distracted, I took the wrapping from my pocket and opened it. The gray pellet, now quite dried up, had crumbled into dusty powder.

THE CLEVER RAIN TREE

Ōe Kenzaburō

Translated by Brett de Bary
and Carolyn Haynes

There are surely few readers of this volume for whom "The Clever Rain Tree" (Atama no ii rein tsurii, *1980) will prove a first encounter with the distinctive fictional world of Ōe Kenzaburō. Published more than two decades after Ōe's youthful "*Shiiku*" (The Catch, 1958; tr. 1959) won him the coveted Akutagawa Prize at the age of twenty-three, "The Clever Rain Tree" represents the mature style of a writer whose prolific output has gained him recognition, both at home and abroad, as one of Japan's leading postwar novelists.*

Ōe, the third son in a family of seven, was born on January 31, 1935, in the village in rural Shikoku that appears, in various mythologized forms, as a recurrent motif in his fiction. Ōe was six at the start of the Pacific War, lost his father and grandmother at the age of nine, and, as a ten-year-old, learned of the atomic bombing of Hiroshima and Japan's unconditional surrender. He has since traced his perceptions of a "void behind the print"—that awareness of the tenuous link between writing and reality which infuses his work—to his childhood in this isolated village from which the world was knowable only through printed words or the occasional, threatening appearance of enemy warplanes.

Ōe's adolescent years overlapped with those of the American Occupation and the abrupt "reversal of values" (kachi tenkan, *as Japanese historians phrase it) experienced by Japanese during the recovery from the war. Ōe entered Tokyo University in 1954, completing a major in French literature and a thesis on the fiction of Jean-Paul Sartre in 1959, as the* country became enveloped in the political turmoil surrounding the renewal of the U.S.-Japan Security Treaty. In 1960, Ōe married Yukari, daughter of the well-known writer Itami Mansaku. His fiction from this early period was acclaimed (and sometimes deprecated) for its unusual combination of sensuous lyricism, sexual farce, and philosophical inquiry incorporating such Sartrean concepts as "authenticity" and "bad faith." These works often included, as well, a dimension of political allegory reflecting concerns that were Ōe's legacy from the Occupation period and the anti-Security Treaty struggle: the multiple dimensions of Japan's postwar dependence on the United States, the attendant confused sense of cultural identity, the persisting questions of war responsibility, the emperor system, and ultranationalist ideology.

Ōe's youthful fiction, however, was radically transformed by two events in the year 1963: the birth in June of a first son with severe brain damage, and a visit to Hiroshima in August to attend the Ninth World Conference Against Atomic and Hydrogen Bombs. In 1964, Ōe won the Shinchōsha Literary Prize for Kojinteki na taiken (A Personal Matter, tr. 1968), a novel that describes a father's nighmarish struggle to embrace the existence of his mentally retarded son. In 1965, an account of Ōe's confrontation with A-bomb survivors was published as Hiroshima Nōto (Hiroshima Notes, tr. 1981), in which Ōe links his journey to Hiroshima with his despair over the son "lying in an incubator with no hope of recovery." This coupling of the motifs of the idiot son, symbol of purity and madness, and the specter of nuclear apocalypse has since become a key feature of Ōe's major work. Moreover, in the years since 1965, Ōe's fiction has displayed increasing versatility of theme and complexity of structure as he has cut loose from the conventions of the realistic novel to explore realms of the fantastic and grotesque more appropriate for depiction of life in the era of nuclear war. Man'en gannen no futtobōru (The Silent Cry, 1967; tr. 1974), the two-volume Kōzui wa waga tamashii ni oyobite (The Flood Has Come in unto My Soul, 1973), and Dōjidai geemu (A Contemporary Game, 1979) are long, multilayered novels with mythical, political, and epistemological themes.

"The Clever Rain Tree" is a shorter, light work published just after Ōe completed the novel Dōjidai geemu. The tale is set in Hawaii, where a cross-cultural confrontation, an "East-West dialogue," becomes an occa-

sion for the revelation of the limitations of human language and the precariousness of the distinction between imagination and perception (a distinction perhaps symbolized by the two differently shaped darknesses, one enveloping the other, associated with the clever rain tree). The pervasive, dreamlike tone of the work is characteristic of the mature Ōe, as is the colorful, parodic sketching in of a political context through allusions to American deserters from the Vietnam War, the Iranian revolution, and the taking of hostages. The image of the cosmic tree that appears in this story has been developed more extensively in his collection of stories, "Rein tsurii" o kiku onnatachi *(Women Who Listen to the Rain Tree, 1982).*

* * *

"You'd rather see the tree than these people, wouldn't you?" inquired the American woman of German descent as she ushered me from the room jammed with partygoers, along a wide corridor, and onto the porch where we faced a broad expanse of darkness. Enveloped in the laughter and hubbub behind me, I gazed into the damp-smelling dark. That the greater part of this darkness was filled with a single huge tree was evident from the fact that at the rim of the darkness the faintly reflecting shapes of innumerable layers of radiating, board-like roots spread out in our direction. I gradually realized that these shapes like black board fences were glowing softly with a luster of grayish blue. The tree—how many hundred tree-years old was it, with its well-developed board-roots?—in this darkness eclipsed the sky and the sea far below the slope. From where we stood beneath the eaves of the porch of this large New England-style building, even at broad noon one could probably see no further than its shins, to speak of the tree anthropomorphically. It befitted the old style of the building, or rather its actual age, that around this house whose sole illumination was so quietly restrained the tree in the garden formed a wall of total darkness.

"The local name for this tree, which you said you wanted to know, is 'rain tree,' but this one of ours is a particularly clever rain tree." So said the American woman, a middle-aged woman whom I called Agatha, since we didn't know each other's surnames. . . Writing like this smacks of a romance set abroad, like those we see from time to time in contemporary Japanese novels, whose hero is a compatriot proficient in foreign languages. In my case, however, it was with no such leisure that I passed these ten days. I was attending a seminar sponsored by the University of Hawaii's East-West Center on the issue of "Reappraisal of Cultural Exchange and Traditions." As for my English ability, it was such that I mistook three delegates from India for delegates from Canada, and didn't realize until halfway through the conference that they were actually from the Kannada region of India. In fact, since the conference was dedicated to the memory of the Indian humanist Coomaraswamy, there were participants from various regions in India, fluent in many distinct forms of English. Listening to the presentation of a Jewish Indian poet from Bombay, for example—his manner of speaking was extremely Indian, yet there was something unmistakably Jewish about it—I was able to enjoy his sense of humor, but if I didn't question him about each point after his lecture, it was difficult to give my response in the following sessions.

The participant from the American mainland, the poet who defined an era as spokesman for the beatnik generation, would arrive at the meeting every morning with a youth who looked physically exhausted and psychologically scarred (at least to me he appeared in this pitiful state) and would cast tender glances toward the youth, who napped on the floor behind the round table where the seminar participants were seated, saying "He is my wife." Although the speech of this New Yorker so combined discipline and unpredictability in its unique way of unfolding that I could hardly follow his English, he elicited my comments on the so-called haiku of his I've inserted below. He even sketched on a napkin from the cafeteria the scene depicted: a snowy mountain glimpsed through the wings of a fly mashed on a window. In brief, he was determined to get an authentic critique from a writer from the land of haiku. Having thus become his friend, I could hardly sit through his presentation daydreaming of other things.

> Snow mountain fields
> seen thru transparent wings

of a fly on windowpane.

At the end of the schedule of meetings that day I returned to the student dormitory which served as our lodging—a girls' dormitory, at that—intending to rest before the nightly party, when I was accosted by an American, a man of small stature with damaged facial muscles, who seemed to be in great torment. He had apparently worked until five years ago assisting deserters from the Vietnam War in a provincial city on the Japan Sea coast. At that time he became aware that rumors were spreading among his co-workers that he was a spy for the CIA, so he quietly slipped off to Tokyo and returned to America from there. "I imagine the leaders of the movement still think of me as a spy. Even if I wanted to renew contact with them now, I can't remember their names myself. I've always been hard of hearing, which makes it difficult for me to understand the English spoken by the Japanese, to say nothing of Japanese itself. Actually, even when I was with the movement, this led to a lot of misunderstandings and I was often confused."

This garrulous young American had become so distraught over the insubstantial rumors that he was a spy that he was now in a private institution for the psychologically disturbed. There are many classes of such institutions here in Hawaii, from the very expensive on down. This fellow lived in the kind that charged little more than the actual cost of living, yet he still went out to work during the day to earn his expenses. But how was I to comfort this poor, tormented young American, this character whose small frame was completely covered with grime (apparently related to his work)? This thoroughly depressed man who kept cocking his head toward me like a bird as if to press his ear to my mouth, yet who still couldn't grasp with his bad ear what my English—a Japanese English—meant.

Engulfing the foreground of the darkness, only the expanse of the margin of the tree's well-developed roots was faintly discernible. . . It seemed that the middle-aged woman who showed me the tree also ran a private psychiatric clinic like those the tormented American had described, this one plainly of the higher class, in this spacious, old New England-style building.

There are often groups of so-called sponsors affiliated with public seminars at universities and research institutes throughout America. Usually late middle-aged or elderly women who have contributed no significant sum of money, they come as auditors to surround the seminar participants. Sometimes they put things in the form of questions, but they are also ready to express their own opinions. Then at night the sponsors take turns inviting the seminar members to their homes for a party. For those participants whose native tongue is not English, especially for those with my degree of language ability, these parties are a mortification no less severe than the days' seminars proper. Moreover the sponsors, having attended the day's seminar, beleaguer one with questions of which they never seem to tire.

The German-American woman whom people called Agatha was one of these sponsors, and her leading me out of the large adjoining rooms where the party was going on to view from the porch the tree in the dark garden was also related to something I had said that day at the seminar. Among the items in a collection of Coomaraswamy memorabilia on exhibit in conjunction with the seminar was a piece of Indian folk art, *Krishna in a Tree*, rendered in a minute sketch on a bound banana leaf. Naked women were calling to Krishna from the river below. "The bodies of these women are typically Indian in every manifestation," the beatnik poet who was also a specialist in Hindu culture stated at the outset. "This has been captured in such a way that the form of an Indian woman's body, especially the breasts and belly, is distinctive from that of women from any other country. And, in fact, when one travels through India one sees women of precisely this physical type." Comments from other areas of the Far East were solicited to reply to this, whereupon a group of Indian women who were auditing reacted against the American poet, and I articulated my thoughts by turning the discussion to trees.

"Regarding what Allen has said, I obviously agree with his point that the style of representing the human form in Indian folk art contains idiosyncracies that are typically Indian. I would even partially support the view that, conversely, the form of the body has itself been influenced. It is probably fair to assume that this means that the physiology of the Indian people determines the style of their folk art, which is a manner of speaking typical of Allen. However, since I myself am not qualified to speak from experience about the bodies of Indian women, I would like to see the same theories applied to trees.

"This black tree Krishna has climbed is undoubtedly what would be called an Indian bo tree in my country. It has certainly been depicted through the sensibility and techniques of the Indian folk art style. That is, its distinctive features are exaggerated, and yet the substantial feel of its trunk and curve of its branches, or again the way the tips of its leaves are elongated like a tail—these are all grounded in realistic observation. Nevertheless, the tree as a whole still strikes me as distinctively Indian. With this concrete example, I would like to propose a hypothesis paralleling Allen's idea. I feel there are close resemblances between a region's trees and the people who live and die there. Don't the trees of Cranach give every appearance of being the bodies of Upper Franconian people standing there?"

I also mentioned the particular fondness I have for trees and the names that identify them in various lands. "When I travel to a foreign country I take delight in seeing within that landscape the trees particular to that region. Moreover, it is only by learning the region's unique designation and thus for the first time really knowing the trees that I feel I have truly encountered them. As I said before, the Japanese call this tree of Krishna's a bo tree. For us, this is a form of expression completely different from its classification as *Ficus religiosa Linn.* As for its scientific name, I interpret it as an explanation of the tree, which is different from the tree's name. . ."

It was with such a set of prior circumstances that Agatha uprooted me from the party to lead me before the huge tree that occupied the garden in front of the building. Nevertheless, since dusk had already fallen when I had been brought to the house, even when I got off the minibus I had been unable to see the entire tree; as a matter of fact even now I was only peering into the darkness where the tree purportedly stood. In any event, Agatha had tried to teach me the local name for the tree.

"It's called a 'rain tree' because, when there's a shower at night, drops of water fall from its foliage until past noon the next day, as if the tree were raining. Other trees dry off quickly, but this one stores water in its closely packed leaves, no larger than fingertips. Isn't it a clever tree?"

At dusk of that day which had threatened to rain, there had also been a shower. The moisture I smelled coming from the darkness, therefore, was the rain that the dense fingertip leaves were causing to fall anew on the ground. By concentrating my attention in front of me and ignoring the din of the party behind, I could, it seemed, hear the sound made by the fine rain as it fell from the tree over a fairly broad area. As I listened, I began to feel that, in the wall of black before my eyes, there were two different shades of darkness. One darkness was something like a giant baobab tree, bulb-shaped; around its rim was a second vortex of darkness which fell away into bottomless depths, a darkness so profound that even if the rays of the waning moon had penetrated it no oceans or mountain ranges, nothing in our human universe, would have been visible. The immigrants who came to Hawaii from the American mainland a century—perhaps a century and a half—ago to build this house must have seen the same darkness on their first night, I mused. But was this darkness that yawned beyond the garden, ready to suck in body and soul of whoever looked at it, an appropriate setting for a home for the mentally ill?

Thanks to my habit of censoring my statements before I articulate them in a foreign tongue, I stopped short of putting this question to Agatha. It was probably just as well, since Agatha, as someone who lived in the building and was responsible for its residents, would no doubt have taken my words as a direct criticism of herself. Nevertheless, I realized that my perception of the two darknesses—the rim of the darkness shaped like the tree I had created in my imagination, and the darkness that engulfed it—was shared by the German-born American woman who stood just behind me. For I could clearly hear the long sigh, like an arrow of darkness released into the universe, that escaped from the sharp-chinned, oval face supported by her erect spine. We turned away from the tree that emanated the smell of water into the night and retraced our steps over the wide, wooden planks of the porch.

Agatha, like all the American women associated with this conference, was a realist, pragmatist, and activist in every sphere, and she could not restrain herself from infusing even the simple, quiet process of withdrawing from the dark garden with a sense of purpose. She came to a halt before one of the many first-floor rooms that lined the long porch and, bending slightly from the hips, peered in at something on the opposite wall with a truly affectionate gaze. Intrigued, I, too, peeked through the door and saw inside a wall covered with bookshelves, dimly illuminated by a lamp that hung from the high, plastered ceiling. (Soft lights, as opposed to the psychedelic lights I had often seen used in Hawaii, had also been used in the rooms where the party was being held, convincing me that this was, indeed, a facility for the mentally ill.) For someone of my height, it wasn't even necessary to bend as much as Agatha did.

As my eyes adjusted to the dim light after staring into darkness, I could see that an oil painting about six feet square was suspended in a most unusual manner, in midair, about halfway down the wall covered with bookshelves, hiding from sight all the books behind it. The painting almost seemed to have been hung at precisely the angle that would make it visible to someone peering in from the porch, as we were, or from the roots of the tree of darkness in the garden. Come to think of it, hadn't I noticed a steel chair, painted in a somber color, among the prolific board-like roots of the tree?

"A *Girl on Horseback*," Agatha intoned, apparently reading the title on the painting; I realized I was looking at a painting of a young girl seated on a saddle that sank deep into the flanks of a sturdy, chestnut farm horse. The girl was surrounded by gloomy, forbidding walls which could have been those of a prison or concentration camp, and were strangely out of keeping with the sporty atmosphere of horseback riding. It dawned on me that this *Girl on Horseback* was a portrait of Agatha herself as a child. I mentioned this and noticed in the dimness that blood seethed up beneath the thin skin of Agatha's face as she answered, "Yes, this is me when I was still in Germany, a girl on horseback, in the days before the truly frightful, unhappy things began to occur." Something intense and powerful in Agatha's burning blue eyes and in her cheeks, so flushed that heat seemed to radiate from the gold tips of her facial hair, prohibited me from asking what those "frightful, unhappy things" were. I knew only that Agatha had left her motherland, Germany (whether East or West, I was uncertain), and emigrated to Hawaii. Yet if I forced myself to make a connection between the two things, I could understand the meaning of the boycott of tonight's party by the European and American Jews at the seminar. (The Jewish Indian poet from Bombay, who deplored taking a single crab from the beach, viewed the lives and deaths of humans in the political context with the detachment of a Bodhisattva.) But some kind of wisdom which makes it possible for seminars and parties like this to proceed peacefully must come into play just one step before a person attempts to scrutinize and pass judgment on such an issue.

When we returned to the adjoining rooms where the party was taking place we discovered that, during our absence, a new central character had appeared and had taken over the role that was previously Agatha's. In fact, the bearing of this new figure contrasted sharply with Agatha's demeanor as hostess; he seemed to constitute a dominating center of the gathering, like a tyrant reigning over the party. He was a dwarfish man of about fifty, ensconced in a wheelchair, who at first glance might have been taken for a child dressed up like a witch for a play. His long, ivory-colored hair had been trimmed and shaped so that it turned under along the collar of his red satin jacket. His mouth, like a dog's, was the largest feature in his face, while his aquiline nose and double-lidded gray eyes had a proud beauty to them. The impression created when his powerfully vibrating voice issued forth from his large mouth was one of arrogance, yet he directed unflagging attention to the young people who sat at his knees and stood around his wheelchair. It was to the beatnik poet, standing directly in front of his wheelchair as if to block its path, that he addressed a steady stream of words. Yet it was clear that the exchange between the two was a sort of game or theatrical performance, and that the man in the wheelchair, if not the poet, was more conscious of his audience than of his opponent.

"The architect Komarovich—our brilliant architect! What high spirits he's in tonight!" Agatha explained brightly, as if displaying her proudest possession. Her voice had instantly adapted to the gay tone of the party before us; the note of exaltation, underlain by pent-up gloom, that suffused her words when she spoke to me about *A Girl on Horseback* had vanished. She left me behind and walked with long, brisk strides to join the young men beside the wheelchair, deftly skirting the legs and knees of those who were seated on the floor.

I stayed at my post beside the entrance to the room and observed the debate between the architect and the beatnik poet, which was beginning to seem like entertainment provided as the party's main event. In fact, if I were to give a perfectly balanced description of all that transpired that night, I would have to present the debate between poet and architect as a one-act play, consisting purely of dialogue without any action. This is because the hour-long debate, after which our soirée in the mental institution came to an abrupt end, consumed the major portion of the evening. However, as I mentioned at the outset, with my level of comprehension it was impossible to grasp precisely the multiple levels of meaning of this dialogue between the architect, with his strangely high-pitched, florid speech, and the poet, who barely opened his lips when he spoke, and whose words combined Manhattan-style sophistication with an unconventionality befitting an idol of the beatnik movement. The only way I could interpret the play of logic and illogic in their words was to follow one step behind, reconstructing whatever I could from bits and pieces of the conversation. Thus, in my own way, I managed to fend off boredom during the hour-long session.

What I have written here, then, is merely a recasting of a reconstruction I performed that evening, no doubt distorted both by memory and the passage of time. To keep myself from degenerating into tedious summarizing, I have interspersed my own perceptions of the atmosphere surrounding the talks. This is also because of the extremely "colorful" nature (to borrow a word used frequently during the seminar), not only of the debaters' performance itself, but of the responses of the guests at the party—who listened intently, and even seemed to participate without actually intruding—and of the waiters and waitresses who were serving them food and drink.

At the feet of the poet, who remained standing throughout the debate, sat three boys of fifteen or sixteen similar enough to be brothers, in the sense that the face and body of each one conformed to the poet's tastes. These boys, unlike the athletic youths of Hawaii, looked as if they had never been to the beach in their lives, and they sat with pale faces cast down, lost in thought. One was a boy who had followed the poet to the seminar that morning, looking as stunned as a virgin who had just been deflowered, and whom everyone tried not to look at. Surrounding these three boys and covering the floor were other young people who were admirers of the poet, among them a girl attired in a Judo outfit (though she showed no traces of physical exertion) who seemed to be trying to attract the poet's attention by acting like a boy. She was, of course, already quite drunk, and no sooner had she nodded vigorously in agreement with something Allen had said than her head would slump and she would doze off, only to struggle awake again, shaking her head as if she had been listening attentively all along.

Encircling the architect in his wheelchair on three sides, like stalwart supporters of his genius, Agatha and the other middle-aged and elderly ladies sat primly on sofas and chairs and cast stealthy, pitying glances at the drunken young woman of the opposing camp in her Judo suit. It was at the poet that they directed their unvoiced disapproval, and they let the architect act as their advocate, expressing the full burden of their moral sentiment. Needless to say, these matrons, whose silence formed a shield for the architect championing their cause, consumed more alcohol than the young people on the floor. Of the three types of drinks—beer, gin and tonic, and whiskey—being served by the bartenders, waiters, and waitresses (apparently students working part-time) in attendance at this midnight party, it was not beer but the more potent stuff that filled the glasses of the matrons, who looked for all the world like spinsters or widows in uniform as they sat in matching girlish frocks with lacy collars. With deft gestures, calculated to escape the notice of the other guests, they drained their glasses and then signaled immediately for refills. Agatha was no exception. In fact, the only people drinking beer at the party were the seminar participants, who formed the outermost flank of those surrounding the debate.

Although I assumed the young people catering at the party were students hired for the occasion, they were a mysterious bunch who seemed to have developed a unique style in their dress and deportment by training together as a group. The men all wore old-fashioned vests and silk shirts with puffy sleeves; the girls wore the same frocks as those of the matrons, covered with frilly aprons. All were pale, terribly thin, and showed signs of what, to a superficial observer like myself, appeared to be autism. For example, they weaved in and out of the partygoers without ever looking anyone in the eye, even when they handed you a canapé or a drink. And despite their graceful bearing, or perhaps even because of the excessive agility of their movements, I detected the sound of violent breathing, as if from sheer exhaustion, whenever one of them brushed past me. A strangely antique, musty body odor, which in no way contradicted their cleanliness, clung to each one. This seemed to mystify those seminar participants whose interest had not been aroused by the debate, and they whispered about it among themselves.

It was against such a backdrop that the debate between architect and poet took place . . . that is to say, the verbal offensive of the architect and the defensive maneuvers of the poet, who managed to deflect the attack without ever appearing underhanded. The following is a summary of what I was able to pick up of the attacker's argument:

"You are a passionate lover of boys and young men and this is a beautiful thing, in and of itself. It is a standpoint we hold in common. Yet it is clear that even here, at our very point of departure, there are insurmountable differences between us. Your passion develops in a direction that debases and corrupts the young. Mine uplifts and enlightens them. Perhaps you will say that you are introducing young people to dark, mystical knowledge and depths of feeling. Just now you insisted that carnal love was as central to human experience as spiritual love, since both were dark and mystical in their essence." (It was by taking the terse, acerbic rejoinders uttered jestingly by the poet and turning them upside down, in this manner, within the context of his own flowery and effusive speech that the architect was able to furnish his alcoholic supporters with a taste of victory. The poet, for his part, actually seemed to be enjoying his successive routs on the surface level of the debate, and made no effort to probe the deep-seated weaknesses of his opponent. Where he could easily have exposed the architect's argument for its imprecision or its fatuousness, he simply shrugged his shoulders and chortled like a Santa Claus.) "But carnal love and spiritual love must be like a spiral stairway, constantly ascending toward their bright, sacred essence. Especially that phyiscal and spiritual love which sees itself as educating the young. . ."

The architect went on to deliver a lecture—he had by now assumed the air of someone speaking from a podium—about the special features of this facility of the mentally ill as he, the designer of the building, had envisioned them, and about how the management of the facility was structured around his vision. "Those who seek refuge in this old house after fleeing the American mainland are the possessors of keen, delicate, ailing spirits. I felt I should provide each one with a place of retreat tailored to his or her own body. If there could be one hill, one valley, for every patient in this facility, what a wonderful thing that would be! Like the castles and estates that insane monarchs in Europe, suffering their various fates, made into hermitages in those wonderful eras of the past! The naked, wounded soul in America today is not even guaranteed a private dwelling place. Accordingly, I've devoted my energies to ensuring that, in this building at least, every person who seeks shelter will have a 'position' of his or her own. For my own 'position' I chose the lowest place in the building: my workshop is in the basement garage. And now, I'd like to ask you to take your cues from me, pretend you're going down to my workshop, right below the floor you're standing on, and from my 'position' try to imagine the 'positions' of the people who live in every partition of every room in this house. My structure incorporates each one of these 'positions' in such a way as to give a sense of constant movement upward. This should strike you immediately. I planned and carried out the renovations of the interior with the aim of providing any individual (particularly a young individual) inside the assemblage of 'positions' with an awareness of existing on a stairway where the self was being elevated on a spiral course into the heavens. Those residents of the facility who are not young people have been assigned to 'positions' that make them a foundation for the constant movement upward of the young. They are primarily ladies in the later years of life who watch with admiring hearts as the children—our youth—ascend toward the sacred heights." (At this point the poet raised several objections. Although he found the conception inspiring, he wondered whether those in the lower "positions" would be happy. Furthermore, as one can see by looking at a pyramid, the number of people who can occupy "positions" at the top is extremely limited. Wouldn't this create antagonism toward the idea in society at large, so that the young people who participated might be subjected to abuse, rather than benefiting from their participation? This could even happen in the closed society of the institution itself. In response, the architect drew himself up with a mighty effort and assumed a godlike posture.) "You are a passionate lover of boys and young men. Yet you are afraid to ask society to sanction the path that leads them to the heights. This is why your love brings them to decadence and degradation. To hide in dark, low places where you pollute and befoul each other—it is this, and this alone, that arouses your passion for the young! The passion of a necrophiliac is no different! But between us there is a fundamental difference. What I have accomplished in this building I wish to propagate outside our 'closed society,' across the American mainland, throughout the world! I am launching an architectural movement to place young people everywhere in 'positions' on stairways of ascent. We must begin with schools, libraries, and theaters for children. The reason I have compressed and reduced my own body, once that of a normal adult, into the child's body you see in this wheelchair is in order to ready myself by seeing and sensing the world from a child's height, from a child's 'position,' from the eyes of a child's body and soul. My goal is to create a model of the entire world on the scale of the child's body and soul, and I am trying to live in the world as a physical and spiritual child, speculating day and night about the types of space and structure most suitable to architecture for children. My compressed and shrunken body itself will be a model for architects of the future!"

As the architect made his proclamation I scrutinized his body more closely: it did indeed seem possible that he had transformed himself into a dwarf by sitting in the wheelchair and compressing the area between his chest and his hips into two or three accordian-like pleats. The wheelchair was merely a device he needed to manipulate his external appearance. Now, raising his arms in their red satin sleeves over his head with a flourish, he became a rose-colored king with the mouth of a small, adorable dog, and the matrons behind him (made even more genteel by drink) let out a discreet burst of applause. Even his debating opponent, the beatnik poet with the face of a bearded Bodhidharma, shouted, "This man is fantastic! He's out of his mind!" Eyes twinkling behind thick glasses, he urged on his disciples, who joined without hesitation in the applause.

It was probably inevitable at this point that the guests at the party decided to tour the inside of the building to see how the architect's master plan had been implemented. With the wheelchair that carried the architect as our masthead, we filed out to inspect the part of the building that was the heart of the architect's vision: the rooms designed to impart a sense of upward motion. Since, aside from the area where the party was being held, the first floor consisted only of conference rooms and a library, we flocked to the stairway and began climbing toward the second floor. The young people who just minutes earlier had flaunted their silent antagonism toward the architect now bore his wheelchair aloft, supporting it on three sides. A mood of exaltation united us as we threaded our way through the vast structure, peering into one empty room after another and discovering, every time we turned a corner, a short flight of stairs. Empty rooms? More accurately, I would describe each room as an assemblage of boxes with bases at differing levels of height. Each of the large rooms of the original structure had been divided into four or five partitions of parallelepiped shape, arranged so that the unit as a whole gave one a sense of moving from a lower to a higher level. This was because, as one went from one of the large rooms to another, one repeatedly had the impression, created through an illusory use of color, of ascending beyond the level of the highest box in the room before (which would have been impossible in actuality). On the stairways, moreover, this illusion of ascent was reinforced by tangible reality, so that while climbing them I had the sense of being suspended in a lofty tower. As we went higher, I even began to wonder if we had been transformed into a herd of rats, racing up the stairs of this tower in the grip of some kind of group insanity. There were, in fact, some members of our band who found the emotion that united us disagreeable and dropped out of the procession.

As those of us who continued in the file reached the top floor of the building (the design created the illusion there was still one more room above) I could sense, outside the darkened windows of the square rooms of ever decreasing size, the dense leaves of the "clever rain tree" whose existence I had merely been able to assent to earlier in the evening. Or perhaps I should say that the rooms themselves seemed like birdhouses enveloped in a vast growth of leaves. We circled around the empty cubicles until we discovered that, in just one of the four partitions into which the corner room of the top floor had been divided, there was someone living.

As I mentioned before, there were a number of people in our group who had gradually become disenchanted with the atmosphere of the procession; still others were by nature apprehensive about the fragility of the wooden corridors and staircases, or had become bored with the unusual but repetitious formula according to which all the rooms had been renovated. Therefore, those who were left to approach the innermost chamber included only Agatha, myself, the Jewish Indian poet from Bombay, the beatnik poet, and the architect in his wheelchair, carried by two young men. I realize now that it was probably better that way. There, in that least accessible of all the rooms—a cubicle that appeared to jut right out from the wall of the house—we saw a woman about forty years old, crouching in a metal washtub which occupied almost the entire area of the floor. To judge from her facial expression alone, she might have been a close relative of those self-contained matrons who had gathered around the architect's wheelchair earlier in the evening, savoring his eloquence with their sips of alcohol. But from the neck down this woman, crouching there completely naked and with one knee drawn up, had daubed herself with a blackish red liquid. Now, turning the small, black holes of her eyes toward us, she smeared a single line of the dark, sticky substance across her narrow forehead.

The beatnik poet was silent, and even seemed impressed by the scene, while the always candid Jewish Indian poet made it known that he found the stench unbearable. This remark shattered the architect's mood of exaltation, and he explained glumly that the room the woman was now in was not her "position"; she had simply been moved here temporarily because of that night's party, and the change in surroundings had disoriented her. Agatha gave vent to the antagonism aroused by the poet's complaint even more bluntly. She told him that it was necessary for the woman to put her stale blood to some use, that no one could reproach her for this, and that she was perfectly capable of doing the same thing with fresh, living blood, but only at very special moments in her life.

Then, as if triggered by Agatha's words, a number of things occurred simultaneously. First the Indian poet, and a few seconds later I myself, came to a similar realization. In that instant of recognition, when we were also communicating to each other with our eyes that the beatnik poet had surely known everything all along . . . at that very moment when we understood that the midnight party had been organized entirely by patients in this mental institution (with the exception of the woman in front of us smeared with blood from her sexual organs) and that these patients were none other than the waiters and waitresses who had served us cocktails and canapés, not to mention the placid ladies sipping their liquor . . . an Iranian journalist who had been a member of the seminar came dashing up the stairs. He informed us that all of the members had decided to withdraw from the premises immediately.

My next clear memory is of the architect, so boyish-looking when he sat in his wheelchair, pulling himself to his feet in a single effort that made his body appear to double in size; I watched from behind as he hurried down the stairs, his surprisingly large body bent forward and supported by Agatha's shoulder. The beatnik poet, mindful not to disturb the woman covered with blood, waited until he had reached the floor below before bursting into peals of merry laughter. The Iranian then told all of us his story. It seemed that when everyone else had started climbing to the upper stories, he and an English teacher from the Republic of Korea, who had already sensed something strange in the air, had descended to the architect's workshop in the basement. There they discovered a scene straight out of an American gangster film: two enormous men in uniform were bound and lying on the floor. In the neighboring compartment, a bathroom, they found three nurses who were also bound. They worked out an agreement with the nurses and night watchmen whereby the seminar participants would return to their dormitories immediately by minibus, on the condition that they would not be implicated in any of the events of the evening. In addition, they requested that any reprisals carried out against the patients who had staged the rebellion would in no way involve the seminar participants. Since the facility was itself subsidized by the high fees paid by the families of the patients, however, it was unlikely that any significant punishment would be meted out to them. Finally, the Iranian warned us that if word that he and the Korean representative were involved in the scandal leaked out to the press, they might find themselves in trouble once they returned home. (This was several years before the Khomeini revolution.)

At that point, without further ado, we began to head toward the front garden, where the engine of the minibus was already humming. Far from bidding farewell to the inebriated women, moving unsteadily down the stairways and corridors in search of their "position," or to the young people, who still walked with their eyes cast down, we simply elbowed our way through them and boarded the bus. I saw no sign of the night watchmen who were supposedly presiding over our departure, and merely glimpsed the heads and shoulders of two nurses who towered over the throng of bent figures. But in my last moments in the building I heard, from the direction of the "clever rain tree" which had never materialized before my eyes out of the darkness, a woman cry out two or three times with sobs so loud it seemed her body was being ripped apart by grief.

Our bus, preceded and followed by young guests escaping on their motorcycles, sped over the steep, winding mountain road as if in desperate flight. But in the darkness inside the bus, reverberations of that sobbing voice seemed to echo all around us, and even the face of the beatnik poet (who had been laughing uproariously until then) took on an expression of pensive melancholy little different from the gloomy expressions of the Iranian and Korean representatives, who were brooding over the possible repercussions of the scandal in their native dictatorships. Yet for all that, I now find it strange that I never once looked back through the windows of the bus to the giant rain tree, which should have loomed up in its black entirety, no matter how dark the night, if I had only gazed into that part of the sky where the day was dawning. Strange, because I frequently picture to myself Agatha, who chose her "position" by setting her chair at the place where tree and earth came together, in among the board-roots that jutted out like great pleats in the ground; Agatha, who stared at the painting of *A Girl on Horseback* in the library across the porch, and looked up at the building designed to spiral endlessly toward heaven like an enormous twin of the tree . . . Agatha, whom I can still see in my mind's eye, although what kind of tree it was that she called her "clever rain tree" I shall never know.

THE SILENT TRADERS

Tsushima Yūko

Translated by Geraldine Harcourt

Tsushima Yūko's writing has grown out of a life of ordinary events, an extraordinary heritage, and an innovative independence. As Tsushima Satoko (her real name), she was born in Tokyo in 1947; she gained a degree in English literature in 1969, married in 1970, gave birth to a daughter and son, and had what she describes as "an ordinary divorce" in 1976. As the daughter of Tsushima Shūji (Dazai Osamu) and his wife Michiko, she grew up with the extraordinary literary legacy of the father she does not remember as she was only a year old when he committed suicide in 1948. She was also greatly influenced by her closeness in childhood to her mentally retarded elder brother, who died in 1960.

From early beginnings as a writer while still at college—her first published story appeared in Mita bungaku *in 1969—she gained increasing success by her late twenties and now supports her family by writing full-time (a fact worth noting in a society that is hard on single parents).*

Drawing on all these elements, a typical Tsushima work will take freshly observed domestic details—dead insects accumulated in a light fixture, say, or a bug being flushed down the kitchen sink—and give them a powerful significance as it develops such themes as blood relations, sexuality and the tie between the sexes that the birth of a child represents, death and the ties between the dead and the living.

These implications are often threaded through a deceptively loose structure reminiscent of the shishōsetsu *but which in fact sets up a resonance or impact all the more powerful because it is unforeseen. The story translated* here, "Danmari ichi" (The Silent Traders, 1982), is a striking example of this technique.

The "mountain men" whose silent trade provides the title were isolated, nomadic remnants of an earlier people driven back by agricultural settlement, and among the village dwellers any recognition of their existence was tabooed. The analogy adds a further dimension to the first-person story, while the symbolism of the nomads' invisibility to the settlement has been explored more fully in the novel Yama o hashiru onna (Woman Running in the Mountains, 1980).

Tsushima's fiction makes many such allusions to tradition and folklore (familiar to Japanese readers) that parallel her contemporary plots; for example, the collection Ōma monogatari (Ghost Stories, 1984) and a novel in progress which will interrelate Heian and modern characters.

Images such as light playing on leaves relieve the starkness of city settings and point up a clear contrast with the literature of urban alienation: this is a world of human connectedness, even if the connections are often tenuous (as in the many telephone conversations that figure in Tsushima's writing).

Water is another recurring motif. The novel Chōji (Child of Fortune, 1978; tr. 1983) has multilayered imagery of water, ice, and snow as the possibly pregnant heroine contemplates having the baby "to escape the molten lava of her own sexuality," and in the 1983 novel Hi no kawa no hotori de (On the Banks of the River of Fire), the author's most complex work to date, she matches a riverside city locale with the momentum of a father-daughter incest and an illicit love affair.

This is not to suggest, though, that the sex in Tsushima's books is decorously draped in metaphor, for at the same time she is attempting to describe sex from a woman's viewpoint in precise language.

Tsushima does not identify herself as a radical feminist, because she is "not part of the feminist movement," but her stereotype-breaking heroines do have a strong appeal for women readers. The 1980 serialization of Yama o hashiru onna in the Mainichi shimbun added considerable popularity to the critical recognition that had brought her the Tamura Toshiko Prize (1976), Izumi Kyōka Prize (1977), Women's Literature Prize (1978), and Noma Prize for New Writers (1979). "The Silent Traders" was awarded the Kawabata Yasunari Prize in 1983.

Women writers in Japan have traditionally been considered to form a "school" of their own, joryū bungaku *(which evolved in an entirely different way from the more recent feminist focus in Western criticism). Thus when Tsushima Yūko is acclaimed as a "representative woman writer" the boundaries of this praise are narrowly defined. Lately, however, Japanese critics have begun to cite her as a "representative writer" of the postwar or younger generation. In a literary establishment that sees* joryū sakka *or women writers as outsiders, this is visibility indeed.*

* * *

There was a cat in the wood. Not such an odd thing, really: wildcats, pumas, and lions all come from the same family and even a tabby shouldn't be out of place. But the sight was unsettling. What was the creature doing there? When I say "wood," I'm talking about Rikugien, an Edo-period landscape garden in my neighborhood. Perhaps "wood" isn't quite the right word, but the old park's trees—relics of the past amid the city's modern buildings—are so overgrown that the pathways skirting its walls are dark and forbidding even by day. It does give the impression of a wood; there's no other word for it. And the cat, I should explain, didn't look wild. It was just a kitten, two or three months old, white with black patches. It didn't look at all ferocious—in fact it was a dear little thing. There was nothing to fear. And yet I was taken aback, and I tensed as the kitten bristled and glared in my direction.

The kitten was hiding in a thicket beside the pond, where my ten-year-old daughter was the first to spot it. By the time I'd made out the elusive shape and exclaimed "Oh, you're right!" she was off calling at the top of her voice: "There's another! And here's one over here!" My other child, a boy of five, was still hunting for the first kitten, and as his sister went on making one discovery after another he stamped his feet and wailed "Where? Where is it?" His sister beckoned him to bend down and showed him triumphantly where to find the first cat. Several passersby, hearing my daughter's shouts, had also been drawn into the search. There were many strollers in the park that Sunday evening. The cats were everywhere, each concealed in its own clump of bushes. Their eyes followed people's feet on the graveled walk, and at the slightest move toward a hiding place the cat would scamper away. Looking down from an adult's height it was hard enough to detect them at all, let alone keep count, and this gave the impression of great numbers.

I could hear my younger child crying. He had disappeared while my back was turned. As I looked wildly around, my daughter pointed him out with a chuckle: "See where he's got to!" There he was, huddled tearfully in the spot where the first kitten had been. He'd burst in eagerly, but succeeded only in driving away the kitten and trapping himself in the thicket.

"What do you think you're doing? It'll never let *you* catch it." Squatting down, my daughter was calling through the bushes. "Come on out, silly!"

His sister's tone of amusement was no help to the boy at all. He was terrified in his cobwebbed cage of low-hanging branches where no light penetrated.

"That's no use. You go in and fetch him out." I gave her shoulder a push.

"He got himself in," she grumbled, "so why can't he get out?" All the same, she set about searching for an opening. Crouching, I watched the boy through the thick foliage and waited for her to reach him.

"How'd he ever get in there? He's really stuck," she muttered as she circled the bushes uncertainly, but a moment later she'd broken through to him, forcing a way with both hands.

When they rejoined me, they had dead leaves and twigs snagged all over them.

After an attempt of her own to pick one up, my daughter understood that life in the park had made these tiny kittens quicker than ordinary strays and too wary to let anyone pet them. Explaining this to her brother, she looked to me for agreement. "They were born here, weren't they? They belong here, don't they? Then I wonder if their mother's here too?"

The children scanned the surrounding trees once again.

"She may be," I said, "but she'd stay out of sight, wouldn't she? Only the kittens wander about in the open. Their mother's got more sense. I'll bet she's up that tree or some place like that where nobody can get at her. She's probably watching us right now."

I cast an eye at the treetops as I spoke—and the thought of the unseen mother cat gave me an uncomfortable feeling. Whether these were alley cats that had moved into the park or discarded pets that had survived and bred, they could go on multiplying in the wood—which at night was empty of people—and be perfectly at home.

It is exactly twenty-five years since my mother came to live near Rikugien with her three children, of which I was the youngest at ten. She told us the park's history, and not long after our arrival we went inside to see the garden. In spite of its being on our doorstep we quickly lost interest, however, since the grounds were surrounded by a six-foot brick wall with a single gate on the far side from our house. A Japanese garden was not much fun for children anyway, and we never went again as a family. I was reminded that we lived near a park, though, because of the many birds—the blue magpies, Eastern turtledoves, and tits—that I would see on the rooftops and in trees. And in summer I'd hear the singing of evening cicadas. To a city child like me, evening cicadas and blue magpies were a novelty.

I visited Rikugien with several classmates when we were about to leave elementary school, and someone hit on the idea of making a kind of time capsule. We'd leave it buried for ten years—or was it twenty? I've also forgotten what we wrote on the piece of paper that we stuffed into a small bottle and buried at the foot of a pine on the highest ground in the garden. I expect it's still there as I haven't heard of it since, and now whenever I'm in Rikugien I keep an eye out for the landmark, but I'm only guessing. We were confident of knowing exactly where to look in years to come, and if I can remember that so clearly it's puzzling that I can't recognize the tree. I'm not about to dig any holes to check, however—not with my own children watching. The friends who left this sentimental reminder were soon to part, bound for different schools. Since then, of course, we've ceased to think of one another, and I'm not so sure now that the bottle episode ever happened.

The following February my brother (who was close to my own age) died quite suddenly of pneumonia. Then in April my sister went to college and, not wanting to be left out, I pursued her new interests myself: I listened to jazz, went to movies, and was friendly toward college and high school students of the opposite sex. An older girl introduced me to a boy from senior high and we made up a foursome for an outing to the park—the only time I got all dressed up for Rikugien. I was no beauty, though, nor the popular type, and while the others were having fun I stayed stiff and awkward, and was bored. I would have liked to be as genuinely impressed as they were, viewing the landscape garden for the first time, but I couldn't work up an interest after seeing the trees over the brick wall every day. By that time we'd been in the district for three years, and the name "Rikugien" brought to mind not the tidy, sunlit lawns seen by visitors, but the dark tangles along the walls.

My desire for friends of the opposite sex was short-lived. Boys couldn't provide what I wanted, and what boys wanted had nothing to do with me.

While I was in high school, one day our ancient spitz died. The house remained without a dog for a while, until Mother was finally prompted to replace him when my sister's marriage, soon after her graduation, left just the two of us in an unprotected home. She found someone who let her have a terrier puppy. She bought a brush and comb and began rearing the pup with the best of care, explaining that it came from a clever hunting breed. As it grew, however, it failed to display the expected intelligence and still behaved like a puppy after six months; and besides, it was timid. What it did have was energy as, yapping shrilly, it frisked about the house all day long. It may have been useless but it was a funny little fellow. Its presence made all the difference to me in my intense boredom at home. After my brother's death, my mother (a widow since I was a baby) passed her days as if at a wake. We saw each other only at mealtimes, and then we seldom spoke. In high school a fondness for the movies was about the worst I could have been accused of, but Mother had no patience with such frivolity and would snap angrily at me from time to time. "I'm leaving home when I turn eighteen," I'd retort. I meant it, too.

It was at that time that we had the very sociable dog. I suppose I'd spoiled it as a puppy, for now it was always wanting to be let in, and when I slid open the glass door it would bounce like a rubber ball right into my arms and lick my face and hands ecstatically.

Mother, however, was dissatisfied. She'd had enough of the barking; it got on her nerves. Then came a day when the dog went missing. I thought it must have got out of the yard. Two or three days passed and it didn't return—it hadn't the wit to find the way home once it strayed. I wondered if I should contact the pound. Concern finally drove me to break our usual silence and ask Mother: "About the dog. . ." "Oh, the dog?" she replied. "I threw it over the wall of Rikugien the other day."

I was shocked—I'd never heard of disposing of a dog like that. I wasn't able to protest, though. I didn't rush out to comb the park, either. She could have had it destroyed, yet instead she'd taken it to the foot of the brick wall, lifted it in her arms, and heaved it over. It wasn't large, only about a foot long, and thus not too much of a handful even for Mother.

Finding itself tossed into the wood, the dog wouldn't have crept quietly into hiding. It must have raced through the area barking furiously, only to be caught at once by the caretaker. Would the next stop be the pound? But there seemed to me just a chance that it hadn't turned out that way. I could imagine the wood by daylight, more or less: there'd be a lot of birds and insects, and little else. The pond would be inhabited by a few carp, turtles, and catfish. But what transformations took place at night? As I didn't dare stay beyond closing time to see for myself, I wondered if anyone could tell of a night spent in the park till the gates opened in the morning. There might be goings-on unimaginable by day. Mightn't a dog entering that world live on, not as a tiny terrier, but as something else?

I had to be thankful that the dog's fate left that much to the imagination.

From then on I turned my back on Rikugien more firmly than ever. I was afraid of the deep wood, so out of keeping with the city: it was the domain of the dog abandoned by my mother.

In due course I left home, a little later than I'd promised. After a good many more years I moved back to Mother's neighborhood—back to the vicinity of the park—with a little daughter and a baby. Like my own mother, I was one who couldn't give my children the experience of a father. That remained the one thing I regretted.

Living in a cramped apartment, I now appreciated the Rikugien wood for its greenery and open spaces. I began to take the children there occasionally. Several times, too, we released pet turtles or goldfish in the pond. Many nearby families who'd run out of room for aquarium creatures in their overcrowded apartments would slip them into the pond to spend the rest of their lives at liberty.

Rocks rose from the water here and there, and each was studded with turtles sunning themselves. They couldn't have bred naturally in such numbers. They must have been the tiny turtles sold at fairground stalls and pet shops, grown up without a care in the world. More of them lined the water's edge at one's feet. No doubt there were other animals on the increase—goldfish, loaches, and the like. Multistoried apartment buildings were going up around the wood in quick succession, and more living things were brought down from their rooms each year. Cats were one animal I'd overlooked, though. If tipping out turtles was common practice, there was no reason why cats shouldn't be dumped here, and dogs too. No type of pet could be ruled out. But to become established in any numbers they'd have to escape the caretaker's notice and hold their own against the wood's other hardy inhabitants. Thus there'd be a limit to survivors: cats and reptiles, I'd say.

Once I knew about the cat population, I remembered the dog my mother had thrown away, and I also remembered my old fear of the wood. I couldn't help wondering how the cats got along from day to day.

Perhaps they relied on food left behind by visitors—but all of the park's trash baskets were fitted with mesh covers to keep out the crows, whose numbers were also growing. For all their nimbleness, even cats would have trouble picking out the scraps. Lizards and mice were edible enough. But on the other side of the wall lay the city and its garbage. After dark, the cats would go out foraging on the streets.

Then, too, there was the row of apartment towers along one side of the wood, facing the main road. All had balconies that overlooked the park. The climb would be quick work for a cat, and if its favorite food were left outside a door it would soon come back regularly. Something told me there must be people who put out food: there'd be elderly tenants and women living alone. Even children. Children captivated by a secret friendship with a cat.

I don't find anything odd about such a relationship—perhaps because it occurs so often in fairy stories. But to make it worth their while the apartment children would have to receive something from the cat; otherwise they wouldn't keep it up. There are tales of mountain men and villagers who traded a year's haul of linden bark for a gallon and a half of rice in hard cakes. No villager could deal openly with the lone mountain men; so great was their fear of each other, in fact, that they avoided coming face to face. Yet when a bargain was struck, it could not have been done more skillfully. The trading was over in a flash, before either man had time to catch sight of the other or hear his voice. I think everyone wishes privately that bargains could be made like that. Though there would always be the fear of attack, or discovery by one's own side.

Supposing it were my own children: what could they be getting in return? They'd have no use for a year's stock of linden bark. Toys, then, or cakes. I'm sure they want all sorts of things, but not a means of support like linden bark. What, then? Something not readily available to them; something the cat has in abundance and to spare.

The children leave food on the balcony. And in return the cat provides them with a father. How's that for a bargain? Once a year, male cats procreate; in other words, they become fathers. They become fathers ad nauseam. But these fathers don't care how many children they have—they don't even notice that they are fathers. Yet the existence of offspring makes them so. Fathers who don't know their own children. Among humans, it seems there's an understanding that a man only becomes a father when he recognizes the child as his own; but that's a very narrow view. Why do we allow the male to divide children arbitrarily into two kinds, recognized and unrecognized? Wouldn't it be enough for the child to choose a father when necessary from among suitable males? If the children decide that the tom that climbs up to their balcony is their father, it shouldn't cause him any inconvenience. A father looks in on two of his children from the balcony every night. The two human children faithfully leave out food to make it so. He comes late, when they are fast asleep, and they never see him or hear his cries. It's enough that they know in the morning that he's been. In their dreams, the children are hugged to their cat-father's breast.

We'd seen the children's human father six months earlier, and together we'd gone to a transport museum they wanted to visit. This came about only after many appeals from me. If the man who was their father was alive and well on this earth, I wanted the children to know what he looked like. To me, the man was unforgettable: I was once preoccupied with him, obsessed with the desire to be where he was; nothing had changed when I tried having a child, and I'd had the second with him cursing me. To the children, however, especially the younger one, he was a mere shadow in a photograph that never moved or spoke. As the younger child turned three, then four, I couldn't help being aware of that fact. This was the same state that I'd known myself, for my own father had died. If he were dead it couldn't be helped. But as long as he was alive I wanted them to have a memory of their father as a living, breathing person whose eyes moved, whose mouth moved and spoke.

On the day, he was an hour late for our appointment. The long wait in a coffee shop had made the children tired and cross, but when they saw the man a shy silence came over them. "Thanks for coming," I said with a smile. I couldn't think what to say next. He asked "Where to?" and stood to leave at once. He walked alone, while the children and I looked as though it was all the same to us whether he was there or not. On the train I still hadn't come up with anything to say. The children kept their distance from the man and stared nonchalantly out of the window. We got off the train like that, and again he walked ahead.

The transport museum had an actual bullet train car, steam locomotives, airplanes, and giant panoramic layouts. I remembered enjoying a class trip there while at school myself. My children, too, dashed excitedly around the exhibits without a moment's pause for breath. It was "Next I want to have a go on that train," "Now I want to work that model." They must have had a good two hours of fun. In the meantime we lost sight of the man. Wherever he'd been, he showed up again when we'd finished our tour and arrived back at the entrance. "What'll we do?" he asked, and I suggested giving the children a drink and sitting down somewhere. He nodded and went ahead to look for a place near the museum. The children were clinging to me as before. He entered a coffee shop that had a cake counter and I followed with them. We sat down, the three of us facing the man. Neither child showed the slightest inclination to sit beside him. They had orange drinks.

I was becoming desperate for something to say. And weren't there one or two things he'd like to ask me? Such as how the children had been lately. But to bring that up, unasked, might imply that I wanted him to watch with me as they grew. I'd only been able to ask for this meeting because I'd finally stopped feeling that way. Now it seemed we couldn't even exchange such polite remarks as "They've grown" or "I'm glad they're well" without arousing needless suspicions. It wasn't supposed to be like this, I thought in confusion, unable to say a word about the children. He was indeed their father, but not a father who watched over them. As far as he was concerned the only children he had were the two borne by his wife. Agreeing to see mine was simply a favor on his part, for which I could only be grateful.

If we couldn't discuss the children, there was literally nothing left to say. We didn't have the kind of memories we could reminisce over; I wished I could forget the things we'd done as if it had all been a dream, for it was the pain that we remembered. Inquiring after his family would be no better. His work seemed the safest subject, yet if I didn't want to stay in touch I had to think twice about this, too.

The man and I listened absently as the children entertained themselves.

On the way out the man bought a cake which he handed to the older child, and then he was gone. The children appeared relieved, and with the cake to look forward to they were eager to get home. Neither had held the man's hand or spoken to him. I wanted to tell them that there was still time to run after him and touch some part of his body, but of course they wouldn't have done it.

I don't know when there will be another opportunity for the children to see the man. They may never meet him again, or they may have a chance two or three years from now. I do know that the man and I will probably never be completely indifferent to each other. He's still on my mind in some obscure way. Yet there's no point in confirming this feeling in words. Silence is essential. As long as we maintain silence, and thus avoid trespassing, we leave open the possibility of resuming negotiations at any time.

I believe the system of bartering used by the mountain men and the villagers was called "silent trade." I am coming to understand that there was nothing extraordinary in striking such a silent bargain for survival. People trying to survive—myself, my mother, and my children, for example—can take some comfort in living beside a wood. We tip various things in there and tell ourselves that we haven't thrown them away, we've set them free in another world, and then we picture the unknown woodland to ourselves and shudder with fear or sigh fondly. Meanwhile the creatures multiplying there gaze stealthily at the human world outside; at least I've yet to hear of anything attacking from the wood.

Some sort of silent trade is taking place between the two sides. Perhaps my children really have begun dealings with a cat who lives in the wood.

THE IMMORTAL

Nakagami Kenji

Translated by Mark Harbison

It is appropriate that Nakagami Kenji should appear at the end of this anthology, for he is one of the new generation of writers, critics, and academics who are preparing to succeed to the positions of Ōe Kenzaburō, Yoshimoto Takaaki, and Yamaguchi Masao in the vanguard of Japanese postmodernism.

Much of Nakagami's reputation rests on early novels, deeply rooted in his own experience, about growing up as a burakumin. *The* burakumin *phenomenon is extremely complex: Nakagami identifies* buraku *with the ghettos of European and American cities, but discrimination against* burakumin, *or ghetto people, has no real ethnic or religious basis. Rather, it is rooted in historical developments that vary from one locality to another, and often, as Nakagami suggests, it arises simply from a shared perception of "difference."*

Misaki *(The Cape), which received the Akutagawa Prize in 1976, and* Karekinada *(The Kareki Sea, 1977) are brutal, naturalistic depictions of the* buraku *in Shingū, a coastal city on the Kishū Peninsula in the Kumano region south of Nara. Akio, the main character in these novels and in the recent* Chi no hate shijō no toki *(End of the Earth, Supreme Time, 1983), is not Nakagami, and Akio's father, his mother, his step-father, sisters, brothers, half-sisters, and half-brothers are not Nakagami's. But the author himself acknowledges that these novels are essentially I-novels, and his depiction of "the Alley"* (roji), *as the Shingū* buraku *is called in these novels, could only have sprung from an intense personal experience.*

Nakagami was born in the Alley in August 1946. His mother, Kinoshita Chisato, registered him under her own name as an illegitimate child, her third by a man known as Suzuki. Kinoshita became Nakaue when Chisato married a local road gang boss, who adopted Kenji, but not his two younger sisters. After graduating from high school, an unusual feat in the Alley, Kenji left for Tokyo and began to call himself Nakagami. The complexity of kinship and familial relationships in the Alley, an important theme of Nakagami's work, is such that the hardback edition of *Karekinada* contains an insert with a diagram of Akio's family tree.

If the Alley is one wellspring of Nakagami's obsession, the "dark land" of Kumano is the other. Since the age of the *Kojiki*, Kumano has always been an "other world." In earlier periods, it was shunned as a place of unknown evils, unbound by the laws of the court and the state Buddhism of Nara. The *hijiri* and *bikuni* of Kumano, who traced their lineage to the semi-mythical wizard En no Gyōja, were revered as holy men and nuns, but they were also feared and shunned as non-people (*saimin*), wanderers in a sedentary society. Nakagami is fascinated with this tradition. The myths and legends of Kumano are a constant undercurrent in his work, and sometimes, as in "The Immortal," they are a dominant presence.

What makes Nakagami more than a *burakumin* version of the ethnic writer is his extraordinary talent and his voracious desire for knowledge. Though he never fails to mention his lack of a university degree, and often poses as an intellectual nihilist, his range of reference is awesome: Bakhtin, Derrida, Hasumi Shigehiko, Japanese literature, Irish folk tales, the legends of Bali. His prolific talent, and his identification with an outspokenly intellectual group of writers and critics, have propelled him into a unique position in the Japanese advance guard.

But Nakagami also has paid a price for his sophistication. His recent work has been condemned by critics who once supported him: "Too much Bakhtin and not enough of the angry, young *burakumin*." More important, it has forced him to question his own inspiration. He has renounced *Misaki* and *Karekinada* as "the work of a child," and *Chi no hate shijō no toki* is a deliberate deconstruction of the earlier Akio novels. Shortly after winning the Akutagawa Prize, Nakagami began to say that he has fallen into a dilemma, that he is trapped on a pendulum that swings between two extremes: in thrall to the Japanese *monogatari*, at the same time he is obsessed *with demolishing "the law, the system, the* monogatari *of Japanese literature."*

"The Immortal" is the first story in Nakagami's recent Kumano-shū *(A Kumano Collection, 1984), which embodies this dilemma. The author himself calls it a linked short-story collection, but, at least superficially, the selection and arrangement of the stories seem chaotic: traditional ghost stories with pre-texts in earlier literature interwoven through a collection of loosely linked I-novels that directly address the self-deconstruction of "I's" literary inspiration. The rich, evocative tone of "The Immortal" is posed against language that bares Nakagami's own soul.*

In "The Immortal," the monogatari *of Japanese literature certainly seems to dominate. The presence of Izumi Kyōka's "Kōya hijiri"* (The Holy Man of Mount Kōya) *as a pre-text in "The Immortal" is unmistakable. The images associated with Kumano (fire, the Nashi Falls, half-human creatures, crows) can be traced back to the dawn of Japanese history, and readers familiar with the Nō will recognize the structure and rhythm of the innovative dramatic plays of Kanze Nobumitsu (1435–1516), in which the* waki *(the hijiri) is the protagonist. But a close reading of the story will reveal that it is Menippean, carnivalesque: Nakagami turns his pre-texts on their heads, and in the process violates every single convention of the traditional supernatural tale. In "The Immortal," he deconstructs the law, the system, the* monogatari *of Kumano as brutally as he explodes his vision of the Alley in the I-novels.*

* * *

To the hijiri, it was not particularly strange to be pushing his way through a dense thicket as he walked on and on in the mountains of Kumano, thrusting aside the top branches of bushes whose leaves shimmered translucent in the sunlight like blazing fire. That is how he had come this far, walking on and on into the mountains. If Amida were peering down from above the mountains, it may have seemed nothing more than circling round and round in the same place, sometimes a profile, sometimes a full figure, like an insect wriggling in the earth beneath the torn grass. But even if that were true, he did not care in the least. *Walking suits me.* He had walked on and on reciting this to himself. And as he walked, he had sometimes reached the top of a mountain pass to find unexpectedly a village on the other side. Sometimes, when he had been in the mountains for a long time, he had suddenly found himself searching for a bamboo grove, wanting to eat something fire had passed through, and wanting to embrace a woman whose body had warmth. *There are always people where there's a bamboo grove.* He no longer knew when he had come to understand this in his bones. To the hijiri, the sound of wind blowing over bamboo leaves was the sound of his own throat, the sound of life rising from every pore of his skin.

The thicket had begun to slope gently upward, but the hijiri's breathing never became labored, and as he traced the faint path that remained where people or animals had trampled the grass, just as he had done up to now, he even raised his voice imitating the sound of the grass brushing against his garments . . . *jaarajaara jaarajaara*. . . He had done nothing to the hair on his face for nearly ten days now, and his demeanor was dark and malevolent. His garments, freshly washed ten days ago, had become filthy with dust and grime. *Jaarajaara jaarajaara*. . . Suddenly, what had happened ten days ago loomed up before him like a dream, and the hijiri closed his mouth, swallowing the sounds. Dense clouds roiled up covering the entire scene. The gentle slope of the mountain, which had seemed to melt into the sunlight striking it until just now, the stand of cypresses spreading out beyond it like outstretched arms, and the naked crags in the distance, to the hijiri's eyes like purple flames, all dimmed, as if their colors had been wiped away. For a moment, the hijiri felt pain bearing down on him. Raising his eyes, he spat loudly, and began to mimic the sound of the grass again . . . *jaarajaara jaarajaara* . . . as if he were chanting a holy sutra.

He had fasted often, abstaining from both food and drink, and besides a devotion to scholarship equal to others, he had been singled out by the person he revered as his master, who had praised him for his speed in learning the sutras. But perhaps because from the very beginning he had learned the sutras only as a child who had been abandoned by hill people, or valley people—or even perhaps by a monkey keeper in favor of the monkey—he always ended up chanting *jaarajaara jaarajaara*, like a lewd growling in the throat, instead of the phrases of the sacred sutras.

Reaching the end of the mountain's gentle slope, he entered a stand of tall cypresses and after walking a little further came out onto the ridge, which was thickly wooded with tall broad-leaved trees. He walked on, stooping so that the garments covering his large body would not be caught in the branches, and on the ground at his feet, where fallen leaves had piled up and rotted, a snake as large as his arm slithered away with a rustling sound to hide itself. There were sounds everywhere, like spattering raindrops—just behind him, something striking the leaves of the branches over his back. Startled, he whirled around, and then realized that he had stumbled into a nest of mountain leeches. He turned to retreat, but when he tried to brush away the branch hanging over his face, leeches fell from its leaves like gentle raindrops, a great number of them striking his head and tumbling into the collar of his tunic. Shouting out, he twisted his body backward, but the leeches, tiny as the seeds of a tree, stuck to his skin and would not come loose. The hijiri had encountered many such things as he wandered in the mountains. And whenever something like this happened, he was struck with wonder at himself, walking deeper and deeper into the mountains and even going through all sorts of hardships when there was no reason at all to be doing so.

He emerged from the cypress grove onto a precipitous cliff. When he looked down, he could see a swollen waterfall that seemed to rend the rocks, and a river. Catching the sunlight, the water shimmered like white silk, and the hijiri felt that even from a distance its beauty was breathtaking. He wanted desperately to dip out some of this water and drink it, and unable to contain himself began searching for a way down. After nearly an hour, he finally reached the bottom of the cliff. First, as if it were a perfectly natural thing to do, he thrust his face directly into the water and drank, kneeling on a moss-grown rock that received the spray of the waterfall. He drank with such force as to gulp down everything in the river into his stomach. When he had finally finished drinking, he washed his face and then his head in the water. Suddenly, as if it had just occurred to him, he plunged splashing into the swift current with all his clothes still on. Standing in water up to his hips, he washed his flanks, his neck, and his back, which were covered with marks where the leeches had sucked his blood. He had stopped the bleeding by covering the wounds with crushed blades of grass, and now the scabs softened and came loose in the water. Blood flowed from the wounds, seeming to dissolve instantly in the water. The hijiri was not surprised by a little blood. Perhaps because he had been in a village ten days earlier, he was fleshier than usual.

The hijiri walked through the water toward the waterfall, which shone with a white radiance like a length of silk. Reaching the base of the cascade, it occurred to him that if he was going to be beaten by this strand of silk, he would profit more naked than with his clothes on, and so he began to take off his wet garments. Just at that moment he heard a sound and whirled around. For an instant the hijiri doubted his own eyes.

Separated by the cliff from where he stood, a woman was dipping water from the river with a bamboo ladle into a wooden bucket. He wondered suspiciously what she was doing here, where there was not the slightest sign of a village, but rather than startle her by making a sound, he watched the weak movements of the woman's hands, bating his breath. She filled the dipper half-full, but apparently it was too heavy for her and she spilled the water. She plunged the dipper into the water again. He saw the ladle floating weakly on the surface, but it was only after the woman cried out and began running downstream along the bank that he realized it had been captured by the swift current.

The dipper was carried down to his feet, and when the woman realized that a hijiri was bathing himself in the small waterfall that plunged into the river, she turned her face away. The hijiri understood what the woman standing before him felt. Fear at having stumbled upon a man deep in the mountains, an ascetic attempting to purify his body in the descending torrent, was clearly visible on her face.

Picking up the dipper, the hijiri straightened his garments and walked through the water toward the trembling woman. Her hair was neatly gathered at the nape of her neck, and the white ankles he glimpsed beneath the hem of her kimono were slender. That alone was enough to evoke from the hijiri's throat the sound of grass rustling, the sound of treetops brushing against each other in the wind . . . *jaarajaara jaarajaara*. Slowly, he stopped in front of the woman, muttering that even a scholar priest bound by high rank at the main temple would violate the commandments if he met a woman alone in the mountains.

The woman raised her face and looked at the hijiri, but now there was neither pleading nor fear in her expression. When the hijiri peered into the reflection of himself in her large eyes, there was even a suggestion of a faint smile playing on her white face. "Thank you," she said, reaching out to take the bamboo dipper. Her hands were too small for her body, as if they had remained unchanged since she was an infant. Staring intently into his face as if to confirm that his excited lust had faltered, the woman took the dipper in her tiny hands and said, "You must forget this." And then she began to climb quickly up into the brush on the mountainside, leaving the half-filled bucket where it had fallen beside the river.

For a moment, the hijiri stood rooted there as if in a trance. But after the woman's figure disappeared into the thicket, it occurred to him suddenly that she had not been a creature of this world. If she were a flesh-and-blood woman, he could rape her. But if she were an incarnation of Kannon, he could save himself from this existence if he but touched her gentle, infant's hands—this existence as a hijiri who could not live in the villages of men but neither was able to devote himself to scholarship. He plunged into the undergrowth after her, then paused to listen, and heard birds taking flight in the distance. He set off in the direction of this sound, without a thought for his soaked garments.

When he emerged from the thicket, the woman was kneeling beside a flat brushwood fence. The hijiri ran up behind her and stopped, standing over her. "Please leave me alone." Her weak, pleading voice seemed to emerge from her lips in a single thread, as if she sensed his rising passion. Here deep in the mountains, she could have escaped had she tried, and even as he lifted the cowering woman in his arms, the hijiri could not suppress the feeling that he was being deluded, though she closed her eyes and weakly gave herself up to him.

Exposing her naked body, he was both disappointed and relieved to find that apart from her hands there was no sign that she was more than human.

After he had sated his passion, he asked her why she was gathering water alone in the mountains, and if she lived here with her husband.

But the woman with the infant's hands only wept silently. He helped her up, but she closed her kimono and said only, "Please, just leave me as I am." The hijiri wondered if she was living alone here because of her stunted hands, to avoid inquisitive stares.

He had no intention of letting the woman go. The grass where she had sunk down was soft and gentle, and the hijiri thought it suited her white thighs. Drawn by their whiteness, he reached out to touch them, but she brushed his hand away, twisting her body back, and said, "Please leave me alone."

The sun was still in the sky but already turning red. When he lunged at her, the woman raised her arms to embrace him, pulling him down with her tiny hands. He thought that to a woman he must appear to be unimaginably crazed, and buried his face in her breasts, pressing his lips against her nipples and biting them lightly. Perhaps because this hurt her, the woman pressed her lips against his and sucked his tongue into her mouth. Just at that moment, he heard low voices around them. He tried to raise his head, but the woman held it down with her tiny hands and said, "Wild boars often pass by here." Not satisfied with this, he again tried to raise his head in search of the voices, but she pressed her body up against his and wrapped her legs around him. "It's only the cries of boar or deer running past toward the ridge."

When she insisted again, the voices did sound like animal cries. But deep in the mountains, with darkness suddenly falling over everything, the hijiri felt approaching danger. He sensed someone standing behind him and whirled around, but the woman wrapped her arms more tightly around his neck to stop him and said, "It is the noble ones." The hijiri threw off her arms and stood up, staring intently into the gloom.

The light that had lingered in the sky until moments before had begun to disappear, the mountains fading into nothing but shifting shadows, so he could not make out their features, but with sounds like the wind rustling in the brush, they were gathering one or two at a time to sit before him. For a moment, he thought he saw their faces, and he felt fear stabbing up from the pit of his stomach—yasha, night demons. Trembling, he pushed the woman away, and clutching his garments tried to run away. But the woman—where did she find the strength?—seized his hand in her own infant's hands and stood up facing him. "Do not be afraid," she whispered. "No one thinks you are a savage like Ise no Gorō." The hijiri had no idea what this meant, but she had drawn nearer, and so he shouted out to the crowd hidden in the darkness, "I am nothing like that," trying to tell them that he was only an ascetic who had happened to pass by this place in his wanderings.

"I won't bother you. I haven't even seen your faces."

From the darkness came voices that sounded like scornful laughter.

"I haven't seen anything. I don't know anything."

He was shouting, but when he heard laughter in what were clearly human voices—had he said something funny?—the hijiri suddenly realized that he was shaking. *What am I doing standing here frightened out of my wits and trying to make excuses for myself?* The hijiri saw himself for the first time naked and shaking, unable even to throw off the grip of the woman's tiny hands. He had valued his own life no more than that of an insect. He had gone down into the villages, and claiming to be a seer with long years of austerities, had wandered from place to place curing nightmares, performing exorcisms, and even telling fortunes. Sometimes, he had stolen the handful of rice that was all a family possessed. Once, when he had left the villages to wander again in the mountains, he had encountered rain, and before he could descend from the peak he had become feverish. But thinking that he had no need of life, he had simply fallen down against the base of a tree and lain there until the fever passed by itself. The hijiri laughed at himself. He, who had thought there was no particular reason to live, was now trembling in fear that his life might be taken by these yasha devils.

"It is the noble ones."

The woman took the garments from his hands and put them on him. And then, as if they had been waiting for her to finish, they all began to walk, making a rustling sound in the brush.

"Come, let's be off," the woman said, taking the hijiri's hand. She started walking, and the clumps of grass around him moved. He heard the sound of many feet trampling the grass.

He did not know how long they walked. It seemed they arrived almost at once, but also that several hours had passed. Though he had wandered endlessly here, the hijiri knew only that they were deep in the mountains, far from the villages that dotted the seacoast. He had no memory of the steep slope they were climbing or of the shape of the mountain that loomed up in the moon he glimpsed hanging in the sky whenever there was a break in the trees. They came to a place where he could hear the sound of spray, and a soft, cold mist struck his face, and he knew they were near a waterfall. "Just a little further now," she whispered in his ear. And as she had promised, they emerged from the grove of trees onto a broad, flat riverbank that opened before them in moonlight, which now covered the entire scene, and above it was a waterfall that plunged down from the heights with the sound of bells, aglow in the silver light. Next to the fall was a mansion, its lights so dim that it seemed uncertain whether it was actually there at all.

"The waterfall turns red, like flowing blood."

As if to show him, she pointed to the waterfall, which was drenched in the light of the moon. He heard a harsh, suppressed voice beside him:

"Have we not sworn revenge on the traitors of Tanabe?"

Voices of agreement rose all around him—"Yes" . . . "Indeed". . . Just then, a person of low stature appeared from the mansion holding two birds in his hands. Knocking the shrieking, flapping birds against each other, he shouted, "There, fight once more." Each time they were knocked together, the two birds kicked their legs out at each other and beat their wings, as if they were terrified of the impenetrable night.

The birds were brought together again and again, until finally one of them lost its strength and was no longer able to kick back at the other.

Apparently there was someone of noble birth inside the mansion, for the little man held the birds up toward it. In the silver light of the moon, which just at that moment hung directly overhead, their blood flowed black.

The voice of a woman weeping inside the mansion reached his ears. The little princess had been put to the sword, she said, and she herself had been forced to flee with the prince, who once had been promised the royal succession. Now they were reduced to living here in hiding deep in the mountains. These people, gathered under the cover of night—how many were there?—were only waiting for the right moment to rise up and attack in force. She spoke as though the capital were just on the other side of the mountain.

A soft, warm breeze was blowing. And with each gust the sound of the brush and the tops of the trees echoed like court music played by noble ladies-in-waiting. As if summoned by the voice of the woman crying inside the mansion, they assembled, pushing through the brush with the same mournful, haunting sound. Suddenly recalling the woman at his side, the hijiri looked at her face. Tears glittered in her eyes. He turned again to look at the people assembled in the silver moonlight and shuddered. Their outlines were hazy, and they could easily have been mistaken for the grass, or the branches of the trees, now only shadows in the darkness, but if he looked at them more intently, they were monkeys and wild boars. Yet they all had the shapes of human beings, no different from the hijiri himself. Some had human faces but the hands and feet of dogs. Whether they had become this way from being in the mountains for so long, or because the nobles living in the mansion had assembled a horde of yasha and devils, they were all weeping at the words of the woman inside. Some of them crouched with their hands together in prayer. Others stood covering their faces with hoofed hands. As he gazed at these creatures, the hijiri thought that it was because such things occurred deep in the mountains of Kumano that the hijiri and bikuni who wandered from province to province longed for and worshiped this land. He did not think that these weird monsters were phantoms. And neither did he believe they were the ghosts of the dead who had been defeated and had fled from the capital in this world. They were here now —the infant emperor who had been carried to the bottom of the ocean, and the slain princess whose blood stained the waterfall red.

When the hijiri stood up to leave this place, the woman with the tiny hands lifted her tear-streaked face and asked, "Where will you go?" In his heart, the hijiri replied that he had had nowhere to go from the beginning, that there was nothing for him but to keep going on and on, but he did not give voice to these thoughts and simply started walking. He sensed that the woman had risen and was following after him with weak, uncertain steps. *If you are some incarnation that is more than human, stay here and cry,* he thought. He was still immature, unfinished, and despite his wanderings and his austerities he could not yet perform feats like En no Gyōja, manipulating devils and flying freely through the air.

Even if he had been beaten by waterfalls and denied himself the five grains, none of it had been more than empty ritual.

Listening to the footsteps of the woman following him, he knew that sounds *jaarajaara jaarajaara* were rising around her. Were they made by the deformed creatures standing behind her, or was it just the wind blowing over the treetops?

He did not know the reason, but he felt ashamed. Unable as he was to live among other people, and at the same time wanting in his devotion to austerities, he nevertheless had an ordinary human body, unlike this woman and her monstrous companions. He could not accustom himself to life in the villages, and he was also incapable of true austerity. He knew that the woman was following him closely so as not to lose sight of him, and the sounds *jaarajaara jaarajaara* rose up even louder in his heart as he traced his way back through the brush from which they had originally come.

The rim of the mountain began to glow, and the hijiri stopped and turned back to the woman.

"Where are you going?"

She smiled and said, "I will see you on your way and then return to the noble ones. That is the way I live."

They had come to a place where the mountain jutted out to form a cliff, and so the hijiri sat down. The woman came up beside him.

"I no longer know how many years I have lived. The noble one mourns her lost children so. There it is."

Peering down from the cliff, she pointed with one of her childlike fingers. The wind blew through her hair, and to the hijiri her face was more lovely than anything he had ever seen before. He found himself looking down from the precipice, as if captivated by her gaze. It was there that he had suddenly wanted desperately to drink from the waterfall, and there that he had been inspired to enter the falls and be lashed by the cascading water. The morning sun had begun to rise, and the rim of the mountain sparkled in golden light. As if night had suddenly become afternoon, birds began to cry out all over the mountain, and the sound of the water reached his ears.

He began to climb down toward the waterfall. Suddenly, he thought that he had seen this thicket before. And it was then that the hijiri realized that the stand of tall broad-leaved trees he had walked through with the woman during the night was the place where he had been attacked by leeches. It seemed strange now that nothing in particular had happened to them.

As he climbed down through the brush the sound of the water pealing in the cold morning air and the woman's footsteps merged with the sounds *jaarajaara jaarajaara* that had begun to rise up again in his body, buzzing in his throat. He emerged from the brush and turned to help the woman, who had climbed down after him. Taking her into his arms, he lowered her from the mountainside and without releasing her laid her down beside the stream.

In the bright morning light streaming down on the riverbank, her naked body breathed colors of peach blossoms, and the downy hair that lightly covered her skin seemed aglow with the color of gold. As if to kneel before this beauty, the hijiri lowered his head and pressed his lips against her skin. He pressed his ear into the valley between her breasts, and the rapid beating of her heart assured him of the woman's arousal. He stripped off the garments he was wearing and stretched his body out beside her. It was enough to do nothing, enough that this woman was there breathing beside him, with her skin of peach blossoms bathed in morning light and her golden down—her red nipples, her navel, which seemed to him the center of this world, the burning shadow of her vagina, and the thicket of hair over it. Not resisting the touch of his lips, the woman opened her legs to the kneeling hijiri and gently stroked his back with her tiny hands. He took the fingers of those hands into his mouth, sucking them one at a time. The woman raised her hips to accept his engorged penis, and pressed her lips over his. He plunged into her, as if by doing so he were arresting the flight of an angel in a feathered mantle, holding her here.

The woman came forth again and again, and with her hands clutching his back, the hijiri thought she was too beautiful in the glaring light of the morning sun. *I don't want to let her go*, he thought. If she was an angel, he wanted to hide away the feathered robe that would carry her to heaven and stay here coupled with her like this forever.

After he too had come forth inside her and the vortex of passion within him had passed, he put his hand on her, and with his fingers stopped the semen that had collected inside and was beginning to flow out. "Stay with me like this forever," he said. The woman smiled, slowly shook her head, and stood up. She said that she would wash herself in the river, and began to walk toward it. As he watched her retreating back, the hijiri was seized with an evil thought. Chanting *jaarajaara jaarajaara*, the meaningless sounds with their lewd reverberations that he chanted instead of the words of the sutras, he saw a vivid image of himself wandering from village to village, from mountain to mountain, like a beggar or a thief, and he thought, *Shall I . . . jaarajaara . . . kill this woman?*—just as the hijiri he saw in his mind, unable to bear his own existence, had once killed a woman. He could see the semen that he had ejaculated into her flowing out and falling onto the sand. As if quite unaware that the hijiri staring at her back was contemplating something abominable, the woman piled her hair up on her head and stepped into the cold water.

The hijiri suddenly felt that the woman was about to disappear completely into the river and stood up to run after her. Looking up at the hijiri, who had come splashing through the current to stand beside her, she smiled and said, "The water is cold." He watched her plunge head first into the water with the same evil feelings and murmured to himself, *She is like the spirit of the morning soaking into your skin.* He splashed her, like a child playing, but she just smiled, not joining in his play. Her demure manner made him uneasy, and his expression became serious. "Come live with me in a village or somewhere.

"Who cares about the noble ones? Let's go to a village and plant fields, and rice paddies. I can exorcise the children's night demons, and I can make medicines for boils and sicknesses of the mind and sell them."

"I cannot go to a village where there are people."

"If you don't want to go to a village, here in these mountains is fine. I could hunt boar, or deer."

The hijiri approached the woman, who was covering her breasts with her infant's hands, and embraced her. He felt it unbearably sad that her skin had been chilled by the cold water, and hugging her more tightly, he thought he was going to cry.

"Stay with me. Live with me. . ." He knew how rash his proposal was. Whatever her circumstances, she must have some reason for being in such a place, and she knew no more about him than he knew about her. The hijiri felt that even now she might disappear from his arms, and put even more strength into them, pressing his stomach against her wet nakedness. His lips on the nape of her neck, he groaned, "Won't you save me?" He knelt in the water and kissed her breasts, pressing his lips between her fingers. She responded to his caresses, removing her tiny hands.

Lifting her in his arms, the hijiri walked toward the garments he had thrown from the stream. Perhaps because he had walked through the night, the roar of the waterfall echoed in his ears, seeming to spread out behind him, and the voices of the birds, more and more of them as the sun spread over the mountain, sounded clear and strong.

He could not suppress his rising passion—it was as if he had not yet embraced her even once. He put her down on a flat rock at the edge of the stream, and not even giving her time to warm herself, spread her taut pink thighs and entered her, unconcerned that the woman was arching her back in pain. But her pain passed quickly, turning to pleasure. She opened her mouth and stuck out her tongue for his and sucked it into her mouth. When he thrust his hips forward like a rutting boar, she closed her eyes and moved her tongue teasingly, as if to say that only she was giving pleasure. He felt himself an animal possessed of nothing but lust. And he thought himself incomparably repulsive.

He looked down at the woman, who had closed her eyes into gentle lines and released her coiling tongue, moaning in her ecstasy. He felt a hatred welling up that was equal to the love seething in his body. Still rutting like a boar, he grabbed her shoulders and butted into her again and again, grunting out loud. The woman just moaned. He knew that he had put his hand on her throat.

Certainly, he contemplated killing her. He put more strength into the hand he had pressed against her neck, and her body stiffened. He felt her vagina tighten hard around him and mounted higher, trying to thrust more deeply into her. The woman writhed in pain. He took his hand away from her throat. He thought he had understood everything from the beginning, and still naked, he raised himself and sat staring down at her body. She was watching his face. With the morning sun striking them, the stream, the rocks, and the woman's naked body were almost blinding. The brush beside the stream rustled in every gust of wind, and though the sound did not reach his ears, he thought he could hear *jaara-jaara jaarajaara*. And though the woman by no means said any such thing, he imagined that he heard her tiny voice saying, "Please let me go. . . Spare my life"—just as he had heard when he killed the woman in the village. She had known he was little more than a thief and a beggar, but every night the village woman had called him "Holy man . . . reverend priest." And when she called him that, he could not bear it. When she called him that, he thought that however much he had fallen, he was still a hijiri, and in fact he had even begun to convince himself that his incarnation as a hijiri was only temporary, that he was really a holy saint, in no way inferior to Kōbō Daishi or Ippen Shōnin. *But it was a lie. I am inferior even to the grass, inferior even to a wild dog, a man who cannot live in the villages with other people, but lacks the wisdom to become a scholar priest. When she nestled her cheek against me and kissed me as if she were receiving it with a reverence that went all the way down to the toes of her feet, when she worshiped me that way, I felt as if I were being mocked, tormented, as if I were being gently strangled with silk floss. And in the darkness of the night, she cried out to me endlessly. "Ah! Save me! . . . Give me salvation! . . . Teach me the way! . . ." She moaned. She trembled. She threw herself on me as if I were the personification of all that was evil and without mercy, groveling and begging for salvation. And sometimes I felt that her voice was my own voice. I was pleading to myself for salvation and at the same time saying the same words in my heart to the woman. "Ah! Teach me! . . . Save me! . . . Teach me the path to paradise! . . ." From early morning that day, I sat in her house with the rain shutters closed, listening to the cries of a cuckoo. As I fondled her dusky nipples while she lay sound asleep beside me, I remember that I thought its cries sounded like "ako, ako, ako. . ." I rolled her nipple around in my fingers for a moment, and then, just as I had done long, long ago, I sucked it into my mouth. She cried out to me again. "Ah! Holy saint! . . ." The rain shutters were closed, and so I couldn't see her face, but the cries of the cuckoo echoed, "ako . . . ako . . . ako. . ." "Ah, holy man . . . reverend priest. . . Save me. . . Save me. . ." Her cries became louder, and with her moaning in my ears, my hand stretched out toward her throat. Save me. . . I was saying it with her as I put more strength into my hand. "Save me. . ." Even after I had released her limp body, her voice remained in my ears forever.*

The hijiri had said nothing to the woman.

His body empty, he stood up, and with the sound of the treetops fluttering *jaarajaara jaarajaara* in his ears, he began to walk toward his garments to put them on. But suddenly he changed his mind and turned toward the water. He stepped into it and then dived, submerging himself. Standing up again, he started to walk toward the waterfall, wiping away the drops of water on his skin with his hands.

Gazing up at the white cascade shooting bright rays of light in the sun, he felt that it was the same waterfall he had seen beside the mansion of the noble ones. It occurred to him that soon it should be stained red with blood, and he turned back to ask the woman with the infant's hands. But from somewhere a great flock of crows had gathered around her, as if to conceal her from him. They had come down near the spot where he had left his clothes and were now hopping around and flapping their wings on the flat ground near the river. Afraid that they would peck the woman's body, he scooped up a rock from the bottom of the river and threw it at them. One by one, they flew up, and squawking loudly to each other, circled over his head.

The hijiri finished putting on his clothes and turned to ask the woman one last time if she would live with him in a village. There was no one there. The hijiri thought he had known that from the beginning, too.

Notes on the Translators

MICHAEL C. BROWNSTEIN is an Assistant Professor of Japanese at the University of Notre Dame. He received his Ph.D. in Japanese from Columbia University in 1981 and is currently researching the evolution of Japanese literary thought during the eighteenth and nineteenth centuries.

ANTHONY H. CHAMBERS, a native of California, received his Ph.D. in Japanese language and literature from the University of Michigan in 1974. He is the author of several studies of the works of Tanizaki Jun'ichirō; his translations include *The Secret History of the Lord of Musashi and Arrowroot* and *Naomi,* by Tanizaki. He is Associate Professor in the Department of Asian Languages and Literatures at Wesleyan University.

BRETT DE BARY is an Associate Professor of Japanese Literature at Cornell University, where she teaches modern Japanese literature and film. She has translated works by postwar authors such as Hara Tamiki, Miyamoto Yuriko, and Ōe Kenzaburō, and also published articles on them. Her *Three Works by Nakano Shigeharu* was published by Cornell University East Asia Papers Series in 1979. She is now preparing for publication a manuscript on Japanese literature at the end of the Pacific War.

VAN C. GESSEL received his Ph.D. in Japanese from Columbia University. He has translated two novels and a short story collection by Endō Shūsaku—*When I Whistle, The Samurai,* and *Stained Glass Elegies*—and written critical articles on modern Japanese theater and Japanese Christian writers. He recently completed a monograph on postwar literature titled *Japan's Lost Generation.* He is Assistant Professor of Japanese at the University of California, Berkeley.

MARK HARBISON, a Ph.D. candidate at Stanford University, is presently studying in Tokyo and writing a dissertation on "Inter-textuality as Method in the *Shinkokinshū.*" He has done a wide variety of translations from Japanese texts, including several volumes of Konishi Jin'ichi's *History of Japanese Literature,* and short stories by Nagai Kafū, Furui Yoshikichi, and Abe Akira. He is preparing a translation of Ōe Kenzaburō's *Atarashii hito yo mezameyo.*

GERALDINE HARCOURT, a science graduate, has been studying Japanese since high school. A native of New Zealand, she now lives in Tokyo. Among her published translations are Tsushima Yūko's *Child of Fortune*, Yamamoto Michiko's *Betty-san*, and Gō Shizuko's *Requiem*. Currently she is at work on a collection of stories by Tsushima Yūko.

CAROLYN HAYNES is a Ph.D. candidate in Japanese literature at Cornell University. Her article, "Parody in Kyōgen: *Makura Monogatari* and *Tako*" appeared in *Monumenta Nipponica*.

AMY VLADECK HEINRICH received her doctorate in Japanese literature in 1980 at Columbia University, and has taught at Columbia, New York University, and Princeton. Her book, *Fragments of Rainbows: The Life and Poetry of Saitō Mokichi, 1882–1953*, was published in 1983. She is currently working on a comparative study of modern women writers and their place in the Japanese and English literary traditions.

ADAM KABAT did his undergraduate work at Wesleyan University. He has recently completed a master's degree at the University of Tokyo with a comparative study of the works of Izumi Kyōka and Mishima Yukio, and is now on a doctoral course there. He is also preparing a translation of a novel by Yoshiyuki Junnosuke.

ALISON KIBRICK received her master's degree in East Asian Studies from Harvard University in 1981. She is presently working in the field of artificial intelligence with a focus on Japanese applications.

STEPHEN W. KOHL is currently Associate Professor of Japanese and Chairman of the Department of East Asian Languages and Literatures at the University of Oregon. His primary field of interest is the interpretation and translation of modern Japanese literature. He is the author of over a dozen articles and translations, including *Cliff's Edge and Other Stories* by Tachihara Masaaki. He has also made a study of early relations between Japan and the Pacific Northwest.

WAYNE P. LAMMERS received his Ph.D. at the University of Michigan and is presently Assistant Professor at the University of Wisconsin. He has published a translation from *Utsubo monogatari* in *Monumenta Nipponica* and is preparing a collection of translations of stories by Shōno Junzō. He has also been an instructor of English language and literature at Iwate University.

KÄREN WIGEN LEWIS did her undergraduate work in Japanese at the University of Michigan, and is now pursuing graduate work in Japanese geography at the

University of California, Berkeley. Her translation of Yasuoka Shōtarō's *Kaihen no kōkei* received the 1981 Translation Prize from the U.S.-Japan Friendship Commission, and was published as *A View by the Sea* in 1984 by Columbia University Press.

VIRGINIA MARCUS is a graduate student at the University of Michigan. Her annotated translation of selected stories from *Yorozu no fumihōgu*, a collection of epistolary tales by Ihara Saikaku, was published together with an introductory essay in *Monumenta Nipponica* in 1985.

TOMONE MATSUMOTO received her doctoral degree in 1979 from the University of Arizona. Her dissertation was a study of modern Japanese intellectual history, focusing on the career of Kamei Katsuichirō. She is currently teaching modern Japanese language and literature at Griffith University in Brisbane, Australia.

JACK RUCINSKI is a Senior Lecturer in the Department of Asian Languages at the University of Canterbury in Christchurch, New Zealand. His previous translations from Hori Tatsuo have appeared in *Poetry* and *Translation*. He has also published articles on Japanese literature and art in *Monumenta Nipponica* and *Orientations*. At Harvard University, he is presently researching illustrated books from the early Tokugawa period. He received his Ph.D. in 1978 from the University of Hawaii.

EDWARD SEIDENSTICKER is Professor in the Department of East Asian Languages and Cultures at Columbia University. His numerous translations of modern and classical literary works have placed him among the foremost interpreters of Japanese fiction and poetry.

CECILIA SEGAWA SEIGLE, a native Japanese, has taught classical and modern literature and language at the University of Pennsylvania, where she received her Ph.D. Her published translations include Shimazaki Tōson's *The Family*, Mishima Yukio's *The Temple of Dawn*, and Kaikō Takeshi's *Into a Black Sun* and *Darkness in Summer*. For the 1985–86 academic year, she is a Japan Foundation Fellow, and is writing her second book on Yoshiwara.

YUKIKO TANAKA was co-translator and co-editor of *This Kind of Woman: Ten Stories by Japanese Women Writers, 1960–1976*. Her Ph.D. dissertation at UCLA focused on narrative technique in the works of Kojima Nobuo. She has translated Kojima's novel *Hōyō kazoku* and short story "Happiness," and is now at work on a book on Japanese women writers.

JOHN WHITTIER TREAT received his doctoral degree from Yale University in 1982 with a dissertation on the literature of Ibuse Masuji. At present he is an Assistant Professor at the University of Washington.

WILLIAM J. TYLER, Assistant Professor of Japanese Studies and Director of the Japanese Language Program at the University of Pennsylvania, did his undergraduate work at International Christian University in Japan, and his graduate study at Harvard. His Ph.D. dissertation was on Ishikawa Jun, and he has published a translation of Doi Takeo's *The Psychological World of Natsume Soseki*. He is currently translating Ishikawa's stories and novellas, and preparing a study of Tōkai Sanshi.

ROBERT ULMER first left his native Toronto in 1973 to study in Japan. He received his Ph.D. in Japanese literature from Yale University in 1982. He is now working for the Japan Trade Centre (JETRO) in Toronto.

Selected Bibliography of English Translations

A number of the authors represented in the present anthology are appearing in English translation for the first time. Through the efforts of qualified and dedicated translators, however, a wide range of modern Japanese literary works has been made available for the interested reader. For translations published before 1978, the reader is referred to *Modern Japanese Literature in Translation: A Bibliography*, compiled by the International House of Japan Library and published in 1979 by Kodansha International. The selected list that follows is a compilation of translations in English which have appeared since the date of that original bibliography.

ABE AKIRA

"A Napping Cove" (Madoromu irie). Tr. by Mark Harbison. *Japanese Literature Today*, vol. 9 (1984), pp. 11–23.

ABE KŌBŌ

Secret Rendezvous (Mikkai). Tr. by Juliet Winters Carpenter (New York: Knopf, 1979). 190 pp.

"You, Too, Are Guilty" (Omae ni mo tsumi ga aru). Tr. by Ted T. Takaya. *Modern Japanese Drama: An Anthology*, ed. by Ted T. Takaya (New York: Columbia University Press, 1979), pp. 1–40.

DAZAI OSAMU

Selected Stories and Sketches. Tr. by James O'Brien (Ithaca: Cornell University Press, 1983). 248 pp. Includes: "Memories," "Transformation," "The Island of Monkeys," "Toys," "Das Gemeine," "Putting Granny Out to Die," "My Older Brothers," "Eight Views of Tokyo," "On the Question of Apparel," "Homecoming," "A Poor Man's Got His Pride," "The Mound of the Monkey's Grave," "Taking the Wen Away," "Currency," "The Sound of Hammering," and "Osan."

Return to Tsugaru (Tsugaru). Tr. by James Westerhoven (Tokyo: Kodansha International, 1985). 220 pp.

Tsugaru (Tsugaru). Tr. by Phyllis Lyons. *The Saga of Dazai Osamu* (Stanford:

Stanford University Press, 1985), pp. 271–385.

ENDŌ SHŪSAKU

A *Life of Jesus* (Iesu no shōgai). Tr. by Richard A. Schuchert (New York: Paulist Press, 1978). 179 pp.

The Samurai (Samurai). Tr. by Van C. Gessel (London: Peter Owen, 1982; New York: Harper and Row/Kodansha International, 1982; and New York: Vintage, 1984). 272 pp.

"The Shadow Figure" (Kagebōshi). Tr. by Thomas Lally, Ōka Yumiko, and Dennis J. Doolin. *Japan Quarterly*, vol. 31, no. 2 (April–June 1984), pp. 164–73, and vol. 31, no. 3 (July–Sept. 1984), pp. 294–301.

"Shadow of a Man" (Kagebōshi). Tr. by Shoichi Ono and Sanford Goldstein. *Bulletin of the College of Biomedical Technology, Niigata University*, vol. 1, no. 1 (1983), pp. 80–94.

"Something of My Own" (Watakushi no mono). Tr. by John Bester. *Japan Echo*, vol. 12 (1985), pp. 23–29.

Stained Glass Elegies: Stories by Shusaku Endo. Tr. by Van C. Gessel (London: Peter Owen, 1984). 165 pp. Includes: "A Forty-Year-Old Man," "The Day Before," "Fuda-no-Tsuji," "Unzen," "My Belongings," "Despicable Bastard," "Mothers," "Retreating Figures," "Old Friends," "The War Generation," and "Incredible Voyage."

Volcano (Kazan). Tr. by Richard A. Schuchert (London: Peter Owen, 1978; New York: Taplinger, 1980). 175 pp.

When I Whistle (Kuchibue o fuku toki). Tr. by Van C. Gessel (London: Peter Owen, 1979; New York: Taplinger,1980). 277 pp.

IBUSE MASUJI

Salamander and Other Stories. Tr. by John Bester (Tokyo: Kodansha International, 1981). 134 pp. Includes: "Pilgrims' Inn," "Yosaku the Settler," "Carp," "Salamander," "Life at Mr. Tange's," "Old Ushitora," "Savan on the Roof," "Plum Blossom by Night," and "Lieutenant Lookeast."

INOUE YASUSHI

Chronicle of My Mother (Waga haha no ki). Tr. by Jean Oda Moy (Tokyo: Kodansha International, 1982). 164 pp.

Lou-lan and Other Stories. Tr. by James T. Araki and Edward Seidensticker (Tokyo: Kodansha International, 1981). 160 pp. Includes: "Lou-lan," "The Sage,"

"Princess Yung-t'ai's Necklace," "The Opaline Cup," "The Rhododendrons," and "Passage to Fudaraku."

KAIKŌ TAKESHI

Into a Black Sun (Kagayakeru yami). Tr. by Cecilia Segawa Seigle (Tokyo: Kodansha International, 1980). 220 pp.

KANAI MIEKO

"Rabbits" (Usagi). Tr. by Phyllis Birnbaum. *Rabbits, Crabs, Etc.: Stories by Japanese Women*, tr. by Phyllis Birnbaum (Honolulu: University of Hawaii Press, 1982), pp. 1–16.

KOJIMA NOBUO

"Happiness" (Happinesu). Tr. by Yukiko Tanaka, with Elizabeth Hanson Warren. *Japan Quarterly*, vol. 28, no. 4 (Oct.–Dec. 1981), pp. 533–48.

"Shōjū" (Shōjū). Tr. by Elizabeth Baldwin. *Faith and Fiction: The Modern Short Story*, ed. by Robert Detweiler and Glenn Meeter (Grand Rapids, MI: William B. Eerdmans, 1979), pp. 213–26.

KŌNO TAEKO

"Ants Swarm" (Ari takaru). Tr. by Noriko Mizuta Lippit. *Stories by Contemporary Japanese Women Writers*, ed. and tr. by Noriko Mizuta Lippit and Kyoko Iriye Selden (Armonk, N.Y.: M. E. Sharpe, 1982), pp. 105–19.

"Crabs" (Kani). Tr. by Phyllis Birnbaum. *Rabbits, Crabs, Etc.: Stories by Japanese Women*, pp. 99–131.

"The Last Time" (Saigo no toki). Tr. by Yukiko Tanaka and Elizabeth Hanson. *This Kind of Woman: Ten Stories by Japanese Women Writers, 1960–1976*, ed. and tr. by Yukiko Tanaka and Elizabeth Hanson (Stanford: Stanford University Press, 1982), pp. 43–67.

KURAHASHI YUMIKO

The Adventures of Sumiyakist Q (Sumiyakisuto Q no bōken). Tr. by Dennis Keene (Queensland: University of Queensland Press, 1979). 369 pp.

"Partei" (Parutai). Tr. by Yukiko Tanaka and Elizabeth Hanson. *This Kind of Woman: Ten Stories by Japanese Women Writers, 1960–1976*, pp. 1–16.

ŌBA MINAKO

"Fireweed" (Higusa). Tr. by Marian Chambers. *Japan Quarterly*, vol. 28, no. 3

(July–Sept. 1981), pp. 403–27.

"Sea-change" (Tankō). Tr. by John Bester. *Japanese Literature Today*, no. 5 (March 1980), pp. 12–19.

"The Smile of a Mountain Witch" (Yamauba no bishō). Tr. by Noriko Mizuta Lippit and Mariko Ochi. *Stories by Contemporary Japanese Women Writers*, pp. 182–96.

"The Three Crabs" (Sambiki no kani). Tr. by Yukiko Tanaka and Elizabeth Hanson. *This Kind of Woman: Ten Stories by Japanese Women Writers, 1960–1976*, pp. 87–113.

ŌE KENZABURŌ

Hiroshima Notes (Hiroshima nōto). Tr. by Toshi Yonezawa; ed. by David L. Swain (Tokyo: YMCA Press, 1981). 181 pp.

SHIMAO TOSHIO

"The Sting of Death" and Other Stories by Shimao Toshio. Tr. by Kathryn Sparling. *Michigan Papers in Japanese Studies*, no. 12.

TSUSHIMA YŪKO

Child of Fortune (Chōji). Tr. by Geraldine Harcourt (Tokyo: Kodansha International, 1983). 186 pp.

"Island of Joy" (Yorokobi no shima) and "To Scatter Flower Petals" (Hana o maku). Tr. by Lora Sharnoff. *Japan Quarterly*, vol. 27, no. 2 (April–June 1980), pp. 249–69.

YASUOKA SHŌTARŌ

A *View by the Sea* (Kaihen no kōkei). Tr. by Kären Wigen Lewis (New York: Columbia University Press, 1984). Includes: "A View by the Sea," "Bad Company," "Gloomy Pleasures," "The Moth," "Rain," and "Thick the New Leaves."

YOSHIYUKI JUNNOSUKE

"Birds, Beasts, Insects and Fish" (Kinjū chūgyo). Tr. by M. T. Mori. *Japan Quarterly*, vol. 28, no. 1 (Jan.–March 1981), pp. 91–102.

"Scene at Table" (Shokutaku no kōkei). Tr. by Geraldine Harcourt. *Japan Echo*, vol. 12 (1985), pp. 42–45.